First Fury

by

Thomas B. Macy
See http://www.firstfury.com for documents, photos, links, etc.

"Blinding vapors of foam and white-
fire...the first fury of the whale's
headlong rush..."
Moby Dick, page 81.

A special thanks is extended to the Nantucket Historical Association and their wonderful library. The whaling scene in the background of the cover is used with the permission of the Nantucket Historical Association. It is referenced as Image Number 1992.0303.003, Sperm Whaling No. 3, The Capture.

Cover design by KatySuzanne: Though Katy makes a living as a graphic designer, she is also a horsewoman, a dancer, a backpacker, a thinker, a photographer, a peacemaker, a biker, a crafter and a shower singer. Many find her serious and hard-working, though she is better known by her trademark laugh. Born and raised in the Midwest, she found home in Colorado where she now delightfully freelances and is the Marketing Coordinator for W.F. Norman Corporation. See http://katysuzanne.com/.

Also, a thanks to the Mystic Seaport's whaling display and their guides on the Charles W. Morgan, a ship of the same vintage as the Christopher Mitchell.

Research in Rochester, New York, was facilitated by Ms. Ruth Tiano.

Research documents, pictures, and more can be found at www.FirstFury.com.

The Erie Canal, New York

Thursday, November 2, 1848

Oh, God! Something's happened to Caleb! This feeling of isolation was new to Ann. She had never been alone—not really alone. She arrived with Caleb three days earlier, and these people were strangers. This place was not home. She gasped, and a tight guttural sound squeezed involuntarily from her throat. No one, not even the bartender, had seen Caleb since yesterday. She quick-stepped back past the inn, forcing herself to take deep breaths.

"Any luck?" asked the inn keeper.

"No." Was her voice shaking? She didn't want to sound like a child. She was 18, a woman now, and Caleb her man.

"Don't worry, Mrs. Coleman. He'll show up. Port Gibson isn't all that big."

Mrs. Coleman. She liked the sound of it. But, as quickly as the thought came to mind, it buried itself in worries of what might have happened to him.

Autumn gusts brushed against her as she hurried down the slope. From the northwest, the Erie Canal approached Port Gibson, then curved at the bottom of the hill, and continued to the northeast. She had left her parents in Rochester and come east with Caleb. During those two weeks with him, her greatest dreams were there to be grasped. She was free to see the world with the man she loved…and, eventually, have a family. But he didn't come back to the inn last night, and now she couldn't find him. When she reached the road that paralleled the Canal through the town, her mouth was dry. In monotonous agony, the surge of Ann's blood carried her worst fears outward, wave upon wave, to every part of her body.

In the warehouse, light pierced the darkness, finding its way over and around goods awaiting transportation to other ports. "Have you seen my…husband, Caleb Coleman? Has a scar." She ran her finger from the corner of her right eye to the bottom of the right ear.

The owner shook his head.

In the mercantile, exotic scents tickled her nose, but they couldn't take her thoughts captive. "I'm looking for my husband." Ann's voice quaked. "Has a scar."

"Sorry."

Behind the businesses, on the docks: ". . . Have you seen him? I'm Mrs. Coleman."

The answers were the same. He was gone. She forced back sobs that sought a way out.

"I think I saw him."

"Where is he?" At last, words of hope. She wanted his arms about her.

The man walked up with the dock master.

"Had a scar just like you described."

Why did he keep staring at her?

"Left last night. Headed east on the Canal. Said if we needed… entertainment…on one of the packets, he knew a certain woman in port who would do nicely." The man smiled as his eyes looked her up and down. "Your name Ann?"

She got a sick feeling in the pit of her stomach. Others on the dock stared now. Her fists clenched and back stiffened. "You're lying!" She challenged them eye to eye.

The laborer laughed. "There is no *Mrs.* Coleman."

"I'm sorry." But the manager's face didn't show it. "Packets come in here full of people all the time. If you need work, there are always passengers on those boats who could use your…ah, services."

Even in defiance, the wind was knocked out of her. She had seen such women on the Canal and heard of houses in Rochester where.... She didn't want to think about it. How could they look at her like that?

"Pay's good!" The men's laughter raked at her back as she left the dock.

Each step to the inn was an eternity. She loved Caleb. What those men said just couldn't be true. And he loved her; he told her so. He gave her the ring on her finger. She turned it slowly, watching the sunlight sparkle. *He loves me!* She had to believe that. He promised to take her all along the Canal and show her places she'd only read about. Life could be so much more than what her mother had, so much more than what her father planned for her. She wanted to see it all, experience it, live it. Caleb would give her all this and marriage, too. Theirs was the perfect match. They both wanted to travel and see the world, and eventually have a family. These were things she'd desired from childhood. The future would be hopes fulfilled, except that he was gone. His kindness had been apparent even though her parents did not see it.

Thoughts of home flooded her mind—the smells of the city, familiar friends, the freedom from worries. She missed her mother. An embrace would give confidence that all was well.

But things weren't okay. She wanted to go back to Rochester. When she and Caleb had arrived in Port Gibson, Ann wrote home to explain why she left. Stealing away with Caleb was a desperate act, but her parents had given no other choice; they didn't approve of Caleb. How could they tell her to stay away from him! Eventually they would grow to accept the man she loved. Then they could all be a family again. Surely, her parents knew that was what she wanted, to be their daughter. Yet she couldn't deny who she was. They knew her goals and plans.

The path left the road and meandered through a small stand of trees, yellow and red leaves still clinging to limbs and quaking in the gusts. Some, having lost their grip, were carried through the air and carpeted the ground. The older ones had turned brown with the start of decay—the soft smell of autumn. The hum of people laughing, talking, yelling, came muffled through the trees, sounds of a world crumbling around her. And no one knew; no one cared that she clung to a thread, that her life hung on the hope of Caleb's return.

That night, she lay alone, in a bed that two had shared. Her mind pictured the one with whom she wanted to build a life. Seconds ticked into minutes, and minutes crept into hours before the room began to lighten.

She could not just wait for Caleb to come back for her.

He WILL! He was probably scouting out a place... Did he really call her entertainment? What the laborer said was a lie. Caleb would never speak such things about her; they were in love. They had the same hopes. She may not be Mrs. Coleman yet; but she would be, soon, when he returned.

Could she go home and wait for Caleb there? Her mother always worried about her; surely she would engulf her daughter in loving arms.

No! Caleb expects me here; here I'll stay. Even though you beg me to come back, Mama, I won't! I can't! This is my choice.

But, if she were to wait for the man she loved, she needed to find work. He kept all their money with him, including what she managed to take from home. Now she required a job, and not the kind the dock workers suggested.

Ann retraced the path taken the day before. In the warehouse, no matter how she argued that lifting bags of flour or sharpening axes would not be difficult, the owner was convinced a man could do it better. In the mercantile, the manager's wife refused to have an unmarried female working with her husband. As far as the woman was concerned, Ann was single if Caleb was not at home. Everywhere, the answer was the same.

She fought back an overpowering urge to grab her hair and just scream. Instead, she slammed the door to her room. She could perform any of those jobs. Yet nothing was available to a woman. Only one choice remained. She shook with revulsion at the thought of strange hands pawing at her. In the darkened room, her loneliness flowed out.

The next day, with morning's light at the window, Ann brushed her thick brown hair. She stroked over, and over again—the way her mother used to brush it—slow, each pull begging for more.

A soft knock startled her from the trance.

"Mrs. Coleman, there's a letter for you."

Her mother had written! Just the sight of the envelope was like the smell of freshness after the storm.

§

Caleb sat on the walk outside the Troy train station. The air was cool but the sun warm, the kind of day where moving was more effort than it was worth.

Ann was a nice diversion, he thought. *Amusing…a good wage for little work.*

But she had grown tiresome, what with her constant talk of their wedding. That was the least of his concerns. He laughed. Life was too full of things to do and experience to be tied down to one woman. They never understood that. But Ann was different from most of the girls he'd had, more determined than the others. Usually, they were malleable; they cooed and fawned over him like dogs trying to please their master.

The three months in Rochester were a collage of delight. Opportunities presented in booming towns were always worth a stay, and Ann turned out to be an unexpected trophy. Finding a job on the Canal building boats was easy, and the owner's niece made the stay even more interesting. At first, she was just a butterfly—coming, going, alighting, watching, listening. But the longer Ann hovered, the more she became one of those opportunities. In this case, finding just the right bait to hook his prey was easy. She told him she was like a prisoner at home. The world was full of things to experience. But she would see none of them if her father had his way.

With a smile, Caleb hugged his knees and nestled against the wall. She was one of those exciting things. Simply by making himself the solution to that problem, he experienced another of those pleasures. Besides, she wanted to see him as the answer. The simple trinket of a ring was all it took. He found it easy to leave other women but stayed with Ann for two weeks. That was more than he'd given any of them.

He still saw her dark brown hair catch the wind and blossom out like wings—like butterfly wings—he laughed again—framing the face of a girl who loved the outdoors. He still felt the soft body of a well-proportioned girl who wasn't tall but was commanding in her presence. She wasn't cut from a genteel mold; quite the contrary, she relished the work of life. Ann had a will of her own. She pursued her desires. She was interesting, a girl with a goal. Yet that difference also made her just as easy as the others. This overwhelming feeling of victory and contentment wrapped about him.

Caleb leaned back, closed his eyes, and let his body soak up the sun. There wouldn't be many more days like this until the Canal froze over. He'd have to do something. Other travelers were full of ideas, but one in particular intrigued him. Of course, it would mean a change in his life, but not too much. The work was easy and fortunes could be made. They told him a man could have whatever he wanted. That was his kind of work.

"Destination?" The clerk's request interrupted Caleb's contented respite.

"Boston."

The man was…fat. Looked like he belonged behind a bar. His smile was framed in rosy cheeks.

"Going for business?"

"In a way. Think I may sign to a whaler."

"Hear there's good money in that." The clerk talked as if by habit while writing on the ticket.

"That's why I'm going. They say the work is easy and the ships are luxurious."

For some reason, the man laughed, as if he'd made a joke.

Caleb took the cardboard pass.

"Leaving anyone?" The clerk smiled. "I hear the voyages are long ones these days."

Caleb thought a moment. "Sure am."

The man frowned and sucked in air through a puckered mouth.

Other men only wished they could do what he did. "Took a girl from her home in Rochester to Port Gibson on the Canal. I suppose you might say I will miss her attention."

"With the Canal what it is these days, her parents must have been pleased to have their daughter in your protection. She have family in Port Gibson?"

Surely the man knew what he meant!

"She wasn't exactly under my protection." He raised his eyebrows.

The man looked at him as if trying to comprehend the words. "You mean you took her from home, knew her, and left her unaccompanied? In Port Gibson?"

He gets it. Caleb smiled and nodded.

"How could you do that? Why?...What?"

"It's not so hard to understand. I gave her what she wanted— freedom from her father and the life he had planned for her."

"But, what's she to do now?"

Why is the man so surprised? Girls like Ann are employed up and down the Canal. "She'll find work."

The clerk frowned and shook his head. "I'd say you picked the right profession."

§

Snip!

Another fistful of long brown hair fell to the floor followed by a tear. As Ann stared at the letter lying open on the washstand, she grabbed another shock of hair and placed the scissors close to her scalp.

Why won't they let me come home?

Snip!

Mama! Oh, Mama! I'm not a ruined woman! I'm not! I'm still me!

Snip!

You know your Annie won't do the work left to her. She took a long quivering breath. The hunger in her stomach told her she was out of time and choices.

Snip! Snip!

She set the scissors upon the washstand and ran her fingers across her brow and down to the nape of her neck. It was done! Her glory, the hair her mother had brushed and braided, lay at her feet. An uneven patchwork of stubble covered her head. Tears pooled and washed her cheeks. She took her mother's letter, crumpled it, and watched it drop. Her petticoats and blouse fell upon the memories of her mother's love, and she stood in the room…naked.

How had it come to this? She picked up the blouse, smelled it, ran it through her hands. Then,

Snip! Rip… rip… rip.

A cotton strip was laid upon the bed. Then quickly another… and another… And, with a fury from a fear she might relent, she turned her lace into the same. There would be no going back.

The task complete, she laid the scissors down, as a doctor might lay aside a saw after removing a limb from a wounded soldier. Her hands moved through the bristles upon her head feeling for a soft caress that was no longer there. She felt down her chest, around her waist, and along her thighs. She paused and considered what she was about to do.

No, this was her only option.

Taking one strip, she placed it against her chest, wrapped it around her back and to the front again, where she pulled, adjusted the fit, and pulled again, finally tying it off hiding one aspect of her womanhood. Then she wrapped a strip about her waist… and another… and another … until its narrowness was gone.

On the bed lay the one set of clothes Caleb left behind. She donned his shirt and pants and pulled on the boots. She smelled him, pictured him with her in Rochester and on the Canal. Never had she been so much a woman as then. Her breath caught in her throat. She looked down and didn't see Rebecca Ann Johnson. Removing the ring, she placed it in the pouch hung about her neck.

My... my name is George.

Wiping her eyes, she took a deep breath and tried saying it. "My name is George." Seeing the man but hearing the woman's voice, she shifted nervously and straightened her blouse. Forcing a lower tone, "My name is George Johnson." She flushed and laughed uneasily. That didn't sound at all right.

§

You can't stay here all day. Get down there!

But every time her feet moved toward the docks, fear stopped her. She stayed in the trees and watched.

She knew the work; that wasn't the problem. Line boats with their cargo, and packets full of people, had continually passed her home. How the hoggees drove the mules that pulled the boats was no mystery.

Women just don't do this kind of work.

Her home on Oak Street, on the Big Bend, right before the Canal crossed the Genesee River, was so far away and inaccessible. The magnitude of this decision flooded her mind. She was about to walk into a man's world, as a man. Home…would it ever be that again? What if her mother saw her like this? Question after question, doubt upon doubt. But turning around was not an option. Live or die, she was now a man.

A team of mules pulled a line boat to the docks. It looked as if the Captain acted as steersman. Perhaps the steersman drove the mules.

Perfect.

George took two deep breaths and pushed aside the doubts. She started down the road willing one foot to follow the other, her insides quivering in step with her knees.

"Sir." She tried to sound sure of herself. "Can you use a hoggee?"

The Captain sized her up. "Driven before?"

She took but a moment to consider. "Yes."

"Name?"

"George, Sir."

"I'm going as far as Troy. We'll winter there. I'll pay $2 for the trip."

"Thank you, Sir."

"If you do well, we'll see about winter work. Could you use that?"

"Possibly, Sir. I'm looking for someone, though. May go off with him if I find him."

"Keep the offer in mind."

"Yes, Sir. I will. And thank you, Sir."

"No. Thank you. I want my steersman back."

To the sound of gobbling, caged turkeys were unloaded along with furs from the west. George grabbed one of the cages. The turkey inside gave a quizzical look at her fingers and pecked them, once … twice. She shook the cage and walked to the unloading area on the dock.

"Don't I know you?"

She had heard that voice and seen that face before. The laborer who saw Caleb looked right at her. Would she really be found out so soon? Not just ruined but dressed as a man? Her face warmed uncomfortably, and perspiration appeared on her forehead. She turned around and set down the cage.

"No." She hurried back to the boat.

Another cage in hand, she faced the unloading area. Staring from across the dock, he still watched her. She would need to go right up to him, again. What could she say? Her skin was too soft. Did she walk like a woman? With a more purposeful stride she marched toward him.

"I know I seen you. What's yer name?"

"George." *Ohh! You sound like a girl.*

The fellow eyed her up and down.

Could he tell she had bound herself? Did he know? Surely not, or he would say something.

She took only a few steps back toward the boat when the dock master walked up staring at her. "Don't he look a lot like that girl that was down here? You said her name was Ann, I think?"

"I knew he looked familiar!"

Where could she go? Was there something else she could do? The other crewmen from the boat helped unload, and the steersman watched. She had to do something. Still looked too much like Ann. Returning would be her undoing. She reached for another cage. This one was covered with refuse from those that had been stacked above it. The smell—the feel on her hands. *Ugh!* She paused and then wiped them clean on her brow, cheek, and blouse.

As she came close to the two men, she knew they smelled her.

"You got relation here in Port Gibson?" The laborer backed up.

"No." She stared right at them.

The dock master frowned. "Let's get back to work." He and the laborer left her with the cages.

Returning for another load, she sighed with relief and gagged from the scent.

"Boy." The steersman backed up. "You've got to learn there's better places to wipe yer hands."

They finished by loading apples and cider onto the boat. Reaching down to the towpath for a handful of dirt, her body throbbed. She rubbed it over the excrement, trying to pull the manure from the blouse. After washing her face and hands in the Canal, she stretched out the kinks in her back and climbed up to the path.

"Here." The steersman tossed her one apple, and another.

"Thanks." They were firm. Her mouth began to water. She loved apples.

"Not fer you! Fer the mules!"

While the Captain completed the selling and trading, each of the two mules got one of the treats. All the time, she paid close attention to the other boats and their hoggees.

"Move out!" The Captain jumped aboard.

She felt a pulsing fear and, at the same time, this addictive excitement. All her sensibility told her she should not be there. So many things could go wrong. But, if they didn't—oh, if they didn't—where would she be tomorrow!

"Heeyah!" She gave the lead mule's tail a twist and shouted out the words she'd heard hoggees yell. "Everybody down!" As the mules stepped out, the rope snapped taut against the boat. Anyone on the docks watched and bent low when the 100 foot rope passed over their backs.

§

"So you think I ought to look for him?"

Joe's left ear rotated back.

"I'll take that for a yes."

Both ears flipped forward.

George was a member of the crew but preferred to keep a safe distance from them. Mules made good friends. Joe was the lead and Sam walked on his right. George stayed next to Joe, on the Canal side of the team.

"Caleb's probably looking for work, don't you think?"

Sam's ears rotated back and forward.

"Come on, Joe. Why else would he leave?"

Joe's ears turned at his name.

"Good. We're agreed then. He's looking for work and when we find him he'll make things right."

The mules plodded on.

Early into the second day, a tender spot formed on each foot and then wetness. She hadn't experienced many blisters but knew the feeling. Step after step. This would be a long trip. She curled her toes to reduce the pressure on the sores that plagued the ball of her foot.

As much as possible, George studied the packets and line boats they met. Such encounters required her to bring Joe and Sam to a stop while the steersman took their boat to the opposite side and let the rope sink to the bottom of the Canal. The approaching boat and its mules passed on the inside while she looked for one face in particular.

Moving on, the heads of her friends bobbed up and down to the rhythm of their step while the rope slid away behind them. Like the boat, attached to the rope and gliding between the banks of the Canal, she was now being pulled along by her own rope of deception, on a path that was surprisingly effortless. But the day would come when this pretense could end, and she would again don her petticoats and lace. Where was Caleb? What was he doing? Was he thinking of her? What would happen if he came back to Port Gibson and found her gone?

A loud wailing sound echoed down the valley. The Captain stood in the bow blowing on the oddest of horns. They approached a lock.

When the boat was situated, George pulled down on the tail. "Whoa!"

They weren't there long, but the Captain had time enough to hire another hoggee. The two of them would take turns working six-hour tricks.

She found a place amidst the barrels of apples and removed her shoes while someone else drove the mules. One and a half days walking, alone, would damage anyone's feet. Her fingers gingerly rubbed around toes, feeling for the blisters. The Captain's horn, a conch shell, lay upon a barrel by the cabin. The tip on the big end was lopped off forming a round hole. She raised it to her lips and blew. Nothing. Then she buzzed her lips and blew producing a weak version of the Captain's sound. The noise was as foreign and striking as any she had ever heard. They passed the hills of upstate New York, but she pictured exotic islands. What if the boat took her to a distant shore? It could. The world's doors were open to her now. She could go anywhere, do anything. Still, thoughts of Caleb lingered. She wanted the man she loved, the man whose clothes covered her and kept her safe.

§

Ann stood face to face with Joe. "You've been a real pal." The mule took an apple out of her hand and chewed, juice oozing from his lips. "Good, huh. Remember to keep our secret." She gave him the rest of the treat.

It had taken ten days to reach Troy, and Ann found no one who saw Caleb. She wasn't sure where to go or what to do. She fed Sam an apple and scratched under his chin. "I think I'll keep on to New York. See about work there for the winter. If you see Caleb, tell him that's where I am."

Sam lifted and shook his head.

"I know you'll miss me. Wish you could come along."

They were ready listeners, never arguing with her when she talked about doubts and concerns. To keep hearing 'No' when she asked about

Caleb, now that was painful. With each such reply, the next question became more difficult. It helped to be able to talk with these two friends.

How long would she overlook the futility of her search? Maybe he really did leave her. *No woman should have to live like this.* She cursed him, and, as quickly, realized she loved him. Eventually, they would be together. Perhaps Caleb searched for her somewhere else. Had he gone west? Had he left the Canal?

The Captain came up. "Thought any more about my offer for the winter? I'll pay well."

"Think I'll move on."

"No luck seeking that friend of yours?"

She shook her head.

"Will you keep looking?"

She shrugged. "Perhaps I'll cross paths with him…sometime."

"A lot of people come through Troy. You could stay and work."

True, but she didn't want to be in one place too long. "Thank you. But I best keep going."

"Well, if you need the work later, look me up, especially in the spring. I know I told you two dollars, but you've done good, even drove the first day alone. Here's four."

She knew she could do the job. Too bad Ann wasn't receiving the compliments. It surprised her how easily the Captain and the crew were fooled.

"Good luck!"

If only the man realized how fitting were his words. "And you, Sir."

George put the money into the pouch around her neck and started off toward the station. The Hudson River took packets north and south while the Erie Canal terminated just ahead in Albany. A railroad paralleled the water-way between the two cities. Here, everyone hurried somewhere. People of means—men, women, families—traveled both directions. Fathers and boys labored; wives and daughters worked beside them. All the activity reminded her of squirrels packing away food for the approaching winter. No one noticed her.

Like them, she had to go somewhere. New York might be nice, but so would so many other places. Wherever she went, it must be busy with people; the more traffic, the less attention.

Then she saw her. A woman alone moved slowly along the store fronts, young and at the same time old beyond her years. Women, whose place was with their men, frowned at her passing. Eyes straight ahead, the woman walked on, her face showing resignation to her position. Waiting to be entreated by a man? Was she ruined?

This feeling of dread crept over George. That woman might be her. A man's clothes was all that kept her from walking under the same judging eyes, looking for fleeting glimpses of love. Her heart beat a little quicker. She had walked the Canal, but only for ten days. This charade could not go on forever. Because of Caleb, she lived a lie that would eventually be discovered. For whatever reason, the man left her in a predicament no lady deserved. Her stomach tightened and perspiration made her clothes feel sticky. The woman rounded a corner and disappeared.

You'll find him. Ann's body trembled as she took a deep breath. *Then it will be okay.* She breathed again and started on her way watching the passing faces. No one gave her condemning glances.

A staging area at the station afforded the opportunity to purchase tickets to any number of cities. Pulling herself onto a large box, she hugged her knees and considered the choices.

"Destination?"

George thought the plump fellow had an inviting smile, and his rosy cheeks fit the bite in the air. "Don't know yet."

He moved on while George looked at the slate with the alternatives written on it. New York, Hartford, New Bedford, Boston... so many places!

Eventually, the clerk returned. "Decided yet?"

"I think New York."

"Family there?"

"Nah. Just want to see what it's like."

"Kind of young aren't we?"

George shrugged.

"Won't your family wonder where you are?" He waited for an answer.

"Can't I just have the ticket?" She wanted to move on.

"Sure you can. But I wonder what it is that takes a gentleman's child out on a journey. You don't have the rough look of most of the young men who pass here."

He gave her the ticket, and she paid him a quarter.

She had asked so often, so many people. She was tired.

"I'm searching for a man."

"No luck?"

She shook her head

"A lot of people come through here."

"His name's Caleb Coleman."

"Don't remember names much. What's he look like?"

"Has a scar." Once again, she drew her finger from eye to ear.

The man gasped. "I know the man! Why would a good boy like you seek a scoundrel like him?"

Caleb had been this way! Her heart soared at last. But he'd called him a scoundrel. Surely that's not … "Why do you call him a scoundrel, sir?" She tried to sound sly in the questioning.

"He ruined a girl and left her in Port Gibson. Men like that should be locked away!"

Caleb, a scoundrel? The words slapped her.

I'm the one he ruined. She was falling with no one to catch her. A storm raged inside and her vision darkened. She wanted safety but the world wouldn't understand. She was neither woman nor man. Ann no longer existed, and this thing in men's clothes had no home…no mother…no father. She had no friends for friends knew each other. Obscurity would be her life. She was alone...because of this man he called a scoundrel.

In her stygian reverie, a light flickered. The man whose clothes she wore, who had promised her so much and taken everything, this man—a deep feeling she had never before felt burned hotter, a desire to see him wiped from the face of the earth—this man must pay. She grasped for the solace of that light and entered the eye of a hurricane.

The clerk was staring at her.

"I am George Johnson, that girl's brother." The strength in the voice surprised her. "Ann was tricked into leaving home with Caleb, and now I seek him to settle matters. Can you tell me where he went?"

"He's gone to Boston. But you're rather young to avenge such a matter."

"I may look young, but my heart is tried. I will find that canal scum and he will rue the day he messed with Ann."

The clerk quickly scribbled. "Well, then, here's your money back, and a new ticket. No charge."

She took the ticket without a word.

"He went to whale. That's what he told me. When you get to Boston, go to the wharf and check out the sailor boarding houses. That's where they wait before shipping. But take care! Whaling is a vile and deadly business." His face was solemn. "How far will you pursue him?"

"As far as it takes!"

§

"Are you sure it was him?" Caleb had been here! He was close. Soon, soon she would make things right.

"Had the scar." The man talked with the oddest accent. He didn't pronounce the r's in words. "Said he was familiar with boats on the Erie Canal."

Finally! In her mind, she saw agony in Caleb's face as his voice begged for mercy, something he didn't deserve, something she wouldn't give. "What ship?"

"Don't know the ship. Wasn't assigned from here."

"It's important that I find him. Can you tell me where he went?"

The man flipped a page in his ledger. "Here it is…Caleb Coleman. Seems he shipped to New Bedford."

"How do I get there?"

"Packet."

George fondled the bag holding what little money she had left. "Cost much?"

The man glanced up from the corner of his eyes. "You can go for free if you sign to a voyage."

"Just want to find the man. Don't want to become a sailor."

"Trust me. He's been assigned by now. The only way to see him is to ship yourself."

"How far is New Bedford?"

"Too far. Best way is by ship; take the packet or sign and go for free."

She was on his trail, at last, and didn't want to lose it.

"How long ago did he ship?"

The man looked at the ledger. "Umm, two days. Trust me. If you sign and ship, there's a good chance you'll find him. Besides, a fine young man like you would do nicely on a whaler. The pay is good and the accommodations are some of the best in the fleet."

"I've been told it's vile and dangerous."

"Nonsense! With all the money made in whaling, the crews are treated very well."

George wasn't sure. The clerk in Troy was pretty convincing.

"Tell you what, I'll help you out. I see you really want to find this Coleman fellow. Sign with me here; and I'll give you a note of release. If you don't like the ship, give the captain this note and he'll put you back on shore."

"A captain would do that? What about paying for the trip to New Bedford if I give him the note?"

The shipper thought but a moment. "If you don't have the money, you can work off the debt. It wouldn't be much. Trust me, friend. They only have your best interest in mind. There are plenty of men who want the opportunity to whale. Signing now just gets you that much closer to the man you seek. And there's little risk."

The offer seemed a good one. Caleb was just ahead of her; she could follow for free, and, with the note, make no commitment. He was close.

§

An evil congregation gathered around lanterns in the Nantucket shipping office. Their hands were rough, faces grizzled and scarred. Laughing danced wildly from these demons in men's cloths as lips curled back over mouths with teeth missing. They talked and joked in language rougher and coarser than used on the Canal. George had never seen so many of this ilk in the same place, and she with them. Their shadows spread and blended into the darkness at the periphery of the room. They waited to ship on the *Christopher Mitchell*, an outbound whaler.

George leaned against the wall in the corner, any cheer long forgotten. She wanted to hide, to run outside and stand alone on the shore. This situation gave reason to worry. But her life did not allow the luxury of acting on such concerns. So she sat in her gloom upon the small trunk purchased from the fitter[1]. Fear or not, to survive she would need the simple items it contained; at least that was what the fitter had said. She fondled the jackknife tied to her waist, not exactly sure what its use would be...holding it, and thinking about how it MIGHT be used.

The voice of a gaunt, young salt named Charlie Eddy, rose above the cacophony. His speech was animated and his accent an exaggeration of that of the other men. "Aye, mates, the Creature waits, hidden beneath the surface. We seek it! But when it is hunted, it becomes the fiercest of enemies." He spit on the floor and wiped his mouth with his sleeve. "Yet it drives us. It consumes us. It is our life."

George's eyes were drawn to the man.

---

[1] Before shipping, whalers could purchase items for the voyage from a fitter.

"Yet, with a swipe of 'is tail or bite of 'is jaw he can destroy us. Be aware! Be very aware! The men of the Essex were just like us. Aye, mates, the same."

The noise in the office diminished, and an air of reverence settled upon the room. George bent forward, drawn to the tale that would quiet such men as these. She listened from the safety of shadows that kept her apart from this life.

"'Thar he blows! Sperm whale. Big one.' But he was not alone. The sea turned black. The whaleboats were lowered and run clear, turning sail to the wind. Even the captain joined the hunt. Only the three tradesmen stayed on board the ship.

"Into the aimless gambols of the whales they sailed. The harpooners cast irons and thrust their lances until the school betook itself below. In the end, the men rested in a sea of blood while the three on the ship laughed at the sight of the success.

"Then…" A wicked grin crossed Charlie's face. "…the beast arose."

George gasped and the hair bristled on her neck.

"So big! So massive! He thrashed about in a maddening sort of way. The tradesmen gripped the railing when the beast made direct for them, not fast, but with a ferocity marvelous to see. The whale drew near the ship's bow…like a fighter might reach out to tap his opponent's fist." Charlie slowly boxed the air. "They stared, eyes fixed on the massive head. His wake was larger than that of any ship. Approaching slowly, he barely tapped the hull. Yet, the men stumbled and fell as the ship quivered beneath them. Then he sank into the waves, and all was still." In the silence, Charlie turned with an outstretched arm and stopped, facing George.

She backed further into the darkness.

His eyes opened wide. "The men pulled themselves up. They looked with disbelief about them. Had it really happened? A whale never attacked a ship! Would the beast be satisfied with this one tap? The water parted off the bow before the rising monster. Aye! The men saw a fire in his eyes, or was it a reflection of the blood? Why? Why should this be happening to them?

"He backed off the bow, lowered his head, and charged the ship. Like a bull blind with rage he came, water rising up and over his back. The men stood on legs that would not move, on the old barky that had served them so well. As the ship exploded beneath their feet, they flew through the air landing amidst splinters and whale oil. The beast, where was he? He was near, an awesome presence in the endless sea about them. They made for the largest chunk of the hull, floating some fifty yards away. Yet the wooden refuge barely grew in size.

"Gasping for breath, they at last drew close enough to make out the cracks and seams in the planks. Safety was within their grasp. Ohhh, something caused currents to eddy around them. The whale breached. The monster's tooth-lined lower jaw rose slowly on their left; and the massive head, with a waiting hole for each of those ugly teeth, rose on their right. Higher came the jaws. Water gushed out the sides. The sea swirled around them. Their mouths opened in screams that died away as they slid into the whale's gullet. The jaw closed, and the creature sank beneath the waves."

George gripped the edge of the trunk. The wrappings about her chest and waist threatened to squeeze the life out of her. She wanted to stand up, rip off her blouse, and shout, "Look! I'm a woman! I don't want to ship!" She glanced about the office. The world had somehow slid into a hell from which she needed to escape. But what would they do to her? Was Caleb really worth what she faced? She stumbled to the door and out into the cold, early morning air. With head down and arms hugging her chest, she steadied herself against the wall gulping breath after breath. When her insides calmed a little, she became aware of the letter of release that the shipper had given her.

How stupid you are. If the paper held any value, she would wave it about and soon be on her way back to the mainland. *How could I believe what that man told me[2]? The clerk was right; these men are vile.* As soon as she boarded the packet in Boston, she was told the note was worthless. Once signed to a ship, she could not go back, like a captive locked behind a prison's bars. But she was a woman. They don't ship women. She could get out of the voyage.

The door opened quietly and a sailor stepped out beside her. He was much more refined than the bulk of the men inside. She hadn't noticed him before.

"You didn't believe that yarn, did you?"

Of course she did. Charlie had spoken as if he knew it to be true. She scowled and looked back to her feet.

The man leaned back next to her. "The Essex was a real ship, and a whale stove her."

The same feelings again bubbled up.

---

[2] Those who signed men onto whale ships often lied to get people to join.

"But that's the only case I know. It just doesn't happen. If you keep your wits about you, whaling can be a great adventure."

For some reason, she found assurance in the man's calm words. He was different from the others, and he didn't have the accent. Still, something inside warned her not to believe anything she heard.

"You'll see places most men haven't even dreamed about." He was an easy speaker with very proper words. "There isn't a better profession to be found."

A touch of morning light appeared through the fog. What should she do? Did she really want to ship, even if Charlie was just telling a story? It seemed so real. But it couldn't be as bad she imagined. She looked up and smiled weakly at the man beside her.

He walked back inside, and she followed. Her life was no longer her own. She returned to the shadows. Where she went, she would be taken. What she did would be directed. Where she stayed, she would be put. She shivered at the thought. If Rochester were the world, it would be enough. The desire to see exotic lands beyond the Genesee was gone. Her deception was no longer a game she controlled.

A laugh. "If harpooners spit their lances, you could be one!"

The men had gathered around a fellow with the look of a farmer, wearing coveralls and boots fresh from walking behind a plow. He was taller than the others, gaunt but muscular, with wavy black hair and stubble on his face and chin. Tom Hally was from Henry County, Indiana. She noticed him when he boarded the packet at New Bedford. The men stood fixed on the farmer as he moved his jaw, focused, and spit. More laughing and cheers followed.

Another fellow put something in his mouth, chewed with careful attention, and finally followed Tom's example, only with jeering and hooting as a result. Soon all the men were chewing and spitting.

"You, in the corner." Charlie looked her way. "Why ain't you over here." Others near him eyed her as well.

The den of pirates! A sickening heat crept from her stomach to her throat like a kettle coming to a boil. No, she didn't want to do this. It was time to back out, to tell them who she was.

Caleb! She pictured him. He had put her here, and he had to pay! *That won't happen if you give in now.*

"If you're to ship on the Mitchell, you best come show us your talent."

Charlie's eyes bore into her. She didn't want to be seen; she didn't want to talk, still sounded too much like a girl. Yet, men saw what they wanted to see. Who would expect a woman? On trembling legs she stood and matched Charlie gaze for gaze.

"Cat got yer tongue, boy?"

George shook her head. *Stop shaking! Just work through this and you can sit back down.*

Tom handed her a pinch of tobacco off the brick in his hand. He smiled as she put it on her tongue. She'd seen the men do that much, but what happened now? Though her mouth was dry, she started salivating. She swallowed once. *Ugh!* And again. She grimaced. Why in the world had the fitter told her to pack so much of the stuff in her trunk?

Tom frowned and gave her a quick shake of the head.

"Avast, mates!" Charlie puffed up his chest and backed away. "Let's see what the boy can do."

A queer sensation gurgled in her stomach. She sucked out what spit she could, aimed for the metal container, and let go the liquid and tobacco together. Some landed a few feet in front but most just dribbled down her chin.

Laughter bubbled up about her.

She longed for her dark corner.

"Again." Charlie pulled her back and handed over another pinch.

Surrounded, with no place to go, she felt tears begin to form in the corner of her eyes. Tom kept something between his lower lip and teeth. She shoved the tobacco there with her tongue and worked on producing juice while the men laughed and spit. Finally, she tried again. This time the tobacco stayed in her mouth and the spit went a few feet.

Tom cheered and slapped her on the back.

A bulge of tobacco slid down her throat and tried to come up again. To laughing and jeering, she shuffled back to the corner, fighting sobs, and cleaned her mouth with a finger.

With her sleeve, George wiped her eyes and nose. She considered these men of uncut quality. They would be her brothers now, no matter how she saw them, no matter how much she wanted to separate herself from them. If it took signing to a whale ship to find Caleb, so be it!

First Days

Friday, December 8, 1848, Day 1

George rocked with each stroke of the long oars that took them further and further from land. The whaleboat rode the swells up and down in a gentle sort of way, but every muscle in her body was drawn taught, refusing to relax. Land was all she knew, and the crew had the appearance of pirates, even in the light of day. She shut her eyes to this world, but their grumbling and cursing were impossible to keep out. She wished for silence but raspy breathing kept time with the movement.

"Seems you've gotten over Charlie's yarn."

The man beside her was the same neatly dressed mate who had encouraged her outside the shipping office. He sat too close; their thighs touched. The fellow was someone she might call a friend, but looks were not to be trusted.

"You're in for an adventure." He smiled. "Ever been on a ship like this?"

George shook her head, short and quick. The *Christopher Mitchell* rested before them, a massive vessel with a slow and stately sway. Though the ship looked big, it would be small. How could she ever hope to keep her identity from the crew of 21 men? On the Canal, she stayed with the mules and found solitude in the woods and fields. On the ship, would it even be possible to be alone? Would she find privacy? She needed a place apart. What happened to someone who didn't belong on a whaler? All kinds of things could be done to her. These were the kind of men capable of anything. She shivered, like a canal rope pulled tight by a mule.

"A ship like this weighs three hundred and fifty tons. It's about one hundred feet long and about twenty-five feet wide."

I don't care. A growing desire to be someplace else threatened to burst forth from her every pore. But where could she go. On shore, running away was always a possibility, but not here, not on a ship. *Ohh!*

The *Christopher Mitchell* loomed close like this ominous thing that should be avoided at all costs. It rode about twelve feet out of the water. The stern was flat. The bow rose up and ended in a scroll work that reminded her of the bottom end of a fancy banister in their home in Rochester. Oh, how she wished she was home. She looked up, straight up, forcing herself to see the ship. Three masts rose from the deck almost as tall as the ship was long. Her insides twisted.

"You'll be up there soon."

Oh, no! Not me.

"Name's Job Rounswell."

He waited for her to say something. In another place and another time she might have enjoyed the conversation.

"I remember my first time. Pretty intimidating. Don't let it get to you. The first days are always the worst."

Ropes ran everywhere, tied off here and there. It reminded her of a spider web, albeit a web by a spider that had never learned to spin one. She saw no order to the mess, though she thought there must be.

"Magnificent, isn't she? Home sweet home for the next three years."

Ohhh!

When the boat came to rest on the starboard side, Job helped pass trunks up a rope ladder to the deck and then, with others, climbed up himself.

"Well, what are you awaiting fer, Christmas?" The gravelly voice bellowed from the deck. "Git up here now and be quick about it!"

George begged her legs to stop shaking. She let the other greenhands climb out first, to taunts and jeering. They all three had the look of farmers. Tom, the last one up, reached back down to give her a hand. She frowned, and refused the help. If she was to live in this world, deferring to men was not an option.

The rope ladder pinched her fingers against the sides of the ship as she inched her way up.

"Boy!" The word cut like a curse directed right at her. "Quit skulking and git up…now!"

Laughter rolled over the bulwarks as faces peered down at her.

When she finally stood upon the deck, Tom was in a conversation with an old salt who had the worst accent she'd heard yet. His words were lopped off and run together.

"Captain's cabin is furthest back. Just fore of that, but behind the mainmast, is the galley. Now you ain't supposed to be back of the mainmast except that an officer sends for you. Remember that, greenie. Peleg knows. Yes, siree, I do."

"Avast, you clod hoppers!"

"That's Mr. Clark, the Second Mate." Peleg spoke softly, almost reverently.

"What are you gawking at? Git your gear stowed in the fo'cstle[3] and tumble back up."

What's a fo cus ul? How do I tumble up? Why did he call me a clod hopper? George had no idea what he meant.

"Now!" Mr. Clark's red beard and hair were like a blaze about his face.

Before she could raise her arms, the back of his hand lashed out and struck her in the side of the head. She grabbed her trunk, stumbled toward a covered hatch on the deck, and followed others down a ladder.

§

After the ship left port, George returned to the forecastle. No light entered there for the hatch was the only link to the outside world. The sun had set and no candle was lit in this new home. She felt in her trunk, pushing aside the blouse. Ignoring the tobacco, needles, thread, string, and other items, she quickly found what she needed. With her jackknife, she cut a piece of old canvas from the roll she had purchased. Feeling with her fingers, she made sure it covered every inch of her bunk's opening and tacked it up so that it gave her complete privacy. She pulled the blanket from her trunk, and crawled in, trembling. Gradually, her muscles relaxed.

George held her hand up in front of her face and saw…nothing. She stretched her arm above her, finding damp wood before she could straighten it. She pointed her shoes and touched one end of the bunk while the top of her head rested against the other end. The hard wooden shelf beneath her provided no comfort. On top of her body was the single wool blanket. An elbow's distance away was the hull of the ship. On the other side was the piece of old canvas. This was her world. Like a corpse in a coffin, six feet below ground, she lay alone.

If darkness hadn't covered this little world, George swore the reeking odors would be visible. She took shallow breaths, afraid that deep breathing would start her gagging again, and doubted that she would ever learn to live with the smell.

---

[3] The forecastle was under the main deck in the bow of the ship and was where the common sea hands had their bunks. It was their home for the term of the voyage.

Below was another bunk. In all, sixteen lined the sides of the forecastle, eight along each side. George had been on the *Christopher Mitchell* but a day, yet already hated the forecastle. She and eleven men called this home; the officers, harpooners, and tradesmen bunked elsewhere. She envied them; anyplace would be better than this. Fortunately, she wasn't the only modest one. A few others had canvas curtains like hers, though she figured her reason was better than theirs. No one had paid her any mind when she tacked it up.

Voices existed in the darkness, just beyond the curtain, but George could not discern words from the grumbling, laughs, and howls. She focused on the growing knot in her gut. Continually, the bunk rose and fell…up and down…sliding…left and right…up and down. She shivered, as much from that uneasy feeling as from the cold and the ever-present dampness that was drawn to her clothes. Up rose the ship. It must have slid down but, in George's mind, it kept rising up…up. Then it began again, over and over.

Nnng . . .

The voices faded from her mind.

Out. Got to get out.

George ripped off her blanket and slid from the bunk. Hers was furthest forward. She stumbled aft toward the ladder until she smashed into one of the beams supporting the deck. Grabbing her head, she momentarily forgot the sickness in her stomach. Bending over, she continued her journey fighting back tears. A single candle burned near the aft bulkhead, the sole source of light and heat for the men gathered around it. By its flicker, facial features became dim forbidding shadows. She took a breath and retched. The stench of the forecastle lingered in her nostrils and mouth as she climbed onto the deck.

"Ah, Johnson, good to see you show yourself willing." Mr. Clark's voice was much too cheery. "The Captain says you must work like everyone else. You may be just a boy, but don't expect any special kindness."

Why couldn't they just abandon her to her suffering? An involuntary, indiscernible plea escaped her lips as she collapsed against the companion way.

"Pull on this!" He held a rope tied off part way across the lower yard[4].

---

[4] A yard is a spar (wooden pole) on a mast from which sails are set.

She found it hard to move, and the motion of the ship made it difficult to stand. But he was the Second Mate. She took the rope and pulled. From the force of a wayward wave, the ship heaved to the side. Her insides heaved with the ship.

Hang on! She told herself.

Laughing? Men on the windlass[5] were laughing. Why was she the only one pulling? She glanced up. The rope did nothing.

"This is going to be a most delightful hunt." Mr. Clark was surrounded cheery faces.

They were laughing at her.

Don't give in! Something hidden lunged from the recesses of her mind and covered up the sickness. She gripped the line and glared at the Mate's back. She hated this ship and loathed the men. She would not let go. But, as the comments died away, the pain inside returned; and her arms felt like cords about to come untied at the shoulder. Finally, she slid to the deck.

When did the comments and laughter cease? She was more focused on her stomach than sounds. Time had no meaning

"Git up, boy! You can't hunt whales if you can't walk. No, siree!"

How could someone not see her wretched condition! She crawled to the tryworks[6], Peleg close behind criticizing her all the way.

"Watch it there, boy. Those pots are fer boiling oil, not holding you up."

She wanted to crawl into one of the two copper kettles on top of the brick structure and hide under its cover. Maybe they could just boil her away. The ship slid to starboard and George whipped her arms out for balance.

The old salt laughed. "I'd say you have more than enough ballast to keep upright."

As he reached out a bony arm to poke her in the side, she stepped around the corner of the tryworks. A sudden slide of the ship to port sent her sprawling to the deck again. More laughing from other sailors busy at work. With a smile, the old salt followed after her.

Again and again she stumbled or fell. And each time, Peleg chastised her.

---

[5] A wheel or drum of some kind on the foredeck, turned by manpower, used to raise and lower the anchor, blubber, and cargo for the hold.

[6] A brick structure used as a fireplace to boil oil from blubber. The blubber hold was just forward of the main mast and the tryworks was just forward of the hold. See www.firstfury.com for pictures.

Why wouldn't he leave her alone to suffer? She rolled onto her knees, head in her arms, moaning, unable to rise. She didn't care if the old sailor was there or not.

§

"You!"

George jerked her head toward the voice. Did Mr. Clark have no one else to pick on but her? She wasn't even out of the companionway, the box like structure two feet wide, four feet deep, and four feet high that covered the entrance to the forecastle. Feeling better, all she wanted to do was come on deck, not be noticed, and breathe fresh air.

"Aye, you!"

The beat of her heart doubled. Men all around her, all day and all night, and any one of them could do worse to her than Caleb, if she were found out.

"Aye, sir!" She came to attention in front of him, her breathing shallow and quick.

"Good boy. Slush[7] these." He pointed to a stack of wooden shafts.

George dropped to her knees beside them, wanting to do exactly as she was told. A bucket full of some concoction was within arms reach, but how was she to apply it? She looked around.

The Second Mate put his hands on his hips and spread his feet. "You have a problem?"

"Uh, is there a brush?"

He smiled and motioned that she should use her fingers.

George looked at the bucket, then back as she dipped in the tips of her fingers. It felt greasy. She sniffed. The scent weaved around her nostrils, over her tongue, and forced its way down to her gut. She tried to expel the rancid sickly smell and gagged.

"Work it in as best you can." If an angry dog could speak, that would be Clark.

She patted some onto the end of one shaft.

"Don't be lazy 'bout it, boy!" He bent down to within inches of her face. "Dig in! Use all the tar!"

Almost as rank as the slush, his sour breath washed by her face. She immediately pulled out a handful of the stuff. It oozed between her

---

[7] Grease collected by the cook as he prepared meals.

fingers as she squeezed around the wood. The other hand pulled the shaft through the mess. Her stomach moved again.

The Mate smiled.

"Andrews!" He walked toward another greeenhand.

"What?"

"What do you mean, 'What'!" Clark's hand struck him in the chest. "It's 'Aye, Sir!'!"

"Aye, Sir!" Gorham gasped.

"Here! Sweep the foredeck!"

"Aye, Sir." He took the broom.

Swack. Swish. Swack. Swish. Stumble. He paused a moment and looked up.

"You grumbling about something?" Clark contorted his face and glared at the greenhand.

"No, Sir." Gorham smiled and moved a bit sharper.

The Second Mate walked aft.

"Mule cock!" Like an unwilling servant, he slapped the broom's straw against the deck and swept George's way. "What you looking at?"

She bent back to the shafts and bucket without a word. *Stay out of the way. No attention.*

"Why would someone as…refined…as you sign to whale anyway? What IS that stuff?" He hit the bucket with the broom.

"Don't know." She spoke softly and kept her head down.

He stuck three fingers into the contents. Holding them to his nose he frowned and shook it from his hand onto her head and back.

George tried to wipe off what she could, but only made matters worse. "What did you do that for?"

"Better on a mule cock than me."

She longed for the security of her bunk behind the curtain.

Jamie Taylor, another greenhand, ambled by with a cask.

"Hey, Jamie, have a look at ol' Johnson here."

Why did they pick on her? What were they going to do? She was only following the Second Mate's orders. Turning her head away from their faces, she rubbed one of the shafts hoping they would just leave her alone.

"What have we here? The boy looks sick. Yes, siree, he does."

Oh no! Peleg was coming. Her arms shook. *Go away! Oh, please, go away!*

She saw their feet. Jamie stood behind her, Gorham beside her, and Peleg in front of her. She glanced to the side. The Mate was nowhere to be seen; he would be no help. When they found her deception, what would they do to her, right here on the deck? Would they throw her overboard? Or worse, keep her on board for their own obscene pleasure? She felt the pulsing fear in her ears. She rubbed harder and faster. Her secret had to be kept.

§

Joseph sat upon the deck, with his knees slightly up, his Bible in his lap, and leaned into the windlass. *A fitting place of rest*. He recalled the hours spent in agony laboring upon its handles. But, even the pain of the windlass, as they pulled up and down raising heavy cargo, would be more welcome than this pain in his heart. Beside him, his supper plate was on the deck untouched.

Lord! Each word was like brine in a cut. *Lord, keep them safe.*

Joseph held the note from home, but he saw the writers, not the words. His sons, one on each side of the woman he loved, wrapped their arms around his wife as she enveloped them, because he was leaving…again. They had parted with tears. The only consolation was the memory of that last night with her.

The first days away were the hardest. His Uncle Isaac had taught him to whale, warning him leaving home would never be easy. *Oh, Isaac, truer words were never spoken!*

Men cleaned the tools that would be needed when fires burned inside the brick tryworks, boiling oil from blubber. Harpoon and lance shafts were being slushed. Mates climbed the shrouds and ratlines to the tops of the masts. Dismissing memories of Nantucket would hasten the enjoyment of this new life, but he missed his wife and sons. He closed his eyes straining to see his family just one more time and caressed the paper with his fingers.

"Considering our mates?"

The voice roused him. "Nay. Home."

Job Rounswell took a spot beside him.

Since they were both harpooners, they shared an aft cabin, but Joseph had been too busy to talk much with his bunkmate. "Hast thou been taking account of the men?" Getting to know the crew was one of the many things he liked about being harpooner and boatsteerer.

"Some. I've been wondering about the boy, George Johnson. He won't talk much. Do you know anything about him?" Job nodded toward where he slushed shafts.

"Nay." But that may change. He learned a lot about people by just observing. A couple of the other greenhands picked at the boy. As Joseph considered how much the boy's chubby form reminded him of his eldest son, Peleg walked up to the three young mates.

Joseph couldn't imagine two more opposite people, yet Peleg and Job had signed on together, as friends. Something about Peleg bothered him. He had proven likeable enough. What the old salt said wasn't the issue; something behind his words, and his walk, just was not right. Joseph absently refolded the note from home. "Now, Peleg is the mate who I wonder about."

"He began whaling as a young man. The woman he was engaged to, left him for someone else. Never did get over that. He blames all women for what happened. Found peace whaling. But told me once he won't sign to a ship where the Captain brings his wife. Thinks a woman on board is bad luck. Good whaler, but he's done some things to kanaka[8] women that would cause him to be cut in and tried out were they done in a civilized port."

The old salt's words drifted across the deck. "Aye! You look a little sick about the gills. Yes, siree, lad. You need a dose of medicine."

George's countenance was that of a cornered pup.

"Didn't the Mate tell you about this here slush being a balm for what ails you?" Peleg stuck two fingers into the bucket and pulled out a healthy portion. The boy scooted away as the old man reached out toward his mouth.

"Hold him down, mates!" Peleg took the stance of a man in charge.

Gorham grabbed a shoulder. Jamie hesitated only a second before doing the same. Instantly, George swung the shaft into Jamie's knee, and he crumbled to deck. Gorham and Peleg jumped back staring in surprise. George took to his feet cocking the shaft back, ready to knock one of them down.

Job ran toward the commotion.

Setting his Bible aside, Joseph followed.

Job grabbed George from behind, holding back the boy's arm, while Joseph stood in front of the lad facing Peleg.

"Let me go!" George fought against Job's arms trying to swing his weapon. "Didn't you see what they were doing? I had to protect myself."

---

[8] A term applied by sailors to island natives.

"I was just trying to help him out." Peleg lowered his head and sounded disappointed. "Slush should bring the color back to his cheeks. These greenies here may have been a little rough." He nodded to Gorham and Jamie. "But, that's no cause to hurt a mate. No, siree! He best watch his self!" He pointed a bony finger toward George.

"Don't pester the boy! Canst thou not see the ship is still foreign to him?"

"Should know it by now." Gorham's voice was barely audible.

Jamie sat on the deck rubbing his leg and stared at George.

"Get him up." Joseph hoped he wasn't hurt too bad.

Grabbing Jamie's shoulder, Gorham helped him to his feet and followed Peleg forward. Jamie hobbled off with his cask.

Job released the hold he had on the boy.

"What's going on here?" Mr. Clark marched up to them. "Heard commotion and saw a ruckus."

George looked as if he was about to say something.

"Just a little teasing from the crew." Job cut him off.

"'Tis okay now." Joseph caught the boy's eye.

Clark gave George an angry glance and walked aft.

George looked pale and his eyes were tearing up. Joseph wanted to comfort him as he would his son. But this was a whaler. The lad would need to deal with it himself. "Thou over-reacted a little."

"They were just having fun with you, George." Job wiped some slush from the boy's back.

"I thought…"

"Thou best finish the job the Mate gave thee."

The boy knelt down again, took a deep breath, wiped his eyes, and began rubbing a shaft. Job went on to another task.

Joseph gazed about him. What a world this was! They would face danger together, experience joy together. Above them, the sails of the *Christopher Mitchell* filled with the wind that would take them places other men only dreamed about. God's hand carried them.

Oh, Lord, bless these mates. Thank Thee for Thy care and concern and bring us Thy whales.

He loved whaling. This crew, good and bad, was now his family. He placed his note from home back inside his Bible, picked up his plate, and ate.

§

The ship plowed along at its own determined pace, up and down swells, heading somewhere, though nothing but water lay between the ship and the horizon. George sat upon the carpenter's bench on the aft side of the tryworks thinking about a man. Did she love Caleb still or hate him? She laughed with him on the Canal. She still had fleeting pains of emptiness, the kind she used to have when parting at the end of a day with him. Was it possible for someone she had loved to be so evil? She took a deep breath and exhaled slowly with a shudder. Maybe he was just misunderstood by the laborer in Port Gibson and the clerk in Troy. When she found him, he might make things right; and they could be together again. She closed her eyes and saw his face, felt his gentle touch.

He ruined you in Port Gibson! The memory of a clerk's words shattered the vision. *If he cared, he would not have left.* She opened her eyes and looked out to starboard for sails, for a ship, for one ship in particular with a certain crewman, the reason—oh, she wanted to see him suffer—the REASON, the ONLY REASON, she was afflicted with this hunt. From seasickness, to slush, to the stench of the forecastle, this voyage was sinking steadily lower into an agonizing pit of pain. She had never experienced such crudeness and malice. The *Mitchell* was an evil place with evil men.

Others gradually settled around her in the waist of the ship since the Captain wanted to address them. The Second Mate focused his attention on Gorham. The greenhand was squatting in front the carpenter's bench, trying to get the attention of the pig in the cage beneath it.

Better not do that, Gorham. This would be but small consolation. With arms crossed, Mr. Clark stood and glared.

The greenhand held out his palm to the pig.

It sniffed closer. With his finger, Gorham rapped the center of the snout resulting in a squeal that stirred up the other animals even more. Laughing at the commotion, he looked up at his mates. Before he could turn around to see what held their attention, Clark gave him a kick that sent him sprawling onto the deck at George's feet. That's just where he belonged.

The Mate moved to within inches of Gorham's face. A look of fear flooded the greenhand's eyes as he lowered his head, cowering against the cage.

After that, the crew remained in somewhat of a respectable grouping in front of the bench but behind an imaginary line running cross ship through the mainmast. George knew she couldn't go back of that line. The quarterdeck belonged to the captain, the officers, and the harpooners as well as the tradesmen. But that didn't matter; what she sought wasn't there anyway.

Gorham scowled at her; but she pictured Caleb, felt his deceptive hands, heard his lying words. A harpooner's lance pinning him to the deck, as a child might pin an insect to paper, would be too good for him.

Captain Sullivan marched across the quarterdeck with a purposeful stride and took a position next to the mainmast. He stood in contrast to the crew. Though he wore no special uniform, he was quite neat in appearance, hair and moustache neatly trimmed and formed. Behind him, the two spare inverted whaleboats rested on what had the appearance of a gallows.

Men stood up around her, so she stood.

He stared with a look of controlled excitement at the crew, moving his gaze from eye to eye. Some of the men shifted nervously, not looking back. George met his eyes with hers.

With a deep voice, he began his speech. "You all may think you know why you came a-whaling. Now let me tell you why you came. You came to make a voyage."

"Aye." Some of the more grizzly members of the crew growled support.

"And on this ship, a voyage means oil."

"Aye!" And Job joined in with a smile.

"You didn't come to play; you didn't come to see the world; you didn't come as a passenger on some merchant ship expecting to be served. No, on this ship you came to work, to work in oil, to be part of a monstrous greasy hunt."

"Aye, Aye." Around her, salts[9] struck fists heavenward in agreement.

He talked on about whaling and duty. George's legs began ache.

"To your benefit, I have provided a small library in the cabin with the slop chest. There is no cost for the use of the library. But, if you lose a book or tract, the cost comes from your lay.

"Sunday will be a day of reflection and meditation, and that begins tomorrow. No loud talking or coarse jesting is allowed. However, the masthead watch will be maintained even on Sunday. That, too, begins tomorrow. You best learn to keep that habit. Should the good Lord see fit

---

[9] An experienced seaman was a salt.

to bring us a whale on His day, we would be remiss to ignore His benevolence."

"Aye." George timidly echoed the loud refrains of the others.

"When it's your watch below, you can stay in the forecastle or forward, just as you please. When you have the watch on deck, you will work on the business at hand. There'll be no skulking. If I see sogers here…" He moved his right arm in an arc over his head and before him encompassing the rigging[10], masts, and all on deck. "…I'll soger 'em with a rope's end. Whaling is why you came!"

"Aye!" Their necks tensed with excitement.

"And whaling is what you will do!"

"Aye! Aye!" Cheering joined the shouts of agreement.

"There is NO OTHER REASON for a sailor to attend to a whale hunt."

---

[10] Ropes and tackle used to support and control the masts, sails, and yards. Vertical ropes (shrouds), with horizontal ropes (ratlines, pronounced "rattlin's") attached, are used by seamen to climb up the masts.

The Azores

Sunday, December 19, 1848, Day 11

Through George's jacket and blouse, the morning sun brought welcome warmth. Patterns of light decorated the sails and shifted ever so slightly as the ship moved lazily along. The masts and yards creaked peacefully; and the rope, rubbing effortlessly against wood, could have been sighing. If it was possible for a ship to lie back and lounge on a sunny day, then that was what the *Christopher Mitchell* was doing. Even the ocean had a peaceful, soothing way about it. She closed her eyes and imagined a cradle being rocked. Other crewmen waited nearby for Joseph's Sunday message[11], but she ignored them.

"Trials…let's talk of trials today." Joseph's words were softly spoken. "Ye travel a path that seeks trials, for we attend to the hunt for Leviathan."

Suddenly, the ocean became a bit more ominous. It had been such a nice morning until this talk of monsters. *It's not whales that I hunt.* The thought crossed George's mind like a cloud across the sun.

"In the days to come, thou knowest well we will be tested; to the depths of our being we shall be tested. To successfully travel this path, we must have a singular purpose and be committed to the hunt. If not, trials shall defeat us. But God has written, 'What is man that Thou dost take thought of him? Thou hast put all things under his feet. Even that which passes through the paths of the sea.' He has put all things under our feet, but not all things are submissive. Danger lurks about us seeking whom it may devour. Be thou committed to our purpose. Be thou committed to our hunt. Remember, our Lord is no less committed to us and desires our love and service as much."

How was He ever committed to me!

Tom bent close to her. "I love the way he talks. Sounds like the Quakers back in Henry County. Glad he's our Sunday preacher."

George didn't care one way or the other.

---

[11] Because the Christopher Mitchell was owned and probably manned to a degree by Quakers, life on board was more reserved than other whale ships.

"No," continued Joseph, "there are things in all our lives that are not submissive to our wills…a thought, an emotion, a habit. What is it for thee? Dost thou want to be rid of it?"

No!

"Whatever comes between thee and thy hunt, or, more importantly, between thee and thy God, must be defeated and brought into submission. If thou canst not do it alone, our Lord can do it. All things are possible through him."

Then, Lord, give Caleb into my hands.

§

The old ship did a slow dance through the waters. The bow cut up and down into the swells; over and over, the ship lurched, rocked, and continued on a promenade under soft and watchful clouds. Joseph's heart moved to the rhythm, as light and gay as the morning. Talking of his Lord always filled his sails with a strong wind. Sunday was his favorite day. He may only be the harpooner on the Third Mate's boat, but the Captain knew—all the men knew—that, as a Friend, the light in his life wasn't whaling.

"Boy!" Gorham's voice sounded like he was trying to imitate Peleg's gravelly speech. The greenhand's mentor followed close behind.

"Move yerself over. Peleg and I need the space." He pressed into George who sat on the carpenter's bench, head down.

Joseph struck the bulwarks with his hand; the dance was over. The other end of the bench was open enough for the two of them to play their backgammon game. Yet they insisted on sitting where George sat. Just like every other day, the old man found some way to have his lap dog aggravate the boy. Joseph focused his thoughts on the work he needed to do. Sharpening harpoons, packing rope in tubs—these things, and more, he ticked off in his mind.

"Children ought to be below." Gorham shoved George to the side and turned his back on him.

The lad, never making eye contact, stood and walked around the tryworks to the windlass.

Why should George's troubles grate on him so? The boy brought it upon himself. Choosing to stay apart just provoked his mates into reacting like this. As harpooner, there were other issues that Joseph would need to deal with, more important than the boy's problems.

"Land Ho!"

As the island of Faial in the Azores gradually grew larger on the horizon, the crew gathered at the bulwarks. Soon, green draped the slopes and the brown of plowed dirt descended to the water. Brilliant white buildings lined a portion of the shore.

The ship rounded the north end, headed south along the eastern shore, and came to rest in the harbor of Horta on the southeast corner of the island. When everything was secured, the men took the boats to shore.

Job gathered them together. "The First Mate gave us money from the Captain and told me to get you supper. So let's be off."

The village consisted mostly of whitewashed stone buildings, not nearly as clean and white as they appeared from a distance. With his friends, Joseph walked along a narrow road to the sound of pigs and poultry kept behind simple wooden fences. Conversations in a language he only slightly understood floated around them. Some of the men, who spoke it more fluently, fell behind, dickering with locals about trades or sales.

Peleg moved closer to Gorham and nodded toward George. "That boy don't belong here, no siree."

"Aye." Like a dog licking its master's hand, Gorham followed Peleg. "Thinks he's better than the rest of us, I'm sure."

"I git the feeling there's no good luck in him. If he complains enough, maybe Captain Sullivan will put him off somewhere."

Gorham nodded.

Peleg glared at the boy.

Joseph found it impossible to just listen. "Thou art like a shark after a carcass. Why dost thou continue to aggravate George?"

"Something about him ain't right. No, siree. Don't know what it is, but there's something wrong with him."

"That's no reason to treat him so."

"Yes, 'tis." Peleg picked up his pace. "Besides, I been treating him real nice so far." He mumbled disparaging comments about the boy, with Gorham hanging on his every word.

§

Entering the little inn last, George thought of better ways to spend her time, more important things to do than eat. She didn't want to be there. *Scum of humanity. Such a sty is fitting.*

Peleg offered her the stool next to him. Gorham sat on the other side of the old man with a most disingenuous smile. As a surge of revulsion washed over her, she gazed about for a…safer seat. She could sit across the table, but that chair was close to the lantern, and Charlie was near it. Too much attention there. No, the best spot was here in the dark, next to Peleg. At that end of the room, shadows obscured the light. And the seat was close to the door.

But why should Peleg offer her a place? Gorham gestured that she should take it. The salt had befriended Gorham, the source of her distress. Gorham's smirk told her no kindness was intended from him. She glanced one more time around. No one made any room. George took the chair and moved it to the far corner of the table. At least she didn't need to sit too close.

"Ah, come along there boy." Peleg exuded a wounded spirit and mumbled his words. "Don't set yourself so far apart. I ain't going to bite." He reached over and pulled the seat.

As the stool slid across the floor beneath her, George grabbed the table. But she wound up beside the old man anyway.

"You're not as heavy as you look." Peleg eyed her up and down.

The owner brought wine.

"Oh, it's been too long." Peleg took the bottle from Gorham's hand just as the greenhand began pouring. "Sullivan don't allow no drinking on his ship. No, siree, he don't. Got to take advantage, while we can." He poured the wine into his mug right to the brim and slid the bottle back to Gorham.

Putting his lips down to the cup, he slurped the liquid and stared up at George. "What! You ain't going to drink with me?"

She smiled politely and held up her hands.

Peleg picked up his mug, gulped down a mouthful, and wiped his lips with his sleeve. "Ah! This is good!"

Gorham did the same.

They hit each other's mug, splashing wine on the table and took another drink.

If they could just keep it in the cups, the night might be bearable. The room was plastered with noise upon noise. Everyone laughed and talked, involved in someway with the vulgar air of the table. Everyone, that is, except her.

Peleg swished the wine in his cheeks and then spit it back.

"Here's to yer first voyage, boy." He leaned toward her and shoved the drink up under her nose. The contents sloshed onto her chin and blouse.

She pushed back on the stool shaking her head. *Disgusting*.

"Captain don't let no alcohol on board. No, siree. Best drink up now." He moved the mug closer to her pursed lips.

As he tipped it up, she turned her head, and the wine ran down her neck. Cotton strips absorbed it.

"Vast there, boy! That's wasting good spirits." He looked at Gorham with a sad face. "He don't want to drink with us."

"Oh, but he does." Gorham stood up. "He just needs a little help."

George's stomach moved to her chest and muscles tensed when Gorham walked around Peleg toward her. The old man wasn't going to stop him. She grabbed onto the table ready to push and run. When Gorham tilted her chair back, she kicked out with her feet for balance and hit the table. His left hand squeezed open her mouth.

"See, he wants to try it."

She grabbed his arm, staring as Peleg's cup came closer. "No!" But the cries were muffled by pinched cheeks. She glanced from the corners of her eyes for help.

"Leave the boy alone!" Job grabbed Gorham's arm.

The chair slammed back upright. Every muscle in her body shook.

"Peleg, my friend, I'm surprised you would force your own good wine on someone who obviously does not appreciate it."

The salt smiled at Job. "Just trying to be friendly to me mate."

"I know." The harpooner put his arms around both of George's antagonists. "But let's keep tonight peaceable. Captain Sullivan wants it that way." He filled both their cups.

When the two were again sitting at the table, he gave George a quick smile that did little to relax her body. She took one deep breath, and another.

For the next half hour, George gradually slid farther into the dark, away from Peleg. Hidden by the darkness of the shadows, she slipped out into the cold night air, shaking off the last vestiges of fear. The street was dark and quiet.

A few of the sailors still talked with the locals. Across the path and down a little toward the shore was a town square with lanterns and a small fire. A handful of men talked and laughed. Women clustered a short way off and chattered merrily. Times with her mother burst upon her. This was just like home, except that she didn't know the language. A young girl looked after children playing near the edge of the square. The vision stood in such contrast to life on the *Christopher Mitchell*! George watched a few minutes before walking up to the girl. "Excuse me, do you speak English?"

The girl giggled something in their language and continued to play with her charges. The women quieted.

"You work well with the children." George knelt down.

Before the young girl said anything, one of the men hurried over, pulled George up, and motioned her away.

"I just want to ask about a whaler."

Shaking his head, the man walked toward her. She didn't like the look on his face. Older youth gathered on either side while the young girl herded the children to the women. George raised her hands. Trouble was the last thing she wanted. Someone shoved her in the back.

"Wait! I just…"

A tangle of arms struck out at her. Raising her arms to ward off the blows, she made for a space between two of the boys. One of the attackers tripped her. Jerking her hands to the side, she blocked a kick and scrambled for safety just as a fist hit her. She tasted blood.

"*Paré!*"

The beating stopped. She staggered to her feet. In a blur she spun around and panned the faces. *Job!* Grabbing his arm she pulled herself close to him.

The boys, some laughing, began to encircle them both. Why did the men in the back just stand and watch? She wanted out, to be back on the ship. She hugged Job's arm a little tighter. At least she was not alone.

In one quick, smooth motion, he pulled his jackknife from its sheath and pointed it threateningly from young man to young man. Her eyes went wide. She carried a knife, but it had never occurred to her to use it. With her right arm, she clung to Job and fumbled to draw her knife with the other hand. The youth began to back off. Still clinging to Job, but with her knife held out, hopefully as menacingly as Job's, she backed into the darkness with him and walked briskly away.

"What do you think you were doing?"

She tried to answer, but Job shoved her ahead.

"Making passes at a girl, in port, with her parents there!" He shook his head and again pushed her on up the street. "You're a whaler, for god's sake! If you want a woman, there are plenty that will do what you want."

What was he talking about? Her mind was a tumble of confusion and uncertainty. Why would she want a.... *Disgusting!*

This was not the kind of night George wanted. She hadn't done much of anything right so far. Everything she tried just brought about troubles. Would she ever be anything more than a woman out of her element? She had to be rescued twice by the harpooner in one night.

"I was just going to ask some questions." She stumbled, attempting to look back at him.

"From the little I understood, that's not what they thought. You're just lucky a mate saw where you were headed." He pushed her onto a side street where the inn was just ahead.

§

With face pressed to the rope and knuckles white, George was near tears, the swelling in her lip forgotten. A breeze whipped her hair and shook her blouse as if trying to knock her loose.

"Move on up the rigging!" The Second Mate's voice bellowed from below, louder now, and his face was redder than his hair.

He yelled; but her hands simply would not move. She clung to the ropes, at death's door. Beneath and back, the cold waves beckoned. She closed her eyes. Tears squeezed out and she didn't care.

"No skulking. Move on up, I tell you. Move up or I'll have you deep-sixed right off the shrouds."

Why had she signed? The ship shook her back and forth threatening to fulfill the Mate's threat.

"George." It sounded like Job. "Don't look down."

She forced her eyes open.

He was beside her. "Just follow me up. If I can do it, you can too."

She loosened the grip of her left hand just as Job stepped on the same ratline clutched in her right hand. With a jerk, the rope gave way along the shroud, and her whole body slipped. Her insides rushed up as if being ripped out from her mouth, and she stifled a scream. She clenched the ropes even tighter. Waves gurgled against the hull.

"George!" Job was talking to her again. "George!"

She wanted to look up but her head wouldn't move.

"Hold the shrouds with your hands. That way, if the ratline should give way, the shrouds will hold you."

"Ohhh!" The unconscious moan came from her throat.

His hand grabbed the shoulder of her blouse and pulled. At his urging she began moving up. With her hands holding the vertical ropes and her feet on the ratlines, she followed Job up the rigging, one rung at a time, to a platform thirty feet above the deck. She stood there hugging the mast.

"Thanks, Job." She barely heard her own words. Every muscle in her body strove to hold onto life.

"We're not there yet. Next one up."

Her eyes followed another set of rigging from that platform up another third of the mast, and, above that, up more rigging to the top of the mast. Her pulse instantly pounded harder and quicker, and her body quivered.

The Second Mate was out of sight. "Can't I just stay here?"

Job shook his head and started up.

George carefully swung onto the outside of the rigging, letting gravity pull her, at least a little, into the ropes, and started climbing up, up. Hand over hand. When she reached the next platform, Job proceeded to climb up even farther. She followed on the opposite rigging. Just about half way up he stepped out on a rope that hung loosely below the yard.

"What are you doing?!" Her voice was more a squeak. "You don't expect me to stand on a rope sixty feet above the deck!" Death behind her, death in front of her, she squeezed the rigging. Where else could she go?

"I'm holding onto the yard, George. My feet aren't going anywhere. It's kind of fun." He rocked back and forth. "Step out onto the rope, grab onto the yard, and I'll show you what to do."

She looked down. The deck was so far away. The world swam around her. *Don't faint! Don't faint!* A slip here and Job couldn't help.

"Get onto the rope, George!"

She gripped the wooden spar; and, testing all the way, gradually slid one foot onto the rope and then the other. For a moment, she thought it might be better on deck. But she didn't look down. The mast wasn't staying still. It moved back…and her legs rocked…and forth…and they rocked more!

"Job!" She fought to keep from crying. "I can't do this."

"You have to!" He sounded irritated. "You'll be fine. Use the yard for balance. The rope will hold you up."

She moved an inch at a time, holding her breath, her eyes glued open. With each step the rope moved a little more. Through the ever-present thumping of her heart, voices rose from the deck.

"Andrews! Pull with your mates!"

Gorham yelped. He must have been hit.

"Heave it up!"

"Ready on that rope, Hally! Yer not hoppin' clods here."

"Harder, men! You're looking like greenhands! HAUL!"

A guttural chorus of men's voices gradually covered the commotion.

"There's whales a waitin' just 'round the Horn,
 A**way**! Haul a**way**!
 We'll heave to the hold oil's better 'n gold.
 A**way**! Haul a**way**! …."

Boots stomped rhythmically upon the deck. She was in a nightmare with no end.

"Anchor's aweigh, Sir." The First Mate's voice stood above the others.

"Very well, set all the canvas flying."

"Set the royals and t'gallants!"

George refused to look down. Her insides quaked uncontrollably. No one cared if she lived or died. She knew nothing. This emptiness welled up inside her. She was nobody.

"George." Job spoke slowly and deliberately. "We're going to unfurl the sail. Untie the rope that winds around it, there, at the mast."

Slowly, and with a very conscious effort, George untied it using one hand, while clinging to the yard with the other.

"Now unwind it and work your way out to the end of the yard, but don't undo the last one till I tell you."

How could he sound so calm? George moved toward the end of the yard, and Job worked to the end of his.

"Ready, George?"

"Yeah, when you say, I'll let it loose." Her arms shook as much as her legs.

"Haul out to leeward!" The command came from the deck.

"Now, George, throw out the line and loose the sail."

George did as she was told and, rocking back and forth, immediately grasped the yard with both arms.

"Knot away!" yelled Job.

With muscles quivering, George inched her way back toward the mast. When she got there, she held on with one hand and reached for the rigging with the other. Not until she felt again the security of that life-saving web did she breathe more easily. The chant grew louder and the yard rose before her eyes. The canvas spread out and opened to the breeze that would take them from the harbor. Other sails blossomed and she found herself caught up in canvas clouds. Beauty and terror together, what an odd sensation!

Back on the platform, George hugged the mast. Her muscles quivered giving the impression that the whole ship trembled. This was not walking mules on the Canal. This was life or death, and death walked too close to her.

The weakness in her arms made it difficult to hold to the mast. Her hunt…how foolish she had been. If climbing the rigging was beyond her, how could she ever expect to kill a man! She imagined her hands squeezing the life from Caleb's venomous neck. If that day were ever to come, she was first obliged to learn to whale. And she definitely required more strength just to survive. She needed someone like Job. She must listen to him, not hide from him.

Gorham and Jamie pulled, up and down, on the handles that ratcheted the windlass in the bow as it lifted the anchor from the depths of the harbor. They didn't sing the chant. Instead, they made furtive glances here and there, pulling, but seldom in unison with the others. The chant continued above the commotion. On every accent, the men jerked the handles and rotated the cylinder that was the windlass. And when the greenhands missed a cadence, they received verbal, and sometimes physical, reprimands. She would do better.

"And that, my friend, is why I'm up here. On leaving a port, that's about the hardest task there is. This is much easier work."

George wasn't sure that she was in a better position, but she listened.

"You needn't worry, though. You'll eventually get your turn at it. When the First Mate gave the order to heave short the anchor, he told the crew that he wanted the slack out of the anchor line. When the slack was pulled out and the anchor was clear of the bottom, the Mate yelled out 'Anchor's aweigh!' That's when we started deploying the sails. I would much rather be here than there. The goal is to plan it so that we're not down before those words are spoken."

George committed the harpooner's words to her memory. The mud-dripping anchor cleared the water. The iron rung at its upper end was slipped over the shank of a wooden timber, coming to rest at the bow of the ship.

"You did well. Keep it up and you'll be noticed for sure."

Sails surrounded her. She had climbed the rigging. The rope that she stood on still hung below the yards. She was far above the cries of her mates. Yes, she had done well. She would become a whaler, but could she do so and remain in the shadows of ship life? She squirmed.

"Being noticed is a good thing."

She disagreed, but didn't want to argue the point.

"Someone said you're from New York."

"Franktown. By Rochester."

"Got family there?"

She nodded.

"They know you're whaling?"

She shrugged. They probably didn't even care.

"Don't talk much, do you."

Talking was dangerous.

"You ought to get to know the crew. Three years is a long time."

Three years! If she'd only known! Three years was forever.

"You can't do that without talking."

He was so different from the other sailors and had already rescued her three times. "Why is it you whale?"

"Sail for my health. There's something about a whaling trip that makes sick men well. I struggled with what the doctors called consumption, a terrible disease." Job shook his head. "And they didn't know why. Someone suggested a sea voyage. I was assigned to a whaler. The air may have been the medicine, or maybe the thrill of the hunt, perhaps the monotony, or the work; maybe 'twas all of these. But that first trip on a whaler turned me around. Came back a new man. I go now because I want to go. I miss it. Never sick when I'm at sea. So, why did you sign on?"

"Don't want to talk about it."

"You've got to let your mates know who you are. The more you get to know the crew and the more they get to know you, the better your voyage will be."

She shook her head. *If only you knew the truth.* The truth? Her hunt would never be "better." The fearful quivering of her muscles subsided leaving in its wake that dull anger which, uncovered, was once again free to re-form and exert itself.

She'd heard some of the crew discussing other ships. That's what interested her. "When will we start seeing whales?"

Job looked at her curiously. "Anytime. But more as we head south and around the Horn."

"Will we gam with the other ships? That's the word I heard used, I think."

"Yes, we'll gam." He smiled. "But what do you mean by 'the other ships'?"

"The other whalers."

"Oh, we may gam with a few here and there. Why?"

"Just curious."

§

Leaning against the forecastle companionway, Joseph considered his mates scattered about the deck, but his thoughts came to rest on George. The boy, as was his custom, sat apart—a dangerous practice when his life would depend upon the men. The boy worked the yards when they left port. Much too early in the voyage for a greenhand to find himself on the rigging, especially one so young. He wondered again why he should feel such anxiety about George. Perhaps hidden innocence drew his attention, or his visible suffering, or the finding of such apparent refinement in the baseness of a whaler.

A scowl shaded the boy's face as he stared out to sea, ignoring his mates. If anger could be directed, it might benefit of the hunt. But, usually, angry men made unpredictable crewmates. And that put others at risk. Whaling was hard enough for a man. A boy on a whaler needed to grow up fast, and whaling was a harsh way to cross that boundary, especially for one like George. Death walked the decks of a whaler as much as any man.

Joseph's mind told him to leave well enough alone, but heart and duty made that difficult. What drove the boy? What caused him to stay so distant? Why the anger?

Maybe tonight. This might be an opportunity to get to know the boy better.

The dogwatch was upon them, the two hours from 6-8, after supper, when all the crew gathered together about the windlass to rest, talk, sing, and dance a little. The mix of men on a voyage always interested him, and George added one more touch to the assortment.

Joking with those about him, Charlie's legs bounced to the beat of a song.

Joseph's heart flew in rhythm with Charlie's bouncing knees. He found himself laughing at the man. Sometimes Joseph wanted to participate as freely as Charlie. Touching the bulge of the Bible inside his blouse, he knew why he didn't. He held himself to a different standard, one that called for a more balanced life not controlled by emotion.

At a break in the music, Charlie settled down. "Eh, Peleg, what do you think of our greenies this trip?"

The old salt scowled. "I say, there's some real tars for ya! They'll be slushin' the top-gallants sooner 'n they can call fer home."

Laughter echoed among the men. "Aye, 'twould be better had they never been weaned than to become slaves on a blubber hunter."

"Ack!" Charlie spit upon the deck. "In short order they'll beg to be let off I wager."

"Are you joking?" Tom Hally leaned forward completely serious. "So far this seafaring work has been quite painless. There's no way I would want off! And go back to farming?"

Charlie was caught speechless.

Gorham stopped his nervous fidgeting and stared. "You're crazy! This ain't nothing like what the shipper told me it would be. Said the ships were luxurious."

Jamie nodded agreement. "Yeah, told me I'd get rich."

"Aye!" Peleg slapped the back of Gorham's head. "And you believed it! That's greenies for you. Yes, siree, that is."

Tom gave Jamie a quick wink. "But can you imagine one of these salts working a plow? I wager they'd beg to be let go real quick like."

Joseph liked what he saw. For a new seaman, that Indiana greenhand was surprisingly comfortable for this early in a voyage.

Jamie paused but a second. "Aye, mate! My problem is not with the simple work, it's the lay. 'Tis downright robbery what these ships pay. On the farm, we gave a fair wage for day's work."

"Avast, there, greenies." Charlie overcame his momentary silence. "You're fools for sure! Just because the shipper said your lay was 300 and mine 200 you thought you were going to make a fortune. Everyone knows your lay of 300 means you get 1/300 of the money left after all costs and profits are taken by the owners."

Joseph laughed. Not everyone knew that, especially greenhands. Shippers lied to get men to sign on. He looked at Jamie. "Son, thou ought to learn the ways of the sea. Since thou signed in the shipper's office, every breath thou dost breathe is entered in a ledger."

"And it's true." Job rested his cup in his lap. "Nothin' in life is free, especially on a whaler. The Captain is noting every hook and ounce of tobacco. He knows what is eaten and where you sleep. All accounts will be paid. What's really distressing…" His brow furrowed and his eyes had a sympathetic slant. "…is that some who don't take care about life aboard ship, will find that they owe the Captain money when the voyage is over."

"That's what we're saying." Tom raised his arms. "Wouldn't you agree that farming is a much more honorable business?"

"Aye, and fairer too!" Jamie slapped Tom's back.

"Honorable?" Charlie fumbled for words. "...You're saying me and my mates ain't honorable?" His hands clenched into fists and his head jutted forward toward Tom.

"Whoa there!" The Indiana farmer could have been stopping a runaway horse. "Farming may be more admirable, but you'll notice we've not talked about the danger. You still need to teach us how to face those whales of yours."

I like him, thought Joseph. *This greenhand fits in as well as any salt.*

Charlie's head took a more natural tilt. "Aye, at least you got that right."

Job waved his cup toward Tom. "In the shipper's office, if you really knew what whaling was like, would it have made a difference?"

"No, though I'd like to return home with at least a little profit."

"So, if not for the money, why'd you leave the farm?"

"It wasn't 'cause I disliked plowing and planting. Henry County, Indiana, is a beautiful place. It's Quaker country." He glanced at Joseph. "I'm here because of a woman."

Peleg laughed and slapped Tom on the back. "Stove by a woman."

"'Tis a sad picture, indeed, of a man." Charlie laughed and nodded agreement.

"What do you mean 'stove' by a woman?" asked Gorham.

"Stove's what a whale does to a boat that gets in its way." The animation in Charlie's hands matched that of his voice. "Whether with its tail as wide as this deck or with its head like a steam engine, or with its jaws with teeth what can rip apart a man quite easily as you squash one of the cockroaches in the forecastle. Don't matter none. Same in the end. The boat becomes splinters afloat in the sea and the sailors but food for the beast. That's bein' stove. An this here greenie was stove by a woman." He laughed again.

Like the satisfaction after a full meal, Joseph's world was at peace. George was the only thing that kept it from being perfect. The boy had a fair, hairless face and sat with his legs pulled up to his belly, neck forward so that he could rest his chin on his knees. He was close enough to hear but remained separate and as silent as the mast in a calm. A mere boy, yet he still needed to fit in. If not, there would be trouble. Joseph squirmed. Such an attitude was pregnant with problems, both for the lad and the hunt. Twenty-two men confined to a space of less than 1500 square feet provided a fertile ground for ill feelings. He wished young Johnson had never signed.

Joseph recalled his son's questions about whaling. It pleased him to have his son desire that work, but the lad would need to mature before actually signing to a whaler. That was something George hadn't done. The greenhand's arms were too thin and his legs too dainty. George could die out here. He wasn't the typical seaman, especially not a whaler. But, when ready, this could be a good living. Joseph imagined a voyage with his son. What more could a whaler want? He missed his wife and their boys.

That shouldn't be! On other trips he thought of them, but rarely had the feelings overpowered the joy of whaling and this life with his sea-born family. Then, like a whale breaching before him, the reason for his anxiety about George was crystal clear. Why hadn't he seen the obvious before? When he saw the boy, he saw his son. What happened to George, happened to his son. The dangers this greenhand faced were dangers his own offspring could be facing. If George were to suffer, it would be like his son suffering. Or, if he were to die….

George needed to fit in. The boy must be able to count on his mates, and they on him. Joseph would do whatever was required to make the lad part of the crew. He moved to a spot beside the young greenhand.

"So, George, canst thou speak of thy family?"

The boy frowned at the harpooner.

"Well, then, what didst thou do before becoming a whaler?"

"Worked the Canal."

"Erie Canal?"

A nod.

"Dost thou know boats then?"

"Drove mules."

"I've got an uncle out on the hunting grounds. Taught me everything I know about whaling. Did thy father teach thee of mules?"

No response.

"What brought thee to Nantucket?"

Shrug.

"Thou ought to be more friendly with thy mates, George. 'Twill be a long voyage for thee if not."

The boy fidgeted.

Joseph leaned back. "There are some interesting mates here. Can't whale by thyself, thou dost know. Tom and Jamie are from farms."

"I can hear."

"Gorham's family raised mules, horses, and donkeys. Perhaps thou didst drive his mules! And that's just the greenhands. Job …"

The boy got up and walked to the forecastle companionway.

§

George lay in the solitude of her bunk. The curtain did nothing to keep out the music and laughter. Her goal was to live apart from these men, except for perhaps Job. So far, she had been successful; no one on deck missed her. But could she continue living in isolation? She missed friends and talks with her mother. She wanted to release the dammed-up feelings before she burst from the unspoken words. On the Canal she walked with mules. They weren't people, but at least they listened. How good it would be to sit without worries on the banks of the Canal with Caleb and just pass time.

Foolish girl! The words came from the back of her mind. *That will never be.* Outside of her bunk, men were everywhere. But the treachery of that creature meant her feelings must remain unspoken.

She may have survived the Canal and almost two weeks on a whaler, but she still sounded too much like a girl. If she grew too close to one of the men, he'd see through her disguise. Simple strips of cotton could not keep a secret. These men were worse than Caleb. What would become of her if she were found out? She didn't want to think about the possibilities. *You better keep on just as you are.*

But Job saved me, two times. Surely, he would be a confidant. Or, Joseph, he couldn't do anything evil. *He'd not allow anything bad to happen to me if my secret were learned.*

Don't be stupid! They are harpooners and would tell the Captain.
I don't have to tell them I'm a woman. All I want is to talk.
You don't NEED to talk. You NEED to keep safe.
But Job and Joseph think I ought to be more open with the crew.
No! You can't do that. You must stay apart.
I can't live like this.

"SHUT UP!" she whispered.

She choked back tears from her eyes as the camaraderie floated into the forecastle from the windlass.

The Boats
Monday, December 20, 1848, Day 12

Gorham sat behind her in the Second Mate's whaleboat. To
practice maneuvering the boats on the open sea was bad enough; but to
put that bilge sucker in the same boat with her just made matters worse.
George groaned. She wanted to be back on the ship where she could find
solitude in her bunk, or on the rigging, away from him. But that wasn't
going to happen anytime soon; they needed to learn the use of the
whaleboats.

Curving to a point, bow and stern, it reminded her of the canoes
that had been used by the Indians of upstate New York. She faced aft,
toward Mr. Clark, who stood at the rudder. Of the five rowing stations,
George sat on the thwart in the center of the 24-foot boat, in the midship
position. She slid aside a paddle under her seat to make room for her feet.
With her arms at eye level, she gripped the rounded shaft of her oar,
which rested in a rowlock on her left and extended out onto the water.

Next to her right side, under the left gunwale, rested three lances
set in grooves, their deadly points facing the bow to her back. She had
probably slushed their shafts. Each was eight feet long. Inside the boat's
hull, on her left, were spare harpoons with tips that looked like giant
arrowheads. She shivered at the thought that these weapons might soon
be used against a whale…close enough to the boat for the harpooner to
strike the beast. The mast, yard, and sail lay across the thwarts from aft to
fore and took up the center of her seat. To her left, on the other side of the
centerboard, the spare line tub rested on the bottom. She had no idea what
most of the other items were used for, but they left no room for any more
than the five oarsmen and an officer.

Peleg sat in front of her in the tub position. She looked aft, past
his seat, into the large tub containing whale line that had been stretched,
tarred, and carefully wound leaving only a cylindrical hole in the center
of the tub. The line, nearly an inch in diameter, left there, wrapped around
the loggerhead in the stern, and then ran fore over the shafts of all the
oars. George lowered the handle of her oar and the rope slid down just

making contact with her wrist. It exited the boat through a lead-lined groove in the bow. A wooden pin kept the line from slipping out. From there, the rope was pulled back into a small pile on the bottom of the boat. Its end was fastened to a shorter line attached to one of two harpoons resting in the bow and easily accessible by the harpooner. Her discomfort rose a notch as she thought about the rope's purpose. Then, as quickly, a feeling of security pushed aside uncertainty as she considered the order with which everything was packed away on the boat. She shifted in her seat.

"Stern all!"

Mr. Clark expected the crew to do something. *Stern*, she thought. *If the boat goes to stern, lean back, dip, and push.*

Not everyone was so logical, and some of the oars were pulled. Charlie let out an excited cry as one boat careened toward his position. George focused on the Second Mate over other cries and other commands.

"Stern all! Push on the oars!"

George raised her oar and leaned back into Gorham's shaft.

He shoved the handle a little harder into her back. "Good for nothin' mule cock!" He spoke just loud enough for her to hear.

"Together, ladies, together!" Clark was definitely not happy. "Follow the stroke position!" He nodded to the sailor directly in front of him, visible to everyone.

George adjusted her movements to match his.

"Avast!"

They stopped and peaked their oars.

"Pull forward!"

Matching the stroke rower's movements, George leaned forward, dipped the oar, and pulled, over and over. On the forward lean, the rope rubbed her wrist. Soon, an open sore scraped against the fibers. How could the men keep pulling! Every ounce of her strength was gone, and just lifting the oar from the water was too difficult a task. The sun beat down upon her. A numbing ache flowed back from the tips of her fingers into her shoulders and down.

"Johnson!"

Abruptly, a new surge of energy shot through her.

The Second Mate's eyes bore into her. "Move with the others!"

"Aye, Sir!" The strength in her voice surprised her.

Gorham sneered something behind her.

Lean, dip, pull…over…and over…George was swallowed up, mesmerized by the pain. A smack as Peleg's oar hit hers and she was back on the boat. The glare in the Mate's eyes renewed her strength.

At last! They stopped in the shadow of the ship. Her arms ached, hands stung, and lungs burned. Leaning upon the oar, George lowered her head and closed her eyes. The throbbing pulse in her temples eased, but she still hurt, inside and out. Every inch of her body rebelled; but she told herself there was a reason—this would make her stronger. Others may complain, but she would not. Exhausted, she looked up at the Second Mate. Mr. Clark always told them to keep their eyes on him.

Gorham's boot kicked her from behind.

How could he, even now, have the energy to torment her?

"Targets!" The First Mate yelled loud enough to be heard on the ship.

Groans arose like a chorus from all three boats.

The Second Mate smiled.

When the carpenter threw in three wooden planks almost 4 feet by 1 foot, Mr. Clark maneuvered their boat in line with one of them. George concentrated on him and his commands, pulling just as he commanded. Ignoring Gorham's periodic chiding, she listened to the Mate's every word, reminding herself again of just how much she needed to learn.

"Stand up!"

George immediately stood, rocking the boat.

"Not you, Johnson." Clark shook his head.

She slowly sat down to snickers from the other crewmen.

"So the mule cock thinks he's the harpooner!" Gorham hit her in the back.

As the Second Mate moved the boat closer to the target, Gorham's chortling and comments continued, loud enough for only her to hear. All she wanted was to do her job and be left alone, but Gorham just wouldn't let it be.

How many times in her life had she wanted things to happen one way, only to have them turn out another! Here it occurred in front of her mates. Besides the harpooner, she alone stood at the command, no one else. *How stupid!* More and more, her life was out of control. Anything could happen, if not here in the boat, then back on the ship; and she was powerless to prevent it.

Fortunately, sweat beaded upon her face and hid her tears. Gorham's comments grated deeper. Either the Mate didn't hear him or he ignored it. She wiped her eyes with her sleeve wanting to reach back and throttle the pest but knowing she could not as long as Clark was watching. The only redeeming aspect to this torture was that Caleb was somewhere out here, just out of reach, and soon she would be avenged.

"Give it to him!" commanded the Mate.

I wish I could!

Job's harpoon knocked splinters from the wood.

"Stern all! …Pick up paddles!" These would be used when a quieter approach to a whale was necessary.

Ah! She had taken enough tormenting from Gorham. *Caleb may not be here, but this might be the opportunity to get the other pest!*

Each of the crew needed to stow their oars, retrieve their paddles, turn around, and take a seat on the gunwale. Hers was the shortest oar. Quickly setting its blade inside the boat, she pulled up the paddle and let it drop from her grip with its handle pointed back toward Gorham. He hadn't yet faced forward and laughed at her clumsiness. Grabbing the blade, she aimed and gave a quick jab back so that the handle slid across Gorham's thwart between his legs. Gorham? Caleb? Pretty much the same. As she pulled it forward, regaining control, Gorham's laugh evolved into a squeak. Releasing his oar, he gripped where he'd been struck.

"Johnson, get control of your paddle." Clark sounded disgusted. Looking at Gorham, he continued in a condescending tone. "Andrews, did we have a little accident? Next time use the head."

During two days of practice, George served in all three boats. On the morning of the third day, she found herself awake and didn't know for sure that she had been asleep. The sores on her left wrist, where the whale line rubbed it raw, had begun to form scabs. As she reached for the cotton strip to wrap about her chest, her hands felt as if they were being pierced by a thousand tiny pins. Her fingers and palms were covered with open blisters. She didn't want to face another day of pulling but couldn't stay in her bunk. Any show of want of spirit could be her undoing. Soggers weren't indulged. She had to tumble up. Torturous moans rose above the silence of the forecastle as men readied themselves to appear on deck, but she refused to suffer audibly.

Dragging herself out of the forecastle, she found an empty spot on the starboard side of the windlass.

Tom took a seat beside her, gingerly rubbing the sores on his hands. "I wonder if this is the way soldiers feel as they train and prepare for battles yet to come."

Face to face with a whale, that was NOT something she wanted to consider. Before she could reply, the First Mate called the men to the waist.

Job jumped to his feet. "This is it."

Joseph joined him. "Been long enough I'd say."

"What's it?" asked Tom

Job and Joseph just motioned for them to follow. George found a place behind Tom in the back, out of the way, and out of sight. The officers stood in front of the crew, Mr. Clark to starboard, the Third Mate to port, and the First Mate in the center. Like a stag watching his herd, Captain Sullivan stood behind them. The harpooners took seats on the carpenter's bench as the officers scrutinized the crew. The First Mate pointed to one of the sailors. "You, Dennison, over here." And one of the older sailors ambled proudly to the First Mate.

The Second Mate chose a man, as did the Third Mate. The crewmen were being sized up, evaluated, and divided into three groups. George shifted from foot to foot.

Tom leaned close to her. "Just like horse sales back in Indiana. Or an ox, so much muscle on the hoof. They're looking over the livestock…"

"Hally!" Mr. Clark interrupted him. "You're with me."

With a look of surprise, Tom walked to Clark.

As each crewman was picked, George's bindings became a bit tighter; and she sweat a little more. Beads of perspiration rolled from her arm pits dampening the cotton around her chest. In the end, she stood alone looking at the deck and hugging herself. Gorham laughed and pointed. Her face flushed, and not from the heat of the sun.

"Johnson!" Will Plass, the Third Mate, picked her. "You're in my watch."

Thankful that Gorham was with the First Mate, she quickly took a position behind Joseph and Jamie, who were also with Plass.

Captain Sullivan stepped forward. "These are your watches. You will man the boat of the officer who picked you. He will assign your seat. Though we are not on our hunting ground, whales may yet be seen. Watches will be by boat crew. The boatsteerers are in charge of each of the watches." He nodded toward Joseph.

The harpooner jumped off the carpenter's bench. "During the day, the senior officer on deck will have responsibility for the watch. When the sail is shortened at sundown, we boatsteerers will command the watch. Each watch consists of four men and a harpooner." He continued explaining the rotations and the use of the dogwatch to assure that all boats' crews shared equally in the night watches.

When Joseph finished, George wondered if anyone else was as confused as she was. But, instead of asking any questions, she decided to follow her boat crew and learn the watches over time. She stayed at the railing staring at the wake being pushed aside by the ship. Others lingered and talked.

"Mr. Clark." Tom had a sheepish look about him. "Why did you choose me?" He looked sincerely embarrassed by having been picked so soon.

"I been watching the greenhands. Some's better than others. You're strong; you listen when I talk to you about whaling; never need to tell you something twice. You're going to make a fine sailor one day." Mr. Clark's mouth actually took on a smile. "Had some trouble when you first pulled the oar, but you corrected the problems quickly. I chose you because I think you have potential. Not all the men are fit for service in the boats." His face transformed into a smoldering scowl edged in red fringe. "Take young Johnson. He's just not good in the boat. Too weak I think. Fumbles the oars."

No way George was going to correct the Second Mate. She would need to prove her worth.

"Well, you know, I hear he was the first up the mast."

Why would Tom defend her?

"Some's meant to be on the ship and not the boats. He's got a temper too."

"I've not seen that. Though some of the crew do pick on the boy a bit much."

"A man's got to control himself. Can't have problems on the boats."

For a minute, neither spoke. "Seems to me, George has done well at most everything he's been given."

George studied the farmer from the corner of her eyes.

"'Tis enough that there's a problem. Look, Tom, when we're fighting a whale, the boat's crew must be working together. No arguments, no misunderstandings. Don't worry about the boy; I have a feeling he will come to no good. When he gets stove, you don't want to be with him."

§

"Huh?" George grumbled. Someone was shaking her bunk.

No, the whole ship gyrated uncomfortably, and sounds like thunder pealed beside her from the hull of the ship. Her eyes burned. She peeked out the curtain through a suffocating haze of un-vented smoke. Crewmen sat around a candle on chests or on the floor talking. Every so often a face lit up in a red glow as a sailor sucked on a pipe.

She dressed in the cramped space of her berth and eased herself to the floor. Holding the edges of the bunks, she made her way past shipmates. They ignored her. After all, that was her goal all along, to be left alone. The dismal light was hardly enough for walking and seeing. Laughter that didn't belong filled the forecastle.

George grasped the ladder and, as the ship bounced awkwardly about, climbed up and carefully pushed open the hatch. She tumbled out onto a wet deck. The wind whipped the top of a gigantic wave into a sheet of water that blew over the railing and soaked her. As they had traveled farther south, the air warmed and the water was not so cold, just wet.

A wave rose before the ship, towering up like a mountain. She grabbed the fore mast weather rigging for support. The *Mitchell* scaled up that swell higher, higher, the bow sprit pointing skyward. The hairs on the back of her neck stood out. Then down the other side it slid, burying itself between two monstrous swells. George gripped the rigging till her knuckles turned white; legs frozen in place. When the ship reached the bottom, she closed her eyes as the water sprayed across the fore deck. It started up the next swell, partially buried but resurrected to rise again. With the stench of the forecastle more inviting than the foredeck, she scurried back through the companionway and retreated to a seat in the darkest corner.

The hatch opened again and the shadowy figures of two men descended into the flickering light of the candle.

Peleg's mumbling rose from the circle of mates. "Job, me friend, how good of you to leave the aft quarters fer our modest home. And you've brought the preacher."

"But no preaching tonight, Joseph," said another voice.

"Why not, pray tell? Who more than whalers need the fear of the Lord?"

Charlie stood hunched over to make room.

"Sit yerself down!" Peleg pushed Gorham to the side. "Make room there, Andrews."

Kneeling, the two harpooners inched into the circle of men.

"You know 'tis a time for yarns and not sermons," someone growled.

Charlie settled down like a bird in a nest. "Aye. These be castle yarns."

Men wrestled for position.

How well the harpooners fit with everyone! Of course, that was their role. Yet it came so naturally to them. She had no one. This feeling of isolation surrounded her like so much more darkness.

Peleg's hunched form stood against the candle's light. "I've got a tale to tell, of old Captain Hiram Gardner and the whale that taught him the truth of the sea."

Peleg told his tale, with loud guffaws and laughter from those around him. A few fists lashed out followed by men wrestling on the floor.

"Let me tell again the story of the Essex."

The noise gradually diminished and Charlie began. "The Creature waits, hidden beneath the surface..."

George remembered this yarn from the shipping office. It captivated her. She now knew the true story was based on a real ship. She pushed aside the endless solitude that nailed her to the wall. Taking the bucket she used for a chamber pot, she moved to just outside the mass of men and sat on it. Some of the crew made space for her; but she chose to stay in the back, listening intently to the tales. Between stories, men shared about adventures and battles, others about home; they wrestled and fought.

There was this exchange going on among them, like nothing she had ever experienced before. They were speaking, but the communication included something beyond just the words. The bravado, the coarse jesting, the physical bantering that bordered on conflict, it all was part of what was happening. She had seen it before but never understood it. Certainly, she had never been part of it. If women were like sunny days and gentle breezes, men were lightning and thunder and...and these waves that broke upon the ship. Storms held a beauty and majesty, though they scared her more often than not.

How could a sunny day bring forth thunder and lightning? The best she could hope for was to pretend well enough to get by. But people see what they expect to see; so, no matter how feminine her voice, no matter that she might make a mistake, they would still see the boy, at least she hoped so. She listened and planned.

During a lull in the storytelling, she cautiously inched her bucket farther into the ring of men. "What's it like being fast to a whale?"

"'Tis a ride you won't soon forget." Charlie accepted the question as if it had come from any of the men. "Aye, 'tis! Like a wagon pulled along behind an unwilling horse…"

"Yes, siree, tis a beast that fights its burden!"

"…It's called a Nantucket sleigh ride. Boat flies o'er the water, up, down, wave to wave. You just hang on for your life."

"Yes, siree, you do. It's fast. Real fast! Had a bow rower one time what didn't hold on. Bounced up high, he did. The boat went so fast he hit the Mate and they both got deep-sixcd."

That raised jeers from around the circle.

One of the men looked at her from across the candle. "You ever seen a whale?"

George pulled her bucket a little closer. "Never even seen the ocean before coming to Boston."

"Then, why'd a boy like you sign on?"

The time had come to test the harpooners' advice. "I heard Charlie say that Tom, here, was stove by a woman, and that's why he signed on."

"Surely, you ain't been stove." Jamie leaned back looking at her.

"Not me. My sister."

"Stove by a woman?" Peleg laughed.

"No. A man."

"Ain't nothing wrong with that. No, siree!"

"I say there is!"

"As do I." Tom rose to her defense.

"Ann was my sister and Caleb the wretch who took her from us with a promise to marry. Then he left her alone on the Canal, unmarried. And she could not return home by my father's command. And Caleb went to whale instead of marrying. She was stove by Caleb. And that's why I am on the *Mitchell*; I hunt not only whales but a man. And, as with the whale, my goal is to cut him in and try him out for what he did to Ann."

§

With the storm over, George held her plate in her lap and rested against the bulwarks near the windlass. She had told them about Caleb because Job and Joseph said she should get more involved with the crew. Still, she wasn't comfortable with the idea and would have rather remained apart. At that moment, the darkness of her berth was preferable to sitting with the men on the windlass. She feared company yet longed for it. Every day brought some new, disgusting aspect of whaling life. No one to talk to only magnified the revulsion. If these harpooners were right, friends might just make the trip more bearable. They each told her to talk with the crew. Perhaps now that she had shared her story, at least a part of it, life would be better. It surely could not get worse.

Dusk somewhat hid her meal from view. This was a good thing. When served in the light of day, other ingredients that clearly did not belong there were revealed in the food. Someone had told her, on whaling ships the cockroaches put up with the men rather than the other way around.

Jamie, Peleg, and Gorham took seats on the opposite side of the windlass, out of her line of sight.

"Do you think it really happened?"

"If it's true, he's a fool. No good in avenging a woman?"

"I'd like to see that boy face a man. What could he possibly do if they met? He's got the physique of a glutton and little muscle on the arms."

So much for fitting in, thought George, keeping her eyes down and trying to ignore the comments. But, her story told, she needed to play it out. She knew she couldn't whale alone. Just to survive required that she become a mate to the other men. She would need to be better than she was, and better than most of the men. She must endure. She had to make things right.

She bit down on something small and crunchy with appendages. *Surely the codfish.* Her throat tightened as she swallowed

Cutting a piece of the hard tack, she dipped it in the cup's contents. That was much better. The sweetness of the molasses added a nice touch to the morsel.

Job took a seat beside her. "So, that's why you wondered about the whale fleet."

George nodded and then looked back to her plate.

More of the crew came forward.

"Joseph, Tom, over here." Job waved to get their attention.

"Quite a story." Tom leaned against the bulwarks. "Do you truly seek to kill a man?"

George felt her face flush but kept eating, not sure this was really what she wanted to achieve. "Yes, I do."

"And for this reason thou didst sign on to the *Mitchell*?"

George gave Joseph a that-was-a-dumb-question look.

"Does Ann know of this hunt of yours?" asked Tom.

She nodded.

"Surely thy parents do not approve. They must worry about thee."

She finished another bite. "This is something I do because it must be done. When Caleb left Ann, she wanted to come home but my parents would not have her, saying she was a ruined woman. Where is she to go? What is she to do? She has no life because of that villain. If I can bring a little justice, she will find some comfort."

Job raised his eyebrows.

Perhaps she had come across a little strong.

"But, George, have you considered the magnitude of this pursuit?" Job sounded like her mother questioning one of her decisions.

She never liked that tone. "He is out here and I will find him."

"Thou best turn thy attention to the whale hunt, son, for it is not likely that ye will meet."

What did Joseph mean by that? According to the shipper in Boston, Caleb would have shipped just ahead of them. Surely they must be close. He would make things right, or she would; and then she could get off this god forsaken ship.

Job nodded agreement, continuing where Joseph left off. "As I told you before, we will gam with some ships. But there are hundreds of whalers on the waters, and these from many countries. Ships from Nantucket hunt from the Arctic to the Antarctic. They hunt in all the oceans of the world. They hunt the line and the south fisheries. His ship could be anywhere."

"There are hunting grounds all over these seas. We could pass near to the ship thou seekest and still not see it."

"Do you know the ship?" Tom leaned forward.

"Or where it's hunting?" Job did the same.

All three of them were focused on her. She had no answer to these questions. Her appetite was gone.

"You could search a lifetime out here and not find his ship," said Job.

George leaned into the bulwarks for support and stared. Darkness closed in about them like a door that could be neither stopped nor opened. Somewhere out there was the man she sought. Somewhere. They were talking but she heard nothing.

No! She screamed into silence. The whole of her life had come to—this! *No!* She didn't want to see; didn't want to hear, to smell, or taste. She remembered the promises and hopes of youth but now ate cockroaches and told herself it was good. She had taken the shards and tattered pieces of a life that was gone and managed to mend them together with hope. She clung to these crippled memories, held onto them, used them to hide the truth of her existence. Now these last fleeting hopes were ripped from her hands by the words of her would-be friends. She clawed for pieces of a life past and strove to clutch them, too afraid of facing what they hid, but they were gone.

You have no hope!

There She Blows

Saturday, December 25, 1848, Day 17

Christmas came, but no tree adorned the deck. And Mama's mincemeat pie wasn't set before her. George picked at the fresh roasted pork in her plate. It tasted good, much better than the usual Saturday meal of salted codfish and potatoes. She just wasn't hungry. The crew was unusually animated around the windlass. But she sat alone on the carpenter's bench. The cage beneath was uncharacteristically calm. One of the pigs was gone.

The ship worked the swells into white furrows that faded into the ocean's gray, but George saw snow covered banks along the Erie Canal. The setting sun brought colors to the clouds, but she saw candle light reflected from the colored decorations on the tree in her home in Rochester. Mom and Dad made Christmas. When she closed her eyes, her mother sat across the table talking with her. Talking. How she missed the chatter of women. She never realized what a joy that sound could be. She longed to hold onto that image, but the guttural noises and mannerisms of men flooded her senses like the endless beating of waves upon a shore. Her breath caught in her throat. She squeezed her eyelids a little tighter.

Strips of cloth bound her as she longed for something she could not have. Like stretching to find saving arms, her heart reached out for tokens of a life lost; she missed her petticoats and lace. Christmas should be a time to dress up, a time for family. She took a deep breath stifling a sob. Her life was slush, swabbing, tar, and death.

A bath! She wanted to be clean again. To smell like a woman, not like this…this unspeakably filthy orphan. Her hair was as matted as any mangy dog's. She had only been gone from home for two months. She remembered what it was to be a woman. She still dreamed of how things used to be. But such memories were becoming dimmer, increasingly veiled by this new life. She didn't want to be a man!

"Merry Christmas, George." Joseph sat down beside her.

She forced a smile.

"Art thou going to eat?"

"Not all that hungry. I miss home."

"It is a hard time to be away. But look about thee. This isn't so bad."

Joseph was an extension of the crew's communal merriment. She longed to be engulfed by it and carried along on its strains of delight.

"Not for you perhaps. But what am I to do? I didn't join to kill whales. I joined to hunt a man. Now there will be no retribution; and, what's worse, I've imprisoned myself in the vilest of jails. There is nothing for me here. Nowhere to go. The man who did this to me—and to Ann—is out there." She looked across the horizon. "And here I am."

Laughter and singing danced up from the ship, but she was not part of that world.

"Take heart, George. God can make things right."

Even if that were true, what satisfaction would there be? And now life had no purpose. "I don't belong here," she whispered. But she didn't belong in Rochester either, nor on the Canal, nor with her mother and father. Where did she belong? In an instant, she was sucked into a void. No one wanted her.

"Thou dost talk as if there is no path to follow." Joseph's voice continued from somewhere.

"There isn't."

"The path thou art on is the path to follow. Thou art a whaler on the *Christopher Mitchell*. Thou may not find that man, but there are great things to see and adventures ahead. 'Tis a great experience for a young man."

"Don't want to be on this ship." But where did she want to be? She had nowhere else to go.

"But thou art, so this is thine."

In a way, she knew he was right; but, if the truth were known, even this would not be hers.

"What dost thou know of Friends?"

"What?"

"Quakers."

They were in Rochester. She even attended some of their meetings. "Filled Ann's head with ideas that women should be equal with men. Caused arguments at home."

A look of surprise passed over his face. "We also teach that there is a Light within us, God's witness. Helps me live my life. It can guide thee on thy path as well, if thou let it."

"My life has no light." At that moment, her life was as dark as midnight.

"Oh, George, I wish thou couldst see. Consider the meaning of the day. For thee, Jesus walked a path much harder than thine. God loves thee. Wherever thou art, He is there. Thou sought revenge. That may no longer be thine. Nevertheless, thou art traveling a path, and it can yield good to thee."

He actually believed what he said. How she wished it were true that God would walk with her, but she knew better. She longed for home and still harbored hope that Caleb loved her. She wanted to be with him. But his actions, whatever the motivation, had brought her here. And she hated the man who had separated her forever from the love of her mother, and her father, and consigned her to serve as a whaler.

"In any case, thou must eat. This life is a hard one. Thy strength will be required of thee. I think Cook outdid himself tonight."

The anguish in her heart was a rancid sauce for the meat.

A fiddle's discordant cry called to them.

"Come, thou, with me to the windlass. We celebrate a great Light tonight."

"I will come, but leave me alone in my darkness. I have no desire to travel any other path than the one I am on." She said the words, but they sounded hollow to her ears. The desire to find Caleb beat within keeping time with her heart. Yet she wanted to be far from this life. This was not a woman's path.

They sat next to Job, but she stared across the endless expanse of water.

"A little downcast, are we?"

Leave it to Job. He's the only one who understands.

"Men have come whaling for all different kinds of reasons. Yours is just one more. Perhaps Caleb deserves the retribution, and perhaps it will come by your hand. Or perhaps not. Still, whaling can be an adventure to be remembered. Few can say they became a man hunting whales. Here's to our hunt." Job took a drink from his cup.

The fiddle's cries grew into cheery strains, and the men joined in, clapping to a wild rhythm. Even the Captain came forward.

Peleg jumped up to "trip the light fantastic" as he put it. George was not quite sure if his step was true or just the whim of some spirit within. In either case, his dance was contagious, and others joined in, laughing.

As if peeking from her place of isolation, George let the music begin to wrap her in its arms. She added her hands to the beat. The heaviness that she had carried for weeks dissipated like a mist in the sun. Eyes twinkled about her like the stars above. They all sought a little of home upon the *Christopher Mitchell*. Laughter echoed into the night overpowering the sound of swells rippling against the hull—her voice mingled with the others.

Towards the end of the watch, when the men began to slow a bit, the Captain stood. "Joseph, could you read the Christmas story for us?"

The harpooner nodded and removed his Bible from his blouse. The men grew quiet as he moved closer to the lantern near the tryworks.

"Saint Luke says, 'Now it came about in those days that a decree went out from Caesar Augustus, that a census be taken of all the inhabited earth....'"

The words brought memories of home, of a happier time, a time when anything seemed possible. When the story was told, still humming the happy tunes and, in her mind, dancing Peleg's jig, George climbed into the forecastle. Behind her curtain, she wrapped herself in thoughts of Holidays past. Lying on her side, she drew her knees up, hugged herself, and smiled. She felt...at home. Tomorrow held no place in her thoughts. The smells of a whaling life were overpowered by the scent of a night well-lived.

§

She sat on the edge of her bunk in the dark. A week's worth of dull, monotonous life replaced the memories of Christmas. Day after day, swabbing, tarring, cleaning, manning the masthead. Whaling had become tedious and pointless, a nightmare from which she would not awaken. She didn't belong here, but here was her place. She had a job to do. But why work? Why continue? Why put her life in danger any longer? She buried her head in her hands.

"There she blows!"

It took a few seconds for the call to sink in. When it did, the words came like a tidal wave, rising from a calm sea and carrying sudden and sure destruction.

"Where away?" The Captain's voice was filled with anticipation and demanded an answer.

"Three points to starboard; about two miles off."

She stood up, muscles taught. The first whale. Visions of Charlie's beast, and the Essex, flooded her mind.

"She blows again."

No more sleeping; men hurriedly pulled on pants and boots.

"She blows again!"

The last of the crewmen stumbled up the ladder with boots yet untied. She was alone in the forecastle.

"Thunder and lightning!" The Captain had never sounded so excited. "Call all hands! Clew up the fore-t'gallant-sail there! Belay! Hard down your wheel! Haul aback the main yard! Get your tubs in the boats. Bear a hand!"

The blanket behind the curtain called out safety, but her place was on deck. She belonged to Plass; the Third Mate's midship rower was her job, her responsibility.

The line tubs were fixed in their places. The cranes were thrust out, and the mainyard was backed. Like baskets over high cliffs, the three boats swung over the sea, and she took her position with Joseph. Mates talked nervously; others kept silence; some ran to fetch last minute items for the boats. None showed the apprehension she felt. How could these men face death as if it were to be no more than another practice?

The *Mitchell* had become a naval man-of-war with men about to throw themselves on board an enemy's ship. The crews waited outside of the bulwarks with one hand clung to the rail and one foot expectantly poised on the boat's gunwale.

What am I doing here? The soft voice called out inside her head.

Her arm quivered as she waited at the ship's railing. Just below her, the whaleboat hung from its rope ready to be launched.

"Clear your falls!" Captain Sullivan was master of the moment. "Stand by all to lower! All ready?"

"All ready, sir!" replied the First Mate.

"Lower away!"

Down went the boats with a splash. Eyes glued to the vessel below her, George held her breath and sprang from the rail along with the others. In an instant, all three were manned. She matched the stroke rower, each pull taking them that much closer to these beasts of the sea. The Mate was fixed on something. She knew what held his attention and wanted to look, but he demanded all eyes on him.

"Peak oars! Take up paddles!"

Must be close. Everything was done to quiet the approach.

Joseph caught her eye. No fear there, all business and anticipation—and a quick smile. George stowed her oar, carefully pulled her paddle from beneath the thwart, and faced what lay ahead.

She searched the water listening for the Mate's command. Then, from the top of a swell, a large rock broke the waters about 200 yards ahead and a little off starboard. But it sank and rose with the swells.

That's no rock! She gasped. *It's a whale's head!*

Plass steered the boat toward the gigantic black object, the size of a locomotive, half buried in water.

George strained against the paddle keeping in rhythm with the others. She glanced back.

"Pull, me hearties!" The Mate stared straight ahead, his voice a hoarse whisper. The veins in his neck stood out. "This whale is ours."

Oh, no!

"Pull! Pull!"

The whale lay almost motionless upon the surface of the wide and shallow swells.

I'm going to die! He's taking us right into its jaws?! She stared, fixed upon the head with its monstrous body, fearing that the beast would hear her heart. A quick glance over her shoulder showed Plass focused on what was coming.

She pulled on. In just a few minutes they were too close. The beast was too big, the boat too small. All was a silence of anticipation. George trembled with excitement. There lay the whale, unconscious of approaching danger, heaving its vast body a little above the surface, then slowly burying its head beneath the wave, as it lazily forged ahead…toward them.

Joseph calmly and quietly set his paddle aside and took the covers from the heads of the live irons resting in their crotch beside him. Unhooded, the razor edges twinkled in the sunlight.

"Hold paddles."

They coasted toward the monster's head. Closer…closer…

"Stand up!"

With line in his left hand and first iron in right, Joseph stood and braced his left thigh into the gunwale securing his right foot firmly in the clumsy cleat in the floor for stability. With harpoon raised overhead, he was the picture of power.

The distance closed between them.

What's that? She leaned to the side for a better look. *Something white just below the surface. Teeth! It's his teeth!* She chastised herself; to be light headed was to court death.

The beast grew larger. For a moment it towered higher than Joseph.

Move! Why don't you move?

Fifty feet. Forty feet.

Turn! The boat approached head on. She couldn't tear her eyes away. There were markings, striations on the whale's skin. She clenched her seat with one hand. The creature was massive. She could reach out and touch this massive mountain of muscle.

Just when George was about to close her eyes and die, the Mate swept the long steering oar to port, and the boat and whale passed in parallel. Instantly, he made another, wider sweep, this time to starboard, to bring the side of the whale bow on.

"Give it to him!"

From a distance of no more than twelve feet, the harpoon left Joseph's arm, flat and hard. He had but seconds to attach to the monster. The whale's flukes smashed to the water with a report like gunfire. Joseph threw out the iron's warp and launched the second iron. Quickly, he threw out its warp as well and about 50 feet of rope from a small tub at his feet. Both irons had stuck in the whale's side.

"Stern all for your lives!"

She gladly obeyed.

In his first fury, the whale thrashed in the water trying to reach the spears that clung to its side. Then, the beast was gone. The line jerked into motion beside her.

"Wet line! Wet line!" Plass's order was to no one in particular. One of the men began pouring water on the rope as it flew by and out the bow.

A kink or twist in the line would be disastrous. It raced out of the tub, in wide arcs, to the stern, around the logger head, and straight forward to the bow past every sailor's inboard shoulder.

George gave a fleeting look up at Joseph. "What happens when the rope's gone?" The whale could do anything…*anything.*

"Thou need not worry." Joseph yelled above the rush of wind and water. "There's 1800 feet in the tub."

In moving from the gunwale to her seat, George took special care not to get near the rope as it blurred past her. She held onto her thwart, the boat now flying up and down over the swells. By the time half the line was out, they matched the speed of the beast.

"What do you think of our Nantucket sleigh ride!" Joseph

glanced back wide-eyed, hair flying in the wind.

She just held on. Others cheered and laughed.

The line, no longer unwinding from the tub, receded from the boat and disappeared in the water ahead. She wondered about the striving of the monster at the other end and looked quickly back at Jamie, seated right behind her in the tub position.

His face showed what flooded her insides. "Do you think the whale may turn and follow the rope back to us?"

George had never considered that possibility. A desperate need for the safety of the ship engulfed her.

The boat rushed on. If the men had their way, the whale would soon be dead. A creature so big…where had it been, what had it seen? All it wanted was to be free again.

That's all she ever wanted, to be free. She had followed Caleb and now a harpoon called "ruined" stuck in her heart. Men pulled on it. If they ever found her, she would be completely undone.

Gradually, the speed diminished.

"Pull, men. Pull in the rope." George reached forward, grabbed on, and pulled. Each such draw brought the boat that much closer to their prey. The sailor in the aft seat carefully replaced the line in the tub.

"There it is." Jamie pointed. "I see the whale."

Still looks mean!

"Let's send it into its flurry," yelled one of the sailors.

What?!

"Avast, men."

George stopped pulling. The boat was within 20 yards of the creature. Too close. The gigantic flukes moved up and down keeping a steady tension on the line.

It breathed a labored gasp, like the rush of a wind…silence…another rush…silence again. It reminded George of a steam engine beginning to pull, the sound of great power.

The harpoons gripped the whale's side with blood streaming from the wounds.

Another gasp.

"Joseph." Plass made no effort to be quiet now.

Joseph moved to the rear of the boat as the Third Mate came forward to man the lance.

"Use oars." Plass took the same position as Joseph had earlier.

"Forward, men!"

Joseph guided the boat to the starboard side of the beast.

Plass picked up the villainous looking lance. With a sweep of the steering oar, Joseph brought the boat's bow to the whale just behind the fin.

"Avast, men." The harpooner guided them. "Hold oars for now."

As the Mate shoved the lance deep into the creature's side, its huge head swung around with jaws snapping at whatever had pierced it. George let go of the oar and gripped her seat as the whale's snapping, death-wielding jaws headed toward her.

"Hold thy oar, Johnson!"

She quickly grasped the shaft again.

Joseph maneuvered the boat back safely out of reach.

The whale slapped the water with his tail.

Joseph swept them back in.

As the boat approached, the wounded creature turned on its side, bent its head, and, with open jaws, attacked again. In slow motion, the whale's head closed toward the boat as it slid toward the whale. Joseph steered directly for the exposed fin.

"Oh, God, no!" George looked into the throat of the beast.

Just before the gaping jaws reached the boat, the Mate lanced the whale again, sending it into such writhing agony that it lost focus of the vessel. This time Plass churned up and down a number of times before Joseph swept the boat back to avoid another attack by the flukes.

"Fire in the chimney." Excitement flooded Joseph's voice.

The whale's breath was no longer a clear mist rising from the nostrils on its forehead; it shimmered a crimson shade in the late afternoon sun. Blood rained down upon them.

Again the boat moved in and Plass churned. This time the labored breathing was filled with barrels of blood. The whale was drowning in its own life flow.

"Stern all, for your lives." The Third Mate's voice carried a command of the situation.

George pushed to the stern as hard and as fast as she could.

"Hold."

She looked aft. A horrendous commotion arose behind her as the whale rolled in a red sea, thrashing wildly with its flukes and jaws. Then, with its head toward the sun, the whale ceased striving and lay silent upon the water.

"Fin out! To the head, Joseph."

"Pull men, easy." The harpooner guided them toward the creature's massive head. Its mouth was slightly open revealing a row of teeth, each at least 6 inches long, in the lower jaw. "Avast! Ready to stern!"

The Mate reached out and pricked the eye. No movement. The whale was dead. Joseph maneuvered the boat to the tail where Plass to cut off the tips of the flukes and attached a towrope to the small, the narrow part where the flukes joined the body.

Plass and Joseph exchanged places.

"Pull men!" They began towing the whale to the ship, whose sails were just visible on the horizon.

George choked back tears and didn't know why.

Cutting In

Saturday, January 1, 1849, Day 24

Joseph climbed from the boat and pulled himself onto the deck. They made it through their first whale; that was good. He reached back down to lend George a hand. The boy hesitated for just a moment, then took it. Behind the lad's eyes was bewilderment, a numbness of the mind. It matched the exhaustion seen in the way his body resisted any effort to move. The harpooner laughed to himself. Every whaler remembered the first time hauling a whale to a ship…hours of pulling with the arms, pushing with the feet, and leaning against the drag of a whale. You pulled until you could pull no longer and then pulled some more. No wonder George looked dazed. But the boy would work through it. All the men did.

The Third Mate's boat was the only one to take a whale. So, while the other two watches prepared for the cutting in, Plass's crew collapsed on the port side of the windlass, out of the way of work. Job brought them the kid containing leftovers from supper. He ladled out codfish and potatoes. With the sun dipping into the horizon, they only had a few minutes to rest and eat.

Joseph chewed on a piece of fish and followed it with a potato, replaying in his mind the attack on the whale. Though just lifting the morsels to his mouth was an effort, excitement still coursed through his veins. He felt again the harpoon in his hand and the draw of his muscles as he hurled it into the creature's side. The harpooner who darts and misses would not long remain in that honored position. He never missed. Euphoria enveloped him; and he rested in its arms, telling himself he should control that emotion but wrapping himself in it just the same.

A moan from young Johnson roused him from his thoughts. George's arms and legs were dead weights pinned to his torso. Periodically, the boy's mouth chewed, but he never swallowed; the look on his face said it all. Joseph remembered his first whale and the scent of oil, slime, and blood drying on his body and clothes. Now, he filtered out these obscene scents and smelled the food alone, but not so the greenhands. Poor George no doubt blended the aroma of food with the sickening odor upon his body. The result was a stink so nauseating that the boy had to force bits of food into his mouth. Even chewing was an effort and swallowing nearly an insurmountable chore. Nothing Joseph could say would help George; it just took time.

But, with the risk involved in every aspect of this life, time was something George didn't have. The lad had wagered his life when he signed to the voyage. This was a business for men, not boys. Joseph's food didn't settle well. He took another bite and considered how much more enjoyable the voyage would be without George. The boy was proving to be a bigger problem than he at first thought possible. Too much was still unknown about him. Joseph took people at face value and didn't like surprises. He and Job had convinced George to share a little more, to become part of the crew. Joseph hoped that would be sufficient. Then George talked and the problem was compounded, not alleviated. Every man on the ship was dedicated to pursue whales, but the boy's purpose for signing was something else altogether. Such divided allegiance did not bode well. His commitment to the boy was now a notch higher, and he didn't like that. Getting close to an angry mate was a bad idea.

The lad should have never signed. Still, he would need help to survive.

Joseph set his plate aside. "Our boat has taken the first whale. 'Tis a good thing for thee."

George raised his eyes. "Better that Gorham's watch got the honor."

"He doth pick at thee like a fish after feed."

"This life is bad enough without being plagued by that man. I long for the day that I will be set free from this voyage."

"Well, a good beginning helps bring a quick end. Canst thou see the end from here?" The boy needed to anticipate something other than his immediate problems.

"Not sure what you mean."

"The sooner we get our ship filled with oil, the sooner we can go home well rewarded. This is a great beginning. Canst thou see the end? It's not that far off, George. And thou wilt go home with money, stories, and a new perspective on life. Canst thou see thyself at the end of the hunt?"

George looked into the distance. "You know what end I want! I can see it even now."

Where strength had been lacking, Joseph saw it appear behind a clouded countenance. He wanted to tell the boy once again the futility of that pursuit. But George had heard, yet still he hoped. In time the lad would need to accept the uselessness of anticipating what could not be.

§

"Job's being fitted with the monkey rope."

While the other greenhands hung on Peleg's every word, George kept her distance.

"You ever seen the man with the monkey at the circus? Monkey moves this way and that." He jumped side to side with a laugh. "And the man pulls the rope. That's just what Job be a doing shortly. Yes, siree! He be a dancing on the belly of the whale. If he slips off the whale, the men on the other side of the rope, they pull it up to keep him from the water."

Still exhausted, George leaned into the bulwarks and looked at the whale. The ship rode up a swell, and the whale's head drifted a few feet from the hull. On the slide down the other side, the whale careened back into the ship. Anyone caught between the two would be crushed. How could Job just stand there laughing at the salt's explanation?

"You're going to work on its belly?"

He looked down onto the whale and nodded. "All three harpooners take turns. This is my turn."

Through a fog of fatigue, she looked at the two huge hooks lying at his feet. Normally kept on a post in front of the mainmast, they each weighed over 100 pounds. "You're not going to carry one of these hooks over its back, are you?"

"I am."

She looked again at the whale, and her breathing became labored. "You jest!"

"No, that's what I do."

"It sounds too dangerous."

"No more than working the tops. And you did that."

True, she had. But it didn't seem nearly as difficult as dancing on the belly of a whale with the hook as a partner. The Third Mate finished fitting him with the canvas strap and secured the rope.

"What do you think of your voyage so far?"

How could Job ask that question? Leaning on the bulwarks, she found it difficult just to hold her head up, and her stomach still called out for food. Every muscle in her body hurt. She was covered in blood and no doubt smelled as bad as everything else. George looked up at him with a scowl.

He raised his eyebrows and looked down, readjusting the canvas and the rope. "Still think you'll find Caleb?"

"Eventually." But she knew it wouldn't be soon. They had made that painfully clear.

His words were never condemning. And he listened when she talked. Conversations with Job, wherever they were, made the voyage at least bearable. The crew had been divided into two shifts for the processing of the whale. She was glad that Job was in hers.

"Johnson!" The Second Mate's voice grated on her.

"Aye, Sir!"

"Go to the windlass!"

"Aye, Sir!"

She stationed herself next to Jamie, on the same side of the handle, and waited, straining to watch Job. The cutting stage, a U-shaped platform, that usually stood inverted over the gangway, was lowered even with the deck and above the whale. The two arms of the U attached to the deck on either side of the gangway, which was left clear for the ingress of the blubber. Walking out onto the stage, with only a flimsy rope railing for support, the First Mate used a long cutting spade to slice into the carcass.

Like a warrior entering battle, Job leaned back into the canvas strap, held the rope with one hand, and rappelled down the side of the ship. In his free hand, he held a boarding knife that looked like a cutlass blade set in a three-foot-long wooden handle. With one last leap he landed on the whale, slipping as his feet met the skin. It took two men to move the hook to the gangway; but Job, alone, dragged it to where the jaw attached to the throat. Standing back of the mouth, he cut a hole at the base of the lower jaw and inserted the hook.

"Heave!" There was that voice again.

Up and down, up and down. George pulled on the handle as the head rose slightly from the water. Officers and harpooners yelled back and forth as a chain secured the head in that position by hooking one eye. More pulling…up and down…a crack, breaking bone…a sound like ripping fabric, only deeper. The lower jaw with its teeth and a large piece of blubber attached, was torn loose from the head and hauled onto the deck.

All afternoon she had pulled in the boat…pulled to where death would have been a welcome release. Now they made her jerk this handle.

How could this body still be working? She was living a nightmare: the work, the movements. The groans…were they coming from her or from someone else? As if on the outside looking into her life, she moved but didn't know how.

"Avast!"

The sky still glowed from the setting sun and a partial moon. They gave enough light to see Job retrieve the second hook and drag it to a crease around the whale's body. The neck! George had seen the whale bend it to attack their boat. The First Mate continued cutting into the blubber, a piece three-feet-wide along that line. Job inserted his feet into the cuts as he made a hole with his boarding knife in the strip being carved by the Mate. At the same time, he controlled the hook with one of his knees. Finally, he attached the hook to the blubber through the hole.

"Pull!"

Up and down, up and down, the driving beat of a shanty filled the ship. George groaned in cadence with the song as her body pulled, and the ship tilted to starboard from the weight of the whale. The First Mate dug his spade into the flesh. Abruptly, the ship partially righted itself as the three-foot-wide blanket piece of blubber ripped free from the underlying flesh. Slow and steady, the blanket piece rose from the whale like the peel off an orange.

The leading edge appeared above the deck at the gangway. Up and up, raise a foot; jerk a little harder; the whale turns; with his long handled spade, the First Mate cuts into the slowly rotating carcass. Joseph stands beside the Mate with a similar spade cutting deep into the neck, deeper and deeper until little must be holding the head to the body.

"Pull, boy! Pull!" The Second Mate yelled into her ear. "Your watch ain't over yet. Pay attention!"

She pulled a little harder. Her arms quivered between jerks and her back was numb.

The ship increased its angle to starboard as the blanket of flesh and fat rose higher.

"Avast!"

The leading edge was nearly to the tackle. George draped herself over the handle and gulped air that hung heavy with the smell of blood and oil.

The Third Mate cut another hole where the blanket piece rubbed the bulwarks. Three men raised the other hook and attached it there. Joseph finished his deep cutting around the neck.

"Secure the head!"

More yelling.

Jamie leaned on the handle, resting his head on his arms, and looked sideways at her. "There's something I've been wanting to ask you, Johnson." He spoke in his slow country drawl between his own gasps for air. "Why is it you're so upset with that guy who courted your sister?"

She didn't feel like talking, especially about Caleb.

"I mean, I think a woman should be treated as a weaker vessel. Certainly you must think similar. If a man is going to win her heart, it should be done respectful like. I enjoy a woman as much as any man, but I don't believe I have ever taken advantage of one in my life. They are wonderful creatures, and I'm glad God made them different from us. But, you know women are just like men in what they want. Your sister was probably as happy with her man as he was with her. Don't you think she knew what she was getting into?"

George didn't want to talk about it. So far, she didn't see any similarity between her feelings and those of her mates. *And, no! I didn't know.* "He lied... Got what he wanted... And left... Thought his hopes were the same as hers."

Jamie gave her a questioning look.

The Third Mate severed the blanket piece above the second hook. The upper piece swung heavily back and forth, dripping blood and oil on the deck. The second tackle snapped taught with the weight of the lower piece.

"Heave!"

George's face dripped sweat as she pulled up, down, up, down. The first piece was lowered into the blubber hold below the main hatch while the second rose slowly above the gangway. Again the whale turned, but now the head remained in place. Up, down, up, down.

"Avast!"

George hung to the handle like a wet rag on a clothes line. The moon was far into the starboard sky and shed an eerie light on the partially stripped whale. Job was gone from its back, probably pulled to the deck.

Jamie breathed heavily. "So." He gasped. "How can you be sure that's what happened with your sister?"

What! Back to that again? She closed her eyes. "I know he lied." She barely had the breath to form the words. "She told me. Wanted to be free, to travel, to visit new places. Promised to marry her." George's eyes ached. "To Ann..." She gasped a breath. "...marriage was most important...no hope without it...She knows right and wrong...He promised freedom AND marriage…How could she refuse?" Her belly tightened and a surge of angry energy rippled through her only to ebb away in exhaustion.

"Heave!"

Up, down, up, down, grunting to the shanty. Her mind could not make out the words, but she knew when to jerk. Up and down, over and over.

"Avast!"

If she let go of the handle, she'd collapse; did her legs still stand upon the deck?

"Ohhh!" Jamie groaned.

Other moans and hoarse breathing rose around her.

"Did she love Caleb?"

Not more questions! How can you still talk? "Yes." Her voice sounded distant even to her own ears.

"How do you know?"

"When he didn't return…her life ended…. Gave up everything for him…. Said he loved her…. Promised marriage."

"But how do you know…she loved him…? Maybe she just wanted…a proper way to be free."

She had wanted freedom. Caleb's promise is what took her away. She loved him then, and maybe even now. She shook her head. How could anger raise tides of vengeance only to be replaced with the longing for his touch? Were those hopes they shared really gone?

Of course they are!

George took a deep breath. She wavered as if balancing on the edge of a cliff. If she teetered one way, ruin and hopelessness awaited her. Stepping the other direction brought her safety and goodness. George wanted life, the days she had longed for, with Caleb on the Canal.

Foolish girl! That will never be!

Maybe not. But that was her desire.

She needed to say something. "Doesn't matter." She took a breath with a wheeze from her throat. "Convinced her with a lie…didn't respect her…treated her like a prize…to be won…once his, she was discarded." She lowered her head and closed her eyes. "Her reasons don't matter….I believe her motives are pure and good….Believe what you wish." She looked away into a dark night. The moon was gone from the sky.

Jamie's head drooped. "Well, I can't argue with you about that…. But wouldn't it be great to have one of those AGREEABLE ladies here tonight…. She'd be a balm for the soul."

George didn't know what to say. Stupid was the word that came to mind. How could he be thinking of something like that in the middle of this kind of work? She shook her head.

"Don't tell me…you've not been with a woman yet."

"Whether I have or haven't…I'd surely not be talking tales about it."

"I don't talk tales! Tell you what…Johnson. Next port, you come with me…. I'll show you how a gentleman…sets anchor…with his lady."

"Don't listen to him!" Gorham's voice sounded behind them. "It'd do you better to be seeing a woman for what she is. But, beings you're just a child, perhaps to have one of these fine ladies would be like having your Ma." He walked off laughing.

"Heave!"

Soon, talk was lost to numbness of mind. Sounds still punctuated the void, but were they from her throat or others? George had no idea how many blanket pieces were raised and lowered. Sometime in the darkness, the watch was relieved. Finding her way to the forecastle, she tumbled into her bunk, welcomed by a deep and glorious sleep.

Groans woke her much too soon. *No! Not already!* Attached to her shoulders, her arms moved like stumps. She willed them to push off the cover. Using her bucket was difficult enough with a rested body. But, that morning, in the cramped space of her bunk, it proved to be a nearly impossible task. Picking at the blouse where dried blood glued it to her skin, she slid to the floor. Her legs threatened to cave beneath her. Slowly, she shuffled to the ladder.

On deck, oil mixed with blood sloshed against the bulwarks on the leeward side. Men slipped about the deck holding onto whatever they could. Amidships, the whale's flukes stretched nearly the width of the ship. At first glance they looked like the tail of any fish. However, upon closer inspection, they consisted of two distinct halves which met in the middle and overlapped. On the trailing edge, they were less than an inch thick. They had a delicate appearance, yet a majestic power had wielded them.

She hobbled to the bulwarks. The whale was gone. Only the head remained—a solitary epitaph. Joseph stood at the bulwarks with some of the crew, laughing over the severed flesh, sliced from the body with his own hands. Her stomach tightened and her muscles tensed. He cut on her sometimes as much as he did on that whale. He had no right to do that. Like a darkly woven fabric, a desire to escape the Quaker's presence enveloped her.

"Johnson! Lend a hand on the windlass." Clark…again.

"Aye, Sir!" She found herself where she had left off the night before. At least Jamie was somewhere else.

"Haul, men!"

A rhythmic shanty began and George jerked again. As the head raised, the starboard side of the ship lowered. Head up, starboard down, the process continued.

"…We've cut off its head and sent it to bed,
Away! Haul away!
We'll dip from its well the oil we'll sell.
Away! Haul away! …."

George stomped her feet upon the deck with the men in the rhythm of the chant. The ship groaned against the weight and took a steady tilt of about twenty degrees. The head continued its upward journey, rubbing along the side of the ship, higher and higher till the trailing edge with its jagged flesh and oozing blood reached the deck. Sliding through the gangway, the mass came to rest just inward from the bulwarks; and the ship gradually righted itself.

While George leaned against the handle, already exhausted, Charlie danced a jig in front of this desecrated piece of the whale. It lay nearly as tall as he stood. With excited cries, he moved about the deck, his fists urging the beast to fight. In spite of the pain in her body, a smile blossomed.

With a spade, the First Mate climbed to the top of the head. He dug in starting at the forehead and slit back. The weight of the flesh helped rend the opening. He dug deeper as he worked his way back toward the forehead. He leaned on the spade. "Enough!"

Charlie stopped careening as fast as he'd started.

"Get the sperm barrels ready!"

Climbing the rigging for a better view, George looked into the slit which had separated enough to reveal a large cistern. Joseph pulled himself to the back of the head, bucket in hand, and lowered it into the hidden reservoir. He retrieved it full of spermaceti and passed it to a crewman as an empty one was handed up. The process continued, Joseph pressing his arm deeper and deeper until it disappeared completely into the head.

Returning to the deck, George helped fill barrels and secure them for cooling. This was much easier work than pulling on the windlass.

Job took a pail from her hand. "He's bailing out the case. Next, they'll cut into the junk in the lower portions of the head."

Sure enough, as Joseph withdrew the last partially full buckets, Wood took a spade and cut a triangular section from the snout.

Plass bucketed from the front. But rather than the clear, pure liquid that had come from the case, these buckets contained a mush of fibers and spongy substance mixed with spermaceti which was poured into the try pots. The heating of the matter would separate the oil from the solid material.

Meanwhile, Joseph attached his bucket to a pole and pushed it deep into the rear of the head, again and again.

"Avast!" The First Mate looked up at Joseph. "Has it all been taken?"

"Aye! Bucket's nearly empty on the draw."

With little ceremony, George helped the other mates push the head overboard producing a gigantic splash. An emptiness welled up in her gut. She, too, was sinking deeper and deeper into darkness. By her father's own command she had no family to return to. Aside from this miserable life, she had nowhere to go. She was a wretched soul, like a ship in a storm with no safe harbor. She bit her lip. This ship was not home. She should be with Caleb, in New York, somewhere along the Canal. Whatever the problem Caleb had, they could work through it. When she found him, he would make things right. He would be her way off this ship and out of this wretched existence. Doubt scrambled up, but she gave it no footing.

Trying Out
Sunday, January 2, 1849, Day 25

"Where's Johnson."

George had just tumbled up from her watch below. She groaned and walked slowly to the Second Mate. "Aye, Sir."

"Get below." He pointed to the main hatch and the blubber hold.

George was sure the lowest of whaling life had already been experienced. She sat down at the hatch to the main hold. Almost before she smelled it, her stomach retched. A scent of rotting flesh mixed in brine sought escape from below and attacked her nostrils. She tried to stand, but other hands pushed her back. Taking a deep breath of momentarily fresher air, down into the dark of the hold she slid. With no shoes, George tentatively stepped onto one of the blanket pieces, warm on the bottoms of her feet. As her head lowered below the level of the hatch, the full force of the putrid flesh assaulted her senses. She gasped for air, tasting what she smelled. Her eyes went wide and unblinking.

She jumped when a blanket piece moved away from her touch. Her feet searched for firm support but found only flesh that oozed oil and blood between her toes. In the dim light, she made out the pieces. A foot slipped and she was ankle deep in gore. Stumbling, her other leg sank knee deep. Blood and oil washed around them.

She knew nothing alive was in the hold, for she had seen the whale die. Yet, the slipping and sliding movement gave the impression that the spirit of the whale still inhabited these slabs of oily meat. Like giant snakes, some over fifteen feet long, they slithered to the vessel's movements. Light from the setting sun played upon the port side. Moving shadows added to the appearance of life. Balancing herself by grasping an overhead beam, she bent low, bringing her head within two feet of the flesh. Testing each of her steps, she slowly moved away from the hatch. Even without the slabs of blubber, the only place to stand straight was between the beams. Now, with the blanket pieces, George hunched over to fit in what had become a space less than four feet high.

Slipping and sliding across the flesh, she moved forward to find a little more room. If the ship were in port, she would have returned to the deck and swum to the beach, but her old life was a world away. With each step, she fought for balance, just as she used to do walking over mossy rocks along the shore of the Genesee River. But her thought of home left as quickly as it had come.

Two spindly legs swung over the edge of the hatch and dangled there silhouetted in the dwindling light. In the quickness of the moment, something about the feet caught her attention, but she had to focus completely on just keeping her balance.

Just as George began rearranging her stance to relieve some tension from her bent back, the ship lurched to a rebellious swell. Her arms, stretching before her to break the fall, straddled a corner of one of the blanket pieces, bringing her face to fat with whale flesh. Frantically jerking her arms up and down, she tried to find something that could support her weight and raise her head from the blubber. Her hands found flesh and she pushed herself to her knees with salt, oil, and blood on her face and the taste in her mouth. She retched but nothing came up; she hadn't eaten in almost a day.

The old feet just missed her face as the body slid down. The right foot had only the big toe, with stubs where the other four should have been. The left had no big toe. These mangled legs, with countless scars, came to rest beside her. She was still staring at the feet when Peleg lowered his head and entered the hold.

"What are you gawking at, Johnson?" The smell didn't bother the old salt.

"Nothing." She gagged as she scrambled to her feet.

"You be the gaff man." He handed George two short poles with sharp hooks on the end. "Hold the pieces steady as I cut." He pulled a cutting spade from the deck. Even in the waning light, George saw the razor sharp edge. The old man, in one smooth motion, cut a piece about 40 inches long and eight inches wide and deep from the end of a blanket piece. "Aye." He stared at the scene around him. "Well, don't be waiting for the Captain. After I cut, you toss the horse piece up and out." The older sailor swung his blade toward the hatch just missing George's nose.

George grabbed low on the gaff, next to the hooks. With a sharp strike she plunged one hook in each side and, kneeling on slabs of blubber, managed to lift the sixty-pound mass up to the hatch. No sooner had it reached near the opening than someone hooked it from above.

George quickly unhooked, and the horse piece was out. "Can you cut them a little smaller?"

"That WAS a small piece. Yes, siree. You're the strapping lad, not me! Be about the work! Secure the blanket!"

George, dropped one hook to steady herself by bracing against a beam.

"Don't drop that hook!"

George's hand stopped in mid-air at the command.

"Pick up yer gaff, boy. That's a tooth ready to bite."

George picked up the tool just as a blanket piece slid over where it had fallen. On her knees, she struck both gaffs into the blubber lying before the old sailor. Approvingly, another cut was made. George wrestled with the horse piece, hitting her head against one of the beams. When she lifted the dead weight over her head, a residue of oil and blood ran down her arms and under her blouse. By the time she had returned to the spade, another piece was already cut. She again dragged it four feet to the hatch.

"Uhh…this piece must be twice the size of the other ones."

"Aye, that 'tis." His voice had the cheer of a dog watch in it. "Get her up."

George slipped, tugged, and pulled the piece to the hatch. Her clothes were soaked in bloody oil, and her hair matted by the same mixed with sweat. She put her hooks in one end and stood up through the hatch to get the piece high enough for the deck hands to get it.

With each piece she lifted, she cursed her existence and the man who put her here. There was no hope, no possible retribution, and there would be no escape. *Three years!* She moaned.

"So, is the mule cock taking a rest?" Gorham hooked her piece. "Do your duty in the hold. 'Member what Captain Sullivan said, 'no skulking!'"

At that moment a battle raged within her. The agony of the purgatory in which she worked fought her anger toward this thorn. Neither won and she just stared back into her antagonist's eyes. He stopped laughing and his face turned sober. He hurried off dragging the piece to the mincing horse attached to the port side bulwarks. George sank back into the torments of Hades.

"By old Nep…"

She hated the old man's mumbling.

"…why did you join our hunt?

You know! "I already told you."

"What you said is no reason. No, siree. Nothin' wrong with what that man did. So, why'd you sign?"

There was nothing to say. She reached for another horse piece and slipped backward just as the cutting spade came down where her hand had been. If not for the fall, she would be missing fingers, or worse. Peleg must have been tumbled by the same swell.

"I asked you a question, boy."

"I got to get this piece up." She crawled toward the hatch with no answer other than the one already given. But she didn't want to antagonize the old man; one enemy like Gorham was bad enough.

She passed it up and bent back for another.

"Again, why?"

"As I've already said, I hunt that man."

"Makes no sense. Something's not right about you, boy. No, siree!"

"Maybe it's that I suffer for my sister."

Mr. Clark's voice boomed down the hatch. "Git those pieces up here. What's the problem Peleg?"

"No problem, Sir. No, siree. I'm a-cutting now. And the boy's a-hauling!"

§

Back on deck, with her watch in the blubber hold over, George fell to her knees. She was beyond tired. Every muscle ached. Two stoking doors hung open beneath the giant copper tryworks kettles. The heat from them took away the chill and soothed her throbbing muscles. Like an empty sail opening to a breeze, she welcomed the warmth and collapsed against the forecastle companionway.

Eyes saw but mind barely comprehended. Someone else lifted horse pieces from the hold. Gorham still dragged them to the mincing horse where Charlie used a two-handled knife to cut one-inch thick slices into the blubber, leaving them still attached to the skin. Another mate moved these Bible leaves to a hopper next to the tryworks. Joseph fed the leaves into the copper kettles that bubbled and hissed as fire extracted oil, like bacon cooked over a fire. Occasionally, Tom lifted from the pots something that looked like the crackling of hogs being roasted. He tossed them through the stoking doors and fed the fire, the fire that gave her warmth and relief.

Blood and oil dripped onto a red-stained deck from flesh hanging overhead. Masses of blubber lay piled here and there awaiting their final end. Smoke billowed from the tryworks flue and around the pots and receded in the flickering rays. Light from the fires flashed through the stoking doors onto the blood covered faces of exhausted men, some working, some lying in the most precarious positions. The flesh hissed and spat as it gave up its oil. Men groaned and cursed with a ferocity in their looks that sent a chill up her back. The hovering smoke held a nauseous scent, as if all the ill odors of the world were gathered together, shaken up, and blown upon this ship. Even Joseph appeared the demon, standing in the red, fierce glare of the tryworks fires.

When Job relieved him, Joseph came and knelt beside her. "So what dost thou think of the profession thou hast chosen?"

"What do I think? I think 'tis hell, Joseph. 'Tis surely hell!" She closed her eyes and let the warmth of the fire carry her on arms of release from the life about her.

A rude kick to George's thigh aroused her. She looked up into the face of the devil. The light from the tryworks fire cast a red glow upon the Second Mate.

"Sleep's below."

She pulled herself up and into the companionway where the familiar darkness of the forecastle welcomed her.

"That you, George?" The voice came from the bunk on the starboard side at the base of the ladder, Tom's bunk.

"Yeah."

"Oooo! George!" Tom's expletive brought her weary body to a halt. "You stink!"

"You mean more than everything else around here?"

"You best clean up a bit before they throw you overboard with the rest of the whale's carcass."

"That can wait till tomorrow."

§

George grabbed the ladder and winced. Her arms barely held. She slowly pulled herself from the forecastle one more time. The flukes still lay amidships, the last recognizable vestige of the whale, unless she counted the barrels of oil still cooling on deck. But the *Christopher Mitchell* was back; the ship from hell was gone. The tryworks fires were out. The cover was on the main hatch. The blubber hooks were at rest in front of the mainmast. Had she really done the work she remembered? A loathsome feeling formed deep within her and, wave upon wave, worked its way out as she began to comprehend. The *Mitchell* must have been where God was not.

The Third Mate cut on the flukes with a boarding knife and handed the small pieces to the crewmen. George rubbed her fingers along the fattest edge. It felt something like a peeled hardboiled egg.

"Take these lippers and scrape the decks free of blood and oil. Use the whale lye." The Mate nodded toward a barrel of water. A crewman shoveled ash from the firebox under the kettles into it.

And George scraped. Before the day had ended, every trace of the bloody ordeal was wiped from the face of the ship. A new ship floated upon the sea. But, looking aft, she saw herself drifting dead and alone, like a headless body of a whale.

The sails were set and the *Mitchell* started merrily on its way south with men at the mastheads looking for more whales.

§

Tom leaned back on his haunches. Some of the crew had gathered around one of the tryworks kettles washing clothes in whale lye.

"Thou wilt soon forget." Joseph saw the ocean in this Indiana farmer. Even the officers treated him as more than just a land lover on a blubber hunter. "The work suits thee."

Tom laughed. "Don't know that I agree with you about the work. I chose this life as a challenge to master, not because it suits me. It's the way I deal with crisis in my life. I would rather choose my struggles than have them imposed on me. You know, I still see her in my dreams."

"What made thee choose whaling?"

"Can't remember who told me about it. Sailing is a most foreign thing to one who grew up as a clod hopper. I can't begin to tell you the times this decision seemed foolish and how close I came to turning back."

Something about Tom set him apart. "'Tis a good thing, I think, that thou didst continue on this adventure. I have seen thee learning the trade."

"Oh, doubts tempted me to turn back, but what would I think of myself if I gave in to their withering allusions. No, once I set to this course, I was destined to see it through." He leaned back and chuckled. "Now, sitting in that boat beside a whale, I thought that perhaps, in this case, I might have been a little hasty."

"That woman must have meant a lot to thee."

Tom nodded. "Jane was everything. How would you feel if the separation from your family was permanent?"

Joseph didn't even want to think it. Three years was bad enough. But, even for him, whaling provided a solace for the separation. "Thou wilt soon see the benefit of thy choice, Tom. The mastheads will give thee time to think, and dangers will consume thy mind. 'Tis a life uniquely suited to thy purposes."

They each dipped a blouse in the lye.

§

Still tired and aching, George lowered her toilet bucket over the railing and rinsed it as she listened to the conversation around the tryworks kettle. Too many men worked there for her to join them. Retrieving another pail of water, she proceeded to wash the smells and stains from her head, arms, and legs. She couldn't tell if she was clean or just no longer able to distinguish the odors of whaling.

When only Tom remained at the kettle, she dropped her soiled clothes to the deck beside him and sat on the bucket. Eyes aching, she stared at the water in front of her, wishing she were still asleep. What an odd combination of thoughts swam in her mind! She hated this life; and, yet, she yearned to look at disaster the way Tom did, to face danger head on and adapt to its attacks, to flourish in trials.

Casually spreading her fingers into the blouse, she felt the stiffness of dried blood and the filmy sheen of oil. *No, I'm definitely not flourishing.* She held the blouse close to her nose and sniffed. The odor tightened the muscles in her neck.

Tom scooted closer to her. "To think you actually wore that."

She smiled weakly. "More whale than shirt." Dipping the blouse in the lye, she rubbed until the fabric was nearly white, gradually working her way higher.

"Amazing how the whale provides most everything on board ship!" He squeezed out the water and, with it, some dried blood. Giving his last blouse a quick glance, he nodded approval and laid it in a pile beside him.

"The way you talk, I wouldn't be surprised to find you signing up to hunt again."

Tom laughingly protested that expectation.

After she worked her way through both sleeves and the body of the blouse, George inspected the fabric. One more rinse. She wrung it out, shook it, and neatly folded it to one side. Then she dipped one of her pants into the kettle.

"What have we here?!" Gorham's voice came from behind her. "Looks as if Johnson worked in a laundry!"

"Nay…"

Charlie was with him.

"…looks more like he was tied to his mother's apron."

As a rising heat began to flush her face, she stared at her hands clutching the legs of the pants in the kettle.

Wash! She told herself. *Keep washing!* She wanted to remove her hands and strike out at her tormentors, but such outbursts needed to be controlled. For some reason, that day, these feelings persisted, and she fought against the rising irritation.

"Boy," said Gorham, "has anybody told you, you wash clothes like a girl?"

Charlie walked around the tub in front of her. "Aye, you'll make someone a fine wife one day."

They laughed as others' attention was drawn to her.

George wrung the legs so hard she thought they might tear. The muscles in her arms and shoulders bulged, a sensation she had never felt before. Setting the damp ball of fabric atop the blouse, she let that feeling momentarily overpower her, the feeling that she actually could throttle these antagonists. She ran the next blouse through the water, washed it out, and laid it, stains and all, atop the others.

When the efforts to get a response from her failed, the rude comments dwindled and Gorham and Charlie walked forward.

Tom leaned toward George. "Looks like you've had some washing experience."

"A little."

"Don't let them get to you. If you want to wash your clothes clean, then do it. You'd surely smell better than they."

"I know, but I don't want to make things any harder than they already are." Squeezing out a pair of pants, she added them to her pile, surprised to find the anger was gone. "I wish I could face this life as well as you do. While I had hopes of finding Caleb, this life was endurable. Now I suffer for no reason."

When they finished hanging their clothing, they settled down under the foremast in the shade of the sails. "You know, George, in a way I admire you."

"What do you mean by that?"

"I mean, you're standing for your sister Ann. Some may say it's foolish, but I say Ann must be proud to have you as a brother. You're risking a lot on your quest. It is a noble thing you do."

"You think my hunt for Caleb is good?"

"Well, I'd not go that far. But you *are* risking your life and giving up years for a battle that is not yours. You must really love her."

"Three years and no hope of finding him? I wouldn't say that's worth admiring. But, what about you?" She wanted to change the subject. "You said that you came whaling because of a woman. How so?"

Tom thought a moment. "I came whaling because I couldn't live with a desire for what I could not have. I couldn't stay where we had walked together and talked together. The memories of her were too strong. I had to go somewhere, do something," Tom's voice grew soft. He closed his eyes and paused as if studying a face only he could see. Then he opened them, and he was someplace else. "We walked hand in hand along the Blue River. Flowers and trees bloomed, but none as beautiful as Jane. The scene and scent of farming is part of me, but all this pales when compared with sitting in her company." The words caught in his throat. "I don't want to forget, and I don't want to remember either."

George nodded. She knew what he meant.

"A beautiful, graceful girl, a Quaker, educated at home by her mother. They farmed near us. Whenever we could, we spent time together. We talked about everything, even marriage. Then, one day, she came to the field I was working. I could tell she had been crying. As we held each other, her tears began again. Her parents told her she was to stop seeing me. She was not to be yoked to someone outside the Friends. I think we could have worked through that. But then, between sobs that wracked her body, she said they were moving to Hamilton County, north of Indianapolis. She might just as well have been moving across the country. I didn't want to let her go. If only the world could have moved on by and left us there."

He was the picture of what she felt. She longed for something taken from her. If a woman sat beside her, George would have built upon these words with her own hurts and hopes and expectations. But she could not. This was a man. Instead, she pushed her silent words down and back.

"She didn't care what her father wanted. She said we should leave right then, together. She couldn't go home to parents who didn't understand. Her desire was to stay with me."

He was describing Ann. She knew Jane. She understood her. George wanted to put her arms around Tom, comfort him, and share her feelings with him.

You can't tell him what you feel! You can't tell anyone! Besides, such feelings are foolish. You're George now. Look where you are.

Tom lowered his head. "That's what I wanted too. We buried ourselves in each other. I longed for what I had only dreamed. We would leave in one week. That gave me time to arrange for money and a horse. Two nights before we were to depart, her brother came to me. He said that leaving home like this would destroy her. But I knew he was wrong. This is what Jane wanted. It's what we both wanted—more than anything. He told me it would tear their family apart. How could that be? I wanted to know. He explained that their father's wishes needed to be honored. But what of his daughter's heart, I asked. He argued that hearts would heal; a broken family would not. I knew Jane; I knew her brother was wrong. Together we would start a new life south of Indianapolis. The family would be fine and we would be happy.

"We put together what few possessions we would take with us; there was little but love. Then, once again her brother came, this time to us both. He said he had not yet told the family. But by night they would know. He reminded Jane of her mother's plans for her, and how much she loved her, and asked Jane to consider how this would cripple her love for her father. That, and more, he shared. With each reminder, her shoulders stooped a little lower under the weight of what he said, until, at last, she wiped tears from her cheeks. I sat defeated."

No! She knew where this was going. *You chose to break her heart?*

"If she left her family for me, that hurt would continue to chip away at our love and eventually come between us." He talked as if trying to convince himself. "I love Jane too much to see her hurt that way; and, to have her turn against kin was a selfish decision. When I told her to go home with her brother, she clung to me and wept, saying she could not live without me. But I knew her brother was right, and she could not live WITH me; I saw it in her face. She said she would never move from the Blue River as long as I was there. If they left, she would stay. Eventually, she would win. That, too, I knew was wrong. How could I remain? I had no reason."

George felt so much like Jane. But Tom was nothing like Caleb. "Will you look for her when you return?"

He shook his head. "She'll find happiness with another…as will

I."

George looked away. An absolute isolation welled up in her gut. Men all around her, and yet none knew her. Though parched, she could not stoop to drink of the water in front her.

§

When George's turn at the tops came, she climbed right on up, hand over hand. She looked forward to these watches above the wretched world. Some things are beyond hope. Yet, alone, at the masthead, anything was possible. She could dream of what would not be. After four weeks of practice, this perch atop the world proved a safe place. Thanks to Job, the masts had become a sure and painless escape. Day by day the climb became easier, not just because she grew accustomed to the ascent, but also because life below grew more unbearable. She may know the crew a bit better than at the start, and they were familiar with her story, but a wall still remained.

Reaching the top of the mast, George crept onto the small platform on the windward side so that she could lean into the mast for support. She inched her way up through the iron ring and rested her forearms upon it. If her eyes should give way to a restful dream, the hoop would keep her from falling. And no matter how vigorously the old ship plunged and kicked beneath her, she could stand comfortably and gaze upon the world. The sleeves were hot on her arms. While the brim of the hat shaded her eyes from direct sunlight, the reflection of the sun's rays still reached her face. She absently rubbed the burns on her cheek and turned, putting the sky's fire to her back.

Like floating on clouds, she looked down fore and aft on sails filled with the trade winds. The *Mitchell* was full ship-rigged, carrying square sails on all three masts. The beauty of white upon the blue of sky and sea! Carried along on gentle swells, her mind envisioned how good life might be back in Rochester…with her parents…and friends…and…. The vision of peaceful white billows on blue became a storm. Thoughts of how she might deal with Caleb filled her mind. George searched the horizon for prey, not only for whales but for a ship and the man upon it.

Even as her eyes followed the horizon, she shifted uncomfortably within the ring. People shouldn't have such teeter-totter emotions. Did she love him, or did he deserve her retribution? More and more these competing dreams fought for dominance. If this kept up, she would go insane before the voyage ended.

As the setting sun cast a golden hue to the west, George looked to the east for whales. The canvas clouds that had separated her from the deck of the *Mitchell* gradually disappeared as men furled the sails. Job worked the yards. The dogwatch was nearly upon them, and she alone remained at a masthead. Joking and talking sounded from the windlass. Tom's laugh broke above the others. Joseph visited with mates. The site of these three men comforted her spirit. They may not know the truth about her, but they were her key to sanity, affording her some kind of fellowship. And of the three, only Job was truly a friend to her, as much a friend as her deception allowed.

§

"So, I thought you Friends are opposed to violence."

This was one of those times Joseph wished the boy was silent. George tested no one else with his questions. But, then, no one else appraised the boy like he did. He leaned into the windlass and nodded. He knew the next question before George asked it.

"How can you justify the hunt or even become accustomed to it? Seems to me you should hate it as much as I do."

He had asked himself this question many times and knew the words he would use to answer. Still, this doubt in the back of his mind kept poking its nasty head into his reasoning. Friends and relatives on Nantucket refused to whale, for the very reason George mentioned, even though whaling had saved Nantucket. "'Tis a good question, George. Some on the island see it as thou dost. Whether for that reason or others, some even removed to other places, like Henry County." He poked Tom. "Thou didst say Jane was a Macy. That family name is prominent on Nantucket."

Job laughed. "By old Nep, had you married that Quaker, you and Joseph might have been related."

"Wouldn't that be a sad state of affairs!" Tom hit Joseph in the shoulder.

Laughter and joking bounced among them, and Joseph loved it. "But, thou dost ask an excellent question, George. We each must evaluate our commitments. I see whaling as no different than hunting wild game for food. Didst thou consider thy decision?" He looked directly into the boy's eyes and saw an adversary. Friends commonly evaluated their lives, at least annually. If George would but weigh his life....

"I did!"

Joseph didn't believe that. But perhaps George would begin to question. "Thou didst tell me thy sister Ann was swayed by Friends. Surely, they did not counsel her to leave home."

"They gave her the idea that women should be free to make their own decisions."

Born and bred in persecution, the Society of Friends believed all people to have been created equal. But they also believed much more than that. The boy's sister must have taken only those teachings she wanted to hear. "We don't believe in rebellion. Ann's choice was strictly her own. She should have considered what her actions would cost her?"

"She did."

"Joseph!" Job spoke before he could continue. "What good does it do to attack the lad's sister?"

"Aye!"

Now Charlie supports George? He must have been listening behind them.

"Don't give up, George. Who knows? Perhaps we WILL gam with his ship. It IS possible. Truly it is."

"Charlie, thy encouragement will come to absolutely no good."

"Ain't you the one who says that God's hand guides the ships upon the sea?"

Why did the man pick this time to remember such sayings? Charlie paid little attention to any of the Sunday teachings. "George is here because of an ill-conceived commitment. This life will not be easy for him. His sister chose her life; he must move on in his." It seemed so obvious. The others should be agreeing with him.

"But this is the dogwatch," said Job. "Leave such arguments for later,"

George settled down, more at ease by the reprieve, and perhaps by the encouragement. But, the boy didn't need "ease." He needed doubt and conviction. He needed to change.

Tom leaned across toward the boy. "I'd like to hear a little more about your sister."

These mates weren't helping matters.

Neptune

1/14/1849, Sunday, Day 37

"Johnson!"

Her gut twisted.

"We were just talking about your hunt." Gorham lounged against the windlass watching her. "I believe Caleb was whaling in Rochester. He sought out his prey and harpooned her." He laughed.

George didn't know how to respond. She'd heard enough talk about the hunt and wished her mates would just forget the whole thing. She wanted to put such futile thoughts out of her mind.

Charlie leaned forward next to Gorham. "But, by ol' Nep, I do feel some sympathy for you and your hunt."

Gorham frowned. "Well, I say Caleb won the prey fairly and earned his lay."

"Don't be so quick to pass judgment." Charlie thought a moment. "Perhaps our young friend will have the opportunity to argue his case before Neptune when the Old Man of the Sea does business with us."

"What do you mean by that?" Gorham's frown took on more of a worried look.

Thankfully, they suddenly were less concerned about her.

"Yes, siree, old Nep's a coming, and he likes greenies."

Gorham's face oozed fear like it did at the start of the voyage. The two salts latched onto that look.

"Especially them that are coofs!" Charlie moved up and down, heel to toe as Gorham sank deeper into anxiety.

Good for you, Charlie. Anyone not from Nantucket was a coof; she was a coof. Before they began picking at her again, George quick-stepped away, and continued to the cabin and the slop chest.

She felt it, inside her. Like a sleeping watchdog. Awake, it might lunge and rip her heart out. But it lay there, quietly waiting. She had suffered its bite before, the pain, the longing. Perhaps it left her to her thoughts because Caleb was out of reach. To stir up anger now would do no good. So, George ignored this friend. Besides, Caleb might still make things right. *He could*, she argued.

§

George squeezed around Tom and Jamie and took a tract from the shelf.

"You want this one?" Tom held a tract out to Jamie.

"No. Can't read past my name. Came for the backgammon board."

"Have you ever tried to learn to read?"

"Never had time for school." He glanced at the booklet in Tom's hand. "Not much need when working the farm."

"We're going to be at sea for a long time. Would you like me to teach you?"

"Why would you do that for me?"

"It opens a whole new world when I read. You might enjoy it. Besides, we should have plenty of time."

Jamie's smile filled his whole face.

Conversations and gaming had spread out across the deck on this Sunday afternoon. For a brief moment, George felt like an orphan looking into a house filled with family and wished she were on the inside.

Gripping a rope, Gorham stood on the bulwarks, and shamelessly relieved himself over the edge of the ship. The bare behind of a man was visible upon the wedge shaped grating laid between the bow and the bowsprit. George found it disgusting that the crew used the head instead of a bucket as she did. Not only was this a sight she didn't care to see, in calm seas the head often became a filthy mess since it depended upon the action of waves washing over it for its cleaning. She climbed to the fore top.

"George." Joseph's head rose above the opposite platform.

What now!

"Mind if I join thee?"

A sinking feeling warned her about the preacher. All he ever did was tell her how wrong she was. She didn't need to hear that. Why didn't he go and save someone else?

"I've been wondering," she said, when it became clear he wasn't going to leave. "I heard talk that you should serve on the Second Mate's boat, not Job. Something about Nantucketers being thicker than molasses.

Since you're from Nantucket, they thought you should have been given Job's position." If she struck first, perhaps the Quaker would go away.

"I've heard it, too. But it's not a problem. God's been good to me in the past, and I know He will in the future. He placed me in this position and I'll serve here as best I can." He thought a moment. "The Bible says He owns the cattle on a thousand hills. I like to look at it as: He owns the fish in a thousand seas. He can give me whatever He wants."

The man was genuinely at peace with himself and his life. George wasn't sure when she had ever really been contented.

"Besides, I wouldn't be able to visit with thee so often if I was on another watch." He settled down as if for the afternoon.

That didn't work. She tried to read, but his silence kept interrupting. Finally, she looked at him from the corner of her eye. "You told me once you have an uncle serving on a whaler. Can you tell me about him?"

Joseph nodded. "My Uncle Isaac, he captains the *Planter*. Haven't seen him for three years." His voice trailed off in thought. "More of a brother than an uncle. Taught me to hunt whales. His wife helped my bride through the farewells when I first left to whale." He stopped and looked at her. "I would love to see him again. His ship always returns full. I had hoped to sail with him but he left in '47, just after I ended my last voyage. But I needed time at home."

"Do you think we'll gam with his ship?"

Joseph shrugged. "Not likely."

"But you do hope!"

§

He had told the boy that being assigned to the Third Mate's boat didn't bother him, but it did. Joseph sat below the mainmast, next to Job, and wondered why. Daily, God blessed him. If he truly wanted to reach George, serving on the Third Mate's watch was the best place to be. He had ample opportunities to convince the boy of the dangers following a path of revenge. Still, he had taken the first whale, not Job. *Pride goeth before a fall*, he reminded himself. The other harpooner was a good whaler and companion. He took a moment to thank God for his friend's fortunate assignment and felt better.

"Canst thou talk a bit about George?"

Job looked back, waiting.

"I worry about the lad and feel some obligation to help him. His discouragement may affect the hunt. I've considered, again and again, his plight and have even sought God's counsel. I want to tell thee what I have determined and hear what thou dost think."

"I think you worry too much about the boy. But let's hear what you have to say."

"We must live with our decisions and their consequences." He considered each word. "We too often refuse to accept the consequences of our choices, or we try to find ways around those we don't like. But we are responsible for our actions. I believe George has made himself responsible for his sister's choices. This has cost him dearly and does nothing to help Ann. That's why he feels discouraged."

"Couldn't it just be that he won't find Caleb?"

"The boy's problem isn't just that his revenge has been thwarted. It's much deeper. It goes to his character. And, if it is not corrected, I fear he will suffer not only on this hunt, but long after. This bitterness is consuming him."

"You make too much out of this, Joseph. He's just a boy."

He had scriptures to quote, words to share, and could have talked for hours about individual responsibility and right standing before God. But if he couldn't make Job understand with short, simple arguments, how could he turn George? "What man sees as right is often what God sees as death. This is especially so when we seek our own desires instead of His. Right and wrong, good and bad, become blurred. What is truly right for George? Dost thou know? I am surely convinced that his present course will come to no good."

"I'll leave such moral discernment to you, my friend."

"George cares for thee more than for the rest of us. I just hope thou dost choose to help the boy, for his own well-being."

Job left him alone with his worries.

"Mr. Clark, Sir!"

Peleg's mumbled shout for the Mate caught Joseph's attention. The old man seldom talked to the officers. In fact, he usually avoided them.

"What is it?" replied Clark.

Shuffling up to the officer, the salt whipped his hat from his head and fidgeted with it nervously.

"It's about Johnson, Sir."

Joseph listened a little more closely at the mention of George.

"What about the boy?"

"Have you heard of his hunt?"

"I'm not here to gossip, man! Do you have something to tell me, or not?"

The old salt cowered under the Second Mate's glare.

"The boy hunts a man, not whales."

When Clark frowned as if the salt was wasting his time, Peleg looked to the deck, his voice becoming even less comprehensible than usual. "It's the men, Sir. Some be arguing about it, for and against. I thought it best you be told, so as you can deal with it proper."

"I'll look into it. Get back forward."

Peleg replaced his hat and scurried away like one of the ship's rats looking for a hole.

§

"Thinking of the next whale?" Gorham draped his arms over the windlass handles.

"Naw. Thinking 'bout the line." Charlie focused on something ahead of them. "We should be crossing it soon."

George thought this sounded more interesting than her conversation with Tom. She saw nothing but water off the bow, not even a cloud.

"Line?" Gorham barely moved his head.

"The equator, greenie." Charlie accentuated the fact that Gorham didn't know as much as he did about sailing. "Don't you know what happens when you cross the Equator?"

Gorham came to attention, eyes wide, staring at the salt.

"Neptune!" Charlie shook his head. "That's when we do business with the…Master of the Sea! Not a good time for greenhands."

"So, what about Neptune? Jamie's been telling me he's real, but I thought he was pulling my leg."

"Nay, my friend. Neptune's real; and, when a whaler crosses the line, ol' Nep exacts his pound of flesh. He knows we take our living from his domain and he wants his due."

"What do you mean?" Gorham turned three shades paler. "What's he going to do?"

"Oh, you poor greenies!" Charlie spoke slowly and looked to the deck, as if hesitant to discuss it.

"What do you mean poor greenies? Why did you say that? What's going to happen to us?"

"That's just the way things is. 'Tis what's expected. We'll just have to wait and see what transpires at this crossing. Oh, my, Gorham, but I pity you." Charlie walked aft.

Gorham hurried to her and Tom. "Have you heard about something happening when we cross the Equator?"

George liked the look on his face. She frowned as if she didn't know what he was talking about.

"Charlie was just telling me about Neptune doing something to us greenhands when we cross the Equator."

Jamie smiled smugly as he mopped an already clean deck around the Carpenter's bench. "He's a comin'!"

Gorham ignored him.

"I don't think there's such a thing as Neptune," said Tom. "They're just having fun with you."

"No! No!" Gorham vigorously shook his head. "Charlie wouldn't do that. Neptune's real and he's going to do something to us."

"Not much we can do if he is real. Won't do any good to fret about it."

"George, what about you?!" He got right up into her face. "What if old Neptune stops your hunt for what's his name, the guy who messed with your sister? He could, you know. He can do whatever he likes."

"Look, I don't know if he lives in the sea or not. I don't really care. I'll hunt what I want, when I want, and there's no god in the sea that's going to stop me!" Oh, this was satisfying.

"Mule cock!" He looked at Tom. "He's real and he's coming. What are we going to do?!"

Tom shrugged.

Standing a good ways back from the bulwarks, Gorham panned the horizon from west to east holding his stomach.

§

"So, you think the boy is trouble?" Captain Sullivan tapped the table with his fingers.

Joseph got a bad feeling about the meeting. The Captain had called him back for a conference with the Mates, and he walked in on a discussion about George.

"I think he's a willing lad."

Clark's response was positive. That was good.

"He has done well in the masts where the other greenhands have not. He works without grumbling, 'tis true. But he has another purpose here. He told the crew about some whaler who wronged his sister. He joined to hunt him down."

This—not so good.

"Not much chance of that." Sullivan twisted his moustache.

Mr. Clark shrugged. "It makes him more apt to be involved in trouble. I've seen him and Gorham head to head. And I've been told he's bringing others of the crew into this hunt of his."

"Joseph?" The Captain turned to him.

He didn't like opposing the Officers.

"We've been discussing Johnson. Have you seen any problems?"

"Well, Sir, Johnson has some trouble with Peleg and Andrews; but, in general, he gets along fine with his mates. He is a bit over concerned about this hunt of his, and I have been working with him on that. Aside from a few comments here and there, I'm not aware of the crew getting involved. But perhaps I'm missing something."

"Mr. Plass?"

"In the boats, he pulls hard. He's weak on the oar but getting stronger. I don't see the problems Mr. Clark has mentioned. But I think it's better to err on caution. A little discipline up front may prevent a later problem."

"I was afraid the boy would cause problems." The Captain rocked back in his chair. "Sounds like I ought to deal with the matter, just to be safe."

The Captain would be fair. And perhaps such a warning would cause George to reconsider his desire for revenge.

"Didn't want him in the first place." Sullivan stood and the meeting was over. "Send the boy aft, Joseph."

§

Just ahead of the bow shadowy figures swam along with the ship. They gracefully darted in and out, crossing paths with other shadows. George recognized them from pictures she'd seen in books.

"Having dolphins follow the ship is a good sign," said Job.

Good sign? "Perhaps we WILL find Caleb's ship."

"Aye, George." Charlie stopped sweeping the deck and leaned upon the broom. "That would be a good day."

"George!" The harpooner's voice interrupted them. "Captain Sullivan wants to see thee aft."

At the mention of the Captain, Charlie immediately focused on his work.

Why did he want to see her? Had her good work been noticed like Job said? Questions flooded her mind with no answers. "Why?"

Joseph shrugged.

She had only been aft for drinks from the scuttlebutt or to get tracts. The Captain didn't talk to common hands. She hesitated at the top of the stairway leading down to his cabin. Her knees wobbled and she held the railing for support. After three deep breaths, she started down the steep stairs. At the bottom, she remembered her hat and quickly swept it from her head. Running her fingers through her hair, she decisively stepped to the cabin door and knocked softly.

"Enter!"

She jumped.

George timidly pushed the door open. A lantern, swinging from the ceiling, lit up the small cabin with living shadows.

"You asked to see me, Sir?"

Captain Sullivan raised his eyes to her.

George shifted her weight from foot to foot. *Why don't he speak?*

"Boy…" The word went deeper than a cutting spade in blubber. "…word has come to me that you are not committed to my hunt."

George's mind went blank, and she concentrated on keeping her balance. "I don't know what you mean, Sir." She forced the words out through a throat almost too tight to breathe.

"Don't lie to me, boy!" He stood and leaned across his desk.

George gasped and backed up a step.

"Haven't you learned yet I know everything that happens on my ship!" He walked around the desk and stood directly before her, rage visible right behind his eyes.

Don't cry, she told herself. Don't cry. The Captain stared at her eyes. She looked down.

"Tears are for women, boy. You don't do that here."

"Yes, Sir." George tried to keep her voice from breaking.

"I hear you are seeking some man on the hunting grounds rather than being committed to my whale hunt."

She hadn't thought this was so important to the Captain. "Sir, that is why I signed on." Her voice trembled. "But I know now that I won't find him. I…"

"You best not even seek him! Do you understand me, boy?"

She understood completely. No doubt about it. She nodded.

"Do you understand me?" He spoke slowly, like a father repeating a question to a child.

"Yes, Sir." Her voice was a hoarse whisper.

"If I hear of this again, you will not get off so lightly."

"Yes, Sir."

"Get forward!"

George exited as quickly as possible, being sure to close the door quietly. She wiped tears from the corners of her eyes and struggled to suck in a breath. She should never have said anything. She knew Caleb was beyond her reach. Who would have given the Captain the idea that she was still focused on the hunt for Caleb?

Luck? Those dolphins hadn't brought her any.

It had to be Joseph, counseled anger.

No one else argued with her about her hunt. The harpooner must have told the Captain. He's the one who came forward with the Captain's message. And to think she had begun to consider Joseph a friend of sorts.

"You." The Second Mate walked toward her. "Johnson, get over here."

"Yes, Sir?"

"The Captain wants no soggers. What are you doing aft?"

"Sir, I was just..."

"You have no business being lazy when there's work to do."

"I'm sorry, Sir, ..."

"You certainly are! Go spin some yarn." He pointed to the waist, between the mainmast and the main hold. "No one is to be idle, boy!"

George scurried toward the tub with Clark shouting criticisms. It contained lengths of old frayed and torn rope. She sat beside the two large blubber hooks, on the cover of the hold, with a leg on each side of the tub. The Mate stayed while she pulled out a rope fragment and began to unwind the strands. She no longer tried to tell him that her watch was not on deck.

Unwinding old rope and spinning it into new lengths was a common job on the ship and took no thought or concentration. Unlike times in the past, however, she did not daydream.

Joseph betrayed you. She ripped on one of the strands.

How could you possibly think of him as a friend! She gave the strand another jerk and unwound two more feet.

He couldn't convince you so he went to the Captain. She jerked again and again.

Probably thinks everything you do is wrong.

Joseph considered her life to be tattered. But what right did he have to take it apart? Her quest had been so simple before he muddied her thinking about Caleb. On the foredeck, everyone was always nearby, but Joseph more than any other. "So why me?" she said under her breath. Caleb was out of her grasp for now, but eventually she would look for him again. And what was wrong with that? George pulled at some more strands, silently cursing the harpooner.

"Mornin', George." Tom took a seat behind the spinning machine. "I see the Mate got you too."

George nodded. She would have preferred sitting alone. But, if a crewman had to work with her, she was glad Tom was the one.

He found the ends of three unwound strands and separated them from the tangle in the tub. Attaching them to the machine, he twisted them together forming new rope. When the end of one strand was reached, Tom spliced in another and continued winding.

"How's the day been?"

She shrugged.

"You seem a little sullen. What's the matter?"

George didn't look up but continued ripping angrily at the old rope. "Had a talk with the Captain."

"What happened?"

"Someone told him I still hunt Caleb."

"But we all know you'll not find him."

George nodded. "I think Joseph told him."

"That doesn't sound like Joseph. He's worried about you."

"Has a funny way of showing it. I don't know who else would have said something to the Captain."

The two worked on, George unwinding and Tom winding.

"Joseph just wants to help you, I'm sure."

"Don't want his help."

"I think he's going to make the voyage rather interesting. He knows so much about the places we're going."

"Probably places I'd rather not be."

"Since you'll not find Caleb?"

She nodded.

"Well, I'm glad you signed. If you hadn't, we'd never have met."

The temperature in her cheeks rose. The comment was just a friend's words. Why did it make her so uneasy? Such emotions had been absent since Caleb left her. *He thinks you're a boy*, she reminded herself. *Get a grip on your feelings*.

She pulled a little faster. "Yeah, I suppose that's a good reason to be here, the only one." *You're just a boy on this ship, nothing more, nothing less. You're a mate. Tom is too.* Over and over, she reminded herself of her position. Gradually, her cheeks blanched. Someday she would no longer be just another mate. Someday she would again be Ann. On the deck beside them lay a growing pile of usable rope made from tattered remains.

§

Job came forward with the other harpooners. Cheer did not accompany them. The dogwatch revelry ceased. "The Captain has informed us that we are approaching the equator. We're about to cross the line."

Four of the salts gasped and drew back.

Peleg stopped laughing and rose quickly to his feet. "Ol' Nep'll get his due tonight, I reckon," He wagged his head, glancing from George, to Tom, to Jamie, and finally coming to rest upon Gorham.

When the salt gave them an I-feel-so-sorry-for-you look, George's insides began to disconnect. Surely, Neptune was just a myth, a good subject for yarns. But why would these men suddenly become so serious?

"I told you he was real." But now Jamie wasn't laughing.

Gorham ignored his friend's words; his eyes were wide as he stared from Peleg to Job and back again.

Tom took a seat next to her but kept his eyes on Job.

She told herself their reasoning was some kind of joke. But the harpooners never teased like this. She was glad Tom was near.

"See!" Jamie pointed aft. "The Captain's looking for him."

The Captain stared through his spyglass off the starboard side of the ship, in the direction of the setting sun. Gorham grabbed the windlass handles and stared to the west.

Captain Sullivan lowered his spyglass and pointed. "The old man approaches, about two points to starboard. Get the greenhands below deck. That is their only hope. We can't afford to lose any of them now."

"Hurry, men." Even Joseph's voice was frantic. "You heard the Captain. Get down into the forecastle."

With nothing but water to the west, her mind said this was not real. But the seriousness in the voices caused her muscles to tense. Something wasn't right.

"Hurry." Job pushed Jamie along as the greenhand stared to starboard. "Move! Move!"

Joseph put his arm around Gorham, whose sinews bulged from his grip on the handle. "Andrews, your only hope is to get below."

Joseph worked Gorham's fingers loose and helped him to the companionway and down, as the greenhand still strained to see the ship. Once on the ladder, the others pulled him into the darkness. George followed last, uncertainty quivering in her legs.

"And, if I were you, I'd keep the candle off down there." Job closed the hatch. Jamie blew out the light. Everything went black.

Her breathing was just like the others', short quick breaths. Muffled commands found their way through the sound of stomping feet and the rattle of the block and tackle. A creak echoed in the darkness— probably the main hatch being opened—followed by a crash as the cover was set aside.

"What do you think's going on?" whispered Jamie.

"Shhhh." Gorham's voice was weak.

"Must be getting things shipshape for Neptune." Tom had the hint of teasing in his voice.

"Quiet." Gorham wasn't visible, but George pictured him cowering against the bulkhead hugging himself. "You heard him. No noise."

"He's coming for YOU, Gorham." Jamie laughed nervously.

When Gorham moaned, she imagined monsters hiding in the darkness.

Stop that! She didn't want Gorham's terror taking root in her. *This is NOT real! There is no Neptune!* An urge to comfort him, as she would a little boy, welled up inside—a desire to tell him everything would be all right. *No!* Why did she feel sorry for him? In fact, she wanted someone's arm around her.

As the minutes ticked away in the darkness, one of Joseph's pithy, pointless sayings came to mind. "God is the measure by which the past can be judged to create new desires and new actions." It said something about what she was going through, but the memory was continually pursued by thoughts of approaching danger.

The deck grew silent.

"Listen!" she said.

"To what?" asked Tom.

"That's just it, all is quiet."

"Ship! Ahoy!" The voice was barely audible, as if from a ship still a good ways off.

"Please!"

Was Gorham begging them?

"Be still! Be still! Please."

No one answered. No one breathed.

"Haul aback your main yard." The voice was a little louder. "I will come aboard."

Tom leaned over to Jamie. "Why not go up for a look?"

"No!"

Gorham moaned.

"Haul up the mainsail." The Second Mate's voice stood out clear. "Haul aback the main yard."

Loud stomps sounded through the deck, followed by scrapes, as if someone, or something, crossed heavily with ... flippers?

"Among you I see no greenhands." A deep, gruff voice echoed in the silence. "Where do they be?"

"Why do you think we have greenhands aboard?" The Captain spoke.

"I can smell 'em. Greenhands always leave a peculiar odor."

"We do have some, but to honor you we keep them below deck."

"All ships must present their greenhands to ME. Perhaps some are worthy to be left as my slaves."

Gorham gasped.

"Shhh!" said Jamie.

"Let me see them. Bring them up one at a time for my appraisal...and be quick about it. I have many ships to see this night."

A commotion of feet overhead filled the forecastle. The scuttle opened and Job's face appeared. "We need a greenhand on deck. Send one up. And hurry. His majesty doesn't like to be kept waiting."

"You go." Tom pushed Jamie. "You aren't afraid."

"No." The words were a squeak. "Gorham should go. He's the one who doubted at first. Gorham's coming," he called up the companionway.

"No I ain't." George heard him crawl deeper into the darkness.

"I'll go." She chastised herself for volunteering. There was no reason for her to feel sorry for Gorham, and yet she did.

A communal sigh of relief went up from the others.

Her heart cried out that a hideous creature waited on deck and that it held her fate in its salty hands. But her mind argued that Neptune was only a legend. Even though fear told her otherwise, George knew that no creature paced the deck to pass judgment. At least, she hoped that was the case.

She made her arms reach for the ladder and climbed into the night. Job's face greeted her all serious and business-like. She considered the possibility that she was wrong. Perhaps she should have stayed below.

"Hold!" Job held a strip of canvas before her. "Greenhands must not look upon the lord of the sea. You must be blindfolded."

She willed her legs to move as she continued on her way, feeling with her feet. The companionway closed behind her.

"He wants to get a good look at you." Job took her elbow. "You need to climb onto the tryworks." Other hands helped her up.

"Stand up tall." That voice addressed her.

She gasped and forced her chin up. She stood on planks across something.

"What have we here? A mere boy among men!"

"A mere boy but one of great courage."

Was that the Third Mate.?

"First to the masthead," he continued. "Pulled fearlessly in the boats. And first to be presented to you."

"I see." The creature could have been rubbing his scaly chin. "Boy, do you fear my creatures?"

"No, sir." She should have said yes but didn't think truthfulness at that moment would do.

"Do you fear me?"

George hesitated. "Y-Yes," she answered weakly.

"It's good you do!" He paused. "When you cross the line, you must commit to seek the whale. He is a noble foe and deserves your full attention."

George nodded.

"Has the Captain treated you kindly on this voyage?"

She still stung from the confrontation with Captain Sullivan but didn't hesitate. "Most assuredly, sir."

"Dost thou attend to his words?"

"That I do, sir."

"Captain Sullivan has always been a favorite of mine. You do well to heed his commands. This shall be a fruitful hunt."

George stood at attention.

"Boy, what be thy name?"

"George, sir. George Johnson."

"Your new name is The Heart. You have courage. This will be your sea name."

She had no idea exactly what all this meant, but something about it satisfied her.

"Thank you, si…" A brush was shoved into her mouth, muffling the word. The smell! She knew it. She had a brush, with slush, in her mouth. She gagged.

"Keep it there!"

Heaving from her gut, her face was covered with coal tar and scraped with an iron hoop.

"Can you swim?"

She quickly nodded yes. Cold water splashed into her face. At the same time, the planks were raised on one side. She tried to scream but the brush and her involuntary retching caused her to swallow clumps of old grease as she slid down, down, into water.

Clawing her way to the surface, she pulled out the brush and sucked in air between choking gasps. She ripped off the blindfold, blowing salt water from her nose and mouth and spitting slush, and found herself in a large blubber tub surrounded by the men. They stomped loudly and laughed.

What?! How could anyone do this to her! No monster on deck? She wanted to hide! She gritted her teeth and looked from face to face. But her muscles loosened and her anger subsided; three other greenhands waited below, and she was now on deck.

Oliver Fish, the First Mate's harpooner, smiled from the starboard side of the tryworks where he sat high above the deck—a regal position for the king of the sea. With canvas flippers, sea weed on his head, a canvas robe, and a long lance for his pitchfork, he had a far from ominous look about him. He smiled at George and she smiled back as the men continued their raucous behavior. Like giant fire flies, the glow of pipes lit up cheery faces.

With a lantern hung on the foremast, casting a warm glow, she climbed out of the tub. Joseph smacked her on the back. "Good job, George. I thought thou might be first."

This was the traitor who got her in trouble with the Captain. Why should he be acting so friendly?

The Captain nodded his approval.

"Can I help with the others?" She turned her attention to what was about to be repeated. This would be fun. She knew what the other greenhands were thinking.

"Surely." Oliver pointed the lance at her. "You're The Heart and no longer a greenhand."

She smiled at that. She, a woman, had signed to a whaler, and here they made her a full sailor. She looked with anticipation to the forecastle companionway.

It was opened and Job called down, "Poor George is done. Neptune needs the next. But, mind you, be of good courage."

§

In the light of day, the previous night stood out to George as one of the lightest on her trip of misery.

"So, they tell me you're The Heart." Gorham sat beside her on the bench.

George still didn't care much for Gorham. His suffering in the forecastle should not have bothered her. "And you're Horse."

"Better that than Mule." He looked a bit uncomfortable and his smile appeared forced. "Why'd you go first?" His voice was muted.

If she could win Gorham, life might be better. "Not sure. Someone had to go, and no one else appeared willing. Besides, I didn't think Neptune was really on deck."

"Job or Joseph told you about this test, didn't they?"

She shook her head. "Why'd you come up next?"

He thought about that. "I think because you went first. To tell you the truth, George, it surprised me that a boy went before three men."

If she were to be stuck on this ship for three years, life needed to get better. She could do little to change the nature of the duty, but she might be able to improve the daily routine. Was it possible to change the way she saw the past, like Joseph said? Was there a God that would do that? But could she even believe Joseph's words?

South Atlantic

Sunday, February 4, 1849, Day 58

"…The king-dom of hea-ven is like unto trea-sure hid in a field; w-h-i-c-h when a man hath found, he hid-eth, and for joy thereof goeth and selleth all that he hath, and buy-eth that field." Shorter words Jamie spoke quickly and longer ones he sounded out.

Tom sat on the windlass with his friend. "Good job."

Jamie leaned back, a look of satisfaction on his face. He nodded toward the main top where George sat. "Has Johnson talked with you much about his sister and that fellow he hunts?"

Tom shifted uncomfortably, wishing Jamie had kept reading. "Not much, really."

"Do you think he wronged her?"

"From George's words alone, yes. Love must be complete and forever. There's no room for divided loyalty. If, together, they were not in agreement with this, it's best that they remained but friends."

"Don't you think a man and a woman can just love each other for the moment?"

Tom pictured the family bull servicing the cows on the farm but didn't think that comparison would be good to share. He searched for better words. "Oh, no doubt what you say is true. There are many things I want. But not everything I want is good for me." How could he explain the importance of staying pure, especially when that wasn't something he wanted to talk about? Most men didn't think as he did and, from what he'd seen, Jamie was in that majority. "It's like what we just read. My purity is a treasure I want to give the woman I marry. I would hope she will be willing to give everything for it. If I give my treasure for a momentary thrill, what do I gain?"

"Pleasure for the moment, and that ain't bad."

"For that moment, perhaps not. But, then, what do I have for the woman I marry?"

"If I find that woman, she'll get the same treasure I've shared with others. Pass it around and make all the ladies rich!" He laughed.

"Think about it, Jamie! When the treasure is gone from the field, it is gone for good. You can only give that treasure once."

Jamie scratched his head in thought. "In any case, I think Caleb took what was not his to take. I do, at least, agree with you that the treasure should be given. And I think Johnson is in the right in his hunt, though I doubt I would start such a hunt, one that will take him around the world, I mean…and with no chance at success."

§

You can't tell him the truth. It would be your undoing.

But Job understood her; he took time to teach her; he had a good ear. George wanted to share her secret with him. A confidant would make this life so much better. She owed him her life.

So? Does that entitle him to know who you are?

She thought about that. Did he somehow deserve to know the truth? If anyone did, he did.

No one needs to understand you that much. That's why you hide here, on the mast.

Hiding? Was she really hiding? She just wanted privacy. That's why she sat on the mast away from the men, or in the seclusion of her bunk. No, she wasn't hiding. But was there a reason for her to stay apart? Job intruded into her isolation and she liked it. She was accepted by most of the crew and knew them all by name. During meals, she even talked of home or whaling adventures they all had shared. So why did she still seek the privacy afforded on the mast and in the forecastle.

Safety, my dear Ann, safety. You are a woman in the basest of professions, serving with the most despicable of men.

But not all of them are wicked. Still, she was safe only as long as they saw her as a boy. Hiding her secret required that she hide herself.

Yes, George. That's right. Everything will be well. You'll see.
Anger soothed her and hushed her fears. Its invisible hands stroked her hair and gently caressed her cheeks.

She breathed fresh air, and the breeze encompassed her. The mast was so much more pleasant than her bunk. Here the sun was merely hot. Behind her curtain, it boiled her. And the odors in the forecastle had grown increasingly unbearable along with the heat. Nearly naked, the men sprawled about the deck after dark trying to sleep. She could not do that. To lie uncovered and unbound was a joy she only experienced in the confines of the bunk. So, she still tried to sleep in her berth. But the mast, this was her release. Her legs dangled restfully over the platform and she rocked with the ship.

"George?"

Job's voice roused her from her daydreaming.

"It would be unwise to fall asleep here."

He pulled himself onto the opposite platform and they sat back to back.

"Just thinking about you," she said.

"Good, I hope!"

"Nothing else. I owe you a lot. From the day you rescued me on the rigging, you've been a faithful friend. You told me something I've tried to live by. You said that if I showed any sign of want of spirit or of backwardness, that I should be ruined at once. After seeing what life on a whaler is like, being ruined here is not something I want."

They both laughed.

"Did I ever thank you for taking me to the mast?"

"Only every time I meet you here."

"Of the whole ship, these are my favorite roosts."

Job nodded. "Perhaps that's why we meet so often above the deck."

To George, they shared a secret, as if only they knew the joys of life on the mast. Like philosophers they sat above the toil of the world, and talked of sailing. Peace billowed up inside her when Job sat nearby. "I wish the whole voyage were like this day."

"Enjoy it while you can. We're getting close to the Horn."

"The what?"

"The Horn. The southern tip of South America. There are two ways into the Pacific hunting grounds—around the bottom of Africa, or around the Horn. The African route is the easiest and safest; the Horn is the fastest but also most dangerous."

"How so?"

"Well, first, the Horn is deep south. The water's like ice. And the currents are as strong there as any we'll ever find. Generally, the water flows from west to east, and we're going east to west. The winds are unpredictable. Squalls can come upon a ship at any time and without warning. The seas are higher than any you've seen; they can toss this ship as if it were a toy in a tub. All in all, it is the most dangerous traverse on the face of God's oceans."

"Then why, in His name, do we take this route?"

"Captain Sullivan wants to spend some time in the Peru hunting grounds. He's had good luck there and believes we shall again. Rounding the Horn is the quickest most direct route. It's called doubling the Horn. Whalers return to the Atlantic by traveling easily from west to east. So we're going to round it twice. Many Captains won't take the chance. But Sullivan has done it before without incident."

"Are you trying to scare me?"

"Not at all. I merely tell you this to prepare you. So you can enjoy today."

She sat with her back to her friend and siphoned comfort from his presence. With Job to help her, the Horn would be passable. Life on the Mitchell was better because of him. Someday she would tell him her secret. He deserved to know. She wanted him to know Ann.

§

"Sail ho." Then louder. "Sail ho! A ship ahead! There's a ship!"

"Where away?"

"Straight ahead, Sir."

The Mitchell approached the Brazil Banks, well into the South Atlantic, and this was the first ship they had seen. The excitement of her mates was contagious. Could this be HIS ship? As she continued swabbing, she looked where the masthead watch had pointed.

Captain Sullivan joined Mr. Clark at the bow.

Soon, George picked out the sails on the horizon, a patch of white that did not ebb and flow with the clouds, but steadily grew larger. The white became distinguishable sails. Then the hull of the ship appeared.

"It's the *Mary Jo*, heavy and outward bound." The Captain stared through his spyglass.

George didn't expect Caleb's ship, but disappointment still washed over her.

By dusk the two ships had hove to and were near enough to allow boats to pass between them. They had but one night together since the homeward bound ship was not willing to delay its return. The *Mary Jo's* First Mate and his watch came to the *Mitchell* while Captain Sullivan and the tradesmen traveled to the other ship with the First Mate's watch. To make room, Gorham and Charlie stayed behind.

On the *Christopher Mitchell,* the men sat between the windlass and the foremast with lanterns hung from the mast and rigging. One of the *Mary Jo's* men began playing "Susannah" on his harmonica. Job began to sing softly here and there. Others joined in, some with him and some singing words where Job was silent.

"Yes, siree! But pick up the beat." Peleg moved his feet and tripped his light fantastic.

George sat quietly on the fringe. This was good. Friends laughed, danced, and talked. She wrapped herself in the emotions without being seen.

The *Mary Jo* was headed home after only two and a half years. She carried a full load of oil. One of the men said he was headed to Buffalo, New York, by way of the Erie Canal.

"We have a crewman from Rochester," said Joseph.

"Where away?" The sailor searched the men about him.

"'Tis our youngest crewman, George Johnson."

Eyes turned her way. She wanted to melt into the bulwarks.

"Can you tell me anything of Buffalo?"

"Well...word along the Canal was of a cholera epidemic..." George's palms began to sweat. She should have just said no. And what she had heard wasn't good. "...It caused great havoc in Buffalo. Apparently, it snatched away a great part of the population of that city."

"Can you tell me any more?" The man leaned forward as if that would urge her on.

"Not about the epidemic. But I can tell you the Canal still runs all the way, though it will probably be closed until the weather warms some."

"I plan to spend a few weeks in port before returning. I would think it will be warm enough by then."

"Maybe he'll find your sister along the Canal."

She wanted away from their gaze, but Gorham just wouldn't let that be.

Peleg laughed and nodded his approval.

"How is it you've traveled the Canal?" The sailor ignored the comment.

"He left home tracking a man," said Gorham between laughs.

Jamie gave him a disapproving look. "He does so to avenge his sister."

George was embarrassed by the responses.

The sailor thought a moment. "What happened? How in the world did you wind up on a whale ship?"

"His sister left home to follow a Canaler." Gorham answered as if it were the most ridiculous of reasons. "Then the man moved on and joined a whaling ship."

Jamie rolled his eyes and frowned. "He tricked her into leaving home with him and then abandoned her!"

Charlie sat back smiling as his gaze moved between Jamie and Gorham, and then to Job and Joseph.

"So, you're seeking that man?"

George nodded, looking up. She didn't want to add much more from fear of looking even more foolish.

"Can you tell me what ship he's on?"

"No..."

Gorham laughed and others began to join in.

Joseph silently shook his head.

"Well, what does he look like?" The man was unusually interested.

George didn't want to dwell on this topic. But, everyone stared at her.

"I can tell you he's twenty-five." She spoke softly and quickly. "He has dark hair, doesn't like beards, and has a scar running from the corner of his right eye to the bottom of his right ear. Got it working in the boat yards." There, she said it. Now maybe they would go on to something else.

The fellow perked up. "I do believe I met the man!"

George choked.

The laughing stopped.

Joseph and Job looked at each other.

Charlie leaned forward with a most serious look and stared at the sailor.

"A man fitting that description sails on the *Mystic*."

George was confused by his words. She had come to believe that Caleb's ship would not be found. Now, this man brought hope. At that moment, she was alone on deck with this mate. "Was his name Caleb Coleman?"

He shrugged. "No idea. But he had that scar, and he said he got it working in the boat yards."

"Where did you see him?" Charlie bounced up and down.

In the pit of her stomach, the oddest sensation began to emerge. She was as elated as Charlie, but something controlled it like reins guiding a horse.

"At Juan Fernandez."

"That's just around the Horn!" Job stood.

"Not much chance we'll stop at that island." Joseph showed no excitement. "Besides, by the time we get there, they'll be gone."

"Don't know as that's so. They took a number of whales just north of the island. Had hunted there for three weeks when we met them. But you could be right." He looked her way. "In any case, you're close."

Excitement rushed around her like a river's current around a rock as the news sank in; she would find him. She caught Joseph's eye. "God's hand guides the ships."

"We're on another hunt." Charlie's enthusiasm matched her spirit.

"What's going on here?" The Second Mate took a seat, smiling about the sailors.

"The boy was telling me about the man he seeks."

"What!" Clark glared at him. "Aren't there better things to talk about? We're hunting whales and that's all!"

"I was just sharing news, Sir. He told me of home so I wanted to help him as well."

"He actually met the man." Job still sounded astonished.

"Boy!" The Second Mate looked right at her. "I hope you have not forgotten your visit with the Captain."

He walked off.

Gorham followed. "I think it's pointless, this hunt of Johnson's."

"Surely it is. It's good to see at least one of you has some sense."

They disappeared behind the tryworks.

The sailor bent into those that remained. "There are some men you tend to remember because of the good they do, others because of the evil. This Caleb falls into that last group. I remember him so well, not only because of the scar, but because he made himself lower than any others in his crew as if that would gain our approval. I believe he referred to the boy's sister as he praised his own escapades. Took pride in having fooled her into paying his way along the Canal."

The waiting creature within her arose. She wanted to cry, but the beast that controlled those reins turned her in circles of confusion. She grasped for the hope that Caleb might make things right and marry her. But that was not to be. She was truly ruined and alone. Sobs caught in her throat, not to be heard. She sank deeper into darkness. Like the muggy afternoons sucked strength from her body, these shadows drained her soul of hope. Nothing remained for her; she was nothing…nothing.

There! The word whipped her. *Now you know for sure! Caleb is scum. It's up to you to make things right. He ruined you, robbed you, and orphaned you. And he's proud of it!*

Anger burst into her mind like a mad dog. The restraint was broken and now, with freedom, it devoured her remorse and pulled her along. She hated Caleb. Why should that…that thing be allowed to sail on, living high and laughing at what he'd done, what he would do to others unless he was stopped. She would put an end to his deceptions. Oh, yes, when she was through with him, he would never again do to another woman what he did to her.

§

The *Mitchell* passed the Brazil Banks and headed south toward Cape Horn. Joseph considered the Maker of the seas, the world, and the heavens. *What is man that Thou art mindful of him?* He reclined on the deck under a majestic starlit canopy that floated just above the top of the masts. *We are all as naught.* Yet he knew his Lord had more concern for each individual on the *Mitchell* than for any part of the creation about them. Even George had a place in the heart of the Son of God. Joseph had seen enough to know that men choose to live in sin; they choose to turn their backs on the God that loves them. How much better life would be for any one of them that would walk by the Inner Light! How much less pain George would have! Experience taught him the stability of a life focused on God's own Son. Yet, in the world were men who would never opt for that security.

Orion stood out to the north, placed there by the gods. Joseph closed his eyes and leaned his head back into his clasped hands. Men were masters of their own lives. Who he was and what he was would be determined by how he chose to live, not by the gods. So it was with all men. You don't blame others for your condition; you take what circumstances you are in and, with God's help, move on.

Poor George sat alone on the carpenter's bench, staring into the dawn-dusk night. The boy let circumstances map his course and refused to see beyond his problems. Ann's pain had become his. He would not let God help him and avoided Joseph as well.

"How passes thy time?" Joseph took a seat beside him.

"Well enough."

"Excited about rounding the Horn?"

A shrug.

"Thought much about what's on the other side?"

"Might say so."

A slap of a sail broke the quiet.

"Art thou still thinking about Caleb?"

A shrug.

"It's not likely thou wilt find him."

Another shrug.

The boy carried an angry face and set his eyes on the horizon. He was still set on revenge.

"Even if thou should find him, what benefit wilt thou see? Revenge may be sweet for a moment, but it does nothing to change thee. Thou shalt still carry thy bitterness. Thy soul is darkened rather than enlightened by winning such battles."

Still no response.

Why didn't the boy grasp it? Instead, he saw Caleb as the problem and was blind to his own transgressions. That fueled his bitterness. George had to see that and move on.

"The end result of a bitter heart is separation from those thou dost love. If anger continues to control thee, a happy life will be forfeit. Let God help thee make for thyself a better future."

"You know, I don't need to hear this preaching. Besides, the Captain has already warned me about pursuing Caleb." George walked angrily to the forecastle.

"A little rough on him, weren't you?" Job took George's spot.

"He must hear it. Bitterness will destroy a man, and those around him. But the lad shuns me of late."

"Perhaps he's tired of your sermonizing."

Joseph nodded. "But I worry about him. He reminds me so much of my son."

The Falklands

Friday, February 9, 1849, Day 63

After nine weeks on the whaler, the savory scent of goat stew startled George's senses. Even though smoke from pipes filled the air, the smell of real food was unmistakable. The well-lit inn was the perfect respite for this long-awaited homecoming of sorts. The only problem with stopping in the Falklands was that it put her even farther behind Caleb's ship. But that was beyond her control, so she drank tea and sat in the midst of men from the *Mitchell* and two other ships, British vessels, one a whaler and one a merchant ship.

Wanting to exchange tobacco for tea, Captain Sullivan had stopped in the Falklands, a small, poor English enclave, frequented by British vessels. The captain of the merchant ship carried tea for the same reason that Sullivan shipped with tobacco—personal trade.

The uniformed sailors of the foreign ships stood in contrast to the free dressing Americans, but they all were men. They drank and laughed, trying to outdo each other with their yarns and stories. Yelling and crude comments bounced from wall to wall with increasing confusion as the night passed. The place smelled of men. And so many in one small room made George uncomfortable. She walked outdoors to be alone, not a man in sight, anywhere.

The farther south the *Mitchell* sailed, the sadder the world became. From the time George had come ashore, darkness lingered just minutes away, yet it wouldn't come till well past ten o'clock. The first signs of dawn would break on the horizon just after midnight. Too much time was spent in that twilight always expecting to reach somewhere but never arriving. Facing north, the harbor was bordered to the east and west by distant black silhouettes of land. Three peaceful ships stood out against the dusky sky. The British whaler, already two years into its voyage, rode high in the water, telling a melancholy story of poor luck hunting. But the merchant ship was headed home to England. With no hearth waiting in Rochester, her life was like the whaling vessel. Waves of sadness washed over her as the sound of the surf, caressing the shore, echoed over and over. Tears welled up in her eyes. The island mourned around her and quashed the sounds of gaiety, as if the world knew something the sailors did not.

The door opened and Job stepped out. Quickly, she wiped her sleeve across her face.

"So, George, you are about as cheery as the night."

"No need to worry about me, Job. No natives here." She forced a weak smile.

"But I do." When he talked again, he was more serious. "It seems to me that this sadness has come about since you began avoiding Joseph."

At the Quaker's name, her jaw tightened. "We all know my pursuit of Caleb is futile. Yet, when he couldn't convince me it was wrong, he used the Captain to trouble me. How can I have fellowship with a man like that?"

In the twinkling of an eye, all the reasons she hated Caleb, every motive to remain on the Mitchell, permeated her like blood in water. She had loved and been scorned. She was rejected as a daughter and stripped of respectability. She dressed like a man and worked like a man. At times, she felt more man than woman. She would never experience honorable love. She would never be a respectable mother. She would never be a lady.

Job raised his eyebrows. "I don't think he told the Captain. You're like a son to him. He sincerely worries about you."

Don't listen to him. The desolate voice spoke with authority. *The preacher is the only one who could have told Sullivan.* "Who else had reason to say this to the Captain?"

"Don't know." He shrugged and looked into the harbor. "But I know it wouldn't have been Joseph."

Harpooners stick together. Don't believe him. She wanted to lash out at Job for defending the Quaker yet something in his words soothed her.

§

Overcoming the urge to pour the liquor into his cup, Joseph instead poured tea. Character was built, not by indulging such whims, but by denying sinful pleasures. The two female servers were a welcome sight to whaling eyes. But, like most Quakers on ships, he did nothing more than look. These women were not only absorbed in their work, but also in avoiding the advances of men who had been too long at sea without such companionship. His wife…they had embraced on shore before he shipped. She had clung to him as if that would keep him with her.

One of the Englishmen grabbed for a server. She coyly responded with flirtatious remarks that left him thinking he had scored in a game which she had already won. Jamie had seen it too. Joseph caught his eye and they both laughed at the boorish overtures, only made coarser by the drink. She had a slight build, light hair pulled back into a short tail, and her gentle features were quite attractive, even to Joseph.

When she brought more drinks to the table, Jamie looked directly into her eyes. "Thank you, Miss." His courteous tone and his smile set him apart from others in the room.

Her walk stuttered.

A young Englishman, next to Joseph, groaned and gulped down more liquor.

"What's thy trouble?"

The fellow ignored him.

"Poor Tristram." One of the man's mates leaned across the table. "Tried to desert. 'Bout a year ago. Balmy! Tried on a small island. Nowhere to hide. Course he'd be found. Flogged near to death, he was."

Sadness wrapped itself around Joseph at the story.

Newly married, Tristram wanted money to start a business and had been tricked into signing to a whaler. They had taken less than twenty whales in two years. Yet, two of his mates successfully deserted, and now their Captain gave no shore leave in ports that might tempt his men. So the only hope held by this young man with a new wife at home was in the pitcher between them on the table. No wonder these Englishmen had a hunger for the alcohol.

Had Tristram been sober, Joseph would have opened his Bible and showed the young man a better way. Yet the drink held a kind of universal appeal to the English whalers as it moved them, for the moment, out of the hopeless life they were living. Of course, their free approach to the ale's bitter escape only encouraged the same from the crew of the *Christopher Mitchell*. The whole inn needed to hear of God's love, but Joseph knew that would be like the Captain dining with Peleg.

§

"Two years we been to sea and only a quarter full." The seaman across from Charlie and George had wavy black hair and carried scars on his face and arms. "'Spect a long voyage." He took a deep draught of the liquor sounding like a hog in slop as he sucked it through his missing front teeth. If he hadn't been such a revolting rogue, his lisping would have been funny. With a thud, he lowered the mug to the table. "If we had more of this…." His voice dwindled away.

George looked into her cup and sighed. The *Mitchell* shouldn't have stopped here. They should be around the Horn, and heading for Juan Fernandez.

The inn reminded her of the Azores. Peleg was his usual jovial self, sloshing the ale around the table and down his throat. But, when the ladies walked by, he took on a grim countenance. He never looked at them unless they were at another table. And then the old man glared in their direction one second, only to raise his cup in a cheery toast the next.

As Peleg had more to drink, words came out of him directed to no one in particular. George strained to hear. He cursed some woman, though it didn't appear to be one of the servers. Odd behavior. George wouldn't want to be one of those ladies alone with him; there's no telling what the old man might do.

The Englishman grumbled something about wasting good liquor on Americans and looked at George. "Your ships take boys to whale now? Can't say much about the profession, but there isn't a better way than sailorin' to make a boy a man." He reached across the table and smacked the side of her head. "'Specially, had he signed to an English ship."

Her temple throbbed but the lisp raised chuckles inside. This made it all the more difficult to ignore the comments. Cradling the cup in her hands, she took another drink as Peleg raised his mug and made a toast to something unintelligible.

§

Joseph didn't like the effect the alcohol had on his mates. The conversations and stories took on a predominantly somber tone masked in its cheer. Jamie was the only one who seemed above it all. His eyes followed one of the servers and he ignored the conversations. He walked to the server he fancied. They talked and laughed together. Joseph strained to hear. The server glanced toward George, with a look on her face like someone wanting to comfort a hurting animal. Calling to the second girl, a red head, they talked longer with her. This server stared at the boy, smiled, and enthusiastically walked off.

When Jamie returned to the table, Joseph leaned over. "What was that all about?"

"Watch and see."

§

The servers cleared plates from the tables and brought more drink. With a full stomach and heavy eyelids, George leaned back not thinking much of anything.

As the red haired server walked by, Charlie reached out to grab her around the waist.

The server deftly spun out of his grip, careened George's way, and landed fortuitously on her lap, the server's arm around her shoulder and the pot on the table. "I'm delivering you some more tea." She giggled.

Speechless, George stared into her sparkling pea green eyes. Why did she just sit there?

With her free hand, the maid sensuously rubbed down George's neck and softly under her chin. "What's your name?"

George gasped. She wanted to get away. She wanted out. But there was nowhere to go. "G... George."

"Well, G...George, I'm Meg. Thanks for stopping my fall." Holding George's face between her hands, she closed her eyes and gave George a long kiss.

Wanting to spit and fighting the urge to gag, George shoved herself back but the chair kept her close to the server. She gripped the seat.

When Meg finally pulled slowly away from George's lips, the room had quieted and all eyes were on them. Her face began to heat up. It had to be as red as the lines on the British Union Jack.

Gorham leaned across the table. "Close your mouth."

"I'm done here soon." Meg spoke softly into George's ear. "I'd like to show you more."

"I... I..."

"It'll be fun. You'll see."

Meg's face came closer, and her arms softly wrapped about her neck.

George raised her hands to ward Meg off, but a man wouldn't do that. So, with her hands flailing to her side and eyes wide open, George could do nothing but accept the kiss, again, before Meg returned to her work.

"You dog!" Charlie beamed from ear to ear. "How'd you do that?"

Gorham laughed. "Better hope she don't have no brother. May track you down."

George's insides shook. She wanted to run and hide. "N...nothing's...going...to happen."

"Americans!" The black-haired Englishman shook his head in disgust.

Charlie leaned close. "She really likes you."

"Like I said, nothing's going to happen."

"Why not? She's doing the inviting."

"I won't do it!" George turned away and caught Peleg's eye.

He stared at her, then at Meg, and back again. Scowled and turned to his drink.

Evening turned into early morning. The room had become a mass of men competing with each other, yelling, laughing, and cajoling. Amidst the noise, the two women worked, cleaning the last of the plates and mugs. When George heard one server ask Jamie to accompany her home, she looked across the room. Meg smiled and George looked quickly away.

Meg walked by, ran her fingers down the side of George's face, and gave her a kind of look she had never seen from a woman before. "Just about done."

A flood of panic coursed over George.

§

Tristram's head bobbed up and down. "I don't want to desert again. Perhaps I could ship with you. Would be home sooner for sure."

Joseph sympathized with the man but knew that wouldn't happen. If the English captain was as bad as it sounded, he would not be able to find a replacement for such a sailor and was already short handed. Still, Joseph wanted to give hope. "I can ask."

The young man smiled and tried to stand but fell backwards over the bench. He grabbed onto his First Mate's table and pulled himself upright wobbling from side to side and saluted. "Sir, I am informing you that I have agreed to ship with my friend Joseph on..." He looked sick. "...his ship." He lowered his salute and vomited goat stew and ale onto the table. Wood and the English First Mate, themselves none too steady, pushed back, stumbling to get away from the stuff flowing across the table top.

"Wood!" The English officer glared at the American. "You know you can't have any of my crew. How dare you offer him duty!" He lunged.

The room immediately erupted into a tangle of fists and bodies.

§

Across from George and Charlie, the Englishman grabbed Gorham by the neck with one hand while pulling the other back to strike. Such an attack tended to sober Gorham up substantially.

Without thinking, George threw her tea into the Englishman's face and immediately urged Gorham to vacate the table.

Gorham took just a moment to yell directly at the sailor, "You mule cock!"

The three Americans weaved through the brawl, which had no order or pattern. Englishmen were fighting Englishmen. Job tried to hit Clark, but the Mate easily avoided the swing and pushed him across a table.

By the time George reached the door both Charlie and Gorham had engaged Englishmen and wrestled and punched with the rest.

The fight made no sense, but at least she was free from Meg. She hurried outside to get away from the pandemonium that filled the room. With the door open, the tangle of men overflowed into the street. As if pursuing her, the battle wended its way toward the beach.

Tom exchanged blows and wrestled in the sand. Job did fine until a large fellow grabbed him from behind so his mate could pummel him freely. Grabbing an oar, George threaded her way through the combatants and gave the Englishman holding Job a sharp crack behind the knees. As the man crumbled to the ground, Job freed himself and fought back against the other.

The man whom George had attacked rolled menacingly onto his side. Looking back with malice in her eyes, she threatened the sailor with her oar, warning him to stay on the ground. He cursed, looked around, turned back to George, and then broke into a loud laugh.

The fight had diminished to a few men shoving each other by the shoulders. Job and his opponent held each other up. Joseph, with a bulge in his blouse, stood beside Tristram. They both had bloody noses. The more sober officers had restrained the serious fighters, those who had threatened with knives. It ended as fast as it started. George didn't want to

fight in the first place. Now that she had been drawn into the battle, it
ended. Her muscles still quivered. She wanted to hit…someone. Yet
everyone else was just fine with the situation. She backed toward the inn,
away from the noise, and leaned on her oar.

A sound echoed from the hill behind the inn…cries of some kind.
She jogged that way, stopped, and listened. A woman's voice, muffled, as
if a hand covered her mouth. In the dismal light of early dawn the figure
of a man leaned over a woman… Peleg and Meg.

An urge to scream for help rose to her throat.

No! The voice of anger rose inside. *If you really want to kill
Caleb, you must be able to deal with this.* Wavering for only an instant
between screaming and fighting, she marched forward with the oar.

"Peleg!" She shouldn't be confronting a mate like this. Her voice
did not exude the confidence of a man. "Get off the woman."

The salt had slit the front of the woman's bodice with his knife
and held the blade under her chin. Meg's eyes were wide with fear,
pleading for help as she glanced at George.

"Away, boy!" At least that's what George thought he said. "I'll
deal with you on the ship."

"You'll deal with me now!" George swung the oar into the arm
that held the knife and knocked the weapon loose.

The salt scurried over the ground looking for it.

"Quick, Meg!" George hurried to help her up. "Run!"

Grabbing her dress with one hand and holding together the cut
halves in the front, she ran toward the beach.

§

He stood, holding the knife. The woman was gone. Was it his
wife? He couldn't remember. Since she left him, his life had been a series
of voyages. Had she left him? Or was she just here? Nothing was simple.
A fog settled in his mind, and he wished he could see more clearly. There
was that boy. He was standing in front of him. *The oar, he hit me with the
oar.* Was he the one who robbed him of his wife? Must be.

"You should not have done that!" He held the knife in his right
hand, ready to make the young man pay for taking his bride. Raising his
left hand to ward off another possible blow from the oar, he glared and
walked warily around the boy; the oar had bitten him once already.

The young man looked familiar. He was from the *Mitchell*. Yes,
Peleg was on a voyage on that ship, and this boy was there. Something

not right about that lad. He remembered, now.

§

George's heart raced. Her muscles tensed. The oar was surprisingly light, and she gripped it a little closer to the center to make it easier to control. Then, matching the salt's stance, she bent forward, standing on the balls of her feet, and followed him with her weapon. She thought about drawing her knife but, if they were in combat that close, she would be at a disadvantage. The blade of the oar was six feet in front of her, a good distance.

He stepped forward. She threatened to swing. Like an animal unsure of the danger, Peleg looked her up and down. "You should have listened to the Captain." The words were slurred, his face contorted, almost tortured. "Women have no honor. You are bad luck, boy. I told the Second Mate about you. Yes, siree, I did. You best let Sullivan put you off the ship."

George heard the words, but paid no heed to them, too absorbed in the look in his eyes.

He charged.

Her heart caught in her throat. She swung. The oar hit him with a force that knocked him to the side. He winced in pain, but his arm gripped the oar's blade. She tried to pull it free, but he held, smiled a wicked smile, and pulled himself one arm's length closer. She retreated to the end of the oar. He pulled himself another arm's length closer and slowly twisted his knife. He could have the oar. She flung the handle between herself and Peleg, turned and ran toward the beach.

§

Like a ship through a foggy sea, Peleg's mind drifted in and out of clarity. *He's running. The coward!* The boy…no, the man who took a wife but hadn't the spine to stand before her husband. Darkness rose from deep inside and blanketed him with hatred. Curses rose to his mouth; and, in a stupor, waving his knife, he ran after the shadowy figure.

Ahead … men. Who? What? "Stop him!" But the words made no sense, even to his ears. "He stole my bride."

These men, they let the fellow go and grabbed me. Why? He fought to continue the chase. They looked familiar. *My mates?* What are they doing here? He fought against so many arms. They called his name.

They know me! His strength left him. Arms, they held him. He couldn't move. Darkness came to his eyes.

§

George ran no more than fifty feet downhill and was met by men from all the crews. She passed them and didn't stop till she reached the inn.

Crying, Meg ran out, threw her arms around George, and held her close. "Thank you." The words gushed out through sobs. "Thank you!"

George hesitantly patted her on the back. "It's okay." But what she really wanted was someone to comfort her.

George got the attention of the other server. She came and helped pry the young woman's arms from around her.

"He won't bother you again, Meg," said George.

Peleg had passed out on the way back to the beach, and the officers all agreed the salt's problem was too much to drink. Still, they wanted no one to remain on shore. George took her oar from one of the mates, retreated to the boat, and crawled in. She was drained and as limp as a dead fish. Peleg was laid in another boat. As soon as the crews had shook hands and shared good-byes, the boats were manned. The two ladies stood in the door of the inn and watched as the boats, none too straightly, wended their way to the ships.

§

George had a scowl that betrayed an attitude worse than usual. Joseph wanted to reach out to him but had been rebuffed so often that he hesitated. The Captains had made the trades and the *Christopher Mitchell* was preparing to leave the Falkland Islands. The boy leaned on a mop just fore of the tryworks. Everyone knew how he had come to the aid of the server. He had no reason to be so dejected. The lad was a veritable hero, though Peleg probably wouldn't think so. Even if he remembered nothing of the night, the mates wouldn't let the salt forget that the boy had beat him.

"Good day, George, I…"

The boy held up a hand. "I owe you an apology, Joseph. I assumed my trouble with Captain Sullivan was due to you. You're the one who keeps telling me how wrong it is to seek revenge and how it could threaten the whale hunt."

"What I've told thee is true. But it has always been between thee and me alone. I would never…"

"I know. Both Tom and Job told me it couldn't be you, but I refused to listen. Last night, Peleg said he told the Second Mate."

"If that is why thou hast avoided me, I wish thou had come to me sooner."

George nodded. "Can't say I've missed your preaching at me. But I have missed you."

"Avast, mates!" Job limped up beside them. "Good to see you on better terms."

The boy looked from Job back to Joseph, and his scowl returned.

Odd character, thought Joseph. His mood could change in an instant. "What's thy problem now?"

"You." George looked from one to the other.

"What do mean us?" Job wobbled in place.

"Look at yourselves. Black eyes, swollen noses, walking with a limp. And yet you wish them well as if nothing happened."

"Last night was a great time, wasn't it?" Job smiled and grimaced.

"How can you say that?"

Surprised by the question, Joseph wasn't sure how to answer. Wrestling was part of growing up, of developing the wild heart of a man. Boys settled disagreements with fists and then walked away as friends. Young men enjoyed proving prowess in combat, even among Quakers. Had George been so isolated as a gentleman that he didn't have such relationships?

"Art thou angry about the brawl? This was just a wrestling among friends, George."

"But look at you!"

"These mementos will pass," said Job.

"Blaming others for our condition does no good. There is only a problem here if we let there be one." Joseph put an arm around Job's shoulders. "Why build a wall between us and them? We may meet again one day. 'Tis better not to dread that gam nor look for it in anger."

Job hobbled on to other work.

The boy was quite a mystery, which was all the more reason to rejoice. They could talk again.

The Horn

Monday, February 12, 1849, Day 66

The world was gray. So far, the *Mitchell* had taken two whales and stowed about forty barrels of oil in the hold. They needed to fill over 2000 barrels and take about 100 whales before heading home. Only one day from Cape Horn, the sky was overcast and the day dreary. Summer had come and gone.

The ship looked so…tight. The anchors were firmly secured on board. Above her, men made a special examination of the spars and rigging to check for any defects needing repair. Any weakened equipment was reinforced. To examine the sails, the harpooners climbed the masts. Any old canvas was replaced with new. The *Christopher Mitchell* was being given her Cape Horn sails, and a main staysail was made ready for the stormy weather. The waist and bow boats rested keel upwards upon the tryworks. As with everything else, they were being lashed down. Everyone worked. Something quite out of the ordinary was about to happen.

George wore an old double-breasted, long, blue wool pea-jacket, with tarnished brass buttons fastened nearly to her throat. She hadn't needed it since the beginning of the voyage. But now, without any fire on board except what the cook kept in the galley, such would provide the only warmth for however long the passage took.

The sky cleared but the sunlight was not bright. Smooth swells, the color of steel, rose high about the ship. They said whales passed these waters; but, if one had shown itself beside them, George was sure that the *Christopher Mitchell* would let it pass and wish it well on its sojourn, at least until they met on the other side. Just like her life, this world had no color.

As she caulked the main hatch, which had already been barred down, her mind wrestled with ideas of what awful seas awaited them only hours away. Jamie and Gorham worked at lashing a water cask forward by the forecastle. As it was three feet tall, two feet in diameter, and still full of water, the two men struggled to move it to the starboard side. The deck slanted down toward port and shifted fore to aft like a teeter-totter as the ship rode the swells.

"Johnson." Clark's voice was all business. "Lend a hand on that water barrel."

With three working, they slid the cask to the starboard bulwarks and lashed the top tight. Around the bottom, Jamie fed George another rope in front, which she passed to Gorham in back. A loud crash caused them all to jump. The whaleboat on the port side of the tryworks slipped partially to the deck.

"You three, lend a hand!" Clark looked right at her.

They helped raise the boat, and George tied the last knot to secure it.

"Get aft and lash down anything that's loose!" commanded Clark.

Normally ready to launch fully armed and fitted boats at a moment's notice, the ship was barred and tied down such that nothing could be dispatched. Men talked in low tense voices, some nervously, some with obvious excitement.

She paused next to Job. "Is all this necessary?"

"You will soon see."

"You worry me, Job."

"Oh, don't fret, my friend. A doubling of the Horn should not be taken lightly. But, if you must make this trip, it is best to do it on a whaler. We can handle gales and squalls much more efficiently than any merchant ship. You see, we carry more men on every watch. If anything serious happens, we can react more quickly. Of all whalers, you're on one of the best. Captain Sullivan has done this many times. Look about you; see how well he's prepared!"

§

"Do I detect some fear upon your face?" Job pulled his way along ropes to where George clung to the weather rigging.

"Perhaps a little. Reminds me of water in a pail that's being shaken." The ship dug its way up another watery mountain. "I don't want to go below for fear the ship will be buried by one of these seas." She gasped as her knuckles turned white. The masts groaned.

The harpooner moved calmly with the ship. "If such were to happen, it would make no difference where you were."

"I know that. It's just that the water—it's so violent. All I really want right now is to see the other side of the Horn. One day of this is more than enough."

Job's smile encouraged her. "Whaling is really one experience like this after another." He paused thoughtfully. "I suppose it's a lot like life."

She knew what he meant but was absorbed in the waters around them. As she held her breath, the ship slid down the backside of a wave. "My life has been one storm after another lately." She planted her feet as the ship rebounded from the trough. "Only it's been mostly down."

"It's the crises that let us see things in perspective. Don't let circumstances determine how you live." He smiled. "I want to hear what you think when we get to the Pacific. Life's good. Even in this stormy sea. The best thing for you would be to go below and get some sleep. You're going to have the next watch and it will go easier if you're rested."

Job was more a friend than she had ever had. Clutching the weather rigging and stumbling she slowly made her way to the companionway and down into the darkness.

§

Though he knew his voice could not overpower the wind and the sea, Joseph yelled a greeting to his friend. Job put his hand to his ear and shook his head. They shared a thumbs-up instead. Joseph felt safer knowing Job had the fore watch. He was a good friend and a great whaler. They both lived for the trials, the tribulations, and the excitement.

Joseph marveled at the sight around him. Straining from the yards, the swollen sails stirred the masts within a cold night sky. With the power it took from the wind, the *Mitchell* assaulted moving mountains of water found only here in all the oceans of the world. The moon shed an eerie light upon their path. Steel gray clouds flew overhead casting fleeting shadows upon the sea and the ship. These ghostly phantoms disappeared deep in the southern sky. In a world of their own, unaware of his ship struggling against the waves, they flew in their courses. He scanned the ship. All looked well.

Clark stood only a dozen feet away, leaning against the cookhouse. He watched the sky, a tense look upon his face. As officer of the deck, he had the responsibility of keeping the boat on course. In his hands were the life of the ship, and, therefore, the lives of all the men on board.

As the ship pulled up and broke through the top of a swell, Joseph thought he saw a tumbled confusion reflected in the moonlight above the horizon. Clark had seen it too and moved to the railing, staring into the dark. Before Joseph assured himself the vision was just spray and foam, the ship began its dive down the other side into a valley between two monstrous seas. When the bow plowed into the next swell and up, tons of water washed over the foredeck and out the scuppers.

He saw the squall just as it hit the ship. The boiling line of destruction screamed through the masts and yards. Snow and ice bit into Joseph's face. The ship rolled to port as the wind's first fury sought to pin its sails. The ropes and sails strained against the onslaught of the storm. The wind howled and screamed and tried to break his grip on the weather rigging.

Clark grabbed onto the cookhouse. "Let go topsail halyards. Hard up the wheel!"

Joseph's body tensed ready for action. He barely heard the commands, and his mind took seconds to process their meaning.

"Job! … Job, let go the topsail halyards." Clark continued shouting.

Joseph jumped to the wheel and leaned into it.

Howling wind whipped the peaks of the swells into white topped mountains. Yet, as the ship rolled farther onto its side, the water and the air next to the deck grew strangely calm. The hull of the turning ship protected it from the onslaught of the wind and seas. A shiver climbed Joseph's back as he recalled his uncle telling him that was the way with a drowning ship. Just feet away, the sails and the rigging groaned against a gale that sought to pound them into the water and bury them forever beneath the icy waves. Ice crystals whipped over the hull into the shelter of the deck. They eddied through the calmer air around the men like snow blowing over a tombstone and meandering in gentle paths to settle upon a grave.

The officers let loose the main and mizzen halyards and sheets, but the foremast was out of their reach. If sails were not freed there, the ship would die.

Job jumped to the companionway to keep from sliding down the deck. The lee rail moved closer and closer to a position directly below him. A few items that had not been adequately secured slid across the deck into the lowering bulwarks. If ever the goods stowed below as ballast shifted to the leeward hull, the ship would be lost along with all the men on board. Joseph yelled encouragement to his friend.

Gorham clung to the whaleboat at the tryworks. Others of the forward crew held onto the weather rigging and whatever else afforded a handhold to life, none willing to let go.

Again Clark yelled forward. "Let go the halyards! The halyards let them go or we'll surely die!"

No one but Job moved. He was in good position. Supported by the companionway, if he leapt onto the starboard side of the tryworks, he would have ready access to the halyards. The deck fell away below him now and the icy waters lapped at the leeward rail. He pulled his legs beneath him and prepared to jump.

Panic erupted within Joseph when he saw what Job did not. His friend was focused on the waves and debris; but, above him, a water cask was starting to slip. The bottom was not fastened tightly enough to handle such stress.

"Watch the cask!" yelled Joseph, just as Job began his leap.

The barrel hit his right shoulder and knocked him over the end of the companionway. Joseph stared, helpless, as his friend cried out and gripped the bow of a whaleboat. His heart sank when Job slid down the deck and into the lee bulwarks wet with ocean water. Protected by the foundering ship, the water was calm. But it had to be cold, so cold. As Job reached up toward the tryworks, Joseph's muscles tensed willing his friend to reach safety. But Job's arms fell short.

As a swell raised the water level, it lifted Job from the bulwarks. He must have grasped a rope; he pulled himself up and held most of his body out of the water that continually lapped over the rail. As the swell receded, the water sucked Job's body from the bulwarks and over the railing so that all his weight was held by his arms and shoulders.

§

Something was wrong. Shaken from her sleep, George braced herself to keep from being dumped out of her bunk. Often in rough seas, the ship lurched ungainly far onto its side. This was different. It wasn't righting itself. Its tilt continued as if in slow motion. She wrapped herself, fumbling with the ties in her haste. She pulled on only what was necessary—pants, blouse, and shoes—and slid down the deck onto the opposite bunks.

Job had told her it would make no difference where she was if the ship were to sink. But the last place she wanted to be was in the forecastle. Using her hands to hold her body from the deck, she half crawled and half stumbled toward the companionway ladder. Bunks opened like pits below her; chests littered her way; and men clung to whatever they could, some groaning, others crying in panic. The shrieking of the rigging and the trembling of the ship made the forecastle appear a haven. But not for her, not with what she feared was happening.

Using mostly her arms, she climbed up the ladder which now tilted ungainly to the side. A few steps up and George pushed open the hatch. With nearly as much confusion behind her as before her, she pulled herself onto the up-deck side of the companionway. Every muscle taught, she stared at Gorham. "What's happening?"

He grasped the weather rigging, a look of panic about him, and glanced quickly down.

Barely audible, Clark yelled through the storm. "Let go the halyards! We'll go down if you don't. Let go the halyards and haul up the main sails!"

Job clung to a rope, desperation on his face. Without hesitation, she descended toward her friend.

"No!" His voice was weak. "Get the halyards first. Save the ship!"

George hesitated. The Second Mate's voice was lost in the roar of the wind through the rigging.

"Go!"

Job's face and command left no other option. She pulled herself back onto the companionway and caught hold of the fife rail around the foremast. With her feet braced against the mast, she sprang toward the starboard side of the tryworks. Her hands just grasped the cooler. She hauled herself up the inclined deck and planted her feet upon the bulwarks. Reaching out, she cast the halyards and main tack from their pins. The foretopsail ran down and the maintack was let go, whipping in the wind with reports as loud as cannons. It quickly shredded, with pieces flying off and carried away by the storm. When the ship started to right itself, George jumped to the deck and slid to the port side to attend to Job. The rope was there, dangling over the railing, which had risen from the water, but Job was not.

"Job!" She slid down the deck to the bulwarks. The deck still remained sheltered, and the water was relatively calm next to the ship. Farther out, though, the storm whipped the tops of gigantic waves into a white froth. As the ship righted itself and the roar of the wind drowned out her calls for her friend, she turned and ripped hysterically at the ropes that bound one of the whaleboats to the tryworks. "Help me." She tried to overpower the storm as Oliver Fish weaved his way forward. "Job's been washed away." She tore at the ropes. They had to hurry.

"There's nothing to be done." His arms fought her. "It's too dark. The seas are too high."

The continuous thunder from the sails and the whine of the wind in the rigging confirmed his words, but George refused to hear. She wrestled against him. Joseph ran up.

"Help! Job's been washed overboard." Her insides exploded when her friend restrained her as well.

"Help him!" She beat Joseph's chest, her face wet with water and tears. "We've got to…"

"There's just nothing to be done, George." Joseph embraced her.

She screamed at him, and then collapsed into his arms, cold and sobbing. A sail ripped loose and was carried into the darkness.

§

The mates were enthralled with Gorham. "If Job hadn't tried, I'd have made for the halyards. I was just about ready when he moved." Then he talked about Job's fall and how he just couldn't quite reach him.

George wanted to scratch his eyes out. Job, her only real friend, had died, and now she was alone, abandoned. Yet the ship sailed on as if nothing had happened. He would never again hunt whales or sit at on the mast with her. She would not hear his laughter in the dogwatch. George didn't know what could be done, but this just wasn't right. Job loved whaling. He looked forward to the hunt to come and the ports they'd see. Now none of this would belong to him. Clouds overhead raced on blindly, and the ship sailed on uncaring. She knew the truth but doubted that she could argue sensibly about it.

As the ship heaved, bounced, fought up seas and slid down them, George made her way to the waist railing just aft of the tryworks. There she found some form of shelter away from the other sailors. Using her boots to keep her back to the bulwarks, she pulled her knees up to her chin and wrapped her arms around her calves. She raised the jacket over her ears, and the warmth of her body warmed her face. In the privacy of this empty little world within her jacket, sobs shook her.

§

Reaching down, Joseph touched George's shoulder. The harpooner knew the ache the boy must be feeling. He felt it too—the loss of a friend—as if he had been turned upside down, emptied out, and then discarded. There was not much to say at times like this, but it helped just having a friend nearby. He sat beside the lad.

The ship sank behind swells and rose abruptly up those ahead. Obliquely smashing into a wave, it lurched to the side. Joseph's firmly planted feet kept him in place. To keep the bulwarks from rapping his head, he leaned forward as a sail gave a loud slap. The wind groaned as it wound madly around the rigging, sails, and spars. Icy mist stuck to their jackets.

"Thou had a hard night."

George just nodded.

"Job was a good man. He lived a good life. He died doing what he loved."

The boy looked away, trembling.

"Dying is part of life. Thou can't have one without the other. It's never easy to understand, but thou wilt learn to accept it. It's part of growing up. It's part of God's plan." He put his arm about George.

The boy looked up and angrily pushed his arm off.

They sat a few more minutes. "Thou shalt see. Each day will be less painful, especially if thou dost let God help. I've had friends die, and I miss them all. But the loneliness, the emptiness—that need not linger. Jesus can fill that space left by Job's death."

"He can't fill me! You don't know what Job's death means." The words were broken. George sobbed.

Joseph had never seen a man act quite like this. Anger? Yes. Bitterness? Maybe. But so many tears? So much emotion? For hours? But George was just a boy. Yet, should the crew see this, the lad would be taunted for days to come.

A tint of orange squeezed its way onto the southeastern horizon. "Thou must know, George, a new day comes and the darkness of the night flees from it. So it will be with thee."

"I can't go on." The boy's words mixed with tears. "It's all I could do to stay till now. You and Tom have shown me kindness, but Job was more than just a mate."

Joseph wanted to be the boy's friend. If only the lad was more willing. "George, there's no going back. And deserting ship in the ports ahead of us would leave thee in a heathen world. And if thou art caught, the punishment is nigh unbearable. Besides, Tom and I cherish thy friendship."

"But, you judge me as a man; Job just accepted me. No one really understands me. I've got to get off."

"Why is that so important to thee now? Others like thee have made it through a voyage and become better men for doing so. And, believe me; the pain of the loss of Job will pass. Truly it will! We men are, in a way, brothers. Let us help."

George looked around the deck and then up into his eyes. "I'm going to tell you something." He wiped away some tears and took a deep breath. "Promise me you will tell no one what I am about to say."

Promises? Secrets? This was childish. He shook his head and said. "Whatever it is, thou canst tell me, George. I'm thy friend."

"I don't care, promise me."

"Okay, okay! I promise thee."

"Other men may have served on whaling ships, but none like me."

Joseph had seen all kinds of men. The boy may be a little emotional but, other than that, he wasn't so different. He waited for George to continue.

"I'm not George. I'm Rebecca Ann."

Did he say he was his sister? What did he mean by that? Foolish words. These would bring him trouble for sure. "Don't let Gorham hear thee say that or thou wilt surely be teased more than ever."

"No." George spoke firmly but not too loudly. "I AM Ann."

He was serious. "Thou art as much a man as I. We have lived with thee for nigh on three months."

The boy continued with a passion. "This is a secret I've well kept. Have I bathed on deck with the others? Have I used the head? Is my bunk uncovered?"

"But thou dost not even look the part of a woman. I don't know what thy reason might be for such nonsense, but speak thou the truth." Joseph felt an irritable anger toward the boy and didn't like it.

§

"Do you really think I am as obese as I appear?" The argument for her case was turning her mind off the problems of the moment. She continued with a purpose, though making sure that only Joseph heard her voice. "With Cook's food, do you think I'd remain as you see me?" She opened her jacket and pulled up her blouse, revealing the thick layer of canvas and cotton wound about her waist."

"But…" Her friend raised his eyes a little higher. "But…" He blushed.

"What binds my waist, can bind other things." She tucked her blouse back in her pants and closed her jacket. "Now remember your promise. No one must know."

"But a woman... Women can't serve on a whaler. It's too dangerous. Thou must tell the Captain. He'll put thee off. That's what thou wanted."

He was right. She had wanted off. In a way she still did. Yet, being able to share the burden of her secret with another person, helped. And, in a flash, the word hit her. Circumstances. You can't let circumstances determine how you live. That's what Job had said. He was right. Circumstances had caused her to give up on the hunt.

What did she really want? She wanted to find Caleb. She was still lonely. She mourned for her friend. She did not belong in this vulgar world. But, if the opportunity were presented to be put ashore, she would not take it. What had been most difficult about the past weeks was having no one with whom to share her deepest feelings and problems, at least no one who knew the truth about her. That was no longer the case.

And now Caleb was responsible for her suffering in the loss of her best friend, just one more reason to find that canal scum. Anger marched about her mind. Like the sun after a storm, it dried up her mourning.

He brings one loss upon another!

How true!

There is no good in Caleb!

Caleb would suffer as no man has suffered.

Leaving Joseph with a bewildered expression, George went below thinking about how she might exact revenge.

§

The evening of the first night in the Pacific, George took a pen, some ink, and a paper with her to the foretop and wrote:

> *I sit alone where we sat. I look for you. But you*
> *don't come. No longer do you take away my problems. And*
> *so my pain stays. What can I do now without you here?*

George reached up and wiped her eyes, a tear marking the words.

> *All I want is to climb the rigging with you just one
> more time. I would give anything to work the tops with you
> again. Instead I sit alone. I can feel you behind me, but
> when I look it's just another mate.*
>
> *Did you know I came back for you? It wasn't but a
> minute. If only you could have held on.*
>
> *They tell me the water cask hit you, the one I
> helped secure to the bulwarks. If only I'd checked the
> lashing when Gorham was finished. I'm so sorry, and I
> miss you so much.*
>
> *The last 3 days have been impossible. You were
> always there for me when I needed someone. Joseph has
> not talked with me since I told him my secret. So, I'm alone.
> I don't know as I can take much more of this. I fear living
> in a man's world will be my undoing.*
>
> *Oh, that you were here. I see your face in the
> passing clouds. I hear your voice on the wind. I expect you
> to be there when I turn. Yet I know we shall never climb
> again.*
>
> *I miss you.*
>
> *Goodbye, my friend. In God's hands may you find
> what you sought here.*

Her nose ran and her eyes filled as she folded it and stuck it in her blouse. Her mind stirred anger and sorrow into an abysmal concoction. She craved justice, and she ached from her inside out. George didn't want to think; she didn't want to move. She just stared at the deck below her.

A handful of men by the main hold threw out fishing lines and cleaned the next day's supper. Intercepting the heads and tails before they could be tossed overboard, Peleg mysteriously wrapped them in a small piece of canvas.

Night came again but not relief.

§

He's a she. George is Ann. For three months, George was a boy to him. Now he says he's a woman. He looked at the boy—the girl—and a knot grew in his gut. George lived a lie. Joseph wanted to help the boy, but how could he help the girl who misled him, pretending to be something she was not. She lied to the whole crew, to the Captain. *She still lies!*

His duty was to tell Captain Sullivan, to warn of problems. What bigger problem could there be than to have a woman serving as a whaler? But he had promised. The knot grew a little bigger.

But, if the boy needed help, how much more the girl! How much greater the danger now, to her and to the crew! But she saved the ship. Had she not been on board, they would probably all be dead. But a woman!

George stood at the railing watching the huge white birds that floated above the ship.

"Gooneys." He joined her.

She stared at the majestic creatures.

It was difficult just to talk to her. "Better known by land-lovers as albatross."

Peleg took the bundle from his shirt. He reached back in and pulled out those heads and tails that had slipped out while stored next to his skin. Setting them all on the carpenter's bench, he picked a couple of heads and tied one at each end of a four-foot string.

When two birds approached the ship, he tossed the string as far out as he could. First one bird flew down and caught a head in his mouth and then the other did the same. Immediately, a tug-o-war began as the two of them each sought to leave with its prize. Eventually, the weaker of the birds was forced to disgorge its dinner as the stronger flew off with a head dangling behind it from a string held in its mouth. Peleg and most of the crew on deck laughed hysterically.

Without a word, George left Joseph and ran to the forecastle, returning with a spool of string and a hook.

§

When had he grown so old? Peleg's fingers ran the string through the gills and tied a knot around the lower jaw. He could tie a fish head to string but his eyes were too weak for much finer work. His heart told him he was young, but his body told him something else. Peleg saw the scars on his arms and remembered other voyages, other adventures. He tied a head to the other end of the string, shaking his right arm to relieve a pain he had suffered with for over a week. Then he rubbed the bruise.

Mates used to praise his strength and prowess in hunting whales. Now he tossed heads to gooneys for attention. But, that wasn't so bad. He had friends on the ship.

"Peleg."

The boy's voice sent chills up his back. For some reason, when Johnson talked, snippets of a life long over bounced about in his brain, faded pictures, fuzzy thoughts of a woman he hated. Such visions were not new, but this was the first voyage where a mate caused them.

Life was lived according to a pattern. Each day should have a sense of familiarity. Then the end could be assured. But when things didn't add up, when life didn't feel right, then danger was near.

And something about George just wasn't right. Whenever he was around, life did not fit the patterns. As long as the boy was on board, the hunt was in jeopardy.

"Can I have one of those heads?"

The voice grated on him. His mates said that the boy hit him with an oar, which was why his right arm ached. He didn't remember it. But, it didn't surprise him. The boy was trouble for sure. He tossed a head. Maybe, the pest would go away.

Instead, Johnson fastened it to the hook on his line.

That was something Peleg hadn't seen before, just one more unpredictable aspect of life on the Mitchell now.

Tom came up and leaned against the railing. "What are you going to fish for?"

"Gooneys."

The boy unwound a length of line as the regal birds circled the ship. When one came lower, he threw out the bait. The line retreated from the loops on the deck. Pulling in the excess, he wrapped it around his hand. Almost before the head hit the water, an albatross swooped down and picked it up. With a jerk of its head, it moved the bait to the rear of its mouth. When George set the hook, the startled bird took to flight only to find it could not leave. As it flew up, tension on the line pulled it back. Flopping between water and air, the bird was drawn slowly and steadily toward the ship.

Not a good omen. No, siree.

Mates cheered and laughed as George stoically pulled in his catch. The gooney tried to dislodge the head but the hook held firm in its beak. Flying right and left, up and down, it soon found the string too short for flight. Quickly, George wrapped its bill with string and held its wings and body under his arm.

"What are you going to do with it?"

"Let's try eating it."

"Better'n Cook's food I wager."

"Put it in the cages."

"Cut it up for bait."

The boy ignored the comments and walked forward to the windlass.

"Not proper on a whaler." Peleg grumbled but no one listened to him. *Something's just not right with him. No, siree.* Tying two more heads to a string, he threw them out to the hungry birds.

§

"That's just whalers talking." George stroked the bird. "You'll be fine."

It fought against her arms, and the warmth beneath the wings felt good. The sun reflected from its unspotted whiteness. With its hooked, Roman bill, it had a royal appearance. "Gooney" just didn't fit it.

Sitting beside her, Tom reached out to pet the albatross.

"Can you hold it for me?"

He put an arm around where George's had been.

She retrieved the letter from her blouse and folded it into a small parcel about three inches long and half an inch wide. Cutting a piece of line hanging from the bird's beak, she tied the note onto one of its legs.

She looked up at Tom. "This is for Job."

"What is it?"

"A letter." Her voice broke. "I would like to talk...."

"I know what you mean." Tom reached out and softly touched her shoulder. "We all miss him."

"I never really said goodbye. Maybe this bird can take it where I can't go." She took the bird back under her arms and carefully undid the string around its bill, cutting it where it entered the mouth. Holding the bill shut with one hand, she gently set the bird onto the ship's head. At intervals it arched its great wings with regal trembling and flurries. With cries of supernatural distress, it lurched from the bow of the ship in an arc toward the water below and then rose on majestic wings, effortlessly carried heavenward. Higher and higher it flew as if it knew it had a message to deliver. Higher and higher until it became a mere spec of white against blue and then disappeared altogether. As the albatross vanished, she wanted to think it emerged in the presence of God and her one real friend. George looked forward so no one could see her face.

"Goodbye, Job." She casually wiped her eyes.

Tom's strong arm wrapped around her shoulder and part of her burden was lifted. He was someone who shared in the loss. She laid her head against Tom's shoulder and, for a moment at least, all was OK.

§

What's he doing? A rush of blood washed over Tom's face as he looked around the deck to see if any mates were looking. A man doesn't put his head on another man's shoulder like some woman that needs comforting. In an awkward gesture, he raised his arm from George's shoulder. *Most emotional boy I've seen.* He patted him. *To act like this he must really hurt.* Finally, he lowered his arm and consoled George, regardless who might see.

Peleg looked up. "What's with them two?"

Another sailor looked up. "That ain't right."

Tom squirmed.

"Let them be!"

Good, Joseph discouraged them.

"Sh...He lost his friend, and Tom's just trying to help him through it."

"Never mind that. Tain't fitting for mates to act that way."

Clark walked into the confrontation. "Don't be provoking the men. You know better than that, Peleg. George just lost a friend, so leave him be. Besides, the boy did more than all the rest of you in keeping us from getting deep sixed."

Peleg scowled. "Still not right. Nothing normal about that. No, siree."

Juan Fernandez Island

Friday, February 23, Day 77

"Slush … the … mast!" Clark cupped his hands around his mouth so that Jamie could hear him over the creaking of the ropes and slap of the sails.

Jamie did not look down, but stared straight ahead, clinging to the wood. With his right arm clutching the mast close to his chest, his left arm felt about his waist for the bucket.

From the safety of the deck, George enjoyed this new adventure; that's what the Second Mate called it. She had experienced enough of these "new adventures" and was happy to see this one from the deck. Since the Horn, life was better. Sure, she would be given this job sometime; but, at least now, she was not singled out.

Jamie stood at the top of the mainmast and Tom at the top of the foremast. Jamie was the most fun to observe given that he hated heights. Dipping his brush in the slush, he carefully moved it up as high as he could. It must have been loaded, since large droplets splattered across the sails and rigging. Staring straight ahead, Jamie moved the brush up and down around the mast. Stopping to wipe something from his face, he ended up jerking and twisting his head and ejecting morning's breakfast across his arms and down into the sea. He never looked down.

George laughed at the thought that he probably ended up painting the slush on his face. "Is this slush only used to aggravate the common hands?"

Joseph casually rested his forearm on the railing. "More often than not. Cook saves all the grease from cooking and there's far more than we can use. In the days ahead, we'll sell the excess."

"You mean people actually want the slush?"

Joseph nodded. "And the money is kept in a fund to buy miscellaneous items the crew might need as the voyage progresses."

When Jamie and Tom finished slushing the upper mast, they each sat in a sling and the crew lowered them by ropes so they could apply it to the masts on the way down.

"Thou dost still look a little melancholy. Dost thou miss Job?"

"It's not gotten any easier to accept. How is it you've gotten over his death so quickly? You worked with him and bunked with him. Surely, he was a good friend."

"Oh, I miss him. And it does hurt when I think about it. But I have a friend who helps me along the way."

George looked up wondering who in the crew he was talking about.

"Jesus, George. He helps me through these times. I mourn Job's loss, but Jesus lets me know it's OK. I don't feel so alone. The Bible tells me that all things work together for good to those who love Him."

She shook her head. Even if God were up there somewhere, he was never close enough for her to feel him. Certainly, he had never helped her through anything. She turned her attention back to the masts. Hanging from the rope, about half way down the mast, Tom was much further along than Jamie and much more at ease.

Can you see Caleb at the end of that rope? The thought left a bitter taste in her mouth as she pictured him hung there, suffering. Then she pictured Tom and a warmer feeling pushed out the anger. At least she had one friend in the forecastle.

"George." Joseph interrupted her. "Thou dost suddenly have a happier look about thee. Dost thou think of what I said?"

Had he said something? What? Oh, that Jesus stuff. Clearing her throat, she looked at the harpooner and smiled. "Uh, a little I suppose." Excusing herself, she went to see if she could help on the ropes.

§

"Land, ho!"

"Where away?"

"Starboard bow."

Now a man short, the Captain stopped at Juan Fernandez to find a replacement. A variety of huts and cottages dotted the shore, nearly a hundred of them. The best looked like those on the Azores, built of mud. Some were whitewashed. However, most were made of posts and branches of trees. On the south side of the harbor was the governor's house with large, grated windows, plastered walls, and a roof of red tiles.

Joseph didn't believe in chance. God's hand controlled everything. Every port held something new, something exciting. Expectation kept him from a fitful sleep.

In the morning, he told the crew what the officers said. They would be in port but one day and would weigh anchor after the First Mate secured another crewman. The next news unsettled his stomach. A rogue ship was in the region. They would all need to be back by the end of the afternoon watch, which gave them seven hours.

Until then, they could follow him inland in search of caves used as a prison when Spain owned Juan Fernandez. Or they could go with Mr. Clark on a hunting expedition, which would start at the cave of Alejandro Selkirk, the original Robinson Crusoe. Those with the Second Mate might explore around the cave or hunt with him. Some, of course, would stay in the port of Cumberland. In such ports, entertainment of every kind was available.

Tom aligned himself with Mr. Clark's expedition. "Hunting sounds great."

Gorham and others followed them back to the boats.

Joseph's gut relaxed at least a little when George decided on the hike. He would be able to keep an eye on her. Jamie and Charlie joined them.

"What's a rogue ship?" she asked.

"Pirates."

§

A small stream of water meandered through the town and emptied into Cumberland Bay. It rippled over gravel and rocks, swirling into small pools behind large stones. Children played in the water. The only concern the youngsters had was that a friend might splash them. Women nearby washed clothes and laughed. The chattering, though in words she could not understand, rang with familiarity. No such sound was found on a ship full of men.

With a longing that would not be fulfilled, she hurried on, aware of a sweet scent in the air. Staring at the trees and bushes, she breathed deeply again and again. A mixture of scents, some pungent, some sweet, some more subtle and yet more startling than any perfume she had smelled, tenderly attacked her senses.

When barking dogs accosted the unfamiliar men, Jamie stooped and held out a hand to one of the mangier in the pack. It licked his hand and he scratched behind its ear. "Think I'll call him Nep."

"Just keep him downstream from me." George knelt for a drink. So sweet, so good. The gradual decline in the water quality on the ship had masked its true condition.

The smells, the taste, the beauty, and the children's laughter…the island exposed her reality. The men around her praised the salty smell of the sea. They could have it. Give her this instead.

The path they followed veered up and away from the creek, over a small rise, leaving the view of the village behind. The land ahead blended into the side of a mountain that towered three thousand feet into the sky. The sound of frogs and crickets, and the impression of trees closing in around her, created a peculiar sensation. Things taken for granted before were new and refreshing. A small waterfall cascaded down a hill in the distance. She stopped and let her senses revel in the beauty.

While her mates hurried up the path, Joseph slowed and waited where the trail lost itself in the woods. Removing his Bible from his blouse, he pulled out a folded paper, opened and read it. With all but Joseph hidden from view, she picked blossoms, cradled them in her palm, and sniffed. Then she did what she couldn't do on board ship, she fit one blossom behind her ear and was, for a brief moment, a woman again. With a sigh, she walked on toward Joseph and let the flower lie in the dirt where it had fallen from her hair.

He folded the paper and put it inside the front cover of his Bible, something George had seen him do many times.

"What IS that?"

"This?" Joseph lifted the cover and pulled the paper out again. "Before any voyage, my wife gives me a note reminding me of our love. This time my sons wrote as well. It's the hardest thing I've ever done, walking away from them to a boat that would take me to a ship for a three-year voyage apart." He carefully replaced it.

"But you're so happy here."

"That's the odd thing about this life. I say goodbye to one family and say hello to another. Few men will understand or experience the wonder, the excitement, and the camaraderie of this life. I love it and live for the hunt. Yet I love Nantucket and live for it as well. This paper…" He patted his Bible. "…reminds me of that. I keep it here because it is God that will guide me and bring us back together."

§

"Take the stroke position." Clark nodded at Tom. "Andrews, you move back."

Other men with more experience were there. Surely one of them deserved the stroke position, the seat nearest the officer. But Tom obeyed, stepping around a red-faced Gorham. He had grabbed that thwart while Tom offered to help the Second Mate pack his gun and ammunition. A number of the crewmen exchanged whispers.

With a breeze from aft, they set the boat's canvas and enjoyed a summer sail out of Cumberland Bay and up the coast.

§

George stood in the crevice, about three feet above the ground. Her right hand stung from a scrape and her left pant leg had a rip across the knee. She grunted as she stretched her left hand up to the next handhold.

She ignored the roar of the water as it tumbled down a fifteen-foot drop onto rocks and into a dark pool. Securing her grip on the outcropping, she moved her right foot up, feeling for something to support it. There, a crevice. Gingerly, she added weight to the foot. It slipped. She groaned.

Nep barked incessantly from above them, and Jamie excitedly urged them to hurry. She just wanted them to be quiet.

Moving her foot again, this time higher, she hauled herself closer. Joseph held down his hand and offered to pull her the rest of the way. She shook her head. He knew better than to do that. Joseph backed up and waited.

With her forearms on loose gravel and her feet holding on opposite sides of the crevice, she inched her way higher to where her waist was almost at the ledge. She started to bend forward when her right foot slipped. She gasped as a rock dug into her knee. Sharp pebbles picked at her arms as she began a downward slide.

Joseph reached out and grabbed her. "I know thou dost need to prove thyself. But there are times when a helping hand should be taken."

Ignoring his comments, she walked off with him following. A bare-chested Jamie met them on the trail and waved excitedly at them. The farther they got from the falls, the louder came the laughing and yelling of the crew. Taking off his remaining clothes, he faced them stark naked. "Come on! I've been waiting for you."

Don't look so embarrassed, she thought. The sight was common enough on board the ship.

Voices encouraged them to hurry.

"Water's great!"

"Get rid of the smell!"

"Whoooeeee!"

Jamie gingerly ran down the bank and dove into the water.

Joseph looked at George; George looked at Joseph.

"Joseph!" Jamie wiped water from his face. "Get on in here. It's great."

"What are you waiting for?" Charlie motioned Joseph to hurry. "George's modesty ain't growing on you, is it?"

George looked down. Joseph stood still.

"Uh, I, uh."

George started walking. "I think I'll go on up a piece and wait."

§

Joseph wavered but a moment between the inviting pool and worry about George. The swim was as refreshing as he expected. But, though he was the last in the pool, he was still the first to start again up the path; he didn't like leaving George alone in the woods on a strange island. About fifty yards into the dense underbrush, the trail came to a grassy clearing. He took a seat on the bank and watched her wade with rolled up pant legs.

As she walked slowly through the water, he tried to picture her wearing women's clothes. It struck him, her face was appealing. Now, her features were delicate, not youthful. The easy smile, the dark eyes, the color of roses that brown skin could not hide—George was pretty. He shook his head as if that would clear away such notions. It made him uneasy to see a mate in that light. In so many ways, George was still a boy to him.

But she was a woman. A woman who had faced a whale and worked in the blubber hold. She climbed the rigging. She labored and ate with whalers. She was a whaler. What woman could do these things? He tried to picture his wife standing before him in this creek. It was a vision too incongruous. Here was a female who had dressed as a man and in many ways became more man than woman. She had accomplished so much, but at what cost!

If it were within his power to make things right for George, he would do so in an instant. How she must hurt! How she must suffer! He wanted to take away her every pain. He prayed for his mate, for the woman who walked toward him in a whaler's garb.

She sat on the bank. "You know, I'm awful tempted to hide up here in the hills and let the *Mitchell* sail without me." Her voice was soft now, not a boy's voice.

"'Tis a beautiful island but thou don't even speak the language."

"I know, I know. Still, it's tempting."

"I can tell the Captain if thou wish. I'm sure he'd put thee ashore. He's already looking for one replacement." Though his voice said he was kidding, he hoped she would agree.

"You promised."

Joseph nodded. He wanted her off the ship; but, even more, he wanted to help her overcome the anger and bitterness that drove her to...this. No, the Captain wouldn't find out from him.

"But, if not for the prospect of finding Caleb, I'd truly consider your telling him." She paused thoughtfully. "And, I suppose, you and Tom keep me from that decision as well."

"What thinkest thou of Tom?" Since Job's death, she had taken advantage of opportunities to talk with the farmer. How did she view this man who would be her comrade?

George smiled and looked down. "My only friend in the forecastle. Someone I can talk to, like I did with Job. He understands me even though he doesn't know me."

What was that look on her face? Was she blushing? Perhaps a good bit of woman still lingered inside this female whaler after all.

"Don't know if I could handle being there alone."

Life in the forecastle was hard for a man. For George, it must be nearly unbearable. "I'm surprised thou hast taken to the *Mitchell* so well. But thou dost play a dangerous game here. Thy life hangs by a thread. Tom and I care about thee, but we could be removed as quickly as Job. Of a truth, George, thou ought to put thy confidence in God."

"Why do you keep after me?"

"Jesus is important to me. I would like Him to be important to thee. Thy greatest joy would be to forgive and go home."

"I know you mean well, but I'd rather you drop it. I told you the truth. I have no home. In my parents' eyes, I'm nothing. And what man would want me now?"

"That has not yet been determined, George. Thou art special in God's eyes."

"What happened to me has brought me to where I am. Even before Caleb, I was nothing in my father's eyes. What hope is there for such a one as me?"

"There is always hope in God."

"If that's so, let your God straighten out my life and make it new."

She spat upon the ground. "Caleb. He's the one to blame."

"George, listen to me. Thy life need not be this way!"

"Joseph, Friend." She looked into his eyes. "I tried to go back and was turned away. With long hair and petticoats I tried to find acceptable work. But to any woman without a man, and especially to one as ruined as me, there is no living to be made, at least not one to which I will stoop. This life I live is the only life left for me, because of one man. Whether here or on the Canal or somewhere else, I have been doomed by Caleb to live life as a man."

"Thou hast chosen this life. Look beyond the hurt and disappointments." To his ears, she sounded as harsh as any bitter man. "There IS a way. God always gives a way."

"I think not for me." She looked off into the distance and then asked, "Why is it you Friends speak differently from everyone else, using the ye's, thee's, thou's, and such?"

"Still thou art not willing to discuss thy plight," said Joseph, shaking his head. Taking a deep breath, he let it out slowly. "As I have told thee before, the Inner Light is within us. We consider all men as worthy. We never want to present ourselves as more important than others. The word 'you' can demean the other person in tone. 'Thee' and 'thou' will never do that."

She laughed.

"What's so funny?"

"I just remembered some of the quarrels with my father. How ridiculous his rants would have sounded in your words!"

"Some Friends also change other words to separate us from the common world."

"Maybe that's why you're so easy to get along with."

"Even though I question thy motives?"

"Even so."

"Why the interest in how I talk?"

"Haven't you ever wondered something about someone but never knew him well enough to ask about it? Well, I've heard Friends before and wondered about their use of words, just never was close enough to one to ask."

"To live life as a man, there will be things about thee that will raise questions. Wilt thou not be close to any so that none may ask them?"

Before George could answer, laughing and jesting echoed up the path. Clean...and clothed...men plopped themselves onto the bank beside them.

"Missed a great time," said Charlie.

"Would have been better had those ladies from the Falklands joined us, eh George?" said Jamie.

She blushed and looked down.

Jamie smacked her across the shoulder. "You almost had your chance in the Falklands. Name was Meg, wasn't it?"

"She did have her eye on you." Charlie leaned back sucking on a blade of grass.

Others laughed and teased the boy. They would help their friend become a man.

Joseph listened and wondered at the upside-down life George was living.

§

Where the valley floor began a sharp rise, they came across a clearing. A large black hole recessed deep into the rock, one of the prison caves. George stood in silence, imagining what it must have been like to be a guard, or a prisoner. Remnants of a fire ring, old wooden bars, and something round and gray littered the ground. She picked up the lead bullet and rolled it around her palm. This relic of violence was so out of place. The island lay in near idyllic beauty. Yet, here was a different scene from the past, one of suffering and violence. She held its evidence in the palm of her hand and saw it on the ground around her. How could Juan Fernandez have harbored such things?

Farther on, through a thin stand of trees, the ground fell steeply down to the crashing ocean below. The distant thunder of breakers echoed upward. This had been more than just a good jail cell; it also provided a lookout over a large portion of the surrounding water. She scanned the horizon, as the guards must have done a quarter century earlier. Smoke! A fire on the water! A whale ship! Which one was having good fortune here? As she considered the ship and who might be on it, Jamie came up beside her.

"Think it's him?"

She nodded, not wanting to take her eyes off the distant plume of smoke. "So near."

"Do you think Captain Sullivan will gam with the *Mystic*?"

"I think he would avoid her just to thwart my hunt."

"We're here for whales." Joseph startled her. "Thou dost know that. It's NOT that the Captain is against thee. He's just FOR his hunt."

"Would he hesitate to speak with the *Planter*? I dare say he'd go out of his way for a gam with your uncle's ship!"

§

George was probably right, and Joseph still hoped to see his Uncle Isaac on this trip. When Joseph shipped on the *Mitchell,* Isaac's wife and children had come to the wharf and stood with his own family. A whaler's wife was a hard calling. Joseph promised them, if he should find the *Planter*, he would remind Isaac of the family that anxiously awaited his return. Joseph had an ache inside him, an unfulfilled desire to embrace him.

Charlie came out of the cave. "What have we here? Trying smoke on the horizon! 'Tis Caleb, I wager. 'Tis Caleb indeed! If Captain Sullivan should see, surely you'll be a-hunting your prey tomorrow!"

"So, you think he'd gam with the *Mystic*?" asked Jamie.

"If there's whales being taken, that's where he'll be wanting to go."

Joseph shook his head. Foolishness! Dangerous in view of the Captain's warning to George.

"You know," said Jamie quietly, "the best hunt of all would be to find whales AND to help right the wrong done to Ann."

"Imagine his face when he sees Ann's revenge out here on the Pacific grounds!" Charlie nearly bounced with excitement.

To Joseph's chagrin, Charlie's enthusiasm caught on.

"Cut him in!"

"Try him out!"

"Throw 'is carcass overboard!"

Everyone laughed, except Joseph. Their encouragement would do nothing but hinder George's redemption.

§

A crack like thunder resounded and another bird fell from the sky into a thicket about thirty yards ahead of them.

"Great shot!" On the frontier, hunting was more than a sport, and Tom appreciated when someone did it well.

"Where did you learn to shoot?" The steady hand, his focus along the barrel, the slow squeeze of the trigger—Mr. Clark took pride in his hunting.

"Lots of practice. Had a captain once that taught me the basics then sent me out in every port we came to. Didn't like fish. He wanted land meat."

Gorham scrambled into the thicket and came back with one more bird hanging from his fist. He carried four and Tom three.

They walked quietly so as not to scare the birds too early. Gorham stopped and pointed. On the hillside, about fifty yards ahead was a wild goat watching them curiously.

Mr. Clark took aim, then lowered the gun and offered it to Gorham. "You spied it."

With controlled excitement, Gorham took the weapon, aimed, and ever so gently squeezed the trigger. Again the thunder clapped. The goat jumped straight up, then fell to the ground.

"Now that was a great shot!" said the Second Mate.

Gorham's face was one big smile.

"You got him. You fetch him."

The sailor ran off leaping over brush and rocks.

"You know, we need another harpooner."

Tom nodded. "There's been talk around the crew as to who he'll be."

"So, what does the crew think?"

"Some say Dennison may get the opportunity. Others think Mr. Wood is looking for one back at Cumberland Bay. I even heard that Peleg was in the running."

The Officer laughed. "It's an honored position with a lot of responsibility."

"Someone said if a man is picked for that position and, early on, mishandles the iron, he can ruin any chance for another try or any promotion."

"That's true."

Gorham held up the goat, each arm holding a back leg, and shook it in victory. They yelled their praises as Gorham started back.

Mr. Clark turned back to Tom. "Who do you think will be picked?"

He had no idea. "There are a few men in the crew that I think have whaled long enough to deserve a try."

"We don't pick a harpooner based on how long they've served. It's based on strength, on their eye, and on courage. Of all the men in the crew, I do believe you to be the most qualified."

Tom didn't know what to say. The Officers had given no indication, nothing.

"Close your mouth before something flies in." The Second Mate laughed. "Even the Captain has seen it in you. We're going to give you the opportunity. That is, if you want it."

Tom did enjoy learning the finer points of whaling but missed his fields and streams. "Sir, you know I've not voiced an interest to continue whaling after this voyage."

"If you are successful on this trip alone, the choice would be a good one. And, who knows, perhaps you'll decide to re-sign." Mr. Clark smiled, obviously pleased. "If you do become harpooner, you'll have a bunk aft."

Removing from the forecastle would certainly be a blessing.

"We'll leave it to the Captain to make the final pick and announce it. Just wanted you to know."

§

The mates joked about different ways to make Caleb suffer; some made George blush. None the less, she accepted their encouragement with enthusiasm. As they walked up the path, the command to stop such talk hung on the tip of Joseph's tongue. He just couldn't give it.

"Look." George pointed. "The smoke's almost gone."

That stopped him in his tracks. "What?"

"The try smoke. It's nearly disappeared."

That shouldn't be! If a ship were trying a whale, the smoke would be visible for more than a day. He strained his eyes and saw just a faint wisp of gray that could have passed for nothing more than a small cloud.

"I don't think that came from a tryworks." Joseph gazed intently at the horizon. Only hours before, black smoke had hung there. "I'd say 'twas an ill omen. Whaling ships can catch fire. And, when they do, with all the oil they carry, they quickly become a blaze upon the water." Joseph made a point to mark its position with respect to main features on the island. "We should start down, now!" Along the opposite coast, a lone whaleboat pulled for Cumberland Bay with the hunters and explorers. The Second Mate would probably beat them back.

§

In Cumberland, the harpooner made straight for one of the boats that the cook had filled with melons, apples, cherries, and vegetables. As the other men followed, George held back. She had questions to ask. Women and children worked around small homes. Men mended nets and worked on boats at the water's edge. Her first thought was to go to the women and children. But that had not worked on the Azores.

"Por favor." She cautiously approached three of them. With signing, simple English, and a few words of Spanish, she asked if they had seen a man with a scar.

They showed little understanding and even less interest in helping. When she pulled out her pouch of tobacco, their faces brightened. One called to a friend and, after some discussion, indicated that, yes, they had seen such a man.

Hope beyond reason! She had not expected this.

"That man. He try to take woman. Good woman. No good, that man!"

"George!" Jamie and Gorham ran up the beach toward her with Peleg walking behind.

She ignored them and tried to find out how long ago they had seen him.

"George, come on! We've got to go."

What were the men saying? She needed to know.

Jamie grabbed her arm. "George! Now! They want us aboard." He pulled her away as the fishermen were still trying to explain what they knew.

He had been here. She tossed them the pouch.

§

Peleg wondered what had interested George. Hanging back with Gorham, he watched them split the reward. They were quite excited about their profit and called another man over.

"Sir!" The new man spoke excellent English. "Mi amigos tell me that your young friend was asking about a man with a scar on his face. My brother tends the restaurant in town and told me about just that man. He hunted whales. He drank too much and caused many problems in the restaurant. He came in two times in the past month. The last time was two days ago. His ship left for a long trip north. Please tell your young friend that information."

"Don't tell Johnson." Peleg hurried toward the boats with Gorham. This would be fun. Besides, the boy's hunt was a bad thing.

Gorham nodded and followed like a puppy dog.

"What were they talking about?" asked George.

"Nothing. No, siree. Just wanted to thank you for the tobacco."

§

The last boat returned to the village to pick up the remaining men. Emptiness had settled in her chest. She just didn't have enough time to get the information she wanted. But recounting the beauty of Juan Fernandes raised her spirits at least a little.

In a great self-proclaimed fanfare, Peleg found his way to a seat bragging about what he'd done to a woman he'd met.

Laughing about something, Gorham took up his oar.

Jamie scratched behind Nep's ear, waded out, and took his seat. Whining from shore, Nep watched his master cross a barrier he could not pass.

The dog paced back and forth, staring at the boat and barking. "Jamie, how could you leave Nep with just a pat on the head? He loved you. He still watches."

Jamie looked up and shrugged. "Just a dog. Fun for the day."

The wind picked up with a distressful howl across Cumberland Bay.

Rescue

Sunday, February 25, 1849, Day 79

Night's curtain fell like a mask of death. Joseph stared toward a dark horizon, guilt and hope stirring within him like oil and water. Should he expect a ship's debris…perhaps survivors? Or should he wish that nothing be found? But if there were no fire and no men to rescue, then he was wrong. The Captain would not think less of him should the night pass uneventful. But this was taking time from hunting whales and had caused the ship to leave the island still a man short. He had convinced the Captain to sail early and look for survivors. What if the fire was something else? It had been obvious as he watched from Juan Fernandez. Yet, in the darkness of the night, doubts formed. He would not wish any whale ship to suffer such an end, but he wanted his interpretation to be confirmed. Unsubstantiated claims might lead to his word being respected less. Feeling like a scale that would not balance, he looked into the darkness.

Not a word was spoken. This fate could be theirs. The ship tacked, crossing back and forth over where he thought the smoke originated. The sliver of a new moon had sunk below the horizon over an hour earlier and stars provided only limited light upon the waters.

"Halloooo!" A light shone from lanterns at each of the mastheads and lit up the faces of the men positioned beside them. Like unkempt angels these mates glowed in the shadows above the deck.

§

With the black of night hovering about her, George stood at the main top. Hugging the mast, just above the bottom sail, she stared into a star-filled sky and searched for shadows on the sea.

"Hallooooo!"

A chill went up her back. She lived aboard a ship whose decks were soaked in oil. Its cargo consisted of oil. This oil lit streets and homes; it burned fierce and efficiently. What would happen to men caught below as fire engulfed the forecastle companionway? What would happen as the barrels burst into flames? How long would the *Mitchell* stay afloat? How hot would it become? And how quickly? She could just as easily suffer the same end as those for whom she scanned the darkness. She stirred restlessly upon the spar.

But who would really care should she perish in some tragedy on the sea? To her father she was as good as dead. She had never been of much importance to him. He told her she had little to offer outside the home.

"Hallooooo!"

She thought of Job clinging to a rope for life, an image she would like to forget. It should have been her. Little the loss if she had died; great the loss of him. A storm caused his death. Joseph might even call it an act of God. The ship could be blown aground. A storm could sink it. A monster from the depths might wrap it in its arms and pull it below the surface of the sea. A whale, such as sank the Essex, could attack them. She thought of any number of possible ways a ship might be stove. No matter how many precautions they took, these things remained outside of her control.

What hope is there when we live and die at the hands of both man and God?! She looked all the harder. Perhaps finding a crewman would make her feel better.

"Barrel to starboard!"

A large oil barrel floated high in the water about twenty yards from the ship. Men gathered at the bulwarks, some pointing it out to others. With renewed excitement, she returned to watching for survivors.

"Light to starboard, Captain." The watch at the main masthead had seen something.

A light twinkled on the water like a star, "I see it too!" yelled George. "And a boat with it!"

"Hallooooo!!"

"Hard down your wheel!" The Captain leaned over the bulwarks. "Haul aback the main yard!"

George climbed to the deck and helped bring the ship to a stop. Four dimly lit figures rowed in the light of the boat's lantern. Why had no one spotted it earlier?

One man remained at the main masthead manning the lantern. "Hallooo!"

Like everyone else, George remained absolutely still straining to hear a reply.

"Hallooo!" The cry was a distant echo.

A cheer arose from the crew of the *Mitchell*; the boat's light went out; and the crew quieted.

"She still comes," called the watch. "I can just make her out."

The Captain came forward and paced back and forth, his concern obvious.

The boat drew closer and became clearly visible from the deck. "Douse your light! Pirates be near!"

The lanterns were put out.

Four men hauled themselves up to the deck.

The Captain ordered all sails set. Whaling ships seldom traveled at night, and, when they did, rarely under a full sail. Whalers had whatever time it took to get to wherever they were going. Whales were the destination, not a place. With extreme care and in complete silence the *Mitchell* sailed swiftly away. This raised a queasy trembling in George's chest.

The man in charge on the boat was the first mate on the ship that sank. While he, the Captain, and Will Wood went aft, the other three men sat around the windlass with the crew of the *Christopher Mitchell*. George stayed in the back.

"It were pirates that done us in."

"Didn't recognize them."

"Half full o' oil, we was."

"Pirates, who would think it, today?"

"They shot us up. Some of our mates hid below. Others took irons and lances to try to protect the ship. The Captain, he took out the few arms we had and gave them to the Officers. But we were no match for them. They had guns and swords...Ain't supposed to be pirates no more."

"Total confusion, it was. Had a barrel of sperm coolin' in a kettle. Hadn't been stowed below. It spilled in the fighting."

"Don't know how it started. But fire spread over the deck. The men hiding below had no chance. The oil seeped into the forecastle."

"Most awful feeling hearing your mates screaming and there being nothing you can do!"

The crew of the *Mitchell* listened in silence.

"I managed to make it to the bow boat. Fire was flying up the masts, sails bursting into flame. I was afraid they'd see me. Cut one rope from the davit; then the other. The boat and provisions foundered. I jumped in and floated beside it afraid to move, afraid they might see me. Pirate ship was on the other side of our vessel. Saw the first mate stick one of them to the carpenter's bench with a lance before two others attacked him. He used an iron to defend himself. They had no gun, them two, but fought the Mate to the head where he jumped overboard. He swam around to where I was floating maybe thirty feet from the ship. I called him. We stayed low behind the boat." The sailor shook his head overcome with the images he was recalling.

"Smoke was everywhere." Another seaman took up the account. "Got to where we couldn't see nothin'. Fire was all around me. Only path was to the bulwarks and overboard. Pirate ship had pulled far enough off to avoid the blaze. So much smoke they couldn't see me."

"Was the smoke I'll remember. Billowed out over everything. Wasn't long and all we heard was the crackling of the fire. No more yells. No more crying. No more gunfire. Just the crackling, and the smoke was all around us. Managed to right the boat and bail out the water. Don't know when the pirates left. But we stayed in the smoke as long as we could, in case they was still hanging around. The ship made the most awful gurgling sound…"

"…as if drowning."

"Then it sank. And most of the smoke stopped, except for a few pieces scattered about the water."

"In places, the ocean itself burned!"

"We just thank God that you came!"

"We waited to light the lantern till we were sure you weren't the pirates."

George went to her watch below and curled up in her bunk with her blanket pulled up and over her head.

§

Pirates? He hadn't heard of pirates for years. Late the next day, Peleg sat on the windlass and recalled the words of the rescued men. What a life that would be! Whale ships floated about like ripe apples on a tree, ready to be picked. He would have his own treasure. Survival of the fittest, and who knew more about sailing than he did? The skull and crossbones! A ship sailing as a law to itself! A giddy feeling stirred up in his chest, until Gorham took a seat beside him.

"You going to tell Johnson?"

He wanted to have that feeling back. Why'd Andrews have to bother him? "Tell him what?"

"About what we heard on the island."

Pirates was a better thing to think about than the boy. But that dream was gone for now.

George stood at the fore masthead. *No merit in his hunt. No, siree.* His sister deserved whatever happened. To bring his personal hunt onto the *Mitchell* was foolishness. What was really disturbing was that there were those in the crew that believed the boy was on some noble pursuit.

"Let's keep it between us for now. Yes, siree." Peleg wondered how he might be able to use what they knew. It had to be good for something.

"What you mates talking about?" One of the rescued men joined them.

Peleg had seen him about the deck, meeting the Mitchell's crew.

"'Bout Johnson, the lad on the masthead." Gorham pointed up with his chin. "Has the craziest reason for signing to this voyage. The boy has a sister who thought she could play with Canalers and not get burned." Gorham looked awkwardly to the deck. "I mean…not get hurt."

"I know what you mean." The sailor smiled weakly. "Messing with a Canaler and being treated badly go together."

"That's exactly what I said." Pause. "Name's Andrews, Gorham Andrews."

"David Sprague. Mates call me Davy."

They discussed George's hunt and praised Caleb's prowess at taking advantage of such a foolish girl.

"Yes, siree. The boy's supporting the wrong party in that union."

The mast head watches were changed, and Johnson returned to the deck in front of them.

"Hey, Johnson." Gorham walked toward the boy. "Got a question for you. We been talking here about your sister."

The lad turned to go.

"Did she ever tell you about how good her lover was?" Gorham called after him.

This could be fun, thought Peleg. He stood and followed the boy. "If she likes Canalers you ought to have brought her along on the *Mitchell*."

Even Davy picked up on the hazing. "She could get what she wants here as well as on the Canal."

The boy stopped and turned on them so quickly that Peleg almost ran into him. The salt retreated into Gorham and Davy. A wild fire blazed behind Johnson's eyes and his hand grasped his jackknife. The boy looked like an angry cat ready to pounce.

Peleg hesitated just a little too long. Tom stood in the middle before he could act. He groaned at the missed opportunity. If the boy had struck first, he could have finished him right there and everything would be back to normal. The Captain's hunt would have prospered. The Indiana farmer just got in the way.

"'Vast there, mates."

Tom should keep to his own business.

"Best you leave well enough alone. I would hate to think what would happen to young George here if he had to cut one of your tongues out."

Foolish farmer. He's got no right to interfere with whalers like this.

"And what would the Captain say? Especially to you." Tom took a step toward Davy. "We just rescued you; and, here you are, bringing a rift amongst the crew."

"No harm being done, no siree. We was just having a little fun with the lad."

"From what I heard, his sister ain't worth defending anyway."

Good. The new mate saw things proper.

When Tom explained George's predicament, Davy walked around Peleg, ignoring him, and up to the boy. "I am so sorry. I had no idea. They didn't tell it to me that way."

What?! The boy's got him fooled too! Something needed to be done. This was not right. The boy was causing even more division in the crew. Did no one else recognize the problem? This support for George was like water closing over his head.

He shuffled to Mr. Clark. "Sir, do you have a minute?" He bowed his head, removed his hat, and looked up at the Second Mate.

"Aye, Peleg, but it best be good coming aft like this. What do you need?"

"Nothing, Sir. Got some more information for you on that Johnson lad."

The Second Mate waited for him to continue.

He shifted his feet. "The Captain's talk didn't help much, Sir. Thought you'd like to know he still pursues that fellow. Was even asking about him on Juan Fernandez. Found out the Mystic is but two days ahead of us. Got some of the crew talking about it. Almost caused a fight just a bit ago."

The Second Mate's complexion blossomed a bit redder as he turned and walked off without a word. Maybe this time the he would do something about it. The boy would see that a whale ship was no place to bring his sister's business.

§

"It's like I'm the one clinging to a piece of Charlie's Essex…out here…alone. It would be so easy to just let go and slide away. But I have this wood to grasp." George clenched here hands into fists. "It's the prospect of bringing some hurt to man who brought me here." If only Joseph really understood her.

A gentle breeze partially filled the sails that periodically flapped as the *Mitchell* lazily slid down a swell. George stood at the foremast lookout with Joseph on the opposite side of the mast.

"Find something else to hold onto. Surely revenge is like an anchor that will drag thee down. What thou dost need is to be lifted up. Thou wilt once again be a woman."

"Look about you, Joseph." She gave a quick wave of her hand to indicate the ship below them. "What is there here that could lift me up? I am just a mate, surely not a woman."

Joseph thought about that for a moment. "Thou art in a unique situation. And it presents thee with unique opportunities. Thou canst find good and bad wherever thou dost look. Even whaling has its good. Thou might find it in the next port…or perhaps in the next fellow thou dost meet."

Tom sat on the windlass. Joseph was right. Warmth flooded over her that was not from the sun. This was good, but she had to be careful. She couldn't let Joseph's words take her mind off the hunt. Too often she listened to these words of his. "I know I shall probably not find Caleb, and I have seen some good in my life on the *Mitchell*. I promise you that I will try to think of Caleb less." She liked thinking of Tom. "Yet I tell you, my Friend. If he should end up within an arm's throw of a lance, I will be avenged. Whalers look for God's providence to supply a whale. Perhaps He'll provide for me." Anger controlled her, but only as much as she allowed.

"As long as bitterness rules thee, thy life shall be lonely. The next port, the next friend won't matter. Thy anger will come between thee and everything else."

"Harsh words, Joseph."

"But true." He climbed down.

George scanned the horizon for spouts, and still, perhaps, a sail.

As she moved down the rigging after her watch, the muscles in her arms moved, and she saw them through the loose fabric of the blouse. Her legs no longer hurt from the climbing. She had never felt like this. As a woman, such work was not required of her.

Holding the shrouds, she swung off the bulwarks and onto the deck.

"Johnson." The Second Mate sounded like a growling dog.

"Aye, Sir."

He walked up to her, fists clenched to his side. "Is it true on Juan Fernandez you were asking about that man you seek?"

"Y…Yes, Sir." Her breathing stopped, and she stepped back. "But only as I waited, Sir." She didn't like his look. "I have no desire to hinder our hunt …"

Before she saw his hand, Mr. Clark backhanded her across the side of her head. "The Captain told you not to pursue that man and yet you persist, even to the point of arguing with the crewmen on deck. Have you no fear about what he will do to you?!"

George raised her arms to ward off another blow.

"Sir…" She had no tears. "…please don't tell the Captain."

"Are you going to continue opposing him?" He raised his hand. She winced. "No, Sir."

"Do you think that because the Mystic is close you can rally the men to your cause?"

She covered her head and hunched away from the Mate.

"Look at me!"

She turned warily toward him.

Grabbing the top of the George's blouse, he pulled her so close she smelled his rancid breath. "You saved the ship. I'll let you off this one time. The Captain won't hear about Juan Fernandez as long as you keep in line. Now get out of my sight!" He shoved her toward the windlass and stomped aft.

He said they were close. What did he mean by that? How close were they? How did he know that? Had Peleg been talking to Mr. Clark again? She must be more careful.

Calf

Wednesday, March 7, 1849, Day 89

From her watch at the foremast lookout, George saw them, playing with the bow of the ship. She had seen them before. Good luck was something she could use more of. "Porpoises! At the bow!" She pointed down. The porpoises rolled and tumbled like sea-going clowns.

As the ellipse of snowy foam grew around the bow, men ran forward. The porpoises jumped and frolicked. Were they performing for the men?

The two harpooners assigned men to a line attached to a harpoon. Joseph stationed himself upon the martingale guy under the bowsprit.

If only the crew would leave these creatures alone, the show might go on a while longer. But they didn't.

Joseph darted the harpoon at two of them in quick succession as they crossed the bow. A third struck a porpoise in the neck. After one twisting leap from the water, the harpoon came out. The wounded creature disappeared into the depths leaving a trail of blood in its path. Others swam after it. Job had told her that a wounded porpoise would be pursued and devoured by his comrades. People acted much the same way.

§

"The mate to starboard, isn't that Johnson?" Davy pointed to one of the mates furling the sails.

Gorham followed his direction. "'Tis for sure."

"Notice how broad he is in the transom?"

Gorham and Peleg looked more closely.

"Yes siree! I see what you mean."

Joseph didn't like where the conversation was going, but he could think of nothing to say.

When the work was done, the crew congregated at the windlass in preparation for supper.

"Ahoy, Johnson." Gorham looked at her from the corner of his eye. "Watched you furlin' the sails. Did a good job."

Joseph made room for her. "George, got a seat for thee here."

Gorham blocked her way. "But, you know, from our perspective, I could have sworn a woman worked the sails," he continued.

Staring without a word, George walked around him toward Joseph.

"A little broad are we?" said Davy.

"No, siree. Ain't supposed to be women on board!"

Smiles and chuckling passed around the crew.

"Take after yer Ma?"

"Let's have a look!"

"Bend over!"

Her brow took on a shiny hue as she sat between Tom and Joseph.

If Joseph hadn't know the secret, he probably wouldn't have noticed. But now he was more aware than ever of the boy's…the girl's predicament. He hated confrontation. "Why pick on the lad because of his weight? Leave him alone. Ye best set thy minds upon thy own business."

"Come on Joseph." Charlie held an exaggerated hurt look.

"Just having fun."

"Boy's got to stand for himself."

The commotion came to an end and the men returned to their own conversations as Cook came forward with the kid containing supper.

"Where's the porpoise?"

"This ain't porpoise!"

"Salt pork, again?"

"Eat the cook!"

"Mind your manners, gents!" The cook stood proudly before them. "Or I'll keep the treats for the Captain and the Mates. The fish is hanging but there is a surprise still on the fire."

"I want it now."

"Me too!"

Tom spoke up loudly and with a full mouth. "I think this is quite delightful."

"Good job, Cook," said Jamie.

"Well, Mr. Hally, Mr. Taylor, leastwise you'll be getting the treats!"

"Yes siree, tis good."

"Three cheers for ol' Cook!"

Cook went aft to his galley, and the men returned to laughing and joking. The porpoise was hung to age and would be served later in the week. Joseph picked at the food. He loved whaling but never found the meals appealing. Fresh porpoise was something to look forward to.

Cook returned with another kid containing half-inch thick squares of something that had a kind of coating. A few of the men attacked the treat.

Joseph jabbed one with his knife and chewed, delighting in a memory confirmed. Others asked about the morsels; but, he didn't want to tell them…yet.

George carefully moved the squares around in the kid with her knife before sticking one and pulling it out. She held it up to her nose and sniffed. Looking at it more closely, she licked it gingerly with her tongue. Staring at it again, she had a tentative smile and carefully bit off a corner. She chewed slowly at first and then more vigorously. Finishing one piece, she retrieved another.

By the time dinner was over the kid was empty. George had eaten three of the squares herself.

"What was that?" asked Tom.

Eyes came to rest on Joseph.

"Thou hast just been blessed with a true culinary gift from God. It won't be found in any inn in any port. As far as I know, 'tis unique to whalers." He enjoyed building the anticipation, especially in George.

"Well, tell us what it is!"

"'Tis porpoise flippers flavored with porpoise brains."

§

Cook came forward with his fiddle to finish out the dogwatch properly. "I invite you gentlemen to digest yourselves into readiness to make a few molestations on the floor."

"Yeoww!" Charlie's feet bounced in time with the clap of his hands.

George loved the dogwatch. This was a time no one paid her any mind. Crewmen around her danced, laughed, and joked. Some sang old familiar tunes. Problems floated into the night along with the music. The taste of the surprise was gone.

"Men." Captain Sullivan stepped forward from the tryworks. "Most of you already know, David Sprague has agreed to join the hunt with us. He will serve in the Second Mate's watch. We will drop the others from his ship at Paita, Peru."

The mates around Davy slapped his back. A smile filled his face.

"Now," he paused, "we need a boatsteerer to replace Rounswell. The officers and I have discussed the matter and agreed that Tom Hally will take that position."

George's insides shriveled.

"He will serve in the Third Mate's watch. Joseph will now serve the Second Mate."

She looked up at Tom. "Did you know about this?"

"They mentioned it to me."

"And you didn't tell me?"

Tom's eyebrows raised. "Mr. Clark just made a comment."

George looked down. Tom had no reason to tell her. She closed her eyes. "It's just that I'm going to miss you."

"I'm assigned to your watch. We should see more of each other than before. Besides, how can you miss someone who serves on the same ship as you?"

§

"Lay down your paddles, men." Tension filled each of Plass's words. The boat glided along the port side of the whale.

George's back tightened and her skin crawled. A whale only feet away placed death too close.

"Stand by your oars. Stand up, Hally!"

Tom took the position of harpooners. He was ready, no visible apprehension.

The beast's back tightened and its skin drew in. It sank out of sight before Tom could strike. Something had gallied the whales. Even the First Mate's prey was gone. Only the Second Mate remained engaged.

Mr. Clark yelled excitedly at Joseph. "Give it to him! Give it to him!" For some reason, their whale remained near the surface. Joseph raised his arm and threw the harpoon straight and true followed quickly by a second.

When the whale raised his fluke to strike, George held her breath, expecting an attack on the Second Mate's boat. His crew pulled stern away, but the beast settled its tail gently to the water as if nothing were wrong. That was odd behavior. The shadow of a miniature version of the monster swam into view beside the stricken whale. "There's a calf!"

Clark's boat was attached to a cow with its calf. For fear of hurting the baby, the mother must have decided against striking out. Instead, she used her body to protect her young.

Plass relayed the message to the Second Mate's boat.

Clark and Joseph changed places.

Joseph swung the boat in and Clark thrust the lance into the whale's side. She arched her back pulling away, and Joseph swung the boat out. But the whale still made no attempt to attack. Instead, she moved between the boat and her calf.

The boat moved in and out, and the Second Mate thrust deep into the mother who opened threatening jaws but closed them without attacking. She hovered beside her calf. The fourth time in, the boat stayed and Clark churned until the mother spouted barrels of blood. And still she failed to defend herself. She died without a flurry, blood surrounding hers body.

The shadow of the calf swam out of the murky red water, and came to rest with its head below George. Shorter than their boat, it must have thought they were its mother. So helpless, it no doubt wanted the assurance of safety only its mother could give.

"Stand up!"

Tom stood.

George gasped. *No!* She wanted to take her oar and warn the baby away.

"Give it to him!"

Tom thrust an iron into the calf's back.

It thrashed about biting water and rolling.

How could they do this! She could have beaten the water and yelled till she was hoarse, but that calf would not have heeded the warnings. It had stayed beside its mother until the bloody water separated them. No warnings would have helped.

"Come aft." Tom and Plass exchanged places. With one thrust of the lance the baby died.

Their boat took only an hour to tow the miniature whale to the ship. They hauled it to the deck and prepared to strip it of what little blubber covered it. The calf intrigued her. The blowhole was at the front of the head and slightly to the left of center. The mouth, so fearsome on the mature whale, was not at all intimidating in the calf. Its tongue and throat were covered with a fine white membrane with the feel of satin. The tongue was small and almost incapable of movement. The eyes were half way up each side and in line with the rear of the jaw. Slightly back from each eye was a small hole less the an eighth of an inch in diameter—the ears. The small fins were just to the rear of these.

What a sad end for one so young! If only she could have warned it away.

Men removed its blubber to the hold. Then they cut open its head and emptied the spermaceti. Just inside the head were two amazing organs, the case and the junk. No one knew for sure how these helped the whale, but they held the valuable liquid. Its insides were prodded and pulled. After abusing the carcass in every conceivable way, they dumped it overboard before Clark's boat finally arrived with the mother.

The overhead sun made the cutting in of the whale a most miserable process. Finally, its head, half baked in the heat, was hoisted to the deck where Joseph directed Tom in cutting into the case and bailing out the easily reached spermaceti.

"Johnson." Clark looked about the deck for her. "It's your turn to dip out the sperm. Remove your shirt and get at it."

George looked incredulously at the Mate, then at the head, and then back again. They expected her to slide her body between slabs of rotting flesh so she could reach deep into the head of the dead whale. She'd seen others do it in some of the larger whales but never considered the prospect that this job may fall to her.

"Get to it!"

Remembering his hand against the side of her head, she had no intention of crossing the Second Mate in any way. "I think I'll keep my shirt on. Rather not feel the flesh."

"Suit yourself. You'll suffer all the more."

She slipped and slid as Tom dragged her up to the slit he had cut. In the light of a cloudless dawn, a cavity opened below the flesh. She inched her legs down into the case. Like a finger reaching down her throat, the smell of rotting meat engulfed her. Deeper and deeper. Tom took her hands and helped her descend. She wrestled with a putrid carcass. As her hips approached the cavity, the flesh squeezed. When her feet came to rest upon a rubbery soft surface, her shoulders just cleared the top of the cut. Straining to keep her head as high as possible, she crouched lower into the severed head and shoved the bucket as deep as she could. As she removed more oil, the bucket was attached to a pole to reach into the furthest recesses of the cavity. This required that she go lower—down, down until her head entered the case to give her arms the reach required. Dark, muffled noises, too long to hold her breath, she had to gasp air from inside a rotting head.

Oil, blood, and sweat soaked her blouse when she returned to the deck. It picked its way through the wraps about her torso, and onto her skin.

"What didst thou think of the job?"

"I thought the blubber hold was bad!"

"Whoever receives the honor to work in there today, will suffer greater than thee."

George had a hard time believing anything could be worse than what she had done.

"Hast thou not smelled the hold of late?"

With all the work and usual smells of the cutting-in, and now the disgusting odors that followed her, George had not paid attention to it. A sickening stench grew stronger as she approached the hold. How had she overlooked the smell!

"I thought…I'd gone beyond…such retching." She gagged and turned quickly to Joseph.

"'Tis called 'stink' now. Been there long enough for the heat in the hold to act like an oven and turn the flesh green. Whoever works down there will truly suffer."

Her watch was over, and she wanted to get below, away from this work, even if the forecastle was also an oven, even if only a bulkhead separated the forecastle from the blubber hold and the stink.

§

Behind her curtain, she removed her binding canvas and sighed. Her strength gave her confidence in climbing the rigging or pulling after whales. And she was secure in her ability to use her jack knife. She struck out at the hull of the ship. Her situation had forced these changes. She didn't want to be locked away on a ship. And something else had begun to happen inside her.

A craving filled her, to be something she was not. She longed to be a woman again, to dress and act as she used to. But more than that, she missed her monthly flow. Sometime in the past two months, the way of women had ceased. She didn't know when. At first, she considered it a blessing, one less thing to hide. Bindings and short hair were an outside disguise. This other was something else. Was she becoming more George than Ann? She didn't feel any different. But doubts still swam in and out of her mind. Maybe she worked too hard at living a man's role.

Joseph had told her that commitments would influence what happens. But the struggles of the day took so much effort to overcome. How could she see where her life was heading? When life became unacceptably bad, who could take the time to consider why?

But she was still…woman. Ripples of excitement coursed over her at the thought of Tom. There WERE good things about her life.

There's nothing good here!

The thought shot through her like lightning.

Caleb is all that matters!

She grasped for the softer feelings.

He manipulated and mistreated you. Your being here is solely the work of one man, Caleb Coleman. It's not your fault.

But, maybe, if I'd listened…

You've been cut in, tried out, and discarded.

Rogue

Monday, March 26, Day 108

"You see it, too!" Charlie surprised her. "Aren't you going to give a yell?"

The harbor was full of ships—loading, unloading, going, coming. One vessel stood out from all the others. Across its stern was *Mystic*.

The vessel was so close. Any one of those men crawling over the rigging or on deck might be Caleb. Her friends had told her the *Mitchell* would not meet with the *Mystic*. Yet three months into the voyage and the two ships lay only a few hundred yards apart.

Captain Sullivan was on deck. He wouldn't want her attention on that ship. But that's why she signed. And the man she sought was there. If the *Mitchell* stayed in port long enough, she might manage to have a boat take her. But, they had dropped anchor in Paita, Peru, to put ashore three of the rescued men. That wouldn't take long. She wiped on one of the ladles from the tryworks and gazed across the harbor.

"Ahoy! Ship *Mystic*!" Charlie stood at the foremast rigging with his hands at his mouth.

She didn't want to do anything that would draw the Captain's ire, but Charlie's yell was in her heart. Her eyes remained fixed upon that ship.

Its crew stowed provisions from a boat that had just arrived from shore. The boat was raised to its davits. *No!* The *Mystic* was preparing to weigh anchor. She had to do something! She looked aft; the Captain was walking their way.

"Ship *Mystic*!" Charlie yelled louder.

One of the sailors on the *Mystic* held a hand to his ear saying he had heard but could not understand.

"Is there a Caleb Coleman aboard?" He shouted slowly and distinctly.

The Captain had a sour look about him. She bent back to her job, much more earnest now. "Charlie," she whispered. "Captain's coming."

He gave her a questioning look just as Sullivan reached them.

"Eddy!" The Captain stood so close Charlie leaned back over the bulwarks clinging to the rigging. "Why is it you call to the *Mystic?*"

"Sir, the man Johnson seeks is on that ship."

George kept her head down and rubbed the same spot over and over.

"I've told him, and I'll tell you, our purpose is to hunt only whales. I want no more talk of this boy's pursuit." His tone left no doubt that there would be consequences.

"Aye, Sir!"

As the Captain walked aft, Charlie straightened himself up. "Captain's none too pleased with your hunt."

George acknowledged him with a glance and continued wiping vigorously on the tool in her hand. When the Captain passed the mainmast, she felt safe again.

A chant arose from the deck of the *Mystic,* and their anchor began to rise. Surges of anxiety washed over her. He was getting away and she could not pursue. The sails receded westward toward the line.

§

"What dost thou think now of George?"

The music of the dogwatch had died away, leaving laughter and talking. The boy wasn't near them. Tom considered the question.

"I like him." The lad was easy to talk with. "I hope he finds this voyage profitable. But he is in such distress over his sister."

"And he suffered a grievous loss when Job died. Looks to thee for the consolation he had from Job."

Tom nodded. "But sometimes he makes me uncomfortable. He's so…" He searched for the right word. "…so emotional. I must continually remind myself he is but a boy."

"He's been dealing with a lot."

"Perhaps." Tom thought of home. He was dealing with a lot too. But things were getting better. Jane did not wear so heavily on him, and his mates' company was pleasant.

"I still am persuaded that his life is headed the wrong way."

Tom wasn't sure. At times, Joseph was too concerned about the boy. "You can't force a mate to change, Joseph. If he's headed the wrong way, as you say, let him bump into a tree, or a wall."

"This life is a dangerous one. A bump could be his end. He needs help."

"If George wants help, he'll ask. I think you're protecting him too much. He chose this life. Let him live it. If you keep coming between him and the crew, how is he ever to become one of the men?"

Joseph was uncharacteristically silent as if he had something to say but lacked the words. That wasn't like the Quaker.

Towards the end of the watch, George plopped himself down between them. His head hung with a gloom that did not fit the dogwatch.

"Why so dejected?" asked Tom.

"The Captain has us staying in these waters, and I think the line would be better."

"And that upsets thee?"

"The sooner we take our whales the sooner this voyage ends," said George.

"We'll do well here." As harpooner, Tom needed to support the Captain.

"We've been this way already and only took a calf and its mother. Besides, it's almost April. Isn't that when whalers move to the line to avoid the South Fishery storms?"

"It's October through April we hunt south," said Joseph, "and May through September that we hunt the line."

"But other ships are already heading that way. I heard Peleg say that the big ones are there."

George quoting Peleg? Tom laughed. "I'd rather put my faith in Captain Sullivan. Besides, the 'big ones' are loners and can be found anywhere."

"I just think we ought to be heading north." George turned to Joseph. "Isn't that what you heard in Paita?"

"Aye. But, ships leaving Paita are usually destined for the line."

"Couldn't it be that's where the whales are?"

The boy's insistence surprised Tom. "You seem quite motivated to head north."

"Especially odd for one who so hates the kill," said Joseph.

Captain Sullivan came forward, and the laughter turned to quiet attention. "I want to remind you all again why we are on this voyage. Some of you have forgotten the purpose of a whaling voyage."

The boy lowered his head when Sullivan looked his way. He must have said something about Caleb and upset the Captain again. This was not the way for George to have a profitable voyage.

"We are here to hunt whales. Nothing else. I want this to be a most greasy hunt, and that means the masthead watches are looking only for whales. That means you are thinking only of the kill when engaged with a whale. We are here for no other reason." He walked aft.

Tom leaned toward George. "Is that why you wanted to go to the line?"

Without answering and without looking at the crew, George retreated to the forecastle.

"See what I mean?" said Joseph. "George must change."

"He'll change on his own. He heard the Captain's words."

§

"I saw him!"

Joseph frowned. Jamie should know better than to get excited about this. Did no one else see the problem here?

"I tell you, Joseph, it was that fellow George seeks. Charlie yelled, and this crewman looked back."

"How did George take it?"

"A bit disappointed when it weighed anchor. But I reminded him that we have a long time to meet the *Mystic* again. That encouraged him a little."

"That is a dangerous thing, Jamie."

"Now, don't misunderstand me, Joseph. I put our hunt first. And I certainly am not one to contradict the Captain. I just believe there is a wrong here that should be righted. It is a noble thing he seeks."

If George's secret were known, would there still be such support in the crew? "George must come to see that sowing bitterness will reap bitterness. Revenge fulfilled is never the answer to hope deferred. He must deal with his anger soon."

"All this…this sowing and reaping stuff…it doesn't matter. There's things that are just wrong."

Joseph fought back the urge to shake some sense into the man.

"Sail ho!"

Good. He had an excuse to move on to something else.

Davy stood alone at the masthead. The dogwatch was over and the sails furled. The edge of night was just ahead. But Davy said he owed the crew his life so he looked when others didn't.

Captain Sullivan climbed to the main top, wrapped his arms about the rigging, and peered through his spyglass. "It's a small clipper-built hermaphrodite brig. She flies a white flag for a gam."

"Sir," yelled Davy. "Can you see the hull? What colors does she show?"

He readjusted his position and took another look. "No colors but the white. The hull appears dark, maybe black."

Quickly, Davy slid down the rigging.

Joseph moved closer.

"Sir." The earnestness in Davy's voice was clear. "That is the description of the rogue that attacked us. May I have a look?"

Captain Sullivan passed the spyglass. "Sir, that's it."

"Are you sure?"

"Beyond a doubt. I will never forget its appearance."

Joseph's hair stood out on his neck.

The Captain turned his attention to the deck. "Mr. Wood, turn us about. We must remove ourselves from that ship immediately!"

"Hard to starboard."

"It's them pirates." Gorham gripped the railing and stared outward. "What're we going to do?!"

"Whatever the Captain says." Pushing down the alarm in his gut, Joseph took a couple deep breaths. Didn't feel relaxed but hoped others thought he was. "Just calm down and listen to the officers."

The First Mate hurried forward. "Set all sail." He started aft, then called over his shoulder, "And be quick about it."

The sun set below the horizon and a sliver of the moon followed in its wake.

§

A bead of perspiration rolled from her arm pit down her side. Another rolled down her right cheek. Sweat soaked her. She would not be able to take the heat for long, but at least she was alone.

"All hands tumble up!" The terse command pierced the sultry darkness.

George rewrapped her body. She hated those bindings. Throwing on her blouse and trousers, she slid from the bunk and slipped on her shoes.

The ship had come about and was on a starboard tack heading northeast. A ship's sails stood out clearly above the horizon to aft. More men crawled over the rigging at the same time than she had ever seen.

Plass grabbed her arm. "Johnson, fetch some buckets from the galley and fill them with water."

The agitation in his voice left no room for questions.

"Set the royals!" commanded Wood.

As quickly as she filled buckets others carried them up the rigging to crewmen on the yards. She glanced aft and saw the sails behind them had grown slightly in size since she came on deck.

"How art thou holding up?"

"It's closing." Every glance back revealed sails that appeared larger. She nodded up at the yards. "What are they doing?" Hand over hand, she quickly pulled up another bucket.

"They're using the water to wet the sails so they'll hold more wind."

The Third Mate came aft.

"What dost thou think of our chances?"

"She still gains on us. I'd say by midnight we'll be within range of their cannon."

George backed up to the bulwarks for support. Flames danced in her mind.

"Don't fret, George. We'll lose them before they get that close."

"Set to run with the wind!"

Men trimmed the sails accordingly. The ship perceptibly slowed.

George looked aft. "What's the Captain doing? Surely they'll take us now!"

"No, no, George." Joseph exuded excitement. "This is brilliant! A clipper can outrun us on the wind. But running with the wind, they lose the advantage. And we've got the royals. Something they lack."

"We should be able to hold our own." The Third Mate patted George on the shoulder and walked off.

She was not convinced. The pirates' sails had been gaining and now the *Mitchell* slowed.

As men sporadically filled buckets and took them up the masts, time slowed down with all eyes glued to the sails behind them. The ship's hull was just visible.

The sky grew dark and hid the world in the falling night. George sat alone looking into the darkness and wondered how much closer the pirates had come. She pictured them, weapons in hand, waiting to board, the way whalers cling to the side of the ship waiting to load the boats in pursuit of whales. They could be anywhere out there, even just beyond her sight.

One of the sailors lit a pipe.

"Douse that light." The First Mate's command was terse but quiet. "No fires! No lights! No smoking!"

The pipe was emptied overboard without an argument.

Tom and Joseph joined her.

"I think we're going to be OK." Tom didn't sound all that confident. "The Captain's smart. See how he keeps us ahead of the pirates?"

George gripped the handle of a bucket. Her body was as taught as a rope attached to a whale.

"He's right." Joseph placed a hand on her shoulder. "No matter how dark the situation, there's always a way through it."

"The slight breeze is in our favor," said Tom.

"And the darkness," added Joseph.

Behind them Gorham moaned.

"Consider poor Gorham. He is so consumed with fear of this rogue ship that he sees no hope at all. Don't let fear consume thee, George. Consider the alternatives. Look for the hope beyond the crisis."

George didn't know how they could remain so calm. "Where is there hope? If that ship reaches us, my life will have come to naught. By midday tomorrow, we may be where Job is."

Gorham moaned. How different was Joseph's approach to such trials than was Gorham's!

Tom put his arm around her. "Everything's going to be OK, George."

She knew that was not a certainty and that Tom was just trying to make her feel better. But the touch of these friends helped...the feeling that she was not alone. She moved a little closer. When he squirmed uneasily, she pulled away and straightened her stance but stayed near. She liked the security of his presence. A question came to mind, one Joseph had asked her weeks ago. "Wilt thou not be close to any so that none may ask thee questions?" She wanted to be close to Tom. But that would never be as long as he saw the boy.

§

She passed Gorham, sitting on the carpenter's bench. Darkness hid his face, but a sigh told her he still fretted, much as she did. She spoke quietly. "It's going to be OK. We'll lose those pirates." She wasn't sure she believed it but tried to mimic Joseph's assurance.

"Mule cock! Peleg told me it's impossible for a whaler to outrun a clipper-built ship! That makes about as much sense as your hunt for Caleb! Ohhhh..."

Peleg's puppy. Slush in the mouth. She was about to spit when Joseph's words eased their way into her mind. How would these feelings toward Gorham help? He remained a thorn in her side and her anger did nothing to change that.

George climbed to the main top and dribbled water down the canvas. The monotony of the work gave her time to think about the torment Gorham caused her, and about the harpooner's words.

He's not worth your time. Anger soared into her thoughts again, and she threw a fistful of water against the canvas.

But life on the ship would not be any better as long as Gorham remained an enemy. Maybe she couldn't make him her friend; but, if she could just make him less an antagonist, her life would improve considerably.

That will never happen.

The voice in her head was probably right. Except for times like this, the routine of life on the Mitchell tended to keep things the same. To change their relationship would require a change in her, and that would take a special effort and a commitment.

No! said the voice. *Don't do it.* Revulsion shook her and she spit onto the canvas.

But she had to try. She was in this mess because of warnings she had ignored. She would not make things worse by again ignoring counsel. Joseph's advice made sense. At least what he said about her future.

She looked down at Gorham and wondered why he took such joy in opposing her. And why did he listen to Peleg? What made him the way he was?

The ship changed direction again. Almost immediately the sails were trimmed to the new course on a port tack. No bells were sounded, but George thought it must be near midnight. A slight cloud cover hid most of the stars and shielded the ship from their glow making it difficult to see beyond a few hundred feet. The Captain had a plan; and, at that moment, her part in that plan was to keep the main sail damp. She poured a little water and wondered...did she have a plan?

She wet the sail again and again before being relieved.

On deck, Joseph rested on the carpenter's bench, head down. She slid up beside him.

"How does the night pass for thee?" he asked without glancing up.

Danger was so close. Her breathing was labored as she worried about what was cloaked in the darkness.

"Not well. Aren't you worried?"

"Worry? I don't think so. This is one of those things beyond my control. All I can do is wait and let the Lord give me peace about it. Besides, He provided the clouds to cover the stars."

She stared into the darkness. Could she ever have such peace and assurance?

Soon men gathered on the starboard side in anticipation of signs of the coming sun. Imperceptibly, the eastern sky lightened and the horizon became visible.

The Captain came forward. "Any sails sighted?"

"No sails, Sir."

"No sails." The words were echoed from the fore masthead.

And a spontaneous cheer arose from the crew.

"Thou must look for hope beyond the crisis."

§

"Can you watch this for me?" Tom handed George a bucket.

The boy poked at the contents. "Kind of on the smallish side."

"Bait." Tom rushed to the forecastle and rifled through his sea chest. He hadn't been fishing—real fishing—in months and wasn't about to waste the small fish he salvaged while cleaning seaweed from the rudder. The hook's point pricked his thumb. With that and the line, he tumbled up and spilled out onto the deck.

George had his finger in the bucket, moving the fish around in their slime. "You expect to catch something out here?"

"Where there's food, there's fish. At least that's the way it is in Indiana." The boy's interest gave him a good feeling. Tom took a seat beside the lad and tied the line to the hook, cutting off the excess at the knot. "Ever fish in Rochester?"

"A little in the Canal. Some in the Genesee. Never liked it much."

Tom smiled. "And here you are, hunting the biggest fish there is." He stuck his hand into the mess in the bucket and pulled out a lively one. "Did Ann like fishing?"

"About as much as me, I reckon."

"A lot of the girls I knew didn't particularly like it. Most wouldn't even try it." Threading the line along its dorsal fin, Tom secured the fish on the hook. The line protruded near its tail, the hook was turned up and back at the front of the dorsal fin.

"Oh, Ann tried it. Had some luck at it, though I don't know as she would have been as forthright as you at handling the bait." George wiped his fingers on his pants.

An almost giddy wave rose within him. He stood...ready to fish.

A crowd gathered around them with no end to the suggestions as to where he should cast. He decided it didn't make much difference and heaved it straight out, landing about thirty feet from the ship. As it sank amidst streaks of sunlight and strands of green plants, the line drew tight in his hand. With a fleeting burst of energy he jerked the line. Weeds! Quickly he cleared his hook and tried again with the same result. Paying no attention to the crew's laughs and comments, he threw his line out a third time. The silvery speck receded into the depths.

From below the ship, a bright flash headed in the direction of the line.

"A fish!" George leaned over the bulwarks and pointed. "See it? There, another one!"

His muscles tensed. The line moved out. Patience...more line...let it swallow the bait. It stopped and he gave a long hard jerk. The line fought him and Tom pulled hand over hand. The fish broke the surface with a gigantic splash. He hadn't hooked one like this even on the Big Blue back in Indiana. George yelled excitedly and cheered him on.

"Here." He handed George the line. "You land it."

Shouts from the crew compounded the excitement. Tom loved it. George retrieved the line and even pulled the catch up the side of the ship. There, on the deck, lay a thirty-five-pound fish all silver and scarlet and blue, at least three feet long. Prettiest fish he'd ever seen.

"Good job, George."

The men praised them both.

Tom caught a few more before giving the bucket and his line to his mates to try their hand at it.

Taking out his knife, he began cleaning his catch.

"This is the part of fishing Ann disliked. Catching wasn't the problem, it was the cleaning."

"You can't have the good without the bad."

George picked up one of the fish and pulled out her jack knife. "I know. And Ann cleaned her share of fish. Sometimes Dad had her clean his too."

"Well, wherever she is and whatever she's doing, if she's anything like you, she'll do all right." He liked George, emotions and all. The boy was a decent whaler even though he hated the work. If his sister possessed half his stamina, she would probably find someway to overcome her problems. How close Ann and George must have been! "In any case, she sounds like a special lady. I'd like to meet her someday."

The lad looked away. What? Were his cheeks turning a little red? *Odd boy*.

"There she blows!"

"Where away?"

Galapagos

Wednesday, April 4, Day 117

"Land ho! Dead ahead!" This feeling of expectation bubbled within her ever since the Captain decided the line was a safer place to hunt. George leaned casually against the iron ring, perched atop the mainmast.

Mist upon the waters to the northwest indicated islands in the direction they headed. Since the Mates said that these waters often raised whales, she kept a close watch; but her gaze was periodically drawn to the mist. There, a little to port! Land appeared as the fog parted. Then, as if smudged by some giant finger, the white merged, hiding the isle. Land emerged again a little to starboard. She knew it couldn't be, but her eyes saw the island move about in the mist. She forced her attention back to the horizon in search of whales.

Life had grown better over the past few weeks. Charlie and Jamie no longer antagonized her. Tom remained a good friend even if he now bunked aft. She talked with Joseph about all kinds of things. If he wanted to argue with her, then she could talk with him about feelings, hurts, and hopes. And that made the trip so much more bearable. She laughed at the irony. His words were to convince her to leave; but, because he talked, she had the motivation to stay.

Thoughts of Tom were fun; she liked being around him. She pictured his arm around Ann, not George. But she had to be careful not to mix reality and imagination. Acting on her feelings was dangerous. She had caught herself embarrassing him by getting too close. That wasn't good. But, when her mind was set on Tom, she left anger behind, and Joseph's arguments had no purpose. Sure, anger visited her once in a while, but it didn't stay. She was its master now. If she took one day at a time, if she talked with Joseph, and if Tom remained near, she might just survive the three years.

The sun burned the mist away revealing a number of islands; how many, she wasn't sure. A mate relieved her, and she returned to the deck. The eastern end of one of the islands rose in a gradual climb. Small rock towers jutted up from the sea like so many miniature islands. The southern side was brown with sparse foliage. To the north, the color became predominantly green. And the higher up the mountain, the greener it appeared. West of the peak, the land dropped more sharply down to the water. The *Mitchell* turned hard on a port tack fighting the current and seeking the shelter of the west end of the isle. Cliffs fell a hundred feet into the sea. Smaller mounds blocked a complete view of the cliffs; and, in front of the coast, a rock stood up through the water as if guarding the cove into which they sailed. A small, brush-covered peninsula formed one side of the bay.

Joseph sat on the carpenter's bench watching the land slide by.

"Why are we stopping here?" she asked.

"These are the Galapagos Islands, also known as the Enchanted Isles. They are the most interesting of islands. A whaler heading for the line will stop at one of these to catch as many tortoises as may be needed on the hunt. These creatures will keep a year in the hold of the ship. Much better than the salted meat."

The ship glided past the silent sentry and entered a sheltered bay. A gradual slope of land, two hundred feet wide, arose from the sea as an inviting way inland. To the left waves crashed against a black smoothly misshaped wall. To the right of the beach a twenty-foot eroded cliff, cut into layers, marked the perimeter. The *Christopher Mitchell* dropped anchor and George helped furl the sails.

Men idled about the deck awaiting orders from the Mates. Most anticipated a trip to shore and talked about other hunts for the giant animal. Tom leaned over the bulwarks with some mates, engrossed in something in the bay.

"See there."

"And over there."

"And there."

Heads of turtles popped up around the ship. Fish darted everywhere. Shadowy figures of sharks swam leisurely below. The bay swarmed with life. George stood beside Tom. She had never seen anything like this.

The boats, under a warm light rain, carried the men to shore. The crew was sent out to search around the base of the volcanic cone for tortoise trails or for the creatures themselves. George followed Joseph and Tom.

"We came to James Island because there are still tortoises to be found here; but, even so, they are not as prevalent as they used to be. In the dry season, they congregate near the peaks of the craters. In the wet season, they will be searching for lower pools of water."

With the warm rain still falling, George didn't need to ask which season they were in.

"Ye will have to keep a close watch for the remnants of trails. Once we find one, we'll follow it to wherever it goes. Hopefully, it will lead us to the creatures. We need to find some small enough to carry."

§

Gorham crawled to the top of a ridge. "Come on."

Peleg lagged behind sweating from the heat of the sun that had finally burned through the clouds. Shading his eyes, he looked into the light blue sky and shook his head. *Poor work for a sailor.*

"Look, look." Gorham pointed and motioned for him to hurry. There, about a mile farther along the south coast, was a small bay where another ship lay anchored.

He had me climb all the way up here for that? "It's just another whaler." He started back down. "Can't you tell a whaler when you see one?"

"It's more than that." Gorham sounded disappointed. "Look. It's the *Mystic*."

Peleg stared more closely. A warm feeling came over him. Motioning for Gorham to follow, he started along the ridge toward the cone and then down into brush and trees. If he handled this right, the boy's time on the *Mitchell* might just be coming to an end.

He didn't know where Johnson was, but Jamie and Charlie were up the cone a ways. He had seen them just a short while before. Sweat rolled down his forehead into his eyes, but he didn't care. Wiping his brow with his sleeve, he marched on through the thickets stopping to listen every so often. Charlie's voice should be like a lighthouse to a ship.

Gorham stopped. "Did you hear that? Sounded like Charlie."

Peleg turned his head, straining to hear. There! Yes! "Charlie!" He headed off in the direction of the laugh, bending low to get through some brush. This was more work than he wanted to do, but it would be worth it…

"Charlie!" He stopped and scanned the slope ahead.

Gorham pointed.

Two men, no more than 300 yards ahead, looked their way. He waved to get their attention.

"Here! Over here!" Charlie's voice was unmistakable.

Peleg stopped to catch his breath.

"Over here!" Charlie's voice was much closer. He and Jamie broke through the brush and met them in a small clearing.

Gorham ran ahead. "You'll never guess what we saw."

Peleg shook his head. Gorham needed to learn to let him do the talking.

"Don't have time to guess."

But Charlie stayed. Peleg knew he would. He was interested.

Before Gorham could continue, Peleg put his hand on Gorham's shoulder. This had to be done right. "We know how important it is for George to avenge his sister. And we know how you sympathize with his mission. That's why we wanted to come to you for advice." He nodded to Gorham.

"The *Mystic* is anchored just to the East of where we are." Gorham grabbed Charlie's shoulders and looked him square on. "Saw it with our own eyes."

"Yes, Siree. Do you think we ought to tell the boy?"

"No...No."

Peleg could see Charlie's mind working on what this meant.

"The Captain wants us hunting for tortoises, not Caleb. We must keep his hunt."

Gorham bent his head to the side. "But..."

Peleg put a hand on his young friend's shoulder and nodded as if he understood what Charlie was saying. This was going to be good.

Gorham followed him back down the hill. "But we want them to go after the *Mystic* don't we?"

Peleg smiled. He knew Charlie well enough to predict exactly what he would do. When he thought they were far enough away, he stopped. "Watch."

Charlie and Jamie talked excitedly and then headed quickly uphill, no longer looking for tortoises or their trails.

§

"Do you think it would carry me?" Tom and his friends stood on the trail blocking the tortoise's way.

"I'm sure it could hold thee."

George stared eye to eye with the creature. "Do you think it wise to do that?"

Its large powerful legs stood out at slight angles, the picture of stability. They held up a huge body covered in a brown dome-shaped shell almost four feet from front to back and perhaps two feet thick in the center. Part of the body was visible in the front giving rise to a two-foot neck gyrating side-to-side. It ended in a smallish somewhat pointed head with two dark eyes peering at them from above a closed mouth. The appearance was like a serpent attached to the body in the shell.

"Probably weighs close to four hundred pounds. Thy weight will hardly be noticed."

As Tom moved near it, the creature gave a low hiss and withdrew its head toward the shell. He took a wide path just to be safe.

George backed up. "Watch that it doesn't bite you or something."

Tom wanted to laugh but avoided the creature's head just the same. Moving around its side, he pushed the creature from the rear. Good, it gave no indication that it noticed. He lifted his left leg and straddled the aft starboard side as he reached forward with both hands grabbing onto the front edge of the shell. Pulling himself upright, he sat astride the center of the tortoise's back. As if on cue, the tortoise's head stretched up, and it lumbered slowly along the trail past the two other sailors, with Tom on top. People back home would never believe this.

"Let's race." He kicked the sides of the shell as if he were on the grandest of steeds. Still the tortoise moved on in a steady uncaring pace with George and Joseph walking slowly behind.

"I'm going on ahead. Thou canst stay and enjoy for a bit, but then we must resume our hunt."

After about ten minutes of taking turns riding, the creature had only traversed about fifty yards. It was time to move on up and help Joseph. "Make this your last ride."

A rustle in the brush behind them startled him. Jamie and Charlie tumbled onto the trail.

"What IS that?" Jamie gawked at the creature lumbering up the trail with George astride.

George dismounted. "Tortoise."

Charlie caught his breath. "We saw footprints back a ways…and knew you were near us…wanted to see how your hunt was going."

George slapped her mount's side. "Pretty good."

Charlie strode up to them. "Well, we can make it even better."

"Aye." Jamie focused on George. "The *Mystic* lies just a couple miles east of us."

Tom didn't like the look on the boy's face. So far the tracking of tortoises had been fun. In fact, this was the most enjoyable afternoon in months. Now, a darker countenance settled upon the lad's face. "Let's head on up. Joseph expects us soon."

Charlie stepped between him and George. "Tell him the boy decided to hunt with us."

§

Go! Anger arose like a whale breaching. It scared her. She remembered the Captain's words. Maybe she should listen to Tom. "You may be right."

Go! The word shook her like the roar of a lion.

But she didn't want to leave Tom. This was the best time she could remember.

Caleb's only two miles away. This is your moment, the one you've suffered for!

Two miles! So close! But Tom...

This could be your only chance. Take it, Ann. Take it!

"Come on!" Charlie pulled at her arm. "That man must pay for what he did to your sister. That's why you signed on."

Yes, Ann. Charlie's right. You need suffer no more!

Jamie spoke in her ear. "With him so close, you're not giving up, are you?"

"You're right." She missed the opportunity in Paita, but not here. She would deal with Caleb, and then Tom could know her as Ann. She pictured Caleb laughing at what he'd done to her. The liar! The thief! This scum of a man was within her reach, and no one was going to keep her from avenging the wrong done. Her hand fondled the jack knife at her waist. "Let's get him!"

Tom stepped in front of them. "You know, mates, I believe I will attend to gathering the tortoises. George, I wish you would come with Joseph and me."

Jamie pushed by him. "George deserves to set things right!"

Charlie ushered her around the harpooner. "May be his best opportunity!"

Tom shook his head. "This does not feel right to me, George. You know the Captain disapproves of your pursuit."

"No one will know," said Jamie.

"Just tell Joseph I decided to hunt with Charlie and Jamie."

§

A branch snapped. All three stopped.

Jamie glanced back and gave an accusing look to a sheepish Charlie.

George's heart somersaulted in her chest, but she did her best to look in control. She followed them to the top of the ridge.

Slowly, they raised their heads above the black gravel to see the men behind the voices. Four sailors from the *Mystic* sat in the sparse shade of a tree, obviously more concerned with the passing of time than with hunting anything. They were about fifty yards away. The three lowered themselves back down the ridge.

Charlie clenched and unclenched his hands. "Could you see if Caleb is among them?"

"Three for sure not. But the other, with his back to us, has the right colored hair."

They could watch all day and not be certain. "Why don't one of you just walk in and check them out? Look for the scar."

Jamie stood up. "Good idea. I'll go. You mates stay put." He walked boldly down the slope.

George stared through the low brush. Every muscle pulled tight.

"Avast there mates. Have you time to gam?"

The four men turned.

"Good day, mate."

"What brings you here, eh?"

"What's your ship?"

"I was up above looking for tortoise trails and saw you sitting here. I'm from the *Christopher Mitchell*." He walked to where the four stood and glanced face to face. "Do you know of any tortoise pools near here?"

When Jamie waved for them to join him, George's hopes faded like fog in the sun.

"Our hold is full of the critters. There's one just a little ways to the west of here."

"It's hidden between two wooded ridges."

"Found it just by luck."

"That general direction." He nodded west.

George and Charlie joined them.

"Looks like another of your mates is coming, eh?" One of the crewmen pointed up the mountain.

A man leaped over a fallen tree and loped madly downhill toward them. "Looks like Fish." Her heart plummeted into her stomach.

"Oh, no." Charlie sounded like she felt. "We're in trouble for sure. Somehow he found out."

Jamie paled.

"Why would you be in trouble here?" asked one of the men.

Her friends gave no answer.

The harpooner was close. She didn't have much time. "Tell Caleb Coleman that Ann's brother is here and his days are numbered." She wanted him to know she was close.

The man gasped. "You're her brother?" He looked her up and down. "He told us what he did. If he were here, we'd gladly give him into your hands. Talks big but not much of a whaler. Course, the Captain wouldn't be too happy about losing a mate."

"Just tell him Ann will be avenged."

Oliver slowed his pace and came to a stop, gasping. "Johnson…the Captain…told you…your hunt…was to be…stopped."

Charlie lowered his head. "We were asking these mates about watering holes."

After a deep breath, "I've been watching from above." He showed them the spy glass. "I saw you tracking these men. You're going to answer to the Captain for this venture."

George knew this wouldn't be good. "But Caleb's not even here."

Jamie spoke more forcefully. "No harm was done."

Oliver stepped angrily toward them and George stumbled downhill. Her friends followed.

George strained to think of something. "There's a watering hole just up here a ways."

Jamie looked hopefully to the harpooner. "That's what they said."

Oliver faced them. "Perhaps some good can come from this. Where is it?"

Maybe they could appease his anger. "From what they said, it would be downhill to the west of here."

"Between two ridges."

"Hidden by woods."

They found the pool. Each found a tortoise they could carry and headed in silence to the *Christopher Mitchell*.

§

George leaned against the bulwarks afraid her legs would crumble.

With his shirt removed, Jamie hung from the portside foremast rigging by his wrists. Only his toes touched the deck. The crew was forced to gather round and watch. Captain Sullivan stood back holding a four foot piece of rope. Nothing but the sound of the world around them.

"Tie those hands tighter!" demanded Sullivan. George and Charlie were responsible for tying Jamie to the rigging. "Climb up on the bulwarks if you need to, but make him secure."

George climbed up. She looked down into the face of her friend. With wide eyes and a look of panic, Jamie glanced up, his face pleading for help. George knew it should be her that hung from the rigging. They had been on her hunt. Yet Jamie took the blame. The only thing that restrained the Captain from flogging all three was that their watering hole helped fill the hold quickly.

George pulled on the rope, and her friend's hand began to darken. Blood showed where the rope dug into flesh, and Jamie winced in pain. Tears formed in her eyes. She lowered herself slowly to the deck beside Tom and looked away. The only noise was a moan from Jamie that came with each labored breath.

"Watch!" Sullivan sounded like thunder as he moved nearer the bulwarks.

George turned. All eyes were on either Jamie or the Captain.

"See what happens when you choose to disobey my orders!"

With a thud, the rope slapped into the man's back, driven by the first fury of the Captain's anger.

George flinched.

Jamie gasped and arched his back toward the rigging trying to get away from the cause of his pain. A red stripe oozed blood.

George closed her eyes.

The next strike produced a painful cry.

George shuddered and stiffened.

Sullivan grunted as he heaved the rope, and Jamie cried out once more.

A tear squeezed from between her eyelids as she clenched her fists.

§

"He's tracked you down for what you did to Ann."

But she didn't have a brother. The islands retreated to aft. Caleb leaned against the railing and told himself this was the same old thing; his mates treated him poorly because he knew so much more than they did. Still, he hadn't talked about Ann for quite a while. Why would they bring her up now? "You mates have three sheets to the wind. You're just trying to worry me, and it ain't going to work."

"Think so, eh?" His mate had a low ominous tone. "He told us your days are numbered."

The words settled in Caleb's stomach like a rock. Who would come out here for Ann? Who would go anywhere for her? She had no one. Her father was too old, her uncle too busy. No! These mates were just telling a tale. His days weren't numbered. Ann no doubt found her place on the Canal by now. And men didn't come to the aid of a woman like her.

"He was with two other salts." The crewman looked out the corner of his eye. "They hailed from the *Christopher Mitchell*."

The *Christopher Mitchell*! He thought he had heard someone from that ship call his name back in Paita. But these mates didn't know that. It could have just been his imagination; who would be seeking him in the Pacific?

"The man was a giant. Looked like he could kill, cut in, and try out a whale all by hisself."

"Saw him single-handedly rip the shell off a tortoise."

"Said that's what he was going to do to you."

A man on the Christopher Mitchell wanted to kill him? For what he did to Ann? Like all girls, she was easy picking. But she WAS likeable. Maybe the man was a friend. But Ann never mentioned anyone. And she wasn't happy at home. She told him so. And, with him, the girl was happier. No! She wouldn't send anyone after him. He gave her what she wanted.

Another of his mates joined the other two. "You been telling Caleb about the man from the *Mitchell*?"

Caleb didn't hear the response. The third mate confirmed their story! He had been the master of his future; he had done whatever he wanted to do. How could little Ann trouble him so? Someone was following him and wanted him dead.

§

"Finally!" The crewman, drenched from head to foot, gave over the wheel. "Thought you'd never get here."

They were on the line, headed west, and George began her two-hour tour steering the ship. No sooner had she grabbed the steering bars than a wave smacked the rudder. The force was transferred to the wheel, and George bounced back and forth across the deck. Her whole body trembled. She glanced at the compass to adjust the course. The path the *Mitchell* traced was more of an S than a straight line. The ship wobbled across the sea much as she had across the deck when the voyage first began. But this rough work was a gift. When the job took little labor, her mind settled on the sight of Jamie hanging from the rigging. His eyes— they were what bothered her—looking into them as she tightened the ropes at his wrists.

"Steady, George. Keep her on course."

She hadn't seen Joseph come up behind her. "Steady?" The wheel pulled her awkwardly forward. "Surely you're joking." The first time she had manned the wheel, she feared harsh words at steering such a wild course. But whaling ships, she had learned, were known for this.

For the longest time, neither said a word. "Jamie's flogging has upset thee."

George nodded.

Back and forth the wheel jerked her.

"Thou mustn't dwell on it. He's already better."

"It's just that the flogging should have been mine. He was fighting my cause, not his. He is the noblest man I know. Could have told the Captain I was at fault, but didn't. He took my punishment. I have made so many mistakes." Her insides were as knocked about as her arms. "It's like there's something out here ready to devour me."

"As I have told thee, Jesus can make a difference in thy life and in thy choices."

"Why should He even care about me?"

"He does. Thou said that Jamie was noble because he took thy punishment. Well, Jesus loves thee so much that he died for thee and thy mistakes. Easter is but two days away. We celebrate that day for this very reason. For the forgiveness we find in Him."

She had heard that before, but now she had a new appreciation for Easter. Still, how could she be at peace while Caleb remained unpunished. "If God really cared for me, I think he would bring justice to Caleb."

"This bitterness will truly ruin thee. Life is full of things that can cause thee anger. It will beat thee up worse than this wheel. It comes between thee and God. It will come between thee and those for whom thou dost care."

"There are time I wish I was free." She fought the wheel. "Sometimes I think it's gone, but it keeps coming back." She was wrenched to the side. "Even should He remove the bitterness, I don't know that I will ever be able to forgive Caleb." She didn't want to forgive him.

She was glad Joseph didn't stay too long.

"Finally!" Another mate relieved her. She was drenched. "Thought you'd never get here."

§

With plate in hand, George sat away from her mates, her back against the port bulwarks near the tryworks.

The Captain had no right to flog him. You brought back those tortoises. She wanted to whip the Captain.

But then she thought of Jamie again. She was in debt to him. She deserved the punishment.

No! It wasn't your fault. Peleg's to blame.

Charlie and she had quickly deduced that the old salt set them up. Her gut twisted. She didn't like the feeling. She wanted the peace Joseph had.

Peleg's little demon is still a bane. You'll never win Gorham. She knew he was part of Peleg's trickery. *And you'll never have that peace!*

Anger pumped within her like blood through her veins.

No! She needed to deal with this. She wanted a difference in her life. She would obey the officers and work as a crewman on the *Mitchell* until presented with an opportunity to be put safely ashore.

But you're admitting Caleb did no wrong! And if he's not to blame than you're to blame for this life in hell.

But, if she found him, did she really want to kill him? She did… She shouldn't… Best not… She didn't know what she wanted.

"Here comes Cook!" Charlie bounced as usual.

"Bring it on!" Davy was just as enthusiastic.

"Let's see what those land turtles taste like!" Even Tom joined in.

She just didn't feel very excited about anything, least of all a tortoise turned into soup. Things just weren't right, not even this meal. This mystical creature had crawled before her much as it could have done at the foundation of the world, an ageless, dateless creature that exuded indefinite endurance. No one could tell her how long they lived. But their appearance alone told of resistance to the assaults of Time. Yet here it had been turned into soup. Others finished their first helpings before George finally took a reverent sip.

Not bad. In fact, it's rather good.

Rank and Splendor

Easter, April 8, Day 121

She had questions. She knew neither Charlie nor Jamie blamed her. But Jamie's eyes, as he hung on the rigging, still troubled her.

The scent of tobacco rose from her mates, like incense from contemplative sages, as they anticipated the harpooner's Easter message. Friends jostled and smiled.

"'And by his stripes, we are healed'." Joseph started slowly and thoughtfully.

George and a few others leaned forward. The background noise from her mates subsided leaving only the sounds of the ship.

"Jesus was a man without sin. He was God come to earth. Yet He allowed himself to be taken, scourged, and hung on a cross. Why would he do that?" He looked from eye to eye and explained that the cords of the scourge were impregnated with metal and chips of bone.

George replayed in her mind each strike of the rope laid to Jamie's back. Why would anyone allow himself to be flogged? Jamie took her beating because he felt partly to blame and didn't want a boy to be whipped. But Jesus had no blame.

"Why?" The ocean lapped against the hull. "For our healing, thine and mine…but healing from what?"

George wanted him to go on. Why did he keep looking at his Bible? She needed answers.

"That same passage says, 'He was wounded for our transgressions'. What sins hast thou committed? How hast thou dishonored God?"

In the past months, George had already formed answers to these questions. *But what is sin? And how HAVE you dishonored God? You haven't. You're here because of Caleb. It's not your fault. You've done nothing wrong.*

But Joseph's questions remained. *'What sins have you committed? How have you dishonored God?'* Had she done wrong? She chose to ignore her parents. She chose to go with Caleb. She chose to pursue him.

'What sins have you committed? How have you dishonored God?'
She had lied. She wanted to kill a man—really, more than one.

Her heart was being emptied, like whale lye being wrung from a dirty blouse, taking with it the filth of this life. Tears threatened to burst from the corner of her eyes and she choked back a sob. This was not the place to break down, not yet. She clenched her hands and stared at the deck.

"Like Jamie's sacrifice, Jesus died for me." She spoke under her breath. "If You're there, I need you now."

§

Tom didn't know what the barrel was for, and Peleg wouldn't tell him. They set it just outside the main hold.

"Oh, no!" Charlie exaggerated his disapproval. "Not the barrel. Ain't necessary yet."

"Best be prepared." Peleg danced a short, excited jig.

"Well, I'm not going to help set it up."

"Got Tom here for that."

Tom wasn't sure about this, especially after Charlie's response.

With shipmates watching, the two of them took it to the bow and lashed it securely to the bowsprit.

Tom tied the last knot. "Going to use it for water or something?"

"Something like that." Peleg motioned with a hand as if Charlie should proceed before him.

Charlie laughed out loud. "You set it up. You should be the first to use it."

With a slow, deep bow, Peleg rose to the occasion, lowered his pants, and proudly urinated into the cask. George turned away. Peleg smiled broadly watching the boy climb the foremast.

The men took turns adding to the cask.

This was not the use Tom had expected. He wanted Joseph to explain it.

"'Tis a urine barrel."

Tom glanced back with a tell-me-something-I-don't-know look.

"We may run on the line and the south fishery for months without setting foot on land and without much rain. The crew will stink perpetually. Some say this barrel answers that problem. Urine will soften clothes too stiff with dirt to wear. It's been said that it extracts dirt much better than whale lye."

Was he joking? "Will you use it?"

"Some say it cleans well." Joseph smiled. "I am not one of those. They will wash well their clothes in the urine and then enclose them in a perforated barrel, tie it to a rope, and drag it in the water behind the ship. Clothes are said to come out more soft and supple than a new cotton blouse."

"Does it work?"

"So say some."

"I'd need to drag mine for more than a few days even if I used my own piss."

§

"That barrel's been up for over a week now." Every time George saw someone use it, her stomach turned. "It must be as full of salt water as it is of urine."

"I haven't seen you using it yet." Tom hit her in the shoulder.

"And you won't." The barrel had become a constant reminder of the nature of a whaling life. "I won't be adding to it and my clothes won't be in it." She lowered her head and continued sewing on the tear in the trousers.

Gorham stepped down from the barrel. "May come the time you need to use it."

Seeing him in a goodly light was a difficult task.

"You're getting along somewhat better with him since we left Las Encantadas."

"I had to do something to mend the rift. Considering the pains of this voyage, I decided to change what I can around me. I know some of the things I do aggravate Gorham. So, I'm trying to control that. Don't know as I can manage. But it's worth the effort." She deftly made a couple more stitches and pulled the two torn edges neatly together.

"Whatever you're doing is working."

"You know how I despise whaling and the shameful behavior that abounds here. If I cannot manage to avoid the ridicule of the crew, how am I to survive?"

Tom just let her talk and that made her feel better. Finally, she leaned back resting her hands in her work. "I sometimes wish we were back in New York or Indiana, someplace away from this prison. There's so much I could show you along the Canal." She started working on her trousers again, quickly stitching along the tear. "It's not as bad as some of the others say."

"Yes, Siree, what have we here? You sew as good as you wash clothes."

A few others chimed in.

"If you hunted whales as well as you mend, we'd have a full ship by now." Charlie hung on the rigging.

A desire to lash out raised its head within her, but she chose to ignore it. Except for Peleg, the teasing wasn't malicious. George bungled the next stitches and the taunting gradually died away.

"You handled yourself well there."

George smiled and tied off the thread.

§

The sun had set. The laughter of the dogwatch faded. The moonless night was dark, lit only by the stars. George sat on the windlass with nothing to do except dwell on the darkness of her life in the late night watch. Since she had duty on deck, sleep could not bury these thoughts.

Men lounged about, curled up on the deck or leaning against the bulwarks. The heat of the day lingered long into the night. Its discomfort often lasted till the rising of the next day's sun.

That night the wind nearly died away completely and the ship rolled along gently on the current. She wanted a house, a husband, girlfriends. A hug from her mother, or even a cross word from her father would be like water on dry and thirsty land.

Weaving through bodies sprawled around the companionway, Tom came forward from a stint at the wheel. "Have you noticed the change?"

George looked around, her mind lingering elsewhere. She had no idea what he was talking about.

"Over the past hour, the water has begun to glow."

How could she have missed it! The water shimmered with phosphorescence that lit their faces. Little fish darted through the sea leaving disproportionately large tracks of light behind them. "Did you see that?"

He nodded with a smile.

"What makes it do this?"

He shrugged. "The Mate didn't know. Called it a milk sea. Bet you never saw the likes of this on the Canal or in Lake Ontario."

George moved closer.

Tom awkwardly leaned against the railing and slightly away.

She gave him more space.

They talked quietly, and sometimes just watched the beauty of the night pass. Their watch ended, yet they remained on deck. The sea grew brighter until they sailed on an ocean of countless candles with soft flames glistening just below the surface. Every little wave that broke against the ship's side filled the air with diamonds that sparkled as they rejoined the light from which they had come.

George tried to find words to describe it but failed. "I cannot imagine seeing anything like this again."

The bleakness of the ship and its crew faded away leaving just her and Tom in their own magical world.

"Look." He leaned closer and pointed a little aft.

There, the sea was set on fire as a school of porpoises leaped and frolicked in the glowing waters. They passed by the bow and disappeared. If that moment never ended, the baseness of the life she lived would be forever forgotten.

The stars dimmed, overpowered by the brilliance of the ocean below them. The ship stood in stark contrast to the brightness of the night. She imagined all that could be. But his touch, for now, remained nothing more than a brother's.

The Storm
Friday, April 20, Day 133

"Tryworks fire, dead ahead!"

George rested against the carpenter's bench, glad that the smoke wasn't coming from their ship.

The First Mate climbed to the main top with a spyglass.

Captain Sullivan waited on deck. "Can you make out the ship?"

"I believe it's the…Mystic, Sir."

"Did you hear that?" Charlie set aside the old rope he was unwinding and craned his neck to see over the tryworks. "Who'd of thought it possible? The same ship… three times… and it's the Mystic!"

Jamie ignored Charlie's observation. "Let's get back to work."

Gorham lounged at the rail beside Peleg. "Wonder what the mule cock is thinking!"

"Cap'n ain't a-going to stop for that ship. No, siree."

They both laughed.

The plume of smoke grew larger until the *Mystic* came into view, but the *Mitchell* did not change its course. They were as close as they would be. The smoke passed aft, far off to port.

One moment she wanted the ship to stop so she could find Caleb. Then, the anger was replaced with guilt for placing herself on the *Mitchell* in pursuit of him. She wondered if Caleb might be suffering, as did she? She hoped so. Regardless, his ship was still close.

§

George tumbled up from the forecastle and took hold of the foremast weather rigging next to Tom. Crewmen moved tentatively about the deck lashing things down. Two mates checked the whaleboats. She looked up into heavy black clouds and gripped a little tighter. They hung so low the skysail poles seemed to penetrate them. She could not see beyond two or three of the bleak and threatening waves. "This darkness worries me."

"Aye."

"I feel almost like a greenhand again." She steadied herself.

The ship rolled to port with a force that promised to take it over completely and then bobbed to a stop preparing to roll back to starboard just as committed to turning in that direction.

A sail slapped above her as the ship bounced off a wave. "There is a definite lack of wind tonight, not nearly enough to steady us under the sail we have out." Words took away the quivering.

The ship pitched its head down about to jab the jibboom into a wave. As it rose, water streamed from the scuppers and rolled back like a tidal wave breaking around the tryworks. The guys and stays dripped after being submerged during the fearful plunges. Like a teeter-totter, the ship's stern settled in the trough with a force that sent water over the taffrail.

"This is not good!" George cringed and pulled herself closer to the weather rigging.

The Captain stood aft in the light of the binnacle reading the compass. He showed no fear, only concern. About four a.m., a streak of light broke into the inky clouds to the south southeast.

"Hard up the wheel! Let go the starboard braces! Man the port main brace! Haul up the main spencer!"

George hurried to bring about what the Captain had commanded. Her muscles loosened as she moved. The ship slowly swung off from the little breeze until the light was directly astern. The wheel was steadied, and the yards trimmed.

"Stand by the braces, men. And never mind coiling the ropes. A hurricane shall soon be upon us!"

All hands were on deck when the wind hit. It started with a puff that slapped the main-topsail against the mast. Immediately, there arose a chorus of screeching from the rigging. George tensed when the sounds brought back memories of the Horn.

A loud crash sounded beside her and she instinctively pulled herself around the foremast away from the noise. The bow boat hung from only the aft davit. The wind flipped it like a woman waving a handkerchief. It smashed into the waist boat leaving a large hole in that boat's bow. The next wave twisted the bow boat off the single davit that held it and carried it away.

Spray and breaking waves soaked her to the bone. For six hours the ship ran on generally northward until the wind shifted to the west, which put the *Mitchell*'s course northwest. When the wind slackened and the sea calmed, the Captain told the men they were free to go down into the afterhatch. It being three p.m., most of the men headed aft, Charlie among them.

"You coming?"

George shook her head. She wanted to be alone.

"Well, I'd rather be drowned like a rat in a hole later, than to drown on deck now." He made his way to the steerage scuttle and dove below with the others.

While the officers and boatsteerers gathered around the wheel with the Captain, discussing the storm, George sat with her back against the carpenter's bench. The tryworks blocked most of the water rushing over the fore deck. Resting her chin on her knees, she took a deep breath, closed her eyes, and sighed.

"Why art thou still on deck?"

"Just thinking. I have this…this turmoil inside me. I shouldn't be here but I am. Gorham grates on me daily. You tell me I must get rid of the anger I have for Caleb. Sometimes I find myself feeling sorry for him, and that is unacceptable. Jamie and Charlie have become my friends but they don't really know me. Tom—I don't know what to make of him in my life." She looked off into the darkness.

"This confusion, it is a good thing. Thy decisions and choices have brought this about, both the good and the bad. When the choices were made, thou didst only look forward to today. Thy future is in thy hands."

"That's what you keep saying," She did her best to hide the frustration. "But you're not me in a man's world!"

"No, I'm not. But we both make choices. And God wants us to choose for Him. He causes storms, like this, about us. And He causes storms within. They can be a gift. He has a purpose for thee. He wants thee to latch onto Him as thy foundation. I think this storm within thee is but a growing light. Thou may yet become a Friend."

His ill-conceived advice nipped at her. But still she liked him. "I count myself your friend already."

With the weather standing thick about them, the ship plowed on, driven by the wind and leaving behind a white and green wake in a blackened sea.

§

In the middle of the next night, the weather finally lifted and the sea calmed. George cleaned the deck on the foreside of the tryworks. Gorham was assigned to wind up rope that had been strewn near the windlass.

In the darkness, two mates cornered Gorham. "We heard tell you said the two boats was damaged in the storm because we weren't seamen enough lash them properly."

George easily overheard the confrontation. A lantern hung near the main mast and shed a faint light.

Gorham stuttered and stammered, giving no response.

He probably deserved the chastising. But, then, it would have been a foolish thing to say, even for him.

Gorham backed up, like a cornered animal looking for a way out.

One mate approached him head on. "Dangerous words."

Gorham looked from side to side. His gaze stopped on her. Looking away, she continued sweeping.

The other mate blocked any escape. "For a sogger to say his mates ain't good at whaling is to ask to swim with the fishes."

Gorham dropped his rope and moved behind the windlass handle putting it between him and the men. One of the mates walked menacingly around the handle after him. Gorham looked at George. This time she locked eyes with him. Even from that distance, she felt his panic.

Let him suffer. He deserves it.

She ignored the voice in her head; set aside the broom; and walked up to the men.

"Surely you mates don't put credibility in such tales." She forced a laugh. "I heard Gorham tell Fish that you did a superb job—much better than he did at the Horn. Why, he said the storm was so bad we could have lost more than two boats had things not been so well fastened down. He should be thanked for what he said!"

The two antagonists raised their eyebrows and looked at each other. And why shouldn't they be surprised? Of all people on board, she wanted to see him suffer. In fact, she probably should have just stayed out of it.

They looked to Gorham, to George, and back to Gorham who was nodding that she spoke the truth.

"See to it you don't bad-mouth the other boats."

"Or you may end up shark food."

They walked off laughing.

"Mule cocks!"

He reminded her of a timid child trying to justify himself after being bullied.

    Gorham turned to her. "Thanks."

Captain Hussey

Tuesday, May 1, Day 144

The ship eased through a cut in the reefs and into a beautiful oval harbor as if gliding across the smoothest of lakes. George worked the upper yards. The storm had driven them west and then north of the line. The nearest place where repairs could be made was this small out-of-the-way place known as Strong's Island.

"Port the wheel!"

"Brace up the topsails, port braces!"

The ship luffed and turned to the head of this lovely haven.

"Clew up the topsails! Stand by the anchor!"

The ship slowed.

"Let go the anchor!"

With a rattle that echoed from the hills around the bay, the chain flew out the hawser hole and around the windlass. They came to rest about four ship lengths from shore.

George furled the sails and got a good view. A small island was part of the reef. It rose to about fifty feet and had a beautiful dark beach all along the shore. Lining the isle was a thick grove of coconut trees that partially hid a large house.

The reef protected the end of a much larger island, which rose abruptly to about two thousand five hundred feet. It had the appearance of a woman lying on her back. Behind the thick tropical vegetation that grew all along its shore, small huts dotted the island. Only a few curious natives hesitantly made their way out.

George had never seen water so clear; the bottom was visible, in places nearly a hundred feet down. Once the ship was put in order, the men of the *Mitchell* were given shore leave.

Taking off her shoes, she walked with Tom on the beach, a mixture of the whitest of coral and black volcanic sands. The grains gently stroked her feet. Joseph headed toward the large house, and they followed. Captain Sullivan had asked him to find whoever lived there and arrange for a meeting.

After calling about and getting no answer, they sat on the steps of the house. In the shade, they broke open a coconut, laughed, and talked.

"Joseph?" A deep soft voice surprised them. "Is that thee?"

A tall, fine-looking gentleman in his early forties stood at the edge of the clearing, completely out of place. Joseph stared at the man who had known his name.

"Joseph, in fact it is thee!" The man beamed and held out his arms.

"Isaac?" As the two embraced, tears formed in the older man's eyes.

This was his Uncle Isaac.

"How…?" Joseph was at a loss for words.

"First, how's my wife, and the children?" With his uncle's arm wrapped around Joseph's shoulders, they entered the house ignoring her and Tom. The walls were thin, and the windows uncovered, so she sat quietly with Tom listening to the conversation.

"Isaac, what doest thou here? Thy wife and children are waiting for thee. I must tell thee they long for thy return. Did thy ship run aground here? Surely, Captain Sullivan will give thee passage home."

"No, Joseph." Isaac's voice was tired. "My ship did not run aground. I am bound to this island and can not go home."

"What sayest thou! Surely we will take thee. Should the *Planter* return without thee, there shall be no end to thy wife's tears. She remembers thy promise to return with money enough to never sail again and to stay at home with her and the children. And thy children, they will grow up without thee. What sayest thou!"

"No. Listen to my story." Isaac sighed and took a deep breath. "For two years we cruised the line and did quite well. I even made arrangements with a Chief in the Marquesas. He was to fill casks with coconut oil that I would pick up later. It would have provided over two hundred dollars toward my goal. Upon returning three months later, the Chief met us in his canoe. He told me that natives from a nearby island had only recently come, killed those guarding the casks, and planned to take my oil to their island. The only way to retake my oil was to arm my crew and drive off the invaders.

"My crew fairly enjoyed acting like military men. From the ship, we had a few rifles, some pistols, and one small cannon. In the dark of night, we crept to the outskirts of their camp. Our natives carried swords and long spears made from shark's teeth. Just as the sun rose, we poured a volley into the huts where they slept. They ran for the shore and the safety of their canoes with our natives in pursuit. The air was filled with frightened cries and victorious yells. My men did little but watch. The last we saw of the invaders, they were paddling madly from the island.

"All was well, I thought. I had my oil. The Chief had regained his honor. And we were hunting in the south fishery. A few months later, we made port in Sydney. Imagine my dismay when I heard an English man-of-war was in search of the *Planter* to take me prisoner to England. It turns out that England claims jurisdiction of those islands. Though I was but taking what was rightfully mine, they considered me an outlaw."

"Surely you are in the right and would be vindicated."

"No, the English would not treat an American fairly. So, that's why I'm here. This island is frequented mostly by whalers, seldom by anyone else, least of all an English man-of-war. Here I am safe. Thou dost know as well as I do that going home would require that I be turned over to the English authorities. So here is where I am, and here is where I must stay."

"Thou art wrong, Isaac. I know it! And what of thy family?"

Silence.

"Tell my children I love them dearly. Tell Isaac he must care for his brothers." Then, barely audible, "And tell my wife that I love her more than life and miss her beyond reason."

Tom was saying something, but George didn't hear what. She stood and walked toward the shore. The story told by Isaac Hussey was surprisingly like her own. She needed to be alone. Here was a man that isolated himself from all that was important to him. He was afraid and let that fear ruin his life, forever banished to this spec in the Pacific Ocean. He was a ruined man. In all ways this could be her.

That is you. Caleb has banished you to the forecastle. Like the gales on the sea, a desire to hurt him rushed over her but was hushed as quickly. For the first time, she actually recognized it for what it was! She wanted to laugh and, at the same time, cry.

Isaac Hussey could have found safety at home. He had only taken back what was rightfully his. And the battle was fought by natives, not his men. In the end, his actions would be justified. Even Joseph had thought his uncle was in the right. The harpooner had told her before about the concern some Nantucket Quakers had of the English. Since the rebellion of 1776, many feared English retribution. They felt the rebellion was wrong, that a great injustice was done, and that the English would therefore seek revenge. In Isaac's mind, fear filled every space. There could be no justice from England. Now this anxiety consumed him and separated him from his family. If nothing else, he could stay hidden on Nantucket while his case was argued.

She saw herself in this Captain. Fear didn't drive her, but she let bitterness and anger make her every decision. Joseph had seen it and tried to tell her, but she was blinded, consumed with anger. She remembered Joseph's arguments, but anger's reasoning had always won out. At the time, its counsel seemed logical, but not now. Now she recognized it. She did not need to let fury drive her. It had been a friend of sorts and found a home within her. She thought she controlled it, and was comforted by its counsel. No longer would she let it roam free.

George remembered wishing that someone would have warned her away from Caleb when her father had already done just that. Nearly the whole voyage, Joseph cautioned her of other dangers, and she did not hear, not really. Now she would listen. She didn't need to hide in the forecastle or on the tops. George spread her arms to heaven and cried. She didn't want anger for a comrade.

§

How much he must fear for his life, to abandon his wife and children! But how could his uncle exile himself here? "My Captain desires to speak with thee aboard ship. Art thou willing?" Maybe on the *Mitchell* Isaac would see the need to return.

"Most assuredly." His uncle's face became at least a little more pleasant. "I love the sea and all there is about it. Ships are not frequent in this port and most that come are quick to leave. I would love to walk a deck again."

"We can go now."

Tom and George caught up with them on the beach.

"Greetings, Joseph..." A smile radiated from her face. "...and to you Captain Hussey."

There was something different about George, but right then his uncle was more important. However, once on deck, as one Captain welcomed the other, he found George.

She was excited about something. "Thou art rather at ease this afternoon."

"I finally understand what you've been telling me. I really have let my anger control me. I see it now. It's so clear and I don't want that to be the case anymore."

What miracle had been worked in George's life? "What brought this understanding?"

"Your uncle."

How could that be? She had not talked with Isaac.

"Fear drives him the way anger drives me."

She implied a lot with that statement, and Joseph wasn't sure he wanted to analyze it. He didn't want to look at Isaac the way he saw this woman-that-would-be-a-boy. She had so many problems. But, just then, she looked to have not a care in the world.

"Surely he could return," she said.

"I think it would be dangerous." His voice broke.

"I would say that Isaac should take the chance. Though this island is beautiful, what kind of fellowship can he have with the natives? And to live apart from his wife and children…"

Joseph turned his face away. How could he tell Isaac's family that their husband and father, though alive, would not be coming home! Quite likely, this was the last time Isaac and he would see each other. They would never have a voyage together.

George moved closer. "Do you remember back when we first left Nantucket? How I stayed to myself in the forecastle? That was a refuge for me. I hid myself there. I felt safe in that abysmal pit. But, thanks to you, I ventured out. Now things are better in all ways." She paused. "Do you think your uncle is hiding here because this is where he feels safe? This is his forecastle?"

He heard truth in George's words. But how could he convince Isaac to leave? "The student teaching the teacher?"

§

George sat on the beach as the shadow from the mountains stretched along the sand and, with increasing speed, coursed east until dusk filled the sky. *If Joseph's uncle is to be in exile then this paradise is not bad.* But how could it compare to what he had given up? What had she given up? Could she have had a life? As she pondered this thought, she recognized her old friend hiding in the back of her mind.

You foolish woman. You may seek peace with your mates, but Caleb will forever torment you. The only hope is to avenge the wrong.

Anger still reached out and struck at her. She wasn't truly free from it yet. And bitterness hid beneath the surface. But she recognized this old comfort and gave it no foothold. Leaning back, she looked at the canopy overhead that stretched from deep purple in the east to gold in the west. Gradually, anger left her. Bitterness could breach into hate at any moment. It still wanted to drive her. It still wanted to consume her. By it she had become known. And after hearing Isaac, she knew it could destroy her. She must be aware, very aware. She must be prepared. No longer would she let it hide. She would meet it face to face. This was no friend.

A lonely figure walked slowly along the beach toward her, head down. Isaac took a seat upon the sand beside her.

For minutes, they sat in silence.

"Joseph tells me thou hast come whaling to avenge thy sister by killing the one who ruined her."

"True. But Joseph has helped me see that my anger will come to no good. I am beginning to understand, I think.

"It's good to see the light. Anger can take away hope. It can destroy a future. Thou might despair of all." Isaac spoke more softly and looked outward past the reef. "We all have dreams of castles and then, for one reason or another, too many of us proceed to build our hovels."

"Sir, may I say something?"

Isaac nodded.

"I believe you have let fear take away your hope. You should go home."

He patted her head like a man tolerating a child's comments, but said nothing. He didn't hear.

It started as a slow, deep thumping beat that grew louder and eventually was accompanied by a howl. The noise overcame the solitude. She had never heard anything quite like it.

"What is that?"

Isaac frowned. "'Tis the natives. They gather on special occasions, like a ship in their harbor. Be assured, many of thy crew will be with them."

The thuds and wailing echoed over the island.

"They call it music."

"I surely would not call it that."

"Nor I. I have been here nigh on a year now, and it still sounds strange. Dost thou wish to attend? I will show the way."

Thinking perhaps Tom might be there, she agreed.

The moon had not risen yet, so they walked through the island's trees in darkness. She could never have followed the noise to its source alone. They walked through some kind of ravine with rock walls on each side stretching up twenty feet. The silhouette of the walls stood out against amethyst heavens. The ravine was about 30 feet wide.

"These don't appear to be natural." She nodded toward the walls. "What are they?"

"One of the mysteries of the island. They were made by some giant race that lived here long before the current natives. At least that's what they've told me."

George stopped for a closer look. The stones were of various sizes, but all fit together as tightly as any stone structure she'd seen anywhere. And some of them were big enough to weigh two tons.

"How old are they?"

"No one knows. A tree, with a girth over sixty feet, is growing in the midst of one of the walls. It must be at least a thousand years old. The walls would then be much older than that to have given the seedling a foothold."

George touched the ancient stone and wondered at the mystery. She would remember this forever. To her surprise, she looked forward to setting sail again. What new adventures awaited?

The beat of the drum reverberated down the corridor. Coming to an opening on the right, about twenty feet wide, Isaac led George into a side passage. It had the same high walls but was only about twelve feet wide. This passage opened into a large grass clearing with a hut about twenty feet wide and a hundred feet long.

§

Peleg's stomach pushed out against his pants. He loosened the rope belt to relieve the pressure. He touched his face and felt nothing, like he was touching some else's. It had taken a lot of drinking but he felt pretty good. "You look a little drunk," he mumbled to the mate beside him.

Gorham stared, as if he didn't understand. "What'd they call this stuff?" A half a coconut shell that contained the thick drink rested on the ground between his legs.

"They called it kava." He wasn't sure Gorham grasped his answer, but that didn't matter. Not as good as wine or ale; but, drinking enough of it produced the same result. These drinks took him to a place he liked, a place where he was always right and he got what he wanted.

"Didn't much care for it to begin with. But now it's pretty good." Gorham took another mouthful and swallowed it in two gulps.

Large nuts tied in strings burned about the room for light. They also put off just enough smoke to hide the activities. Peleg squinted into the dimness. "I wish that fellow would stop his infernal drumming." Each low growl of a beat filled his head.

§

George walked around the essentially naked bodies of native men and women. She was thankful that darkness hid her blushing. The revelry was focused on the liquid in the cups. "What IS that stuff you're drinking?"

"Kava." Jamie burped.

"It's pretty good." Gorham handed George his cup. "Take a drink. Might loosen you up a bit."

Jamie made a place for her. She held the coconut shell to her nose and sniffed. There wasn't much of a smell. She poured just a taste of the thick, slimy mixture into her mouth and moved it about—almost as bad as the slush. Wiping her tongue on her sleeve she passed back Gorham's cup.

One of the natives laughed, which started the other islanders laughing.

Jamie whispered to her. "That's the Chief's son."

He had one of his men bring George a shell of her own. "Drink. For you, good."

Jamie leaned close. "Better do what he says."

The stuff caught in her throat and came back up. Closing her eyes, she forced it down. Disappointing the Chief's son was probably a bad idea. The natives and her mates laughed as if she were the entertainment. When the cup was finally empty, she set it on the ground and thanked him. Quickly another shell was passed to her. Maybe, if she moved further in, she wouldn't need to drink it.

Cradling it in her hands, she walked deeper into the building to check out the source of the persistent beat and the wailing, and to see if she might find Tom. There, in the recesses, a native hit his drum, a log over twenty feet long, cut off about two thirds of the way around and hollowed out. The remaining shell was about three inches thick. Beside the drum ten men and women moved slowly and gracefully. Dressed only in island jewelry, they gyrated as if caught up in their chant. That scene faded into the darkness as another revealed itself. She took a sip from the cup. The taste was getting better.

Past the singers, women sat in a circle around a large open bowl carved from a block of wood. They all meticulously chewed on pieces of spider-like roots that lay in a pile beside the basin. Each periodically removed the contents and tossed the dark stringy affair into the bowl. Then the process began again. They must have been chewing for quite a while since the bowl was nearly full.

She took another drink.

A native carried the bowl to the side and poured in some water massaging the damp stringy mess with his hands. It reminded her of some childhood game, mimicking the preparation of food. All kinds of things would be mixed together as food and served but never really eaten. At some point the mixture reached the right texture—it looked like a sickly porridge—and the fellow gave a yell. The contents were poured through a fibrous sieve into cups. The nectar flowed into the same kind of half shells that she held in her hands.

Dropping it, she stumbled back toward the entrance. Outside, she knelt on the ground breathing deeply, welcoming the urge to vomit.

§

She exited the manmade canyon. Captain Hussey should never have guided her to that party.

"George?"

With a partial moon peaking over the island's mountains, she just made out Tom sitting atop the wall on her right. She found enough handholds in the debris from the crumbling wall to scramble up to where her friend sat.

"I was wondering where you went." She moved a pouch to make room for a seat next to Tom on his left side. The wall was about twenty feet thick at this point and not quite flat. While the tops of most of the foliage were below their view, the fronds atop the coconut trees decorated the starlit sky. The silhouette of the ship in the harbor was the perfect picture of a world at peace. They were alone above the island's life.

Tom spoke quietly, as if sound might disturb the night. "Went to the party but only stayed a short while. Not the kind of thing I like."

"The Chief's son made me drink some of that kava." She still tasted the mixture.

"Pretty bad, wasn't it? I'd say this is a bit nicer."

Yes, this was much more pleasant. With no one here but Tom, she let her imagination fly.

Tom leaned back and looked up. "Have you ever thought that

some of these same stars are visible from home?"

She made out the Big Dipper and thought of Rochester. Two of her fingers touched Tom's. When he didn't move them, she got this queasy feeling inside. Looking up a little at her friend, she imagined what he would say if she told him her secret. Her breathing was quick and shallow. She felt closer to him than to any other man and wanted to share so much more with him. If only he knew her as Ann! She wanted someone to understand her. Joseph did, but it wasn't the same thing. Tom looked at her, and she quickly turned her head toward the familiar stars but saw nothing except this friend. Her heart was beating as loudly as that drum, and much faster. Why didn't he hear it? She closed her eyes and tried to calm herself.

Tom said something but she didn't hear. "What's that?" She turned toward him again.

"I said, are you all right? You look flushed."

"I'm fine." She was short of breath.

Tom took his right hand and placed it across her forehead bringing his face within inches of hers. "A little damp. You sure you're okay?"

What? Sitting next to Tom, and now so close, alone, in the moonlight, in the beauty of this remote island? Of course she wasn't okay. They had never really been alone before. At that moment, they were the only two people anywhere. Their hands were touching. This would never be possible on the *Mitchell*. Her imagination took her where she could not go.

§

Holding his hand upon her brow, Tom looked into the George's eyes, concerned that the boy may be picking up some sickness. There had been talk of malaria being caught on some of the islands, and other diseases that plagued sailors. With his right arm, he reached across George for his pouch. He wanted to get the boy back to the ship where Cook might recommend a medication if required.

§

As George watched, heart pounding, Tom took his hand from her forehead and reached around her waist, leaning in toward her. *How could this be happening?* Tom's face came down toward hers. She didn't know and, at that moment, really didn't care. She reached up, threw her arms around his neck, closed her eyes, and kissed him.

When Tom stood, spitting and sputtering and wiping his mouth, George wanted to be somewhere else. The beauty of the moment was gone carried away by her imagination as it flew into the shadows. Now her heart raced for another reason.

"Why'd you do that? What kind of man do you think I am? Why hunt Caleb? You have enough problems of your own."

She had to say something but didn't know what to say. Tears came uncontrollably. What words would do? Her mind raced. "Meg! Meg, don't be upset!" The first thing that came to mind was the Falklands.

"What are you talking about?" Tom grabbed his pouch and made his way down the edge of the wall.

"Ohhhh!" She didn't know what else to say. But, once spoken, it was done. She would stay on the wall till morning. If she had been in some kind of delirium, she would have returned no sooner.

§

He stumbled through the rubble. He needed to get far away.

"Watch where you're going, mate. It's dark out. Yes, siree. A man might get hurt if he's not watching."

"Peleg? What're you doing just standing in the dark?"

"There's all kinds of mysteries on this island, especially for one who heeds what's about him. Yes, siree. All kinds of mysteries."

"Rather late to be looking at rock walls."

Tom hurried toward the boats wiping his mouth.

"Some mysteries you don't need to see."

He heard Peleg's unintelligible comment, but other things filled his mind.

§

She sat alone as the stars passed overhead. An ache surged from her gut to her chest and wouldn't go away. Tom didn't see her as a woman. How could she have kissed him! What must he think of her? If she revealed her secret, she would be put off the ship. That would take her from him forever. Hugging her knees, she rocked back and forth.

A red twinge led the way for a rising sun.

§

"Hast thou seen George?"

"No!" Tom didn't want to talk about the boy.

"He didn't return to the ship."

Why was Joseph so concerned about him all the time? "You watch him closely."

"He's but a boy. Wouldn't want him to find trouble."

"He'll find trouble enough himself."

"What dost thou mean?"

Tom shrugged. Joseph should have seen it. They all should have seen it.

"When didst thou see him last?"

"He was acting real funny last night. Called me Meg or something. Acted crazy." As far as Tom was concerned, the boy wasn't acting. But how could he tell Joseph what he suspected. He wasn't sure he could ever sit with George again.

Jamie walked up. "Meg, hmmm."

He must have overheard.

"If I remember," said Jamie, "that was the name of the girl on the Falklands that had her eyes set on him."

That's right. Maybe the boy was feverish. Then Tom shook his head. No, George had known exactly what he was doing. Still…. "Last place I saw him was at the wall."

§

Joseph hurried up the beach toward the path inland. When George walked slowly out, head down, lightly kicking sand, a wave of relief stopped him. He let go a pent up breath. "What happened? Tom acted very odd this morning."

"You wouldn't believe me."

"Tell me and see."

"I kissed him."

"Thou didst what!?" George was a woman, but still it didn't sound right. He thought of the Falklands and almost laughed. Then pity overwhelmed him for what George had been through. Then he almost laughed again.

"Shhh." She vehemently shook her head as if fearing someone would overhear. "I kissed him. I know that was a stupid thing to do. But it seemed right at the time, at least until he gagged."

"So what art thou to do now? Can't let on to the truth. And men like that have no place in the forecastle."

"I didn't know what to do. He thought I was sick, so I acted feverish. Called him Meg."

Again Joseph fought back chortles that nearly shook him. "Well, I don't know what will become of thee. We will need to be watchful and correct any problems. Let's hope for Tom's discretion."

They walked a ways in silence.

"So, thou dost think of Tom in that manner?"

George nodded.

"Difficult."

"At best."

"Thou hast a problem."

She nodded.

"I mean…a problem."

A questioning look.

"Revenge."

"It's beaten."

Joseph wasn't so sure. Recognizing it is one thing, defeating it is another. "Be sure. Revenge can yet come between thee and him. Remember on the Galapagos? Thou chose to pursue Caleb over walking with Tom and me. What wilt thou choose should the opportunity be given again?"

§

The question stopped her. What would she do given an option to dole out retribution or walk again with Tom? Obviously, she would choose Tom. But she knew the strength of her anger. The choice wouldn't be so easy if Caleb stood before her. What would she do?

"As long as thou dost carry this anger toward Caleb, thou won't have a good relationship with any man."

"I want to be rid of the bitterness. I've told you as much."

"Thou must do more than desire it. Thou must do it."

She mulled that over… and over. What did it mean to really be rid of bitterness? "You're telling me I must forgive the man who ruined me?" She didn't like the words. "The scum who turned my mother and father against me? The one for whom I was condemned to serve on a whaler?"

"Yes."

She thought of Peleg. Was it even possible to truly forgive? "How? There are times I rid myself of the anger only to have it return even stronger."

He took his Bible from under his shirt and thumped its cover. "The Bible tells us in Matthew that a man can clean his house of demons; but, if he doesn't fill it with something else, they can return even stronger. Thou must do more than clean. Thou must fill thy life. Thou dost know the answer. I have told thee many times before."

"Jesus? The Light?"

Joseph nodded.

"Don't know that I can."

§

The damaged boat was repaired and another procured. The ship spent another two days in the beautiful harbor of Strong's Island, giving the men time to relax before the long cruise back east. It also gave the captains time to visit. In the end, Isaac refused to see that he could safely return home. He and Joseph said their tearful goodbyes with Joseph promising to relay his uncle's message to a wife and boys who "will suffer greatly from the message." The *Christopher Mitchell* pulled out of the harbor and Strong's Island was left behind. Joseph watched the island shrink aft and, with shattered hopes, longed for a hunt that would never happen.

§

"Now don't you boys be soggerin' down there." Clark leaned over the main hold hatch. "Watch the end of the hose and don't waste no oil."

George held the end of the hose with Gorham, as the men on deck funneled the cooled oil, from another whale, into the other end. It gurgled down to the bowels of the ship…to them. Hot, dark, and humid, the belly of the ship reeked of all sorts of smells. Shallow breathing didn't help. She contorted her face but that brought no relief. The liquid sloshed down and into a barrel. Some seeped through and made her clothing all the more uncomfortable. The canvas bindings around her chest and waist dampened with sweat and oil.

Tom's voice echoed from the hatch and an empty feeling spread out from her chest and consumed her. Especially in this darkness, her loneliness was magnified. Since the kiss, he avoided her, as much as he

could on the ship. More oil sloshed down the hose. The canvas moved
upon her shoulder with the approach and passing of the oil.

§

"It's tough sometimes."
Tom paid attention when Mr. Clark spoke.
"As boatsteerer, you have authority over the crew but are still one
of them. Don't let them think they can fool you. Gotta be hard on them."
So far, he'd not had any problems, other than with George, and
that really wasn't with regard to whaling.
A crewman readied a bucket over the end of the hose. The Mate
prodded him. Tom looked into the hatch. "Here comes the next bucket.
Stow it all or we'll be hunting whales till the cows come home!"
"It's good to see the boy getting along well with Andrews. Started
out at each other, but now work well together."
Tom's sight followed the line of the canvas hose as it disappeared
into the darkness of the hold.
"He's making an effort to apply himself to the hunt," continued
Clark. "This pleases the Captain."
The hold was dark. And it smelled.
"Hally." Clark looked at him curiously. "It wasn't that long ago
you were telling me how I should be more concerned about the boy. Why
you being so sullen now?"
"Hard life for a boy. Some people would do better on shore than
on a ship. I just wonder if that might be Johnson's situation."
"Well, that isn't going to happen. Anyone can learn. He's on for
the duration. Besides, he's doing rather well lately."
If the Second Mate knew what had happened, he would probably
want the boy off. Should he tell Mr. Clark? Was the kiss an indication of
the boy's character or was it the result of a fever as Joseph assumed?
George's behavior was strange ever since the voyage began. Things
would just be simpler if he were not part of the crew.

Joseph met George and Gorham on their way up. "Johnson, canst
thou come and lend a hand? I've got to seal the barrels."
She wanted out, but this was an opportunity to talk about his
uncle. Besides, the smell was becoming less obnoxious. Gorham scurried
on up. She led him to where they were working. "I am sorry to see that

your uncle decided to stay on the island."

"'Twas probably the safest choice."

"You don't think it's a mistake, then?"

"He shows understanding in many things. Who am I to find fault with him?"

But he found fault with her. A mallet sealed a barrel. On the island, she found real freedom from her exile and was certain his uncle could have obtained release from his as well. But whatever she said would not change his situation now. Maybe that was why Joseph refused to fault his uncle; it would accomplish nothing.

But what of you? The voice struck her from out of nowhere. *Aren't you just like Joseph? Failing to face the truth about Caleb because you won't find him?*

But she really wanted to forgive him.

Ha! She felt like laughing at her own naiveté. *Until you know his end, he can never be excused. And there's only one end that will satisfy. You know that!*

But she was familiar with this anger. She must control it.

§

Like some kind of conspirator, Charlie kept his voice low. "Think we'll yet find the Mystic out here?"

"Rather gam with a whale."

"Nah!"

"Hope not for the boy's sake."

Peleg gritted his teeth and cringed. Conversations often centered on Johnson's hunt, but only when the officers were not near. And the Officers paid him little heed lately.

Charlie barely swallowed a bite of food before he shoved his knife forward. "I'd love to see Johnson run him through."

"Hear he's not on that hunt."

"Given up is what I hear."

"Flogging will do that."

"Don't know that I think the man did such a bad thing. But what the boy seeks is noble." Even Gorham teased the boy less since the storm.

Some of the mates nodded.

Peleg knew what he had heard. Something not normal was happening atop that wall on Strong's Island. *Why is it none of them see the boy for what he is?* He had to say…something! "But I hear he's got no right." He looked to the deck, away from his mates, focusing on the words. "No, siree. No right at all to hunt him down." Maybe the men would begin to see things his way and the Captain would put the boy off. Then the *Mitchell* could get down to the business of whaling.

Charlie scooted closer. "What do you mean? I agree with Andrews. 'Tis noble to right a wrong."

"That's just it." Peleg tilted his head up. Had to be careful what he said. "He's not so noble as you might think."

That got their attention. The boy's defense of his sister never was proper. She was clearly no better than the woman who had left him. Just the boy's being on the ship was an abomination. He had always known something was wrong with Johnson, and now his mates would see it too.

"No, siree. Not justified in his pursuit. And here you are, Charlie, following him and arguing as if he is the most noble of mates on a most noble cause. He's got you fooled."

No one spoke, and Peleg waited, looking from eye to eye. "We all know that the boy has enjoyed the company of our newest harpooner."

Some of the men nodded.

"Did you see how the boy was a little too familiar with him?"

Others nodded.

"A normal man don't hang on a mate like..."

"Avast there, Peleg." Charlie interrupted. "He's just a lad grieving the loss of a friend."

"Nay, it's been too long for that. And have you noticed that since leaving the island Tom has avoided the boy?"

Some had seen it.

"I know why. Yes, siree. I do." He paused and looked again to the deck. This was great. He had them.

"Back on the island I heard something. Just the two of them was sitting on the wall. All alone, nice and cozy. The boy did something that angered our harpooner." Peleg raised his eyebrows.

"What did he do?" One of the mates spattered half chewed food to the deck.

"Something not natural. Had Tom spitting and wiping his mouth. Left the boy alone and hasn't talked with him since."

"I don't believe it!"

What's this! Gorham arguing with him? "I know what I heard. Yes, siree, I do"

"Then you heard wrong." Charlie's defense didn't surprise him.

Others just listened.

"I tell you mates, there's something not right with the boy, and he best be put ashore."

"There's Johnson," said a mate.

The boy had just exited the companionway.

"Well, well, here comes the noble hunter now!" Peleg wanted to make sure Johnson heard him. "How does it feel for your secret to be out?"

The boy stared from mate to mate as if he had been caught doing wrong. Was that panic in his eyes? Serves him right, after getting the men to feel sympathy for that wicked sister of his. If he'd just kept his hunt a private matter it wouldn't have been a problem, but the boy had to go and bring everyone else into it. Even Job had died supporting the boy's foolish adventure.

"Not so noble are we? No, siree. Not even Hally supports you now does he, since you've shown him what you really are?" The boy's face turned a shade of crimson.

"Leave him alone." Gorham rose to George's defense.

"Avast, Andrews!"

"What kind of lad are you, Johnson!"

"Shameful!"

"Disgraceful!"

Peleg stood up. "What do you have to say for yourself?"

"I still don't believe it." Charlie stood beside Gorham.

"Here comes Hally."

"Tom." Gorham waved him over. "Peleg's been talking about Johnson."

George looked like a dog with his tail between his legs. But the boy was trouble. Tom didn't want to get involved with him again. "What's he been saying?"

"Uh…well…uh…something about the wall on Strong's Island."

The mystery that Peleg had been studying was he and Johnson. Tom wasn't sure how to answer. The boy had caused questions enough in his own mind. He looked at Peleg. "What do you think you saw?"

"What I heard was not natural. No, siree. Tell us what the boy did to you back there."

What could he say? The voyage would be better if George were put off the ship, but not this way. He wasn't sure himself what happened on the island. He looked at Johnson. The boy's head was lowered as if beaten down by the accusations of these mates.

"Like you said, Peleg, the boy and I were on the wall talking. But he acted funny. Had a fever. And I heard he drank some of that kava."

"That natives made him drink it!" Gorham nodded as if vindicated.

"Between the fever and the drink, George acted crazy."

"What did he do?" asked a mate.

"That kava was bad stuff," said another. "Gave me bad dreams all night."

"And there's all kinds of fevers on these islands." Charlie looked from Gorham to the others.

"No!" Peleg jutted his head forward. "Wasn't those things at all. You came down spitting and sputtering like someone had just stuck slush in your mouth."

"So what did he do?" asked the mate again.

"He called me Meg and tried to kiss me."

"No!" exclaimed a mate.

Others groaned in disgust.

"Be thankful I don't have a fever now." George raised his head with a tentative smile. He no longer looked downcast.

"Must have been some fever for him to kiss you!" Gorham laughed.

Tom still wasn't comfortable with George, but at least this problem with Peleg was over.

"Avast! Mates." The old salt just wouldn't let it be. "If it were only the fever or the kava, why is it you avoid the boy now?"

"As boatsteerer, I must work with all the crew, not just one. For now, I must go aft to talk with the officers." He walked off glad to be away from them.

Back on the Line

Monday, May 14, Day 157

Days blended together and everything stayed the same. Attached to the outstretched arms of the ship's masthead, like an offering to the sun god, George gazed across a sea that must have been boiling in the heat of the sun.

Little trickles inched down her hips from between her waist and the wrappings. Before tumbling up, she had applied them with slack, yet not so loose that they would become obvious under her blouse. Still, they were too tight. She squirmed trying to find some form of comfort. Oh to be free of them. Maybe then her body would act as a woman's. She fought the urge to scratch the itching, throw water on the burning sensations, and rip those bindings from her body.

A lone barrel bobbed at the end of a rope behind the ship as a testimony to life on a whaler. Tom talked with her but only when required and only about whaling. With her hunt for Caleb over, what reason was there to remain upon the *Christopher Mitchell*. On shore she might find shade, breeze, and water for a bath.

When relieved, she returned to the oven of her berth. In that heat, Cook could have prepared the kid without a fire. The deck above and the sides of the ship radiated inward onto her. With only the companionway open to the outside, existence in the darkness of her bunk had become the epitome of hell. The place burned all day and through the night until the rising sun started it all over again. She existed within these two inhospitable worlds, masthead and bunk.

As soon as she closed the curtain behind her she laid bare her torso, and gently rubbed the sores that had formed on the skin of her waist. In the darkness, away from the eyes of the men, she moved her hands from her sides up over her breasts. Yes, she was still a woman, which could explain why tears had begun to flood her eyes again even though she had told herself she was long past that. No one comforted her. No one embraced her.

Joseph had told her that she could determine her own future and that his God could make things right. Yet, not much had changed. If God were real, surely He would have provided a solution by now. Six months was a long time. Another two years like this—she groaned, turned on her side, and hugged her knees. She once more cursed the man who had taken her from her home. But she had signed on. She pushed anger back. More tears streaked unseen down her cheeks. Oh, how she wished for someone to wipe them away. The heat pressed in. Each breath was a struggle.

She thought of Tom and breathed a little quicker which only aggravated the pain in her chest. He was the vision of a gallant, sensitive hero. He had rescued her so many times. Everyone liked him and he got along well with…most of his mates. She took a trembling breath. He was so easy to like.

Without grief, he accepted the loss of the woman he had loved. But, George could no longer ask him about such things. Sadness settled like a rock in her stomach. When she closed her eyes, she still felt his closeness. She wanted him to be the one to wipe away her tears. She wanted to be able to replace Jane. She dug her fingers into her legs.

Crying was not a pleasant sensation in her bunk, but she did it anyway. And, in some odd way, it felt good. Not knowing who else might be in the forecastle, she wept in silence. When her tears were done, she wiped her eyes with the damp canvas wrappings and dabbed her face dry. The irritation of sores in the small of her back overcame her thoughts.

§

Another morning came, just like so many before it. They were alone on their own watery world, going nowhere. Tom worked at the carpenter's bench sharpening harpoons and visiting with men who passed by. He had time for everyone but her. Something in the back of her mind kept repeating, *This ought not be*. But what could she say to him?

She walked up to him resolved to do what should have been done days earlier. He was sweating profusely and his shirt and pants were soaked.

"Looks like you just had a bath." She forced a smile.

"I wish that were the case."

They discussed the weather and other pointless topics, not what she really wanted to talk about.

"Back on Strong's island…." She fumbled for the right words.

"I don't really think we need to talk about that. Let's just say it was your fever or the kava."

"It must have been that. I don't remember much about it."

"Let's leave it there."

"Okay. But it's been hard. Your friendship has helped me bear these first months. I don't like it when we can't talk."

Tom squirmed as he ran the tip over the stone. "We can talk…whenever you want."

"Like we used to?"

He pushed the harpoon a little harder into the stone and shrugged.

§

Tom was glad George had come to him; he missed their chats. Yet, he didn't like talking about the kiss. For sure, he didn't want the boy touching him. He wasn't sure if they could ever have the friendship they had before. But, if the fever or the kava had controlled the boy, ….

§

George awoke in a sweat in the stifling darkness of her bunk. Something wasn't right. The side of the boat was much hotter than usual to her touch and the bunk was flat and still. The ship wasn't moving. The sound of the bow cutting the swells—the sound that had become her bedtime song—was not being played. Wiping the sweat from her brow and away from her eyes, she wrapped her waist, and forced her hands to apply those that concealed her breasts. The sensation was almost more than she could bear. Bound as she was, even perspiration would not provide relief from the unbearable heat. She eased into loose pants and a blouse.

The only sound in the forecastle came from bunks where others on her watch still tried to extract whatever restless sleep they could. Squinting against the brilliance of the day, she climbed into a heat fed from a ball of fire in the sky. She could almost reach out and touch it. The rope wasn't rubbing against the masts. No breeze wiped the sweat from her brow. The sails hung limp.

The watch on deck was busy at a job she had not seen before. With buckets on ropes, they dipped water from the face of the mirror-like ocean upon which the ship was set. The men poured it over the deck, which gave some relief to the feet. But the sides of the ship found no reprieve. The heat caused the pitch in the seams to swell, bubble, and run down the sides as it melted. Men sought the shade of useless sails. And still the watch was kept at the masthead.

She relieved a mate and lowered the bucket over the bulwarks. When it filled, she drew it up. Over and over until her arms ached.

"Heat getting to thee?"

"You know it does. And more today than other days. What is this we're in?" She moved a hand about her.

"We've fallen into a dead sea."

"How did we do that?"

"Just happens. No telling how long it will last…Thou dost look about as dead as this sea."

"I don't feel all that great either." She emptied a bucket upon the deck. Resting her arms on the railing, she stared down at a face buried somewhere beneath the surface of the water. A boy that was woman gazed back as if in some sort of trance. "I talked with Tom a while back."

"I know. I saw thee. How did it go?"

Lowering her bucket, she took a deep breath and let it out slowly. "Well enough for now."

Joseph nodded. Another bucket was emptied.

And again, George slowly lowered the bucket and let it rest just above the surface of the water. "I wish you hadn't told me that stuff about getting close to people…I am living a lie here…like this. When Tom finds out the truth, I worry that this will become a wall between us."

"Well, first, thou can hope that the revelation is a long ways off. But, when it does become known, perhaps thou wilt have been able to prepare him in some way."

"How?"

Joseph shrugged.

The day dragged on. The watches changed. The sun sank lower and lower toward the horizon. Laughing and talking came from the windlass, but no one was ready for song and dance. The night was no cooler.

George went below to the privacy of her bunk, stripped and lay naked. Whether a fever plagued her or just the awful heat, she didn't know; but she surely did not feel well. Sleep came, but not much rest.

She found herself on deck early the next day, still suffering the godforsaken heat. Even sitting in the shade did little to help.

"Land ho!"

"Where away?" called Clark.

"Aft, Sir," was the surprised reply. Without a point of reference, the ship had no visible motion, no forward or backward direction. So aft had meaning only with regard to the ship. Now, however, George saw the ship was moving; the current was carrying it toward the island stern first, a very unusual approach. A low mist just on the horizon had not yet burned off. Soon land replaced the waning fog. As the ship turned on the current, the island moved to starboard. George lowered the bucket and drew up another pail of water. Her eyes dimmed, and she staggered into the railing. She took a moment to rest.

The Captain and the Mates gathered about the carpenter's bench discussing the approach. Captain Sullivan called the boatsteerers.

A thin line of white appeared along the island's reef where the current caused the sea to break upon it. Between pails of water, George listened to the officers.

Captain Sullivan sounded unusually worried. "We can pray for wind, but, without it, we're at the mercy of the current. Mr. Wood, I need you to put our strongest rowers in two of the boats. Mr. Clark, Mr. Plass, you steer them. Tie the boats to the bow with long ropes. We need to pull the ship north to get around that island."

George groaned. This was just one more thing to bother her. But she was glad she would not be called upon as one of those to man the boats. She was strong, but there were others much stronger. When her watch on deck was over she adjourned to the shade of the foresails in the bow of the ship.

If pulling a whale was hard work, she wondered how the men on those boats must be struggling to pull a ship around the tip of the island. She leaned into the bulwarks for a good view of the rowers. The distance between the ship and the reef was still too far to see which would be victor.

"Pull, mates!" Charlie yelled from beside her and motioned them on. "The island is winning. Pull or we'll end up livin' on this pebble in the ocean."

There was no indication they heard. The looks of pain and exhaustion were evident.

If she were on the boats, she wouldn't want such cheers. "Why do you taunt them so?"

"'Tis not taunting. I encourage them. If we don't get around the reef, your hunt will be over."

"My hunt for Caleb already has ended." Her knees weakened, and she held to the bulwarks for support. "Now I hunt whales. I want this to be a remarkably greasy hunt." She didn't really, but it sounded good.

"So, you see it my way, eh?" Gorham joined them with the tone of a teasing friend.

"I'll leave it to Charlie to do him in."

"What do you mean?!" Charlie was all business. "There's a good chance we'll find the Mystic again. Aye, there is. Then you can get even for sure. May even find it at Paita if they're still on the line."

The thought raised a sudden thrill like a whale just breaking the surface of the sea. But she pushed it back below the surface. Mustn't let anger win. "No matter. It would do no good. My future doesn't depend upon Caleb." She told herself again that this was what she believed.

"Aye, I think you're right, George." Jamie added his expertise. "But it would be enjoyable to see his end."

"Perhaps, not your future." Charlie argued with her. "But what of Ann's?"

"For Ann's sake," said Jamie, "it would be…ah…entertaining."

"The poor fellow would be strung up by this posse!" Gorham hit Jamie's shoulder.

"She's probably gone on with her life by now." George looked into the distance. "I was foolish to seek Caleb on such a reckless venture."

"No, you weren't!" Charlie got up in her face. "She was wronged. It should be made right. No matter what these mates say, 'tis the noble thing to do."

She took a deep breath. "It will be made right in good time. I would like to have my hand in it, but don't want my future to depend upon it." She didn't feel well and arguing just made her more uncomfortable.

"Don't give up. We'll find him yet!" Charlie almost pleaded.

George shook her head and lowered her brow to her knees.

"What's the matter? You don't look so good." Gorham actually sounded concerned.

"Not felt well for some time. This heat is just making things worse."

"Maybe you should go below and rest."

Jamie's suggestion sounded good. But this was a bad time.

"Got to be in good condition when you meet Caleb," said Charlie.

"Not now. Too much going on."

Charlie turned aside to the boats. "Ev'ry mother's one of you, give it a pull! The ship's barely moving and the reef approaches."

They were within two miles of the island.

The Captain yelled for Charlie, Gorham, and Jamie. "Take the sounding ropes and call out the depths." Gorham went aft and Charlie forward. "Taylor, stay in the waist and tell me what you see in the water. Johnson…"

Ohhh. She wished he had not used her name.

"…get up the mainmast and yell down what you see coming between us and the reef."

They were within half a mile and losing the tug-o-war. Each step up was a deliberate motion as she told herself to focus on the job regardless of how she felt.

Charlie leaned forward on the verge of jumping up and down. "Pull! Pull!"

§

From the bow of the boat, Joseph faced aft. Every back strained. The look of pain mixed with fear in the eyes of those who turned to see the approaching reef. They pulled as hard as ever they had, yet the ship showed no perceptible movement.

"Keep at it…men!" He wasn't sure he heard himself.

Plass steered to keep the boats apart. "You do well!"

"Say a prayer!"

It came from someone on the boat. It didn't matter who. "For God's sake, then…" Each word squeezed through neck muscles drawn tight. "…pull on!"

Pull, raise, bend, dip, pull….

"Pray…each of you…as well. Pull and pray!"

The small breakers. So close. Doesn't look good. Without noticing, silent prayers became audible as his anxiety rose a notch.

Sweat and prayers.

§

"I see the reef in the water!" George's stomach caught in her throat. "About 300 feet ahead!" It veered away to the north.

The men, wet and laboring, pulled in unison, leaving eddies in the water.

Raise, bend forward, dip, and pull.

Their faces showed red. Whether from the sun or from blood in their veins, she could not tell.

"I see the reef!" Jamie pointed and turned a worried face to the Captain.

Gorham: "Twenty feet!"

Charlie: "Thirty feet!"

The approach of shallow waters was obvious from the patches of green water. They weren't going to make it! George was certain. Not enough speed to miss the northern side. "Reef bends away! But we've got to go faster!" *Oh, God!* It was there just ahead. "A rock! Just below the surface! Hundred fifty feet. We're headed right for it!" They just weren't moving fast enough.

"Pull! Pull!" Charlie's voice was as close to a shriek she had ever heard from a man.

Raise, bend, dip, and pull.

Raise, bend, dip, and pull.

The rock! "Hundred feet!"

Charlie: "Sounds to twenty five!"

Gorham: "Fifteen!"

What! The ship was making markedly better movement against the oncoming breakers. There was hope! "What is it?" She could not hold back her hope.

"The water itself, the current is moving us around the island," The Captain yelled for all to hear. "But it will be close!"

The water broke upon the reef within one hundred feet. The ship's stern was going to clear it.

"The rock!" Jamie ran aft along the bulwarks, no adherence to protocol now. The Captain joined him staring at the approaching obstacle hidden just under the water. The shadow beneath the surface came closer…closer.

"Pull!" The Captain yelled still gazing into the water.

The reef would be cleared, but the rock… George gripped the ring.

"Hard to starboard!" The Captain's focus did not change.

Mr. Wood turned the rudder. The stern moved to port, slowly, slowly. George watched the stern magically move and the rock—she gasped—just slip by. As shouts of victory arose from around the deck George breathed a sigh of relief. Her knees buckled and the ring caught under her arms. She had to get down.

"Free the wheel!"

Gorham: "Twenty five … twenty seven … thirty five!"

"Bring the men in!"

"Yes, Sir!"

George climbed down on shaky legs. To a man, the crews from the boats fell to the deck exhausted. She helped Gorham, Charlie, and Jamie raise the boats to the davits and secure them. The slap of canvas signaled a slight breeze and the sails began to fill.

Cheers continued all around the deck. Even George raised a weak fist triumphantly into the air. She shuffled slowly to the scuttlebutt, took a long drink, and brought a dipper full back to the men on the deck. Tom hung in a daze over the windlass. "Good job." She gave him a drink but not a hug. She held Joseph's head and poured swallows until he turned aside. "You saved us!" she said.

Joseph looked up. "I'll tell you who saved us. Every one of us was calling upon the Keeper of the Sea for help. He's the one who carried us past those breakers. Whoever shall call upon the name of the Lord shall be saved!"

George went back to the scuttlebutt, took more deep drinks herself, then carried the dipper back to the men. Handing it off to others, she went below; she didn't feel at all well.

Revelation

Monday, June 25, Day 206

The dark moved about her. Keeping one hand on a bunk for balance, she took one determined step after another through the forecastle. The familiar rocking of the ship was just noticeable along with a welcome sound of the bow cutting newly forming swells. Her bunk felt good. A gyration in her head made it difficult to remove her clothing. She loosened the bindings and let them fall where they might. Had she called upon the name of the Lord? Would she be safe? The danger of the reef was past. What of Tom? Would he ever know her as a woman? What of Caleb? How would she react should she find him? Thoughts and images flooded in and out and she really didn't care. Visions of these thoughts dallied with the darkness.

"…George?"

She heard the name. *Why didn't the fellow answer?*

"George!"

That's her. She's on the *Mitchell*. Jamie's calling her.

"Hmm?" She sounded weak even to her own ears.

"Are you okay?"

"I don't think so. I can't get out of the bunk just now."

"Here, I brought you some water." He reached in the corner of the curtain and found her hand.

"Thanks." Her hands trembled. "Tell Mr. Plass that if he needs me I'll try to tumble up. But, if not, I want to rest."

"I'm sure it will be okay. But I'll tell him."

§

"He's quite feverish." Jamie was definitely concerned. "Unless he's needed on deck, I think he ought to stay below."

Tom wished the news had been taken to one of the other harpooners. Now he needed to get involved and took the word aft. Since the dead sea, George didn't look well and the officers agreed the boy should rest, at least until another whale was spotted.

Seems they were more concerned about George than he was. This feeling that Tom didn't like rose within him. Perhaps George really was sick on Strong's Island. How much harder had he made the boy's life because of his wild imagination? Poor George suffered from fever even now. Throughout the day Tom considered that perhaps his analysis had been wrong.

The boy should have been up at least for the dogwatch. Maybe he needed something.

"George." Tom called softly at the curtain.

No answer.

"George!" He called more loudly.

There was a sound of stirring.

"Huh?" was the weak reply.

"It's Tom. Can I get you something?"

§

It took a moment for George to comprehend the question.

"Tom? Uh, yeah. Let me dress a little and you can help me up for something to eat."

"No, you can stay. Let me bring it to you."

"No, no." George tried to sound strong. This was Tom. "It will do me good to move about." She hurriedly put on her bindings and clothes. Tom helped her from the bunk and steadied her as she walked toward the ladder.

"What did Cook prepare?"

"It's Thursday, what do you think."

"Corn, beans, …"

"…and pork," they said together.

"And no one else is sick?" George forced a weak laugh. She had no appetite but would try to eat a little.

"George!" Jamie stood and made room.

"Feelin' better?" Gorham scooted over.

"Sit thee down!"

"I'll see what Cook's got left." Tom headed toward the galley.

The air was still warm, but not the blazing heat of the days before. Yet, a chill raised bumps on her arms. The fresh air must have been good for her, but her head still swam. She leaned on her knees to steady herself.

Tom returned with a ladle of water and a cup with a mixture of food. Her mouth was dry, the water good. But just the sight of the food turned her stomach. Licking the blade, she forced in a little of the meat. The saltiness gagged her. She took another drink of water and then used what was left to wash her face.

"I'm sorry." She wanted to stay next to Tom, but darkness assaulted her eyes. "I've got to lie down again."

"Let me help." Jamie reached down for her arm.

"No." Tom put his arm around her shoulders. "I brought him up; I'll help him down."

She leaned heavily upon him and used all her strength to pull herself into her bunk.

"Thanks, Tom."

"I'm sorry for the way I've treated you."

George thought she heard an apology. As in a dream, she undressed, unbound and drifted away on her blackened sea.

§

The next day, under a full sail, the sun beat down upon the deck, and the men worked at the usual jobs. Rope was spun; decks were washed, and washed again; the watch was kept; the sides of the ship were tarred. But George stayed below. The dogwatch passed.

Late in the middle watch, Charlie leaned peacefully against the carpenter's bench. He loved the excitement of whaling. One day he would be harpooner. He knew it. And maybe even a Captain. The sound of the ship…his mates…this was the life.

The wind had slackened and the sea was calm. Jamie was at the wheel with nothing to do but lean over the spokes and keep himself at least half awake. Poor fellow, with Mr. Clark next to him he couldn't doze. Clark leaned on the main rail with his arm over the monkey rail. Every so often, his head bobbed down, and he began humming the tune of some song to show that he was, in fact, wide awake. Charlie smiled.

A smoke would be good. Taking a cup of water with him for the boy (as hot as was the night, surely George could use a drink), he lowered himself into the forecastle and took the candle from the post. In the dim flickering shadows, he stuffed some tobacco into his pipe. After lighting it, he took a few long puffs. Peace filled him like the smoke he drew in.

With cup in one hand and candle in the other, he stood outside George's bunk. "George." His teeth clenched the stem of his pipe. He called quietly again with his head closer. He didn't want to wake the other sleeping mates. Still no answer. Carefully, he pulled back the canvas to rouse the boy. In the faint light, George lay uncovered and unbound. Charlie closed the curtain and backed up. The pipe hung loose in his mouth. When he stopped sucking air, it went out. He gasped. Trying to put the candle back, he fumbled it, and it fell to the floor, extinguishing itself. Should he pick it up? He hesitated. *That is a woman!* He tumbled up the forecastle steps with a bound and rushed aft, past Joseph, without a word.

Startled, Clark stopped his humming and stared as he ran up.
"There is a woman in the forecastle!"

§

Peleg fought sleep on the windlass. Supposed to be quiet on deck. He would give someone "what for" about this noise. "What's going on?"

Gorham stood near the forecastle companionway staring aft. "Don't know for sure. Charlie shot up out of the forecastle saying something about a girl below."

"What did he mean by that?"

"Don't know. Maybe he had a dream."

"Look! He's talking to the Second Mate!"

"The mule cock! Mr. Clark will have him swabbing the deck for weeks!"

"Yes, siree, he will!"

§

Joseph followed. He had a sinking feeling that Charlie knew something he shouldn't.

"What in creation is the matter with you?" Mr. Clark sprang off the rail and stood in front of Charlie ready to knock him down. "You're making no sense at all."

Charlie backed off. "George is a woman, sir! Come forward and you can see for yourself that he is!"

"You're speaking nonsense. Show me what you mean." He grabbed the lantern that hung by the wheel.

Joseph's stomach flinched. "It's not possible!" He followed after Clark and Charlie. Others joined the parade as they passed the mainmast heading aft.

"I know how you feel." Charlie bounced as he walked. "He had me fooled too…. Had us all fooled."

§

The growing throng of crewmen parted and let them past with Peleg close behind. Mr. Clark followed Charlie down into the forecastle.

"Do you think there is a woman down there?" Gorham's eyes were wide open.

"Nah! Where'd she come from?" Peleg had seen foolishness before. Charlie would get flogged for sure. If a woman had been on board he'd have known.

"Joseph." Apparently, Gorham didn't like his answer. "Why's the Mate in the forecastle?"

"Thy guess is as good as mine. I did hear Charlie say something about a woman in a berth below."

"How's that possible? How could a woman stay below, unnoticed!"

Whispers rushed about the deck like a summer breeze.

A revulsion of what he heard weaved its way through Peleg. "Someone's going to get flogged." He peered down into the forecastle. Others crowded next to him. But no one moved to follow the Second Mate. Peleg didn't want to be any where's around what might happen. Nothing was right about what was going on. Men huddled together on the deck or just stood in open-mouth amazement at the accusation.

No! Peleg shook his head. No woman could be on board the *Mitchell* without being found out.

§

Charlie quickly descended into the forecastle and pointed towards a berth that had its curtain partly drawn. He stepped quietly to the side. Everything was silent, except now and then one of the men, who had the watch below, tossed around in his sleep, uneasy in the heated quarters. Nothing had disturbed them. When the lamp shone into the berth, Mr. Clark stood dumbfounded. Charlie smiled. He was right. And the Mate knew it. There lay before them a beautifully formed woman. Clark just stood in the silence of the forecastle, staring, for what seemed an eternity. Impatience quickly overtook him; he wanted Mr. Clark to go on deck and tell the others he was right.

"How did she manage it?" Clark spoke quietly. "With 14 men in the forecastle." He blinked his eyes as if that would change what he saw, but the facts remained.

Handing the lamp to Charlie, he motioned for him to back away. As fringes of darkness settled upon the curtain, Clark closed it, moved back a step, and quietly called, "George!"

Sounds of stirring came from behind the curtain.

"George!"

"Aye?" The boy's…her voice was worried.

Mr. Clark moved his head nearer to the curtain. "Hurry on enough clothes to appear on deck. You do not belong in the forecastle and must go aft with me."

Charlie stood back. George was a woman. He shook with excitement. This had never happened before. And he had found her!

§

Joseph leaned against the carpenter's bench and looked around the tryworks. Would his deception soon be revealed. Charlie came up the steps first, with a smirk on his face, followed by Mr. Clark. The crew had expected some kind of verbal or physical discipline following such a preposterous accusation. When the two came up, one vindicated and one dumbfounded, they quieted and backed up.

Peleg alone approached the Mate. "'Tis true, Sir?"

With a motion of his hand, Mr. Clark quieted him. No one else said a word, waiting to see what would happen.

Joseph had kept a confidence although, as a boatsteerer, he should have revealed the truth. While he knew George would not expose him, his complicity ate away at him. He stood alone in the darkness. While he had wished this day to come months earlier, he did not expect it to come so soon. He was relieved that George … Ann would be put ashore soon in safety. If he just hadn't promised her.

§

Reaching for the canvas strips that had bound her for 8 months, she held them in her hand and quickly decided they were no longer needed. The Second Mate had told her she didn't belong in the forecastle. Somehow, he found her out. Happily, she set them aside. Worried, she hurried on her clothes. What would happen to her now? She was on a ship full of men. Would she still be a friend? Her legs still threatened to give in as she pulled herself along and up to the deck.

§

"George." Gorham drew close speaking in whispers. "What's going on down there. Is there…" Peleg nudged him. His friend stared at George's chest. He looked. His chin dropped. "You're a …." He looked up to her face unable to finish the sentence.

Peleg stared wide-eyed beside him as she hurried aft with the Second Mate.

"I told him! He didn't believe me. But it's true. You all saw it! George is a woman!" Charlie's words bubbled out of him.

Gorham remembered Neptune. A woman had shown more courage than he had. He was relieved that, besides George, only Tom and Jamie knew what happened below deck as they waited. She had a woman's shape. How could he have missed that?! George was a woman. She had served where no woman should have ever found herself. How could she do that! She had waded through blood and slime in the blubber hold. She had been a whaler. He walked as far aft as allowed. Nah! George couldn't be a woman.

§

Jamie put his thumbs in his rope belt and stretched out his queasiness. He had stood before her, NAKED, and encouraged her to come swimming with him. He closed his eyes and moaned. She deserved whatever punishment the Captain gave her. He had arranged a rendezvous between her and Meg. He remembered the look on George's face and chuckled. As he replayed that night in his mind, his body shook as he tried to stifle outright laughter.

§

As his mates walked to the waist, to see what followed, Charlie pictured the woman he had seen below deck, behind the curtain. George wasn't seeking the man who ruined his sister. She was searching for the man that ruined her! Not only was he feeling satisfied about his vindication with the Second Mate, he felt like a knight facing an evil enemy. What a noble hunt this had become! Wouldn't it be great to find Caleb!

§

"Captain!"

Thomas Sullivan sat up on the edge of his bed, rubbing his face. *Too early*, he thought. "Is there a problem, Mr. Clark?" He got up and walked to the door trying to wake himself up.

"I do believe so, Sir," The Second Mate stepped aside revealing George in the dim light.

"So, why did you bring the boy aft?" He yawned.

"Sir." Clark looked about the room but not at him. "Sir, this lad is not what he appears."

He didn't have time for this nonsense, not in the middle of the night. He looked squarely at Clark's eyes, wishing his Second Mate would get to the point.

"Sir, George is a woman. He, I mean she, is Ann, his sister."

Ridiculous! Now, he was awake. "What are you saying, man?"

"Look, Sir! He's a she."

A ludicrous accusation, but Captain Sullivan looked. It wasn't a cubby boy that stood before him! He reached out and turned George to the side. Her profile in the dim light showed a shape that did not belong to a man.

"I see what you mean." He had seen many things in his years on the sea, but nothing like this. What should he do? Where should he set her ashore? "Sit!"

§

The room was hot. Her legs weaved. If the Captain hadn't told her to sit she would have fainted right there. She buried her head in her arms upon the table at which the officers ate.

Twisting his moustache, the Captain stared at her.

"Rouse Hally and Fish. Have them prepare the spare stateroom."

She had been there for the slop chest. Other items were also stored in the small cabin next to the Captain's.

"Have them make a bed for her there. She can't stay in the forecastle."

With sleepy eyes and only wearing shorts, Tom and the other harpooner came in. Fish stared at her. "Why is the lad aft? Is something wrong with him?"

Tom's face was drawn in concern. "He'll be all right won't he?"

"She'll be fine." Mr. Clark spoke slowly.

George didn't want Tom to see her like this. She kept her head down and buried in her palms. Tears wet her hands as she imagined what he must be thinking.

§

It took a moment for Mr. Clark's words to sink in. Tom looked up to the Captain at the same time as Oliver.

"Men, it seems we've had a female serving on board these eight months. George is a woman."

Tom blinked again…and again. The boy looked like the same George. Surely the Captain had misspoken. Still, the command was to clean out the stateroom and prepare a bed. He went to work and, with Fish's help, quickly had it prepared as the Captain had requested. They stood back as Sullivan gently raised Ann to her feet. Against the light from the lantern, he saw it. *He really is a woman! But…* He stared as the Captain led her to the door of the stateroom.

Ann had wet streaks on her cheeks. Sobbing, she put her arms around the Captain's neck. "You have been so good to me and I know you will hereafter."

A surge of revulsion washed over Tom. A boy shouldn't act this way. *But he's a girl.*

"Yes, I will, you are a sister of mine as long as on board this ship."

"Thank you." She wiped her tears with trembling hands. "I don't think I could have stood my life much longer in the forecastle, if I had not been taken sick. I am glad it has been found out and would have told you before, but was too ashamed and wanted to reach some port and get away without being discovered. What are you going to do with me?"

"We are nearing Peru. I shall immediately shape the ship's course for Paita, and put you in the hands of the American Consul, who will send you home to your friends. Now go to sleep, you are as safe as if you were at home with your mother."

Tom had questions. He wanted to talk with the boy…the woman. Yet this loathsome energy filled him at the thought of George. He went back to bed, but didn't sleep.

§

Joseph slowly knocked on the door. He had never felt free to see George as Ann. When it opened, she still wore her seaman's garb. "Brought thee some breakfast."

She took it to the single chair beside her bed.

"It's good to see thee so much improved these last few days."

"Having this room, and the kindness of all the officers, has been a blessing to me. I can open the door and get at least a little fresh air. I even have a small porthole. I'm feeling quite a lot better. Captain Sullivan says we should be in Paita in about six days."

"Looks as if thou wilt have thy wish."

"A pleasant enough thought." Pause. "I will miss you. You've been a good friend!"

"What of Tom?" The question was to tease her, but he realized it had a serious side as well. "Wilt thou miss him?"

Ann took a few bites of the food. "I will…"

Her downcast countenance was not what he expected. Ann's journey as a whaler was coming to an end. But he hoped she would take something positive away with her. If she truly loved Tom, she would need to take steps to cross the gulf between them.

"…Why hasn't he come to visit? The other officers and boatsteerers have."

He shrugged. Ann wouldn't want to hear it. "I suppose thou wilt just have to ask when on deck next. If thou dost truly care for him, thou ought not part without making the effort to reconcile." He had another matter to ask her about. "Now that thy secret is known, what of thy hunt for Caleb? Hast thou forgiven him?"

Ann stopped eating and stared at her plate. Then slowly shook her head. "I believe I can overlook the fact that I will not find him. I should be able to go on."

"But hast thou let God remove the anger inside thee?" He tapped his chest.

She stared at the plate.

"Thou must let the Lord remove that bitterness, or it may surface and destroy that for which thou carest most."

Ann nodded and gradually returned to picking at her food.

Joseph wasn't sure she fully understood the importance of dealing with the bitterness. Still, if she wouldn't talk about it… "Think thou wilt feel up to coming on deck soon?"

"Soon. I want to finish my dress first."

A half finished dress draped over the edge of the bed, made with the Captain's calico and cotton. "Thou hast a good start."

Using a fork and spoon, Ann continued eating. Joseph noticed that, like a true whaler, Ann still carried her jackknife at her waist. It was, after all, a useful tool.

"Has anyone asked about our friendship and how it could be I didn't know thy secret?"

"No. No one. Have no fear. It is my turn to keep your secret."

§

When Joseph left, his words remained and bounced around her head. The time was short. In six days she would be off the ship. What a blessing! But, she only had six days to make things right with Tom. Where should she begin—and how? Now that her wish was a reality, and she was to be released from the *Mitchell*, she only had a few days. To Tom, she was the woman who pretended to be a man. She fidgeted on the bed, wishing that, at last, Tom might accept her as a woman. And she wanted to be rid of the bitterness that still crept into her heart when she thought of Caleb.

§

Tom sat upon the windlass running an oil stone over the point of an already sharpened harpoon. Over and over he ran it along the edges. The work kept him busy, too busy to possibly be tempted to go below and confront George.

He had sincerely enjoyed George's company. Then the lad kissed him on Strong's Island, a disgusting event. Now he tells us he's really Ann. Where George had said he did not know what he was doing on the island, did Ann actually know? What would that mean? For eight months, he had lived side by side with George, walked with him, ate with him, he had even relieved himself in his presence. He groaned. How could he see George as a woman! For eight months she was a man to him.

"I do believe thy harpoon is sharp enough to cut the toughest hide." Joseph took a seat beside him as Tom kept working. They sat for some time in silence.

Perplexed, Tom set the harpoon aside. "How is it you and the others can accept so easily that a woman served among us?"

"I can't speak for others. But, for me, I believe Ann did this because of a wrong done to her. And then I think of what she must have endured. She served in the blubber hold; she slushed the masts; she pulled after whales and cut them in; she worked the tryworks. No, Tom, I have no problem accepting her for who she is. I do believe Ann is an amazing woman."

Tom applied himself to the blade again, considering what Joseph had said. "To do what she did, she must be more a man than a woman."

"Hast thou talked with her yet?"

Tom shook his head.

"Thou canst not avoid her forever when we bunk near her stateroom. Besides, she may give thee a different understanding."

What he said sounded right, but Tom did not want to think about that. "How long will we be in port?"

"Probably just long enough to place Ann in safe hands and find a replacement."

Ann! The boy's name is George.

§

Ann walked forward from the cabin wearing the day dress she made. Oh how she had missed such attire…a high-waisted, loose fitting bodice with simple sleeves and a skirt with a sash tie and a slight train. Her stomach felt queasy; how would her mates react to her? Her garments were as foreign to the ship as they were to her after 8 months. Passing the carpenter's bench, she smiled at Peleg. He merely scowled and looked to the deck. Men with whom she had worked stood at the lookouts. She gave a timid wave and smiled.

"You! On the masthead!" Clark yelled upward. "There ain't no whales down here. Keep your eyes peeled toward the sea!"

She walked past the forecastle companionway and had no misgivings about not calling that her home.

"Well, would you look at that!" Jamie rose up before her.

"Mule cock! Is that George?"

"Quite pretty, for a whaler." The Second Mate stood next to Tom.

"Quite pretty for a woman." Jamie stared at her.

These were comments from her mates. It didn't seem right. Her face blushed, but she didn't try to hide it. She drank in the familiar scenes. From being the actress, she had become the spectator. It felt wrong walking past her shipmates as they toiled at jobs she had done by their side.

When Gorham moved a mop out of her way and extended his hand to help her over a pile of rope, her heart tried to leap from her chest in gratitude for this unexpected act of kindness. He had to shake his hand before she finally moved to take it.

"Thank you." Her voice almost broke with the words.

Gorham backed away as she passed. The man she wanted to see was just ahead.

"Hello, Tom."

§

Tom saw a woman. The dress she had made from the Captain's calico didn't belong amid the working clothes of the crew, and the person wearing them looked just as out of place.

His mates excused themselves and walked a short ways away but kept their eyes on him and Ann.

"Hello…George."

"It's Ann. I prefer that name."

Tom shrugged and tried to look away from her. "Hard to see you as Ann."

"Perhaps I went to too much trouble hiding who I am." She leaned against the bulwarks facing him.

"You know what I mean." He stared out to sea wishing she would go away. "I've looked at you as a boy. You weren't a woman. It's obvious what you are, but it's George I see."

"I wanted to tell you the truth, but how could I? I couldn't take a chance on being found out."

He turned toward her and looked her up and down. "Why did you do this!? Was your story true?"

Ann took a deep breath and looked down. "I started out hunting Caleb with every intention to kill him. What I found was a deeper understanding of myself. And I found friends. At least I hope the crew will still see me as a friend. I will always remember them."

She grew silent, and Tom turned his gaze outward again.

"I met you, Tom. Your friendship gave me strength. You're a wonderful man. You're caring, your family is important, and you have a passion for whatever you do! When I remember this voyage, I will remember you."

Tom didn't want to hear that. He didn't want to be remembered by this boy-woman. He felt himself blushing. To be sure, this person made him uncomfortable. But he had one question. "I have to ask, on Strong's Island, did you really have a fever?"

"No."

He joined this hunt to be the master of his life. Destiny was something he determined. Yet, since the kiss, life was not clear. This…this boy-woman caused him no end of turmoil. He walked off. What he was thinking had no business being voiced. But what else could she have done? He shook his head. Her face still bore the rough and sunburned look of a seaman and her hands the signs of hard work. But, with her canvas wraps off, she was far from a chubby boy. She radiated a beauty that went beyond her physical appearance. Her dark, short, rough-cut hair gave a carefree look that just added to her character. Had this been a different place, a different time….

§

That night, Ann couldn't sleep. She put on her dress and left the cabin. The boatsteerers' door was shut and the room quiet. Snoring came from behind the Captain's door. Except for the sounds of sleep, all was silent. She climbed quietly to the deck. Stars filled the sky and reflected from the water all around the ship. Most of the crew was either below or resting around the windlass. The ship rose and fell, gently rocking with the swells. Such a peaceful night. They would be in port in two days. If this were the typical life of a whaler, she would beg to stay on board. Her right hand moved along the railing, feeling the wood, feeling the ship. When she got to the rigging, she placed both hands upon it and pulled, recalling her first climb and Job.

"Whaler is no place for a woman!" A low, threatening voice shattered her reverie.

She spun around face to face with Peleg. He glared at her.

"Bad enough having the boy on board."

She didn't like the old man's wild look and tried to move aft, toward her cabin, but he stepped to the bulwarks blocking her way. She fought back the urge to yell for help or run, choosing instead to meet the problem head on.

"Having a woman on board's bad luck. Nothin' good can come of it. No, siree." He glared at her. "I never serve on a ship with a woman on board. You ain't supposed to be here."

Looking him in the eyes, she said with a strong voice that surprised even her, "I will be off soon enough and out of your hair."

"Nay, not soon enough!" He took a couple of steps toward her.

§

All along he'd known something was not right about that boy. Hadn't he said so? Ship's no place for the likes of her. Got to be rid of her once and for all…for the sake of the ship and the crew. He pulled his knife from his belt. She gasped and jerked back. He twisted it within inches of her face. Easy enough to be rid of a woman. Yes, siree. He knew. "Job's not here to rescue you this time."

As he was speaking, the startled look on Johnson's face transformed into one of guarded anticipation. She pulled her knife from the sash about her waist and backed up, giving room between them.

He hadn't expected that. A woman never did that before. Just the same, this was only a female. He aimed the knife for her throat and thrust. As she stepped aside, her hand grasped his arm and stopped the knife

What's this! Some men didn't have grips that strong. He shook his arm, but she refused to let go. He stared at her. She looked back with no fear on her face. Surprise maybe, but no fear. This wasn't right! As he tried to break free, she smashed his hand into the bulwarks, shooting pain from his wrist up to his shoulder. Anger shook him from the inside out. A woman couldn't to this to him! She took a step closer, her knife shimmering in the starlight before his face. He lunged for that arm, but she agilely avoided his attack. She twisted his arm and pulled. It hurt. She spun him into the bulwarks. His buttocks hit the railing. He reached for her hair. Then his feet were off the ground…falling backwards.

"No!" He dangled above the water. The woman still had hold of his wrist and quickly reached over with her other arm grasping him tightly. He didn't want her help, but if she let go he'd drown for sure. He looked down and the dark swells lapped at his feet. He reached up, trying to find her with his free hand, and kicked wildly for a foothold against the smooth side of the ship. "Don't let go."

§

Tom tossed and turned in his bunk, unable to sleep. Thoughts of George…Ann…had plagued him all night. She even kept him from sleeping. Hearing noise in her stateroom, he listened more closely; it sounded as if she was going up on deck. He needed to talk with her. Pulling on his pants, he followed her to the deck.

"Someone help! Over here!"

It was Ann's voice.

"Man overboard!"

Racing to her side, he helped pull Peleg back to the deck.

"What happened?"

By this time, all the men on deck had gathered around them with questions.

"The old man must have dozed off." Ann smoothed out her dress. "Happened to be walking by as he fell over. Managed to grab his arm."

"You fell asleep on the rail, Peleg?" Charlie shook his head.

Peleg grumbled something as he reached down and picked up his knife. Then he walked off rubbing his arm and shoulder.

Some of the men tried to follow, but he was in no mood to talk.

Others stayed and praised Ann for her help. Gradually, all left but Tom.

"Best pick up your knife." The blade just showed from under the bottom of her dress. She had not told the whole truth—again.

She stuck it back under her sash.

"So, we're alone. What really happened?"

Ann hesitated. "I just would like to leave this ship without any more trouble. I've had enough already, especially these past weeks."

If she didn't want to tell him, that was fine. There were other things he wanted to discuss. He didn't know where to begin, but he wasn't happy the way things were between them. "Ann, these past days have been miserable for me. I've missed your company." Her eyes began to water, and he choked up. "I… I just don't know if it's the boy or the woman I'm missing."

"I'm the same person, Tom."

"But I don't know if you are to me. The problem is, I want to find out."

"I would like that too. What's wrong with that?"

"We only have two days."

He walked aft with her, away from prying eyes.

§

Ann dined with the Captain and the officers. "What's to be expected of me?"

Captain Sullivan lowered his fork. "We will contact the consulate, and they will arrange passage on a ship back to the states. Can I make a request of you?"

"Certainly, Sir. You know whatever I can do for you I will."

"Would you wear the rig of a sailor for me when leaving the ship?"

Such clothing was not her first choice. She frowned, and then smiled. "I will, this one last time. But know that I hope never to wear anything but my own outfit after that."

The officers feigned hurt attitudes.

"No more sailorin'?"

"You don't approve of our profession?"

"Ann!"

Captain Sullivan quieted the comments. "Where do you want to go? They can make arrangements for wherever you would like."

The First Mate leaned forward. "Nantucket's a great place."

She didn't really have anywhere. "I have no one there. I suppose New York. That's where I signed on. From there I can go most anywhere easily."

"You're going home, aren't you?" The Third Mate asked the question she had mulled over for days.

"Probably start there. Don't know that my parents will welcome me, but I do have an uncle I'd like to see. And there are friends along the Canal."

"Anyone that don't want to know you will be missing out."

"Thanks, Mr. Clark. But, if you think about it, what I have done would shame many families."

"Well, I for one," said the Third Mate, "count it a privilege to have served with you. We will be hard-pressed to find a replacement as good as you."

The others agreed.

Her face flushed, and she excused herself, offering to take the dirty dishes to the galley. It just didn't seem right to sit with the officers after having served so long as a common hand. She gathered up what she could carry and left the officers as they lit up pipes, talking.

§

Tom sat alone, back against the front of the galley. He looked forward to where the men had gathered to eat. He wasn't hungry and just picked at his food.

After leaving an armful of dishes with Cook, Ann took a seat beside him. "Captain says we'll be in port tomorrow."

"Excited about going home?"

"Don't know for sure where I'll go. But it will be exciting. What about you?"

"It's a little soon for thinking about going home. There's still two years left on this voyage."

"I know. But do you think you'll sign on again?"

That was a difficult question. Probably not right away. Maybe later. Maybe not. He might want to find Ann. "I think once is enough. But who knows?"

"Have you decided yet whether you miss Ann or George?"

Tom looked into her eyes for the longest time. He wasn't sure any more. "Tomorrow comes quickly, Ann. It's difficult to reshape an eight-month relationship in just a few days."

She looked up. Tears had formed.

"Now don't do that." He put his arm around the woman. "You know how the crew will tease a mate that cries like this." He smiled and remembered the past months. The look on her face was one he had not seen before. She appeared content but the tears didn't stop. He began to choke up as well.

Ann wiped her eyes and forced a smile. "You ought to go on forward with your friends."

"Aren't you coming?"

"No, the Captain said he wanted me to wear a sailor's outfit. I've got to get my cleanest clothes ready. May take some washing. They're pretty stiff."

"Don't want to use Peleg's barrel?"

She frowned.

Tom remembered a chest he had seen under his bunk. "Say, I know where Job's clothes are. He was about your size. There may be something in his belongings."

She hesitated.

"He was your first real friend. What better way to leave the ship than wearing his clothes."

Avoiding the officers, Tom helped her down the ladder, through a small hatch beside the galley, to the boatsteerers' quarters. The scent of pipe smoke filled the air. With the sun setting, the portals gave little light so Tom lit a lantern and led her into the quarters shared by the harpooners.

He knelt down in a corner and rummaged through some chests

and old clothes. He glanced back at Ann. In the twilight of the cabin; she looked almost angelic. This warmth spread over him, a feeling he'd not had in over a year.

§

Peleg leaned against the carpenter's bench ready to begin a game of backgammon with Gorham.

"Heard you lost your footing last night."

What! Does the whole ship know?

"Cursed woman." Peleg slammed his pieces onto his starting position.

Gorham looked startled.

Why did that surprise Andrews? Peleg shoved the board toward his mate.

"So what do you think of actually having Ann on board?"

Peleg tensed and felt anger rise to his face. "That woman is a disgrace." He barely got the words out. "She should be doused like the forecastle candle before something bad happens to us all."

"Come now, Peleg. She's quite the woman. May not agree with her hunt for Caleb, but she is remarkable." He looked off into the distance.

"Fool! You should be put off with her." He hit the game and the chips scattered across the deck.

Gorham stood up. "We're going to be in Paita tomorrow. She'll be off then."

Peleg tried to explain to his young mate about the problems with women on a whaler, but Gorham just stared back, gaping. There! He'd said it. Surely, Andrews would appreciate the argument.

"You are one bitter old man. Sounds to me like you're a smoldering wick that needs to have its fire relit or be put out yourself."

Fool! He'll learn soon enough. He stomped off. Gorham could pick up the pieces.

§

Laughter from the aft dining area was lost to her hearing. This tall figure bent low in the dimness was the whole world. She watched and wished things could be different.

"Here it is!" Tom pulled something from the corner. "I knew I'd seen it. Never thought we'd need it."

Just the two of them, alone. He saw her as Ann. This was a moment she had longed for. He looked at her, holding the chest. If only he held her. *Not yet!*

She cleared her throat and backed away. He set it on the floor. Clothes she hadn't seen for six months brought back memories of a friend lost in the cold waters off the Horn. But, looking at Tom, she wondered, when she left the *Christopher Mitchell* this one last time, would these friends be as dead and gone, though they lived?

She ran her hands over the contents, a blouse, a kerchief, stained pants. She heard Job's laugh and his chastising. She saw him sitting at the maintop, hair rustled by the breeze. She touched the fabric and touched him one more time. She closed her eyes, but tears still slipped out and rolled down her cheeks.

In the end, she pulled out a blouse and pants that were nearly new. "These ought to work."

§

One moment she wanted to cheer and the next she fought back tears. Leaving the ship should be easy, except for Tom. Yet the Christopher Mitchell had been her home and life for eight months. It carried her through storms, to new worlds, and changed her. The work was worse than bad, but these men were her friends. Emptiness welled up inside her, bursting within the joy of expectation. This Thursday, July 5, was different from any other day of the last eight months, for the end of her voyage was actually in view. And she wasn't sure this was what she wanted. With all hands on deck, the ship slipped slowly into the harbor at Paita, Peru.

"There 'tis again!" Charlie stood on the balls of his feet and pointed. "She's passing to port!"

Just one more emotion thrown into the mix. The *Mystic* passed not more than fifty yards away. Faces turned her way to see what she might do. What could she do? She stayed sitting in a chair in the shade of the cabin. The *Mystic* slowly approached. She would not see it again, nor the man it carried. She fondled her knife.

Peleg watched from the railing. Oh, how she didn't want to wind up like him. Anger held him. It no longer hid beneath his surface; it swam freely in his life. Bitterness had its way in Peleg. *Oh, God, if you're there, I need a work in my life. Don't let me end up like that old man. Let me forgive Caleb. As he passes out of my life here, let it be for good.*

Captain Sullivan walked up. "So, Ann, you showed no anger at the passing of this opportunity."

"Sir, I just hope it is forever gone."

"So do I, Ann. So do I." He paused. "Do you know what you will do when you get home?"

"Not sure. But I know there are needs out there that I can meet. There is a place for me."

"Don't just seek a place, Ann. Don't force yourself into a mold defined for you by the world. Ask yourself what makes you come alive and go do that." He spoke to her with an insistence she had not seen before, as he might talk to his daughter. "That's what the world really needs, people who are alive in what they do. If nothing else on this voyage, I would hope you have come to understand, that doing what you love makes all the difference. Why, I'd wager that most of the men on the *Mitchell* would not be here if it were not something they loved."

§

On Friday, Captain Sullivan and the First Mate traveled to the consulate and scheduled a meeting for Monday with Mr. A. Bathurst, the American Consul. While the consulate would ultimately take responsibility for returning Ann, an issue remained around reimbursement for the cost of shipping her home and her board while at the consulate. Such a discussion could delay her return. Surely, it would determine the nature of the passage she would receive.

On Sunday, Joseph talked on the importance of friendship. Everyone attended; Ann wore the dress she had made and sat a little aft of the crew, with the officers. At the end of the meeting, Jamie helped her from the chair as men gathered around to wish her well.

"We ought to give her more than just words," said Tom.

Jamie's agreed. "Aye. We wouldn't be here but for her."

Charlie pulled off his cap and threw in two cents. "Let's take an offering to help with the cost."

The men pulled out what change they had and tossed it into the cap.

"What's going on?"

"Mr. Clark, sir. We're taking an offering to help with Ann's fare." Charlie held his hat between them.

The Officer looked in. "You'll need more than that."

Where else could they get money? Tom moved closer to the Mate. "What about the slush fund?"

Mr. Clark nodded and took the cap aft and returned with it nearly full. "We all gave. Even Captain Sullivan put in from his own funds."

Charlie took it and did a little jig. "Sir, can we go to the other ships?"

Mr. Clark looked to the deck in thought.

"I could go and be back before eight bells."

Jamie hurried over. "We could all go and be back in no time."

The crew set out on Sunday afternoon going from ship to ship. The word spread that a woman, dressed as a man, had shipped on the *Christopher Mitchell* as a common hand and that she was to be disembarked in Paita for return to the States. She had done so to search for the man that ruined her. The intensity of the *Mitchell*'s men convinced other crews of the truth of this unbelievable story. They returned Sunday evening with over $500 given by the officers and men of the other ships.

§

Ann had just finished packing her things when Tom came to her dimly lit stateroom.

"I wanted to see you before you left with the Captain."

She had this empty place in her bosom that only he could fill. And now she was leaving. The past night she had cried enough. She smiled up at him.

"You know what I said the other day, about not being enough time to change how I see you?"

Of course she did.

He just stood looking at her, hands twisting his pants, not speaking. If anything was to be said, he would need to say it; she had no words.

"I want to see you as Ann."

She gasped. She had been holding her breath and didn't know it.

"You have been a great friend and I have truly enjoyed your company." The words flowed from him as if rehearsed. "I would like you to write to me. And, if you're agreeable, I would like to meet again when my part of the voyage ends. I care about you and …"

The words were a blur but Ann knew what he meant. Before he could finish, she reached up, put her arms about his neck, pulled herself close to him, and did something she had wanted to do for a long time. She gave him a kiss, which he knew was coming from a woman. He kissed her back.

"I wish we had more time."

She did too. "I know. I'll see you on deck." She sat down on the edge of her bunk as Tom left with her trunk and closed the door. She had kissed Tom and he kissed her back. Tears of happiness mixed with those of sadness. This parting would be for two years.

§

Captain Sullivan came to bring Ann forward. Striking! For him, she had dressed one last time as a sailor, at least somewhat. But her beauty began on the inside. She carried herself with confidence and assurance that the outward appearance simply framed. Caleb was such a fool.

"Ann." He held out his arm.

"Sir." She took it and he led her forward.

The darkness of her tan had lightened a little from days recuperating away from the sun. Her cheeks showed a fine blush of roses. On her head she had a braided Timor sennet hat, made of sail cordage. Around it, was a black ribbon an inch in width, the two ends hanging three inches over the rim from a double bowknot fastened behind the hat. Job's blouse was white with a wide collar of blue hanging well over the shoulders and down the back. Under this and around the neck was a black silk handkerchief. Captain Sullivan recognized it as one he had given her. She tied it in a sailor knot. The ends hung halfway to the waistband of her pants. The bosom of the shirt was also of blue, with cuffs of the same color turned back on her arms three inches. She dressed in the rig of a sailor but didn't look like any sailor he had seen.

Job's pants were of black broadcloth. Since he was not quite as wide as she was in the transom, they fit her form without a wrinkle. From halfway down her thighs they widened to where they reached the heel, so that when she pulled forward the bottoms would just overlap the toe. On her feet she wore a pair of white socks and low-quartered shoes.

He had wanted to present a seaman. Here was a lady, a beautiful woman! The outfit hid nothing.

Everyone listened as Captain Sullivan talked. But the men kept stealing glances her way. She tried not to laugh. These were the men with whom she had whaled. Eyes struggled to see her, a quick turn of the head and then back. The overall appearance was far from an official attention. Yet she gave every indication that this was the most serious and well-presented formal staging as any on any ship.

Captain Sullivan faced her head on. "…Ann, we owe you our lives. None of us would have chosen to take a woman as a hand, but we are glad you served with us. As you take your leave you are dressed as a sailor, which is only fitting."

When his hand snapped to his forehead, a blush washed through her face. Salutes weren't part of ship protocol, but here was the Captain saluting her. She tentatively raised her right hand and returned it.

"Your mates wanted to help you on your way. Here is a gift." He handed her an envelope with two hundred dollars.

Tears formed and she didn't need to hide them. Her mates smiled, obviously pleased with the response. She wiped her eyes with the back of her hand.

"This is for you to use however you see fit. They raised over five hundred dollars but three hundred will be given to the consulate for your care and transportation home."

Each of the hands had wishes for her. Captain Sullivan proudly stood beside her as the men filed by. She bowed her head. They shouldn't have done this.

The men came aft one at a time. When Jamie stopped and reached to shake her hand, she leaned forward and kissed him on the cheek. "You shall carry always the stripes earned from our adventure on the Enchanted Isles. Yours are on the outside; mine are on the inside and will bleed anew every time I think of what you did for me."

"I would take them again a hundred times, Ann."

By the time Charlie reached her, the fellow could hardly contain himself.

"I shall miss you," she said.

"If we find the Mystic and Caleb, we shall do him in for you."

The Captain frowned.

Charlie blushed.

She smiled and hugged him.

Peleg walked up, head lowered, refusing to look at her. He had nothing to say, but she did. "Peleg, some of us fight bigger monsters than others. Let Joseph help you as he helped me."

When the old man raised his eyes to hers, he looked to Ann like a cat in the rain. "I will pray for you."

He said not a word.

Gorham stood before her face to face. "You taught me a lot about men," she said. "But, if we meet again, let me ask one thing of you."

"Ask, Miss Ann."

"Please do not refer to me by that anatomy of a mule."

The men nearby stifled laughs as he turned red and smiled.

Last of the crew were the boatsteerers.

Tom stood before her for the last time on the *Christopher Mitchell*. "You are lovely in every way." He choked up and wrapped his arms about her. She collapsed against him and they embraced. "Please write. I will wait for each letter from you. Now I have a reason to not sign up again."

She didn't want to let go.

The Captain cleared his throat.

Tom walked off, head bowed.

Fortunately, Joseph was next. He understood why she was flustered. "Ann, great things are in store for thee. Just remember what hides beneath the surface and Who it is that can remove it."

She wiped her eyes and took a deep breath. "Joseph, my Friend, you saved my life. You are my friend forever. May God bless you abundantly."

"On this trip He already has. Here." He handed her a note. "Read it and, whenever you do, remember me."

She hugged him tightly. "Goodbye and thank you."

She waited for one officer in particular. They were next. When Ben Clark stopped in front of her, she clung to his hand for a few moments and lowered her voice. "The officers of this ship are Gentlemen, and have my heartfelt thanks, but you in your kind actions on the night of my discovery, I shall remember as long as I am alive."

When all the men had passed by, the Captain went to the side where the boat waited for her. She walked towards him smiling, thankful for his kindness. Usually a reserved man, he caught her in his arms and kissed her. "I beg your pardon, Miss Ann, but I just had to give you a good down-east kiss."

What...He was her Captain....But no more...and she was not a sailor. Granting the pardon, she reached up and kissed him gently back on the cheek as she might have kissed her father. She liked being a woman again. "God bless you who have been more than a brother to me, a poor ruined girl." She hoped her coy smile told him that she no longer considered herself to be such.

"If at all possible, Miss Ann, come to Nantucket and visit my home when we return. I would so enjoy you meeting my wife and children."

"I will see what is in store for me."

They went down the side into the boat and started for shore. Ann refused to look back. Tears picked at her eyes. After turning Joseph's note over and over, she opened and read.

> *You have finished one voyage and begun another.*
> *Let the Light be your Captain and your Mate. You will*
> *have choices to make; choose wisely, seeking your*
> *Captain's purpose. When storms come and you are*
> *tested and tempted to your old ways, remember who it is*
> *that leads you. When danger seeks you, count on your*
> *Captain's counsel. I will pray for you each day.*
>
> *I shall remember you always and will proudly tell*
> *all I meet of your courage and your victory over the*
> *beast within. It has been a privilege to know you and to*
> *be counted as your Friend and friend.*
>
> *Always yours, Joseph*
> *Hussey*

She wasn't sure she had been victorious over the beast, for she still felt its presence. Folding the note, she placed it in her blouse.

"Sir." She looked back to the Captain. "Why do you suppose all those people have gathered around the landing?" On the shore, a large crowd looked their way.

"I'm not sure. But we shall soon find out."

They were interested in her. The news had spread about a woman who passed eight months on the *Christopher Mitchell* as a common hand. Men, women, and children strained to catch a glimpse of her. The crowd parted for them. Children reached out to touch her, and she shook the hands of those who were willing.

Upon entering the Consul's home, Captain Sullivan bid Ann goodbye and was taken to Mr. Bathurst's office while she was whisked away by his wife. A warm bath had been drawn and caressed her every pore. The perfumed water teased her nose. She washed her hair and relished the feeling. When she left the tub, she left the remnants of a whaling life, reborn. She was clean for the first time in eight months.

Mrs. Bathurst and her daughter of eight doted over her, as if she were a giant doll, trying to find the perfect attire. Ann had never worn such magnificent clothes.

And the words—she had been away from women far too long. She covered herself in the soft chatter of mother and daughter, no longer needing to guard what she said.

Timidly she followed them to the garden where the three sat in the shade, mother and daughter listening to stories of natives, whales, storms, and sailing. Late in the day, the Consul joined them.

"Where's Captain Sullivan?" she asked.

"Returned to his ship. They will continue their hunt tomorrow."

"What of me?"

"We will send you home on the next ship upon which passage can be arranged. Until then you are welcome to stay with us. I believe you have already found your way into the hearts of my wife and our daughter."

Mrs. Bathurst smiled approval as her daughter squealed excitedly.

That evening, for the first time in months she slept on a soft bed. Halfway through the night, when she would normally rise for a watch on deck, she looked out upon the peaceful harbor lit by a nearly full moon. The *Christopher Mitchell* was held at anchor like a majestic beast hitched and awaiting the start of a new and exciting hunt. She knew every mast, rope, and yard. She thought of Tom and closed her eyes imagining what the future might hold. Was he thinking of her?

Finding the bed too soft, she fell back to sleep lying on the floor and dreamt about the man she would see in two years.

§

He lay in a dark, dismal room, alone though others were there. His mates on the *Mystic* had done this to him. They said he was growing tiresome. *Bah!* The crew would have done well to heed him, but they just didn't like someone around who knew more than they did. And the Captain didn't believe him when he said the dogwatch fight was planned and the mates broke his leg on purpose. When he was carried away to this hole, no one bid him well. No one would miss him in his absence. The fools!

He was alone in a foreign port. No telling how long he would be in bed. A fever made his sleep restless. He could call for a nurse and one might come, or she may not. Quiet conversations swam in the darkness. Some he understood; others were in languages he did not know. If they talked to him it mattered not. He was of no mind to answer back. His body hurt in more places than he could count, which tended to keep him in the twilight of sleep. He stared into the darkness imagining his knife at the throat of those who put him here. The injury had ruined his chances for riches on the hunt. And the care on the *Mystic* surely hadn't helped the healing of his leg. If it didn't mend properly, it might ruin any prospect for future work.

He moved in and out of sleep, finding it difficult to tell which was which. His dreams were far from pleasant; most were upsetting, which blurred the boundary between them and the reality of where he was. A distant shanty drifted into his darkness. Dream or reality? Sleep or waking? The chant was mixed with other noises, sounds of early morning business. It repeated and came more clearly. Dream or reality?

> A wonderful woman our sister Ann
> Haul him up and try him out!
> Was wronged and wounded by a scandalous man.
> Haul him up and try him out!
>
> Went a whalin' she did but not for a fish.
> Haul him up and try him out!
> To run the man through, that was her wish.
> Haul him up and try him out!
>
> Now what was his name, this unfortunate foe?
> Haul him up and try him out!
> Who was the scum who would sink so low?
> Haul him up and try him out!
>
> Caleb by name, we hunt him the same
> Haul him up and try him out!
> For the things he has done he is surely to blame.
> Haul him up and try him out!
>
> Rebecca Ann, for you we sail on
> Haul him up and try him out!
> For whales and Caleb, hither and yon.
> Haul him up and try him out!

At the last stanza, his eyes opened wide, and he knew he was awake. He grabbed the dress of a passing nurse. "Did you hear that. What did they say?"

"Calm down." She extricated herself from his grip. "Hear what?"

"That shanty."

"Aye, mate," said the man in the bed next to his. "I miss the chants meself, I do."

The woman straightened out his sheet. "Never pay attention to them."

Caleb frowned and mussed up his sheet again. "Listen! It begins again."

She paused. "Ah." She laughed. "The story is that a woman sailed as a whaler on the *Christopher Mitchell* to hunt down the man that ruined her. Don't know that it's true, but that's what I heard."

He knew the truth of what she said. Ann was the man his mates warned him about. What must she have done to survive in the forecastle with all those men, to have them keep her secret! A woman like that would do anything. Since the Galapagos Islands, he had worried about meeting with the *Mitchell*. The only good thing about being put off in Paita was that he would certainly be safe. Ann would not find him here. His muscles relaxed.

The sailor beside him rolled onto his side. "She must be some woman to work as a tar on a whaler and win the hearts of her mates. Did you hear the words?"

The nurse rearranged his sheet. "The woman was put ashore yesterday." She turned and left.

Immediately, his muscles tightened. Pain shot up his leg.

"Some shanty, eh mate?"

The prattling from the fellow next to him didn't help.

"She's got a ship full of blokes on her side! I would hate to be that Caleb fellow."

The *Mitchell* had come close three times, and now Ann was here. How did she know where he was? She had tracked him this far. What would she do? His mates told him she wanted to cut him in and try him out. If she found him like this… He tried to sit up. He had to get away.

"Avast there." The mate reached across and grabbed his shoulder. "What's your problem? Want I should call the nurse back?"

He shook his head and collapsed back onto the cot.

"What's your name, mate?"

How could he tell him his name!

"Eh." The man drew out the word. "You ain't the Caleb in that there shanty are you?" He laughed at his joke.

Caleb's leg hurt too much to stand. He stared at the ceiling. His heart thumped madly, and he felt drained, like he was running a race—and losing. Ann was coming.

§

"Do you hear that?" The young girl ran to the window.

"Aye." How could the Captain allow such a shanty?

"That's about you, isn't it?"

"Aye." She wished they had used another song.

"Wow!" The youngster listened to every word.

Ann smiled as the sails unfurled, stretched to their full length, and filled with the breeze. She pictured her friends raising the anchor. As the last repetition of the chant was dulled by the canvass and the turning ship, the *Christopher Mitchell* sailed majestically out of the port of Paita, Peru.

Ann hoped they would not use that shanty again.

§

The consul's wife took the basket and led her daughter and Ann toward the hospital.

"I'm glad you decided to come with us." The girl tugged on her arm.

"I should do my part to help." She knew the sicknesses and injuries sailors experienced. "I am put off in Paita and experience such kindness as I shall always remember. Not all people are so fortunate."

Mrs. Bathurst's face was filled with concern. "From what sick seamen have told me, the hospital may be dreary, but it is still a far cry better than the forecastle of a whaling ship."

"You have no idea!"

They walked down the dirt street, Ann hand-in-hand with the youngster, carrying sweet breads made by the servant staff at the consulate. Every Tuesday, Mrs. Bathurst took treats to the hospital. Her daughter often attended as well to learn the benefit of a good character in helping those less fortunate. Starting with those who were there longest, she was greeted with cheers and halloos.

She teased the men, flirted, and shared the bread they had brought. She was appreciated. This was good.

"Who's the new angel?"

"This'll help recovery!"

"Avast, over here!"

Mrs. Bathurst spoke softly to her. "What a good example for my daughter..."

How could she say that of her?

"...I am amazed how such loveliness could be born from such a beginning and radiated from such roughness."

But the lady was sincere. Ann smiled back.

"You are a beautiful woman, Ann."

The next ward contained the newest arrivals. Most had not been treated to the Bathurst kindness. As Ann walked among the beds in the dim light, eyes watched and soon saw these ladies as bearers of treats. They tasted the gifts and wanted more. The level of cheer rose visibly. Ann liked being seen as an angel of goodness.

She stopped beside one of the beds. "What's your name?"

At her voice, the man tensed and gasped, as if choking?

What had she done? "Nurse!"

One of the aides in the ward came with a lantern. When the light reached the bed, the sailor had covered his head with the blanket. It took the two of them to pull it down.

The scar! Caleb!

The aid left to help at another bed.

You have him now! The beast breached higher and higher till it hid everything else. *End it now and you need only wait for Tom!* As the first fury again enveloped her, hair bristled on her neck and her skin crawled. *That's it! Your knife!* Her hand grasped the jackknife, hidden beneath the sash that encompassed her waist. *Pull it out. Now! Before someone comes. HE RUINED YOU!*

The knife was in her hand in front of her. She had used it to kill, to disembowel, to slice, to do most everything. Blood wasn't a problem for her. It would be so easy to finish what she had started. Like a harpooner ready to cast his iron, she stood before her prey.

Caleb stared eyes wide.

Ann smelled perfume, her perfume. Petticoats caressed her legs, not bloodied pants. Her dress picked at the edge of her vision. A woman held the knife. To her friends on the *Mitchell* she was a lady. To the Consul's family she was an example. *Who am I?*

To Caleb you are a diversion! Finish it! Now! HE RUINED YOU!

Ruined? She thought of Tom; she saw Peleg; she heard Joseph's words.

No! She cried inside. She recognized this monster. *Away!* If she did THIS, she would be ruined. *Lord, I've sinned.* She felt the desperate beating of her heart. *I'm sorry. Remove this thing.* The beast had remained hidden. She didn't want it to control her! "Take it away!" she cried. "Take it away!"

Something happened inside her. The beast was gone. It just wasn't there! Finally! Cut in and tried out. Her Captain had heard.

§

Caleb gripped his sheet looking up into Ann's eyes. She yelled. Did she want him away? That's what he wanted too. She looked the part of a proper woman but held a jackknife in her hand, the mark of a whaler. The sick bloke next to him had said she won the hearts of her mates. But Caleb knew what she had done to win their hearts. She wasn't the lady. Oh, no! She was the girl from the Canal, here in Peru. She wanted him dead. He tried to speak but had to breathe to form words. He did nothing more than sputter. *The knife! No!* She was going to kill him right here, in the hospital.

He couldn't take his eyes off the blade. It was coming down. The woman he had left in Port Gibson followed him to Paita. She was smiling. How could she take such pleasure in killing him! He felt himself getting faint.

No! No! Don't close your eyes! Fight back.

He raised his hands to ward off the attack.

§

Caleb was white as new canvas. He wasn't breathing, but stared at her knife. He shook uncontrollably, like an animal caught in a trap. He tried to push himself away from her and voiced a scream, but nothing sounded. He pulled his hands up to protect himself from something. She tried to calm him with her smile and proceeded to cut a slice of bread from the loaf in her hand.

Mrs. Bathurst ran up. "Is anything wrong?"

Ann shook her head, staring at Caleb.

"Why don't you go outside and wait."

Ann needed to finish this. "No. This is something I must do."

Caleb's voice was hoarse and barely audible. "Don't go!" But Mrs. Bathurst had already headed toward her daughter and didn't hear.

In the faint light, Ann saw his eyes darting from side to side longing for someone as if he didn't want to be alone with her. She sat down beside him and returned the knife to her sash. He still disgusted her, but for the first time she was free from the anger that had accompanied her memories of him. "I have brought you a treat, Caleb. Here." She picked up the slice. "I brought this for you. Don't be afraid."

He was too upset to eat. As she pulled his hands together and placed the bread between them, a new friend brought to mind a memory. The leather thong still hung about her neck, something that had become part of her over nine months. She pulled the pouch from under her blouse and massaged it in her hands. Yes, it was still there. She knew it would be. She removed the ring and placed in on his little finger.

"I don't think I need this any longer."

She walked outside into the sunshine, leaving the darkness behind.

Bibliography

Ahab's Trade, Granville Allen Mawer, St Martin's Press, 175 Fifth Avenue, New York, N.Y. 10010.

Etchings of a Whaling Cruise, Browne, J. Ross, the Belknap Press of Harvard University Press, Cambridge, Mass, 1968.

In the Heart of the Sea, by Nathaniel Philbrick, Viking Penguin, 2000.

Incidents of a Whaling Voyage, by Francis A. Olmsted, Rutland, VT., 1969.

Life On a Whaler, by Nathaniel W. Taylor, The New London County Historical Society, 1929. Press of the Case, Lockwood, and Brainard Company, Hartford, Connecticut.

Men and Whales, by Richard Ellis, New York, 1991.

Men & Whales, by Richard Ellis, The Lyons Press, 1999.

"Seamen and Their Treatment," by Wentworth, Rev. E., D. D, The Ladies' Repository, vol. 13, iss. 4, pp 297-298, Methodist Episcopal Church, Cincinnati, Apr 1874.

"The 100 Barrel Whale," by Nordhoff, Charles, The Ladies' Repository, vol. 17, iss. 12, pp 708-712, Methodist Episcopal Church, Cincinnati, December 1857. Found at http://moa.umdl.umich.edu/

The Charles W. Morgan, by John F. Leavitt, Mystic Seaport, The Marine Historical Association, Incorporated, Mystic, Connecticut,1973.

The Cruise of the Cachalot, Round the World After Sperm Whales, by Frank T. Bullen, F.R.G.S. First Mate, June, 1998 [Etext #1356], Project Gutenberg Etext of The Cruise of the Cachalot, by Bullen.

"The Story of the Second Mate", by Alden, William L., Overland monthly and Out West, vol. 4, iss. 5, pp 423-429, May 1870, San Francisco.

Two Years Before the Mast, by Richard Henry Dana, Jr., as edited from the First Edition, with Journals and Letters of 1834-1836 and 1859-1860, Ward Ritchie Press, 1964.

Whale Hunt, by Nelson Cole Haley, Mystic Seaport Museum, Inc, 1990.

Hunting Neptune's Giants, by Gourley, Catherine, The Millbrook Press, Brookfield, Connecticut, 1995

www.ingramcontent.com/pod-product-compliance
Lightning Source LLC
Chambersburg PA
CBHW070900180626

46817CB00003B/843